LAST CHANCE

Chloris heard the scrape of the iron gates in front of the house that she had left unlocked, and she drew open the front door a bit more. In the light of a new moon, she could see the whiteness of Wrexford's shirt front. When at last he stood before her, she caught her breath.

He closed the door quietly behind him. He took her in his arms and kissed her tenderly and lingeringly. "There is no need to be afraid," he said, and kissed her again.

As they stood in the pitch-dark hall, their kissing took on increased fervor and neither wished to stop long enough to mount the stairs. But at last he released her. "This is your last chance to show me the door," he said with a soft laugh.

Wordlessly, she took his hand and led him up the stairs. . . .

LADY CHINA

Elizabeth Hewitt

A SIGNET BOOK

SIGNET
Published by the Penguin Group
Penguin Books USA Inc., 375 Hudson Street,
New York, New York 10014, U.S.A.
Penguin Books Ltd, 27 Wrights Lane,
London W8 5TZ, England
Penguin Books Australia Ltd, Ringwood,
Victoria, Australia
Penguin Books Canada Ltd, 2801 John Street,
Markham, Ontario, Canada L3R 1B4
Penguin Books (N.Z.) Ltd, 182-190 Wairau Road,
Auckland 10, New Zealand

Penguin Books Ltd, Registered Offices:
Harmondsworth, Middlesex, England

First published by Signet, an imprint of New American Library,
a division of Penguin Books USA Inc.

First Printing, June, 1991
10 9 8 7 6 5 4 3 2 1

Copyright © Mary Jeanne Hewitt, 1991
All rights reserved

 REGISTERED TRADEMARK—MARCA REGISTRADA

Printed in the United States of America

For Sally Genova,
my friend and mentor

1

"I CANNOT CREDIT it no matter what you say, Mr. James," Amelia Rawdon said hotly. "Papa would not have left matters in such a state if he had been in full possession of his faculties."

Mr. James coughed discreetly. "I understand your surprise, Miss Rawdon," he said, displaying a gift for understatement. "But I have no reason to believe that Sir Clive was in any way deprived of his faculties before he died, and the will he made shortly after his marriage to Miss Tennant is in perfect order."

"Then I think it must have been an infection of the mind from which Papa died," Amelia said scathingly.

Sir Amery Rawdon, not yet twenty years of age, was only ten months his sister's junior, and though he was neither timid nor disinclined to speak his mind, he balked at giving reproach to Amelia in front of the solicitor and the other family members who were gathered about the wide oak table in the morning room at Ferris Grange, the principal seat of the earls of Wrexford, to hear the reading of the last will and testament of Sir Clive Rawdon who had died of an unspecified infection in Macao, China, some two months previously.

Shock, dismay, and grief all contributed to Amelia's outrage and disbelief. Communication between England and China was occasionally erratic, and it was not surprising that they only had learned of their father's death a little over a fortnight ago when Mr.

James himself had journeyed to Hampshire to convey the unhappy news. Of the three children of Sir Clive and Eugenia Rawdon, Amelia, as the oldest, had known their father, who had spent most of the past fifteen years abroad, best, and it was she who had taken the news of his untimely death the most to heart. Her grief had turned to anger during the reading of the will, for Sir Clive had not left his property as Amelia had expected he would, and the fact that her expectations were neither realistic nor reasonable mattered not at all to her in her present state.

Amery saw his aunt, the dowager Lady Wrexford, cast him a helpless look that clearly bespoke her expectation that Amery, who was now the head of his family, would take his sister in hand before an unfortunate scene was created. "I can't say I like it all that well either, Amy," he said, his voice placating rather than remonstrative, "but what's to do? As his widow, Lady Rawdon has every right to a fair share of our father's estate. It is not as if he took anything away from his children to enrich her. Annabelle's and your portions are considerably increased over the amounts set forth in the original marriage settlements between Papa and Mama, and I have the entail, which is most everything else and a bit of additional property that I never expected. Lady Rawdon has mostly father's foreign interests, which we scarce knew anything of in any case."

"She has Rawdon House in town, which was not protected by the entail," she replied, in no way appeased, "and Myerly in Nottinghamshire, which I had hoped to persuade Papa to deed to me as a bride gift when Prentice and I are wed."

"But Amy," Annabelle said, with a fifteen-year-old's gift for unfortunate frankness, "you know the only time we spent the night at Myerly you said it was too old and drafty and that you hoped you would never have to stay there again."

Anger flashed in Amelia's eyes and Amery said hastily, "You and Pren will want to purchase a far snugger bit of property than that old ruin. The extra you have added to your portion, Amy, is worth far more than Myerly."

"It is not a question of value or of money at all," Amelia said, getting up from the table at which they were gathered and going to the window which overlooked the park, lush and green in the fullness of summer. "It is That Woman. Why should an adventuress who seduced a lonely, aging man into marrying her take from Papa's family the legacy which would have been theirs if Papa had not had the misfortune of being duped by her wiles?"

Amery was not without temper, and his sister's unjustifiable venom caused it to flare. "Come now, Amy," he said with sudden sharpness. "You're behaving like a dashed spoiled child. Can't go accusing Lady Rawdon of being an adventuress. For one thing, we have never set eyes on her and know nothing of her character for good or bad, and for another, she's our stepmother and it's dashed poor *ton* to say nasty things against a member of the family in front of others, whether you like her or not."

Amelia turned, her eyes bright with unshed tears. "What power this Siren must have," she said derisively, "that she can hypnotize yet another man at a distance of thousands of miles with only a few words penned on paper."

"I'm just trying to give her a fair chance, damn it," Amery returned, himself forgetting the presence of the solicitor. He stood abruptly, almost overturning his chair. "Do you think I am delighted any more than you are to find a woman I have never met suddenly set over me as guardian until I am of age and with control of my purse strings until I am five and twenty unless I marry before with her consent? For all any of us knows she may be Haymarket ware or a cursed termagant, but to judge her before we have set eyes on her and cast aspersions against her character changes nothing of the reality of her existence in our lives and makes accepting matters as they are all the harder.''

"It is intolerable and should *not* be accepted," Amelia said, her voice rising in pitch, a clear warning that she was perilously close to a fit of the vapors. "I certainly shall not accept it, and shall do everything in my power to overturn the will and prevent that scheming doxy from getting so much as a farthing of Papa's money.''

"Amelia!'' Lady Wrexford said with genuine horror. "You forget yourself.''

"She dashed well does," Amery said, his fair complexion turning crimson with his rising anger. Amelia's lower lip trembled ominously at the reproach from her aunt and her brother, but Amery was in no humor to concern himself with his sister's sensibilities. "If you go on like this you'll make us all a byword in the *ton*. There's nothing the gossips and harpies love more than to see families washing their dirty linen in public. You heard Mr. James tell us that the will was in perfect order. If you insist on fighting it, you will likely accomplish nothing beyond casting us all into a wretched scandal. I won't have it, Amy. If you try anything of that nature, I'll make it known that I oppose you. You don't have to like Lady Rawdon, but she was our father's wife and at the least you will respect his name and his memory.''

Amelia recoiled from him as if he had struck her. "You may say what you will of me," she said, tears already beginning to spill from her eyes and her voice catching on a choked sob. "The world will know the truth for itself soon enough when that scheming lightskirt comes to England—*if* she ever has the courage to show her brazen face. I have no doubt it was fear of facing us that caused her to prevent Papa from visiting us since he married her.''

Amery's face was flushed and dark and his eyes bright with anger. Knowing that Amery was about to forget himself as much as Amelia had done, Lady Wrexford stood suddenly and pounded the table with one delicate fist. It was such astonishing behavior for the usually self-effacing dowager countess that both combatants forgot their anger for a moment to stare at her in astonishment. "It is I who will not have this behavior," she said, her voice uncharacteristically stern. "From either of you. You disgrace not only yourselves with your vulgar and ill-bred brangling but me as well, for Mr. James knows full well that since the time your mother died and your father left England, I have had the raising of you. Your language, Amelia, is more fit for the stable than for this house and sets a very poor example for Annabelle, who very naturally looks to you as a pattern. You do neither yourself nor Belle any service if you prejudice her against Lady Rawdon for no better reason than your own jealousy and unwillingness to accept the fact that your father chose to marry a woman unknown to you."

Not conceding the floor, she turned to Amery, who still stood beside the table, spread-legged as if braced for the onslaught he expected. "And you, young man—you are now head of your family. The sentiments you have expressed on behalf of your stepmother are admirable, but losing your temper is to no purpose. You have had the example of both your cousin Morgan, who is head of the entire Rawdon clan, and his father before him, of mature self-discipline and consideration. With your new position comes responsibility, and a part of that responsibility is self-restraint."

The young baronet opened his mouth and closed it again, swallowing with some difficulty. He glanced from his elder sister, her face red and tear-stained, to his aunt, who was also pink from the effort of expressing her feelings, to Annabelle, who was wide-eyed and avidly attentive, and finally to Mr. James, who was making a fine show of sorting the legal papers spread before him on the table. Amery was very aware of the responsibilities that had suddenly descended on his youthful shoulders at the death of his father and his succession to the title. He also possessed enough self-honesty to know that he lacked years and experience to handle the charge laid on him with the maturity with which he would have liked to carry out the task.

It was true that his cousin Morgan had been only a few years older than Amery was now when he had succeeded to the earldom of Wrexford, but Morgan's father, the fourth earl, had been an invalid for several years. It had been expected that Robert Rawdon would suffer an early demise and Morgan had had ample time to prepare himself for the obligations he soon expected to inherit, but Sir Clive at eight and forty had still been a relatively young man at the time of his death, enjoying, as far as his family in England had been aware, superb health and a sturdy constitution.

All of the many duties and obligations of administering the properties and fortune of Sir Clive had been given over to the very capable expertise of his men of business and stewards and bailiffs whose own families had a long history of serving the Rawdons. The care of the family itself had fallen to the Wrexford branch of the Rawdon clan. Alyce and Robert Wrexford had literally had the young Rawdons trust upon them by the distraught Sir Clive when he had made his decision to leave England, but Lady Wrexford, who had been told after the birth of her only child, Morgan, that she could bear no other children, had been only too happy to take on the charge. But the result of all this was that Amery at nineteen had had very little experience of responsibility and he was very unsure of his ability to acquit himself well. Thus, he was very much upon his dignity and his fragile pride easily wounded. A defensive retort formed on his lips and this was what he forcibly swallowed. He was equally conscious that he was not behaving with the maturity due his position and that he and the whole of his family owed a great debt to Alyce Wrexford in addition to the genuine regard in which they all held her.

"I beg your pardon, Aunt Alyce," he said stiffly as soon as he could trust himself to speak, "and yours as well, James. Are there details still to be discussed? It might be best if you and I adjourned to the library." He cast his elder sister a fulminating glance and turned to leave the room. As he stepped away from the table, his gaze rested briefly on Annabelle again. "And you, urchin," he said addressing her. "I am certain that Hoppy must be waiting for you in the schoolroom. There is no reason for you to be absent any longer."

The young girl's disappointment was plain in her expression. She knew perfectly well that this discussion was far from over and she wanted very much to hear what her sister would say when their brother, become suddenly very grown-up and censorious since they had learned of their father's death, left them and Amelia felt free to speak her mind again. "Miss Hopper must realize that I am not a schoolgirl any longer," she said primly. "I am nearly sixteen and Aunt Alyce has said that I may come out at least in the neighborhood next fall."

"If you are ignorant and lack deportment, it will be a waste of time, Belle," her brother informed her as he paused at the door. "No on will want to marry you and I'll have you on my hands forever. Upstairs with you, brat."

Annabelle, with her rich chestnut hair and startlingly green eyes, was unquestionably the beauty of the family. She pouted prettily, but rose and walked toward the door which her brother stood beside, holding it open for her in a speaking manner. She would not deign to look at him as she passed, but put her pretty retroussé nose in the air and flounced out in a

manner that was superbly theatrical. A faint smile was
forced from Amery and his own gray-green eyes held
a decided twinkle. He bowed very low as she passed
and left the room after her followed by the solicitor,
who tactfully closed the door behind him.

Lady Wrexford saw the thundercloud in her young
niece's face and sighed and sat down again. Alyce was
a good-natured creature, agreeable almost to the point
of being irritating at times. Her philosophy, if it could
be said that she had one, was live and let live, and
fighting or fussing in any form was generally abhor-
rent to her. Her duty to correct her charges carried
out, she felt quite drained and subsided into silence
while Amelia, no longer tearful but still extremely ag-
itated, paced about the room in a nervous, intense
manner as if she were caged in the pleasantly ap-
pointed room.

So preoccupied was Amelia that two or three times
she brushed perilously close to a small occasional table or one of the spindle-back chairs left drawn out
from the table.

"Please pay attention to what you are about,
Amelia," Lady Wrexford pleaded as her niece once
again nearly collided with a chair. "You know how
easily you bruise."

Amelia, who was chewing absently at a thumbnail
as she paced, removed her hand from her mouth and
waved it dismissively, having no concern for something so trivial to her at the moment. "There must be
some means of stopping That Woman," she said,
speaking for the first time since the others had left the
room.

"Mr. James has said—"

"Oh, fiddle. I don't care what that pompous old fool
has said. If I have no means of knowing for certain
that she is an adventuress, neither do he nor Amery
know that she is not."

Always ready to be fair, Lady Wrexford allowed how this was so.

"Nor do they know that she did not coerce or in some way trick Papa into marrying her and including her in his will."

"But we do not know that she did, dear," Lady Wrexford reminded her.

Amelia ignored this remark. "What we need to discover is the Truth."

The word was plainly capitalized and Lady Wrexford had a sudden premonition that Amelia, who had been headstrong even at the age of five when she had first come to Wrexford to live, was again about to do something uncomfortable to her peace. "Short of journeying to China ourselves, I don't see how that is to be accomplished," the dowager said waspishly, anxiety making her tone sharp. A light sparked in Amelia's eyes and Alyce Wrexford had a sudden pain in her lower stomach. "And that, of course, is completely out of the question," she said with a haste and firmness that was as uncharacteristic as her earlier outburst. "I have a slight acquaintance with Sarah Weston, who last I heard lived in Macao with her husband, who is associated with the East India Company in Canton. But we have never been great correspondents and for me to write to her out of the blue and ask a great many awkward questions would be unthinkable."

But Amelia was no longer listening to her aunt. She subsided at last onto a stuffed chair near the empty grate at the far end of the room. One or two words in Lady Wrexford's speech had caught her imagination and she settled to the task of applying the ideas they engendered to her purpose.

In the library at Ferris Grange, a dark and heavy room that still somehow managed to be comfortable and inviting, Sir Amery handed Mr. James a brimming glass of his cousin's finest Madeira and sat in the chair facing the one in which he had placed the solicitor. "I beg your pardon for that little display in the morning room, James," Amery said gruffly, a little embarrassed and uncertain that apologizing for his sister's behavior was the right thing to do. "The truth is, Mr. James, you behold us astounded. It is not just the unexpected death of Sir Clive, but the situation as a whole. When our father wrote to us last year to inform us that he had remarried, we could scarcely credit it. He had always declared after the death of our mother that he would never marry again and then to do so thousands of miles away and to a woman about whom we know nothing . . ." He broke off, his hands rising as if in helpless credulity. "It was most difficult for Amelia because she has always regarded our father in the light of a tragic romantic figure—you know, he left England because he could not bear to remain here after the death of our mother."

He sighed deeply and the solicitor wisely kept his counsel. He had been fairly well acquainted with his client before Sir Clive had left England, and it was his private opinion that Sir Clive had been a self-absorbed man who had no taste for facing the responsibility of raising his children alone and who had gladly seized on the excuse of his grief for his wife to push this responsibility onto his older brother and his wife. Sir Clive might have loved his offspring—Mr. James did not care to pass judgment on this—but that love had not been sufficient to cause Sir Clive to spend more than a month or two at a time in England at infrequent intervals after which he once again pursued his penchant for travel.

"We know very little of father's life since he left England," Amery said after taking a long drink from his glass. There was no censure in his voice, but perhaps a note of regret. "Nor was he much of a correspondent. He always used the excuse that the post from the remoter parts of the world—which is where he always seemed to be—was erratic. Oh, he would return from time to time—every other year or so—for a month or two at best, but then you know that. But I was only four when father started his travels and Annabelle was still a babe. I know nothing of him as a man. For all I know he had a wife in every blasted country he lived in for more than six months together.''

The solicitor permitted his usual impassive expression to be altered by a slight upturning of his thin lips, which was doubtless meant to signify a smile. ''I shouldn't think so,'' he said, making a steeple of his hands and then pressing his palms together. ''Like you, I was quite surprised when Sir Clive wrote me of his marriage to Miss Tennant. He was as fond as any man of the company of the fairer sex, but he claimed to be devoted to the memory of your dear mother and I doubted he ever would set anyone in her place again. Perhaps this marriage occurred because Sir Clive tired of being alone, or it may have been the result of a natural healing process.'' He paused and then said carefully, ''Or Lady Rawdon may be a remarkable woman whom your father found worthy of the position he conferred upon her.''

Amery considered this for a moment. He glanced at the solicitor's scarcely touched glass on the small pie-crust table beside his chair and almost defiantly poured himself a second glass of the amber wine. ''You must have had a greater correspondence with Sir Clive and Lady Rawdon that we have—matters of business, I mean. Will you tell me what you honestly think? Is it possible that Lady Rawdon is the adventuress that Amelia thinks she is?''

Mr. James looked pained. It was his profession to ask awkward questions, not answer them. He said with caution, ''I have known Sir Clive since he was a boy— I was just taking my place in my father's firm when your grandfather first came to James, James and Landry. It was always my belief, despite his decision to leave all his responsibilities and to travel for the remainder of his life, that Sir Clive was a very sensible man and quite capable of seeing to himself in all circumstances.''

It was not a direct answer, but Amery understood him well enough. ''No. I agree. What I do know of my father, I can't imagine that a scheming lightskirt would be able to bamboozle him to the point that he would offer her marriage. Even if she enflamed him, I don't think he would have married her just to bed her.''

James coughed discreetly. ''When your father first wrote to me that he had married Miss Tennant, I took it upon myself to do a bit of investigation, being concerned myself that nothing out of the ordinary had occurred. Miss Tennant—that is, Lady Rawdon—is of impeccable, if unremarkable breeding. Her father was of a branch of the Northumberland Tennants—that would be Lord Calabrae's kin—and her mother was a Ryden of Cornwall. No nobility there, but landed gentry since the time of the Black Prince at least. As I have said, unremarkable, but certainly not unworthy of bearing the Rawdon name.''

''What does that say of her character though?'' Amery said after staring moodily into his glass for a silent minute.

''Why nothing in the least,'' James returned. ''But none of my inquiries turned up anything against her, and both her parents were dedicated Methodist missionaries, or so I have been informed. They shared a mutual interest in imparting the Gospel to heathens and thus lived abroad for virtually all of their married lives until they both succumbed to a fever within a week of each other in Kowloon. Miss Tennant herself actually lived in England for nearly eight years, spending some of the time with her mother's family in Cornwall and most of the rest of it at Miss Grayson's Academy for Young Ladies of Quality in Bath, which is not a school of the first stare, but quite respectable and unexceptionable. Other than that, she too has lived abroad for most of her life. It must have given them a common ground to begin with.''

The solicitor glanced down at the table and looked at his still-filled glass as if he had only just discovered it. He picked it up and raised it to his lips, sipping so sparingly that the amount of wine in the glass did not appear to decrease. ''In lieu of any evidence to the contrary, there is every reason to believe that Lady Rawdon is a woman of upright and moral character. In fact, if there is anything that one could object to, it is the strong possibility that her upbringing may have resulted in an excessively pious nature which, it has been my personal experience, is all too common in those possessed of an evangelical bent. However,'' he added with a lawyer's inbred caution, ''that is a personal prejudice of my own, and not to be regarded as in any manner intending to defame the lady's character.''

Amery chuckled aloud. ''As I have said, I did not know my father very well, Mr. James, but I can't imagine him taking a woman of excessive piety to wife any more than I can imagine him being duped by a clever Cyprian.''

Mr. James took another minute sip of his wine and then set his glass down on the table again, straightening his position in his chair and leaning forward slightly as if to hint to his host that he thought it time for their interview to end. ''Whatever Sir Clive's motive when he married the present Lady Rawdon, it must now remain forever speculation.''

Amery was quick to take the hint. ''Quite,'' he said, rising and extending his hand to the solicitor, who stood simultaneously. ''I am certain that you have more to occupy you than idle speculation, James. I thank you for coming to Ferris personally to see to this matter for us. I wish I could persuade you to remain the night, but I understand that you have other clients' affairs to see to.''

The solicitor took the baronet's hand and applied exactly the correct pressure for a man who was neither equal nor subservient. ''As you say, Sir Amery,'' he agreed politely, ''though I do thank you for the consideration. Unless I am unfortunate enough to draw lame horses at a change, I should be back in town in time for a late dinner. At this time of year there is light enough for the journey for several hours yet at least.''

''One last thing,'' Amery said hesitantly, just before he drew the library door open for the solicitor, his hand actually on the handle. ''Is there any likelihood at all that this will may be overturned if it is fought?''

James's eyebrows rose a perceptible fraction. ''Is that your intention, Sir Amery? In law there are no true impossibilities, but as your solicitor, I would strongly advise you against it. It would be expensive and very probably futile.''

Amery sighed. ''No, it is not *my* intention. But my sister will soon be of age and free to act as she chooses. It does not always matter to her that her choices are ill-advised.'' He finally drew the door open and personally escorted the solicitor to the door while a footman sent word to the stables for Mr. James's carriage to be brought around. Such an action was a mark of considerable distinction and gave Amery a decidedly satisfying sense of *noblesse oblige*.

While Amery was still in the library with Mr. James, Amelia returned to her sitting room, which commanded the same prospect of the park as the morning room. She sat at once at her writing desk which stood before those windows, but she spared not even a glance for the charming sunlit vista spread out before her. She pulled out the largest drawer so quickly that it nearly fell into her lap and removed several sheets of monogrammed rice paper, then rummaged about for a pen that appeared to her sturdy enough to withstand considerable use. When she found it she mended it hastily, but with skill.

Yet when she had removed the stopper from the standish and dipped the pen in the ink, for all her haste she sat with the pen poised over the paper for several long moments before she wrote. She chose her words with care, not because she was unsure of what she wished to write but because of her understanding of the character of the person she addressed.

Like his mother, Morgan Rawdon, fifth Earl of Wrexford, was possessed of an agreeable nature, but unlike his mother he did not permit his good humor to be taken advantage of. He could be persuaded, but never pushed; he was amenable to suggestion, but never susceptible to control. Raised with her cousin and close enough in age to regard him as an older brother, Amelia, with her strong will and determination to have her own way, had had ample opportunity to test the limits which Morgan would permit her. And so she weighed her words, hoping to convince him, but avoiding any hint of command.

Morgan had begun a career in the diplomatic service when he had come down from Magdalen, and despite inheriting both titles and estates from his father at the age of two and twenty, he had continued on in the service of His Majesty's Foreign Office. His mother had declared that wanderlust must be in the bloodlines of the Rawdons, for like his uncle Sir Clive, Morgan had chosen stewards carefully and had spent the past six years since he had received his first appointment to a foreign embassy mostly in countries other than the one of which he was a native. He was currently assigned as special advisor to the ambassador in Madras and had lived in India for just over a year.

Unlike Sir Clive, Morgan was an excellent correspondent, proving that communication between East and West was not always as unreliable as his uncle had claimed. With some regularity, Lady Wrexford and the three Rawdons received letters from Morgan detailing the more amusing and interesting aspects of life in India and of the people with whom he lived and worked. Amelia, with a mind more inquiring than the others and a greater perception, suspected that there was much in India that he did not find amusing and which he did not choose to share with his family in England, for she recognized an increasing note of cynicism and something of dismay in each missive she received from him. It was only a matter of time, she suspected, before he would be with them again at Ferris or at Wrexford House in London, though whether or not this time he would finally be ready to heed his mother's entreaties and settle in England to marry and secure the succession was questionable.

For now, though, while he remained in the East, Amelia hoped to persuade him to put his numerous contacts there to good use. She was cautious in how she approached Morgan because, like Amery, he did not share her conviction that the widow of Sir Clive could not be other than an unscrupulous adventuress. Attempts to influence her cousin to her way of thinking had met with short shrift and a tart recommendation that she recall her Bible lessons on the inefficacy of hasty judgments.

But matters were changed now, she reasoned. Morgan, with his excellent understanding and insight into human nature which had made him a first-rate diplomat, must see that personal gain had to have been the motive of Chloris Tennant when she had married Sir Clive. Sir Clive's will, made, according to Mr. James, within a sennight of his marriage to Miss Tennant, proved that, at least to Amelia's satisfaction. With the idealism of youth, Amelia believed that her stepmother, if she were an honest woman, would not have permitted Sir Clive to leave so much a penny away from his children. She neither knew of nor cared about laws of entitlement or the obligations of affection.

She was still writing—on the third page of her letter, for she wanted it to be completely legible and did not cross it—when Annabelle slipped into the room. If Amelia heard her sister's entrance, she made no note of it. Annabelle did not go immediately to her sister, but made a circuit of the room, stopping to examine a painting or to pick up a figurine as if unfamiliar with the room and its contents. By this route she was finally brought to the windows and subsided in a chair beside the writing desk. Amelia did glance up at Annabelle as she sat, but made no comment.

Silence continued but only for another minute or so. "Mr. James is leaving," Annabelle informed her sister. "I sat near the top of the stairs where they couldn't see me and I saw him and Amery come out of the bookroom a few minutes ago."

There was an eagerness in her voice, but Amelia's tone in response was dampening. "Then no doubt he is gone by now."

"Don't you mean to speak with him again?" Belle said, surprised.

"Mr. James is the executor of Papa's will. No doubt I shall be speaking with him often."

"But I thought that you intended to contest Papa's will," Belle said, sounding disappointed. Though Belle was thoughtful and responsible for her age, at fifteen she did not have a true understanding of the value of her own dowry and therefore had no personal interest in the amount of her own legacy. Nor had she anything in the least against her unknown stepmother. She had been less than a year in age when her father had left her and her brother and sister to the care of their Aunt Alyce, so Sir Clive had never been more to her than a large, handsome gentleman who had visited Ferris infrequently, showering them with exotic gifts and then departing again so quickly that Annabelle would not have remembered his face next time he was at Ferris if she had not been brought down from the schoolroom and told that it was her father who had come to visit. Her interest in her sister's desire to contest the will was solely because it promised to add a bit of spice and intrigue to their usually quiet existence.

"You know nothing of such matters," her sister said repressively.

"I know more than you think," Belle returned with a hint of petulance. "I am not a child any longer, you know."

Amelia made no response and Annabelle watched her as she complete the third page and began on the fourth. "To whom are you writing?" she asked, her injured esteem forgotten in curiosity.

"Morgan."

Annabelle thought on this for a moment and then said, "You are telling him about the will, aren't you? Do you think he'll take your side against Amery? If it is a great deal of money that Papa left to Lady Rawdon, he might not like it, I suppose, for he is very protective of our interests." Her voice did not sound hopeful and after a moment of further thought she added, "But then he did write that very quelling letter to you when you were so upset that Papa had married again."

At these words, Amelia put down her pen and turned to her sister with a darkling expression. "What do you know of that letter?" she demanded, her tone ominous.

Belle's eyes went round as she realized that her curiosity had caused her tongue to be careless. "I just caught a glimpse of it. It was lying open on the desk one day when I was in here," she said hastily.

The sisters shared the sitting room, which adjoined each of their bedchambers, and it was a constant source of friction between them that Annabelle with her inbred inquisitiveness could not be persuaded to see that there was anything in the least wrong for her to read her sister's correspondence or rummage casually through Amelia's other possessions to discover items of interest to her. "It never was," Amelia said positively, but more with resignation than with heat. It was an old argument. "It was in the drawer with my other letters, which I suppose you read as well. It is time I spoke with Aunt Alyce about a new desk. One that locks."

Belle was pleased that Amelia did not intend to ring a peal over her head for snooping, but neither did she wish for the desk to be replaced with one to which she would have no access. She quickly brought the subject back around to Amelia's intentions concerning their father's will. "*Do* you think that Morgan will help?"

"I don't know," Amelia admitted. "But I think he will feel differently to some degree when he knows that she persuaded Papa to change his will so much in her favor. I have not told him precisely that I think we should contest it, but I have asked him to discover, if he can, anything more specific about her conduct since Papa's death. If she has displayed no grief and is living high on her expectations, that must be a sure indication that she deluded poor Papa and cozened him into making that will. I only hope that it is not more than that, for it does not bear thinking of."

Even at fifteen, Belle's quick mind grasped Amelia's dark hint. "Oh, Amy," she said, genuinely shocked, "you do not think . . ." She could not even bring herself to voice so horrible a suspicion.

Neither could Amelia, when pushed to it. "I don't think anything specific yet until I can garner more information. That is why I am writing to Morgan. Positioned as he is in the East, he should be able to learn more than we possibly could from here." She picked up her pen again and turned pointedly away from her sister to signify that the conversation was at an end, but she could not resist adding, "But I put nothing at all as being completely beyond That Woman."

2

CHLORIS RAWDON held the letter so loosely between her fingers that it finally fluttered to the ground at her feet. John Reid, who stood beside the stone bench on which she sat, bent to retrieve it. He didn't even glance at the contents but folded it slowly, abstractedly watching his fingers crease the paper. He did not give the letter back to Lady Rawdon. He walked a little away from her and then turned to her again and regarded her for a few moments before speaking. "I think you're brewing a tempest in a teacup, China. Lord Wrexford is the head of the Rawdon clan; it's only natural that he should concern himself with meeting you."

Chloris, who had been known to family and friends as China almost since birth, gave him a swift, characteristic smile. "I suppose," she said, with a faint shrug, which conveyed less concern than she felt. "I would be more inclined to that view if his letter had not come to me so hard on the heels of the one from Mr. James, Clive's London solicitor. Is it really concern, or does Lord Wrexford propose to visit Macao because he wants to see the scheming adventuress for himself?"

"What if he does?" Jack returned with a shrug of his own. "You have nothing to blush for, China. Perhaps you haven't the grand connections of the Rawdons, but your marriage to Clive was hardly a *mésalliance.''* He took a step nearer her and finally handed her the folded letter.

China took it and sighed, but more in a philosophical than a dismal manner. "The letters I received from Clive's family in England were always couched in the most civil terms, but I know they have judged me and think that at best Clive was foolishly besotted to marry me or at worst tricked into it by some Machiavellian ruse.''

"I don't think the dowager Lady Wrexford feels that way,'' Jack said, seeking for something positive to say, though he knew through conversations with the late Sir Clive that the news of his marriage to China had been greeted with less than enthusiasm by his family. "Clive told me that she wrote to congratulate him in the warmest terms.''

"She said she was very glad if he had found some measure of happiness and meant to stop racketing about the world,'' China said with another, drier smile. "Though not, of course, in precisely those words. But I suppose it is unfair of me to expect her to fall into transports when she knows nothing of me other than what Clive may have written,'' China conceded. A breeze stirred the tendrils of flaxen hair that framed her heart-shaped face.

"In any case,'' she said, rising from the bench and drawing her shawl more closely about her, "it is not so much whether or not I am liked by the Rawdons that concerns me at the moment but rather the degree to which they are willing to take their dislike of my marriage to Clive. Mr. James was very careful in his phrasing, but I think he was giving me the hint that they may contest the will, or at the least that they are exploring the possibilities. I would wager on it.''

A servant came out of the house to inform them that other guests for dinner had arrived and China took Jack's arm and they returned to the house. Neither the Westons nor the Fitchley-Gores, who joined them for dinner and an evening of music and conversation, guessed that behind Lady Rawdon's vivacious charm and ready laughter lay a disquiet that had been growing, feeding on the veiled hints of the solicitor and the letter she had received from the Earl of Wrexford informing her of his intention to visit Macao to make her acquaintance.

In her heart, China did not believe she had anything to fear; Sir Clive, a man who had served his country well enough to have a baronetcy conveyed upon him before the age of thirty and to have acquired a fortune as great as the one he had inherited before his untimely death, had been an astute man who would not have made a will to be easily broken by avaricious heirs. Nor did she really dread the judgment of Morgan Wrexford. What could he, or for that matter any of the Rawdons, do except make matters unpleasant for her by their blatant disapproval of her and their dislike that she had inherited such a large portion of her husband's estate?

But China had grown very comfortable in her quiet, well-ordered life, if a little bored by it, and she abhorred unpleasantness. It was her nature to like people and in general she found herself equally regarded by all she met. It had hurt her more than she had permitted her husband to see that she had not received a ready welcome from his kin, for his sake more than for her own. This did not make her anxious to meet any one of the Rawdons, least of all the Earl of Wrexford, whose few letters to her and to Clive she had judged to be decidedly cool. She would have much preferred it if Clive's family had chosen to ignore her existence altogether.

Her earlier conversation with Jack could not be immediately resumed, but Jack lingered in the hall when Sir Vernon and Lady Weston were leaving, giving the impression for propriety's sake that he too was about to depart, but in fact he remained to join China in a glass of brandy before retiring for the evening.

In fact, the salve to propriety was merely inbred in both of them. Jack had been Sir Clive's closest friend since the baronet had first arrived in China at Shanghai, and when Clive had moved to Portuguese Macao, preferring the more settled quality of life there to the erratic and sometimes dangerous streets of Shanghai, Jack had gone with him and had found a warm welcome in the small, closely knit English community banded together against the hostility of both the Portuguese and the Chinese on the outskirts of the city.

As a second son of a well-to-do country squire in Sussex, Jack Reid had studied medicine to carve out a career for himself, and though he had never completed his degree, he was the nearest thing to a doctor that the English in Macao had, or at least felt they could implicitly trust in this outlandish place, and since medicine was often more common sense and a knowledge of anatomy than a true science, he was valued in the community. He had an agreeable personality and his deep-rooted cynicism born of experience rather than inbred, was never cutting, making him well-liked and a valued dinner guest in a society too narrow and closed not to grow occasionally bored with itself.

Sir Clive had suffered from gout and a passion for chess which Jack shared, and he had spent so many quiet evenings with Clive and China that he might as well have been a member of the family, and was thought of in that way not only by the Rawdons but by most others as well. While Clive lived and encouraged Jack's visits there had been no occasion for gossip, but now that China was widowed there were those who suggested that there was more than friendship between China and Jack. Perhaps it was unpropitious for Jack to continue his frequent visits to China, but China refused to bow to idle gossip and their comfortable relationship continued much as it had before.

Jack sat in an over-stuffed chair in the room that had been Clive's study and which China had altered only slightly to make it her own sitting room, enjoying the memories of happy evenings spent there with her husband. "I don't think it matters if the Rawdons do contest the will," he said, as their conversation came back around to the earlier topic. "Clive told me himself that he had taken great pains to see to it that you were well endowed and well protected if anything should happen to him. He never said outright that he feared his family would not accept you, but he had too much sense not to realize that you might not have an easy time of it."

"I have not so much concern that they will overturn the will, but I should dislike it excessively if scandal were made in the process," said China. "It would be unfair not only to me, but to Clive's memory. There would doubtless be questions about Clive's state of mind when he married me and made his will, and perhaps about his illness and death as well."

"Is that what troubles you?" asked Jack, enlightened. "I thought you had ceased blaming yourself. It was not your fault, you know that. You couldn't have known how bad off he was. Clive concealed the truth from all of us."

China regarded him unblinkingly. "But I was his wife. I should have known him better than anyone."

Jack's smile was wry and a little self-mocking. "If a man is sufficiently determined, he may keep an unpleasant truth even from those dearest to him. None know that better than I. It is always the untoward event that does him in. Then the truth will out. When Clive's condition unexpectedly worsened, he could no longer conceal it. Or face the reality of it, for that matter. It really had nothing to do with you."

"Oh, I have come to accept that in my mind," China said with a faint upturning of her lips, "but will the Rawdons be as generous?"

"They might if you told them the complete truth."

China shook her head vigorously. "You know I cannot. I promised Clive I should not. He knew his family better than I could ever hope to, and he did not want them to know."

"But Clive is dead," Jack said, "and you should use your best judgment."

"I won't play him false." China sighed again. "I supposed the Rawdons were all in England and not likely to travel such a distance merely to make my acquaintance," she said, sipping the warming spirits. "But I had forgotten that Wrexford is in Madras." She smiled, and her one dimple peeped and her eyes sparkled with self-amusement. "Suddenly the safe distance is considerably shortened."

"Why should you assume he will disapprove of you? And what would it matter if he does?"

China shrugged. "Not the least thing, I suppose. Certainly, I would prefer if Wrexford and the rest of the family liked and accepted me, but with so many miles between us, the opinions of the Rawdons caused me no more than a passing concern while Clive lived."

"Nor should they now," Jack affirmed. "Is that why you have not wished to return to England after Clive died, because of the Rawdons? I would have thought that you would wish to see your property there and take charge of the guardianship of Clive's children. Given the increasing difficulties of remaining here, it might well be a prudent move."

"My dear Jack," China said with a wry laugh, "do you imagine that the Rawdons would welcome me to take charge of their affairs? I leave that to Wrexford, who is also named guardian in Clive's will. As to the problems we have here, even if the Portuguese and the Mandarins make remaining impossible for us, I have been informed by James, James and Landry that I am rich enough to live most anywhere I please. It need not be England."

"That's crying craven, China. You used to talk very

wistfully about returning to England one day while Clive was still alive,'' Reid reminded her.

China laughed again, knowing he would not let the point go. ''All right, Jack, I concede. I am cow-hearted and quake at the thought of meeting the Raw-dons. But now it seems that I have no means of es-cape—unless I do go off to some other part of the world, and that would likely confirm their worst sus-picions of me. Wrexford is coming here and the day of judgment is at hand.'' She got up and began to pour more of the brandy for herself, but thought better of it and put the stopper back in the decanter.

Jack finished the last of the brandy in his glass and then rose and took her hands in a warm clasp. ''Don't tease yourself, China. When Wrexford comes, he will not be displeased with what he finds. If anything, he will return to the others singing your praises.''

''That's doing it rather brown, Jack,'' China said, returning the pressure of his hands. ''But you are right. Let Wrexford come and be damned to him.''

Reid laughed, pleased at her spirit. ''That's more like it. Clive loved you for your bottom as much as for your beauty.'' He released her hands. ''I had best be gone, before the vipers begin to whisper that I have spent the night.'' He gave her a brotherly kiss, which she returned in a like spirit.

China did not ring for a servant but walked to the door with Jack herself. Her house was a large one by the standards of the neighborhood and she had the means to employ several inside servants, which, since the Chinese and Portuguese were united in wishing to make life as difficult as they could for their English competitors and would not work for them at any price, was an expensive luxury that few could afford. All of her servants were imported from England and paid an exorbitant wage, and were well aware of their value. Like other of their friends and acquaintances who had had to adjust to the very different employer-employee relationship in Macao, China rarely called upon her servants to perform tasks that she could as easily do herself.

As they walked down the curving stair that Clive had had built in the house in reminiscence of the stair at Cedar Hill, his principal seat in Shropshire, they talked of other matters, but China's thoughts were still preoccupied with their previous conversation. "Have you ever met Wrexford?" she asked when they reached the mosaic-tiled floor of the front hall.

"If you mean been formally presented, no. We did not move in the same circles," he added dryly. "But I know who he is; he was an undersecretary in the Foreign Office during Canning's administration and they say his work in Spain and Portugal at the end of the war was such that he might have held an actual Cabinet post if he had wanted it, which apparently he did not. He isn't the sort to puff himself off in public. He's very social, with a mild reputation for being a rake, but that sort of thing can be an asset in diplomatic circles if one is discreet. He is."

"Well, then at least he is not likely to make a scene and publicly declare me to be unfit to have been Clive's wife," she said with a smile as they stood before the door. A large mantel clock in an adjacent room chimed the hour. It was later than usual for a guest to remain; the uneasy toleration of the separate communities occasionally became openly hostile and it was not considered safe to be out on the streets alone as the night advanced. With concern for his safety, China asked Jack to spend the night in a guest room.

He had done so a number of times while Clive had lived, but now he would not put China's reputation at risk by giving the gossips grist for their mills. He tapped the head of his walking stick, which China knew separated by means of a small catch from the remainder of the stick and contained a small but lethal sword. "It's a short distance and I make my defenses known abroad. I shan't be accosted."

He put his hand on the doorhandle to open it, but China touched his arm to stay him. "Is Wrexford an attractive man?" she asked, as if continuing an unspoken thought.

A faint self-mocking smile touched Reid's lips. "I would say so. So would you, I think. He has a little of the look of Clive, much the same coloring and the Rawdon eyes. Why? Do you mean to use your wiles on him to get him to convince the other Rawdons that you are not such a bad lot?"

"He would be convinced that I was a scheming lightskirt if I did that," China responded with a brief, caustic laugh. "No. I just wondered because you said he was something of a rake. I've never met one before. Or at least I don't think I have."

Jack's eyebrows rose. "Piques your curiosity, does it? That's half the attraction of the breed, you know."

"Perhaps to a more conventionally bred female," China agreed, "but I was raised with a daily warning against the wickedness of the world and the sins of the flesh. Libertines hold no allure for me."

"Then since you do not intend to be cowed or seduced by Wrexford, you have nothing to worry you when he comes. Good night, my dear, and sleep well. There is nothing in the least to disturb your peace."

China obediently agreed, but when she closed and locked the door behind Reid, she returned immediately to her sitting room to respond to the earl's letter, knowing she would not recapture her serenity until she had done so. Though she had no personal knowledge of the man, like Amelia she took great care in chosing the words that she wrote to him.

The object of China's disquiet was in his comfortable book-lined sitting room in the suite of rooms allotted him in the small palace that served as a residence for English officials not formally attached to the Embassy in Madras when he received China's response to his letter.

Morgan Rawdon, fifth earl of Wrexford, was alone as he read the letter, but his valet, Gilley came into the room just as he let out a sigh that was plainly one of exasperation, followed by a softly spoken, "Damn." Gilley, a small, cadaverously thin man, unobtrusively placed the bowl of rose-scented water on the table near the window to catch the breezes which would spread the fragrance throughout the room, and then cast a covert glance at his employer to see if he could gauge the earl's temper.

Morgan chanced to look up from the letter at that moment and, noting the look of assessment in his valet's eyes, he smiled. "I'm not going to throw any books at your head, Gil," he said, the pleasant quality of his baritone voice making it seem unlikely that he would ever be given to such an act.

"No, my lord," the servant agreed with a dry inflection. Though the earl was never given to violence and his temper was fairly equable, he could be formidable in certain humors and not even Gilley, who had been in his service since Morgan had come down from Oxford ten years ago, would have cared to push his tolerance to the limit. "Do you wish me to exchange the Madeira for cognac, my lord?" he suggested, nodding toward the table beside the earl's chair which held the wine and a glass ready for him but still untouched.

Morgan's brows went up suggestively. "Look as if I need it, do I? Very well. No doubt you are right."

When the valet left the room again, Morgan resumed his rereading of China's letter. It was as civil as his letter had been to her and it disturbed him almost as much as his had disturbed China. Damn! The word again punctuated his thoughts. Never before had a woman who was neither a blood relation nor a lover or potential lover cut into his peace to such a degree.

He had not been as surprised as Amelia or his mother had been when news had reached them that Clive had remarried—he knew the ways and yearnings of his sex too well for surprise. Nor had he found anything to wonder at that his uncle had married a younger woman. Most likely a very pretty young woman; Clive, he knew, had been a connoisseur of the fairer sex. Chloris Tennant, a young woman of acceptable birth and connections, was very likely an English flower standing out in an exotic garden, ripe for picking at exactly the time when the restless baronet was beginning to find that his nomadic life had lost some of its attraction.

Morgan found in this no condemnation of China. Unlike his cousin Amelia, he did not believe that the mere fact that China had married a man more than twenty years her senior branded her as an adventuress. An opportunist, perhaps, that he could understand and accept. Both from his own contacts in the East and reading between the lines of Clive's letters he had formed a fair idea of China's background and situation before she had married Clive and guessed that Clive had been a godsend to her.

And what if China had viewed Clive as a savior more than a lover? In his class, marriages were predicated on far worse than that. It was unfair to Clive, in any case, to assume that he hadn't the power to attract a woman of his choice by other than being a means of rescuing her from an unattractive future. No, he could not with good conscience condemn China solely for marrying Clive. And if she had brought the restless baronet some measure of happiness or comfort before he had died, it was to her credit.

Yet, however much Morgan intellectualized his feelings toward China, he was not easy about them. He had corresponded directly with her only two times before, and though her letters were always unexceptionable, he had sensed a care, a guardedness behind the civil phrases and responses. It might mean nothing—it probably did mean nothing—he himself had been a bit circumspect in his congratulations, knowing nothing as he did about his uncle's bride. He gave no credence to Amelia's vituperative characterization of China, which she had not hesitated to pen to him, and he harbored no dark thoughts or unspeakable suspicions about his uncle's death; he knew firsthand how susceptible even a seasoned Englishmen could be to the myriad fevers and strains of influenza that abounded in the East.

He had not been deceived by Amelia's carefully written letter, which was clearly meant to persuade him to discover something to Lady Rawdon's discredit. He had no intention of doing so, but he acknowledged to himself that he would be far more sanguine if he could meet China and know something of his uncle's widow firsthand. Yet if Clive had not died so suddenly so soon after his marriage, if such a comfortable portion of his estate had not been left away from his children and gone to this woman who was unknown to them all, he knew he very likely would have felt no uneasiness at all.

China's response to his letter, though very politely phrased, was clearly intended to put him off from visiting her at Macao, and this made him more rather than less determined to make the journey. He folded the letter and tapped it against his knee for a moment before uncrossing his legs and getting up to go to the window which looked down on the courtyard. The palace had once belonged to a minor raja who had had it built for his favorite concubine, and erotic scenes set in mosaic graced the courtyard. Immediately below his window was the vision of an exceptionally well-endowed female displaying her unclothed attractions to a very interested male. He smiled at the beauty and simplicity of the design, which robbed it of crudeness. He found himself wondering if anyone really understood what attracted a man to a woman or a woman to a man.

In spite of his reputation as a rake, he did not agree with the popular maxim that all cats are gray in the dark. In his thirty years he certainly had found himself in sexual situations with women toward whom he felt a tepid attraction at best, but for the most part for him there had to be some special spark or he did not consider the conquest worth the effort. With all the women who had crossed Clive's path in his travels and doubtless shared his bed, what had it been about Chloris Tennant that had led Clive to offer her marriage? He wanted to meet this woman for himself, for reasons quite apart from what he felt were his responsibilities as head of the Rawdon family.

He heard Gilley reenter the room but did not turn from the window. His one fear of meeting China was that he would find her unremarkable after all, and really rather ordinary. Clive would not be the first man with a reputation for conquests of exceptional women who finally settled down with a female who offered him comfort rather than excitement. Given China's upbringing by missionary parents, this was the most likely, yet he didn't believe it of her—or didn't wish to believe it.

Gilley came up behind Morgan and stood patiently waiting for his attention. Pulling his gaze away from the courtyard and his thoughts away from his reflections with some reluctance, Morgan turned away from the window and took the glass of cognac his valet handed to him. Morgan drank and felt the familiar warmth the liquor imparted. In his chosen profession, a man had to have a hard head, and the ability to drink deeply and still keep one's wits about one was simply a matter of survival. But the amount that he drank and the increasing amount he needed to drink to feel the effect of the spirits bothered him, and it was one more thing added to many others which had made him decide that the time had come for him to leave the diplomatic service and become what, after all, he had been bred to be—an English gentleman and land owner.

When he had inherited his dignities at the age of two and twenty, the prospect of no occupation other than management of his estates, which were already very well seen to by a superb staff, had bored him. But of late, that style of life had come to seem increasingly attractive and he had already begun to make arrangements to give up his post and return to England. He had not intended to detour for a visit to Macao until he had received letters from his mother, Amelia, and Mr. James which had given him sufficient concern to think that a face-to-face interview with Clive's widow might be in order.

Amelia would have been offended if she had known it, but it was Mr. James's letter that had caused him to write to China suggesting a visit far more than her own. James had not stooped to any unfounded suspicions of Lady Rawdon, but he clearly believed that it was in the widow's best interests to return to England for various reasons, some clearly outlined, some merely hinted at, and he had written to Morgan in the hope that he might approach China to persuade her to that course. He appealed to Morgan as head of his family, of which China as Clive's relict was now a part, to see to her interests. But Morgan's letter to China had been no more than exploratory; he had not been entirely certain if he meant to bestir himself to go so far out of his way—until he had received her intentionally discouraging response. He could not imagine why she would wish to put him off, but it was plain that she did, and this stirred his curiosity sufficiently to move him to action.

"Have you ever been to China, Gil?" he asked before he finished the contents of the glass.

"Not yet, my lord. Shall I be going there?"

"Yes. I think so. To Portuguese Macao. Find out how passage there may be arranged."

"Very good, my lord," Gilley responded, his voice carefully impassive. He suppressed a sigh and took the empty glass from the earl, returning it to the tray on the table. Though his loyalty to Morgan was unshakable and he would have followed him to any place on the earth that the earl chose to go, he had been counting the days until their return to the green, misty landscape of England. He never stooped to reading his employer's correspondence when the earl left his letters carelessly lying about, but he knew enough to guess what this was about.

Well, Gilley thought philosophically, it would be something, he supposed, to rest his peepers on the chit that had brought the roaming baronet to heel. All the Rawdon servants had thought it a sad turn that Sir Clive had gone off like that and left his children to the care of relatives and servants and then had just up and married some green girl no one had ever heard of. Like the earl, though for slightly different reasons, he too thought that China must be rather remarkable.

He followed the earl's instructions to the letter, as he always did, and at the end of a sennight, all the details for their journey to Macao were completed. Having made his decision to leave the diplomatic service, Morgan made the break cleanly and quickly, and it was little more than a fortnight after he received China's letter that he and Gilley boarded the English merchant ship that would take them, at last, to China.

3

IT WAS Boxing Day, or would have been if one were in England, and the determined festivities that the English in Macao had busied themselves with to forget that they were so far from their loved ones at home and the gaiety and beauty of a real English Christmas had dwindled to an end. They always did their best to maintain some semblance of the polite society they had left behind and small entertainments at each other's homes were commonplace, but at this time of year they were concentrated, leaving most feeling a little tired and a little saddened when they drew to a close.

China found herself a bit restless this morning. For the past few days she had had the sensation of waiting for something to happen—something she felt might not be pleasant. Her friend Sarah Weston, and Jack as well, scoffed at her uneasiness, but China was convinced that it was a premonition.

She dressed with extra care, donning a lovely celestial blue morning dress, one of many dresses and gowns Clive had had made for her in England by sending her measurements and instructions of what he wished made to one of the finest London modistes. Madame Celeste had proven herself worth her exorbitant charges, for everything she made fit China to perfection without so much as a single fitting. China had been raised to believe that money was unimportant beyond what it could do to further the missionary cause, but, she thought wryly as she stared at her reflection while Lucy, the housemaid who also served her as an abigail when required, brushed the tangles out of her long, naturally curling, guinea-gold hair, it had other advantages as well.

China had mostly lived a life of intentional deprivation, for her parents had lived by personal vows of poverty, but she had had no difficulty at all adjusting to being the wife of a rich man and she had not the least compunction in admitting that she liked it very well. She supposed she could go back to her former life if she were left without a choice, but it would be harder now to bear scrimping and subservience. It was always easier, she mused as she stared back into her own brilliantly azure eyes, when one had no idea what one was missing.

When a blue ribbon that matched the one at the high waist of her dress was tied in her shining tresses, which fell in a mass of rich golden ringlets over her shoulders and back, China rose from her dressing table and went to the cheval glass across the room to better view the overall effect. It was not vanity that prompted this attention to her appearance—that had been another sin in her parents' long catalog of unfitting behaviors— but a need to boost her confidence, to counter the lowering feeling which she could not seem to shake off with the ease to which she was accustomed in dealing with such things. If being pleased with her appearance alone was sufficient to raise her spirits she should have been in alt, for the long glass reflected a vision of loveliness that would have struck envy in many a female heart.

It had amused Clive to say that her sobriquet was appropriate, for with her delicately fair complexion, thick golden hair, and wide-open, guileless blue eyes she looked like a china doll come to life. Her unconsciousness of her beauty and her ebullient personality made her all the more attractive, and China had spent a good deal of time since she had first begun to mature warding off unwanted advances from men who yearned to possess her.

The gossips were always ready to whisper about China and every man who cast her lingering glances, and after she had married Clive it had troubled her for fear that he would think that she encouraged the advances of other men. But Clive had laughed and said let them talk; those attentions had appeared to increase his pride in his beautiful wife, and China had learned from him to have an aristocratic disregard for *on-dits*. She also learned to take pleasure in the attentions of attractive men, but she was careful that nothing concrete could ever be said against her character—she flirted, but singled none of her flirts out particularly, and no man who wooed her won her, save her husband. Only on Jack, who had had the complete approval of Sir Clive, had she conferred the privilege of intimacy, and that entirely platonic.

China usually had an excellent appetite for breakfast, but this morning she scorned all food other than a slice of toast with the morning cup of the pungent China tea she had come to love. Jack called shortly after she had eaten, and though she was feeling restless, she declined his offer to drive her into the city to shop and instead, when he had gone, returned to her bedchamber for bonnet and pelisse to pay a call on her friend Sarah Weston.

But when she arrived at the Westons' she discovered her friend was from home. China's disappointment was severe, for she had been counting on her friend to talk her out of her megrim, and the prospect of returning home again with her distemper intact was dampening. She stood in the front hall for a few moments, irresolute, while the male servant who served as butler, footman, and, occasionally, groom, waited with practiced disinterest.

A clock struck from somewhere inside the house and China broke out of her distraction. Taking a small wallet from her reticule, she extracted a pencil and on the back of one of her visiting cards she began to write a brief message to Sally when the sounds of arrival proclaimed the return of her friend. China greeted her gratefully but sensed that Sally was a little rushed and flustered and that it was probably not a good time for a visit. She offered to return later, but Sally refused to hear of it.

"Nonsense," Sally said roundly. "You looked as if you beheld a savior when I came through the door. Come up to my rooms and we'll have tea and you can tell me what has happened."

"Nothing in the least," China assured her with a dry smile. "I am just feeling bored and blue-deviled, with nothing whatever to do, and I need you to restore my spirits, Sally."

Sally laughed indulgently. "Blue-deviled? You, China? We can't have that. We'll see what the latest fashions can do to make you feel more the thing. Elise Lytton has just received the latest edition of *La Belle Assemblée* and I have wrested it from her for us to pour over, and I just have purchased some of the loveliest figured silk I have ever seen in the market. I want your opinion on what you think I should do with it, because Vernon always says that you have the best taste of any female he has ever met."

She linked her arm in China's and they started up the stair as she spoke. A door opened below them and a few moments later Sally's butler/footman called after her. "I beg your pardon, my lady—Sir Vernon wishes to see you in the bookroom."

"Oh, bother," Sally said with annoyance. She turned to China. "He probably wants to know what I have been spending his money on in town. You know what Vern is. He would give me the earth and everything in it, but first he would make sure that I appreciate the expense involved. Wait for me in my sitting room, dearest. I'll join you in a few minutes." She turned and retraced her steps, instructing her servant as she did so, for tea and cakes to be made for her and China.

China continued up the stair and let herself into her friend's sitting room. It was pleasant and sunny, reflecting Sally's own charm and character, and China felt her spirits rise slightly just crossing the threshold.

China had lived only eight years in England after her infancy, but she had learned to love the hominess with which even those high in rank seemed to like to surround themselves, at least in their private apartments, however grand the remainder of their household. Even here, in their small, beleaguered community on the western edge of Macao, the English had managed to satisfy their tastes to a remarkable degree. With a relaxed sigh, China lowered herself into a comfortable, overstuffed chair upholstered in a pretty flowered print. China might just as well have been in Miss Grayson's room in the Grayson Academy for Young Ladies of Quality, where she had been sent to receive a proper English education and which her mother, with a view to her daughter's future, had insisted that she attend over the vociferous objections of her husband, who regarded the school as elitist.

Those days figured among some of China's most pleasant memories and more than once she wondered what her life would have been like if she had accepted the proposal of the drawing master and eloped with him and remained in England. The prospect now made her laugh softly. Who would have thought then that she would one day be a rich widow at the age of six and twenty?

It was only the unpleasantness she feared she would face from Clive's family that kept her putting off her return to England. Living in exotic cities had been very different when her parents and Clive had lived; now she was mostly bored and restless. She felt rootless and at times had the feeling that she had yet to truly begin her life. Eventually she would have to screw up her courage and face the Rawdons and their condemnation, or live with the fact that she was wasting her days for no better reason than cravenness. Perhaps the attraction of England would prove no more than a romantic fantasy, but she knew she wanted to make some sort of permanent home for herself somewhere, a thing she had never in her life known.

Her thoughts came full circle from pleasant memories to imagined misgivings. It was at this point that Sally came into the room and one glance at her expression told China that something was afoot. "What is it, Sally?" she said, with more urgency than the situation warranted. "Is something amiss?"

Sally smiled, wiping away her solemnity. "My dear, the most amazing thing," she said brightly.

China laughed uncertainly. "Sally, you wretch! Tell me at once, before I have a fit of the vapors."

"No. No. There is not the least need for that," Sally said in a soothing voice. "It is just Wrexford."

"Wrexford?" exclaimed China in genuine puzzlement. "What has he to say to anything?"

"He is with Vernon."

China's expression cleared slowly. "Dear lord," she said under her breath, and then to Sally's amazement, she laughed. "So Wrexford is the cause of my half-acknowledged dreads. I suppose I should have thought of it, but I confess I did not. When did he arrive in Macao?"

"Today, I suppose. We should certainly have known of it if he had come before then."

"But why has he come here instead of directly to me?" China asked, wondering if there were something ominous in this behavior

Sally knew that China had misgivings about the earl's visit, supposing that its sole purpose was to inspect her for later reporting to the remainder of the family, and she wanted to treat his arrival as lightly as possible to prevent any concern in her friend. "We are acquainted with Lady Wrexford, his mother, you know," she said casually, "and had met him several times in town when we were in England. No doubt he thought it more proper to come to us first, since he is not at all acquainted with you other than by post. Vernon has asked him to stay with us since it would not do for you to have him in the house without any sort of chaperone. My dear, wait until you see him," she added in a confidential tone. "He is quite, quite handsome. I had no idea."

China had no interest at all in the physical attractions of the Earl of Wrexford. "He may be Adonis for all it matters to me. I wish I hadn't to set eyes on him. There was no need for him to come here at all."

"Apparently Wrexford does not agree," Sally said with a note of impatience. "Whatever does it matter, China? Send him to the devil if that is what you wish to do."

China smiled wryly. "I only wish I might. Did you tell him I was here?"

"No. I said nothing, not knowing what you would wish. But if you like, I shall send word that you are here. He will doubtless wish to meet you."

China felt there was little point to delaying the meeting. Like having a tooth drawn, it was best gotten over with as quickly as possible. "By all means let us beard this dragon at once."

Sally wrote a brief note to her husband informing him of China's presence and leaving it to his judgment whether or not to impart this information to the earl. Apparently Sir Vernon had no qualms about doing so, for only minutes later the servant returned with the message that Sir Vernon wished them to come to his study.

Morgan stood as Sally and China entered the study, and turned from his host to face the ladies. China's first impression of him was not the one she had expected. She felt a sudden increase in her heartbeat and realized that the physical attractiveness of the earl did affect her after all.

Morgan Wrexford was an undeniably handsome man. He was tall, over six feet, and well formed. His broad shoulders needed no padding and his moderate wasp-waist coat required no corset to show his figure to advantage. His hair was a rich auburn in shade and gently and naturally curling, his face finely featured yet unquestionably masculine. His eyes, China thought as she met them, were cat-green.

This coloring with a fair complexion, only lightly tanned by the hot Indian sun, created a startling effect. But it was more than this that disconcerted China. She had never seen a likeness of Clive in his youth, but she felt sure that in a more subdued way, for Clive's coloring had not been as striking, this was just as Clive must have appeared before maturity had mellowed his youthfulness into distinction. There was something similar in the eyes and general cast of features that had made her feel for the briefest of moments that it was Clive himself who stood when she entered the room.

China extended her hand to him, but instead of bowing over it in the usual manner of a man greeting a woman, he merely took it in a firm, masculine clasp. If he did have the practiced wiles of a rake, apparently he wasn't going to waste them on her. For some reason this small slight of gallantry had a calming effect on China and she greeted him with complete composure. "I had not expected to see you so soon, my lord."

"Or at all?" Morgan said with a slight sardonic upturning of his lips. "You seemed to think the last time we corresponded that I would be making a wasted journey. I hope I may prove you mistaken."

China was not offended by his directness, but rather impressed that this obvious man of fashion was given to plain speaking rather than airs and graces. To physical attraction was added a deeper affinity; she knew at once that she was going to like Morgan, and suddenly his approval was of even greater importance to her. But she would not pander to her need. She raised her brows slightly and gave him a brief smile to match his own. "I hope you may," she said civilly, but without giving him any encouragement in her tone to make him think she thought it likely. "Since you are come, I bid you welcome. It is a pity that you did not find yourself able to visit us before Clive died. It would have pleased him, I know. He thought very highly of you."

Morgan smiled faintly again at the setdown; it was not undeserved. Whatever else Clive's widow was, she was not missish. His opinion of China was not dissimilar to hers of him. He liked her at once, and the physical attraction was as strong for him as it was for her. He had expected Clive's wife to be attractive, knowing his uncle's taste in females, but he had never expected such a delicate vision of loveliness. She had to be at least six and twenty, but with her striking fair beauty, dressed in a demure style that became her, and with her hair tied back in the style of a girl not yet out of the schoolroom, she looked more like sixteen. This was clearly mere illusion. He saw intelligence in her eyes and a degree of worldliness at odds with her appearance. It was a seductive combination, and though seduction was not yet in his conscious thoughts, he was aware that she stirred him. Morgan had no difficulty at all understanding why Clive, no doubt jaded by his travels and wealth of experience, had found her sufficiently attractive to be a fair exchange for his freedom.

"As I did of him," Morgan said politely, not at all put out of countenance by her remark. "The Rawdons appear to suffer from a surfeit of wanderlust. It was rare that Clive and I were in the same part of the world at the same time, but we were ever faithful correspondents. The reason I have come to you, Lady Rawdon, is that I am returning to England and hope to persuade you to make the journey with me. You have inherited considerable property in England as well as abroad and we stand as joint guardians to Clive's three children, who are doubtless anxious to meet you at last.'' He saw China's brows rise skeptically. She was definitely no fool. ''Mr. James, our family solicitor,'' he continued smoothly, ''has requested me most especially to do what I can to persuade you to accompany me at the very least for an extended visit to put your affairs in order, if I cannot persuade you to make your home in England with us.''

Skepticism was replaced by a guarded look in China's eyes. She remembered well the veiled hints in the solicitor's letter that she might have to defend her inheritance. Was this what Wrexford was telling her as well? ''I have thought of it,'' she admitted. ''But I don't know that I have decided yet to visit England again. Since the war has ended, travel is much easier and safer, and I have been pondering visiting Italy or Austria first.''

Morgan inclined his head in acknowledgment that this was a reasonable alternative, but said, ''All of England has flocked to the Continent in the last two years since the war has ended. You would probably meet more of the *ton* in Rome or Vienna than in London, but since you have yet to take your place in society as Lady Rawdon, you might find the transition easier if you began it at home.''

China knew he was telling her that she needed to establish her acceptance in the world since the world knew nothing of her, and though she knew it was true, she found she resented it. ''My purpose, my lord, in visiting the capitals of Europe would not be to attend fashionable balls, but to view firsthand the art and culture that has always fascinated me but which has only been known to me in books.''

Morgan's smile broadened. ''Of course, Lady Rawdon," he said with unimpaired cordiality, "but as a woman traveling alone, I fear you might find it . . . ah, inconvenient to be entirely without friends in unfamiliar surroundings."

Sally Weston was also no fool, and was in fact a very astute woman. She had sensed the spark of attraction that had passed between Morgan and China and recognized that her friend was seeking to deny it by finding offense in everything Wrexford had to say to her. "My dear, Lord Wrexford is right. It is the most uncomfortable thing. But you are very independent, of course, and no doubt you would fare far better in such circumstances than I should."

Having hopefully defused a potential quarrel that would have gotten Morgan and China off to the worst possible start, she turned to Morgan and informed him that she had requested her housekeeper prepare him a room and that he might wish to go there to refresh himself before luncheon. "Though if you are hoping to taste the fabled cuisine of China, I fear you are in for a sad disappointment. All of our servants, including Mrs. Haggerty, who serves as both housekeeper and cook, are English. The Chinese and Portuguese resent our presence here in Macao very much—Vernon says it is because we are such better traders that we make all the money—and do everything they can to make our living here as difficult as possible. No Chinese or Portuguese will work for an Englishman at any rate, for it would mean complete ostracism from their own kind, and so we must import our own laborers on every level. China, you must join us as well. No doubt you wish to further your acquaintance with Lord Wrexford."

In part this was true, but China felt the surprise of his visit and the fact that she had met him at her friends' house instead of having him come to her in her own home gave him an advantage of sorts over her which she could not like. It would not do to be defensive with him from the start. "I should love to, Sally, but I fear I have another engagement."

Sally's eyes widened with surprise. "But you said only before that you were feeling fidgety because you had nothing in the least to occupy you this afternoon."

Whether Sally's wits had deserted her or whether she was trying to force China's hand, China couldn't guess, but she could have shaken her friend. Knowing that there was color in her fair cheeks and that Lord Wrexford must know she was lying, she said, "I am promised to Mary Fitchley-Gore. Andrew Creeley is still delayed in Canton on business and she asked me to join her and Caroline Creeley for luncheon to see if we might raise Caro's spirits." It was true enough, but the engagement was for the following day.

"Send a note to Mary," Sir Vernon suggested helpfully. "She won't mind putting it off for another day. Very easy-going sort of woman."

China felt positively beleaguered, but she held firm. "Nevertheless, I feel I should keep my promise to her. I am sure Lord Wrexford will excuse me."

Morgan's face was solemn, but there was a light of amusement in his eyes that China detected and could not help but find attractive. "Of course. If you permit, Lady Rawdon, I'll call on you tomorrow some time during the morning. We do have much to discuss, I think."

"I shall be at home, my lord," China replied, extending her hand to him before her friends could find some other excuse to detain her.

This time Morgan bowed over her hand in the more accepted fashion, but his eyes remained on hers and China knew instinctively that the attraction she felt for him was reciprocated. Her pulse increased and she was very glad to leave him before she betrayed herself in some way.

When they quitted the room, Sally admonished China in the hall. "Why on earth are you turning tail,

China?'' she demanded. ''He won't take a bite out of you, you know. And even if he meant to, surely you would be better off here with me and Vernon rather than facing him on your own.''

China shook her head. ''It isn't that; I am hardly afraid of him. But I wish to be more collected before we discuss anything of importance. He has not come all this way, Sally, to exchange polite nothings with me.'' She gave a short, mocking laugh. ''I wonder that I did keep a straight face when he said that Clive's children were anxious to meet me. I'll wager they would not have wished him to come here any more than I did.''

''I hope you do not mean to say so to him, though, love,'' Sally said, her brow knit with concern. ''Your directness is generally most charming, but Lord Wrexford is unacquainted with you and might be a bit taken back by it. Even if he has no power over you, I still think it would be politic not to offend him unnecessarily. You know you will wish to return to England one day, even if not just now, and it would be much more comfortable for you if you were on good terms with Clive's family.''

A martial light flashed in China's eyes as she retied the ribbons of her bonnet beneath her chin. ''Lord Wrexford will have to take me as he finds me. It is the Rawdons, not I, who are guilty of prejudgment. When he returns to England he may say whatever he wishes about me, but at least it will be the truth and not speculation.''

''Do you know, I was quite flustered when Vernon first presented Wrexford to me,'' Sally said as she escorted China to the door. ''There is such a look of Clive about him. You must have noted it.''

China acknowledged that she had. And that, no doubt, was the reason she felt so unsettled. She picked up her reticule and kissed Sally's faintly rouged cheek. ''To please me, dearest, try to steer the conversation to neutral topics tonight. I would prefer him to meet me tomorrow free of prejudice even if it is all in my favor.''

Sally gave her word, but unfortunately she had no control over her husband, who even as she made her promise was regaling Morgan with China's history as far as he knew it. ''Such a pretty little thing, and sweet-tempered besides,'' Sir Vernon said as he poured out another glass of his favorite Canary wine, which he had brought with him from England. ''Can't say I blame Clive in the least, though when he first brought China here from Kowloon we wondered if it was another case of the old man's lament; she looked more like a school-room chit than a young woman who was fully of age. Not that Clive was that old, mind, but he wouldn't be the first man who took up with a girl less than half his age to restore his tired virility. But it turned out, of course, that China was not as young as she appeared nor was she any bread-and-butter miss. She has a head on her shoulders, that one.''

Morgan considered this remark. Given Sir Vernon's obvious preference for China, he could not have meant it to be disparaging, but Morgan was not yet prepared to acquit China of being a clever opportunist. He also thought that little was not a word he would have used to describe her, nor simply pretty, for that matter. She was a little above average height for a female and it was his guess that she weighed eight stone at the least, but her exquisite coloring, porcelain complexion, and air of fragility made her appear delicate and would cause many men to regard her as more diminutive than she was in reality and awaken the masculine instinct to protect. He was not immune to her attractions him-self. If China were not a near connection of his, if they had met in different circumstances, he knew that at the least he would have pursued her for the purpose of flirtation or, if her inclination permitted, something considerably more.

"You will think it impertinent of me to ask this," he said as he sipped the Canary, "but I do so as Clive's nephew and with a genuine interest in his welfare. Do you think he was happy in his marriage to Lady Rawdon?"

Sir Vernon considered his reply for a moment before he spoke. "Such things are often difficult to gauge. If a couple wishes to fool the world about their relationship, it is not impossible to do. But China is a woman who I believe could bring happiness to a man without any great effort. She is not only a beautiful, desirable woman, she is a delight and a pleasure to know. She is a kind and gentle woman, her temperament is sweet, and her sense of humor enchanting, if a bit out of the ordinary at times." He saw that Morgan was regarding him noncommittally, and added with a slight defensiveness for China's sake, "You did not see China at her best today. She was taken a bit off guard, I think, meeting you so unexpectedly."

There was a hint of reproach in his voice which Morgan felt obliged to respond to. "I should have written Lady Rawdon again, I suppose, to apprise her more exactly of my arrival," he conceded, "but my plans came together rather quicker than I expected and I likely would have arrived myself as soon as any letter."

"No harm done," the baronet said in a fatherly way. "For all her outward fragility, China's a good strong lass. Had to be. She's been through a lot in her young life."

"Quite." There had been such a wistful note in Sir Vernon's voice when he had extolled China's virtues that Morgan suspected that Sir Vernon was at least a little infatuated with his former friend's widow himself. But the fact that China seemed to be on such good terms with Lady Weston could not lead him to suppose that it was more. "I notice that you always refer to Lady Rawdon as China. Is that how she is usually called? Clive always referred to her as Chloris in his letters.''

"He was the only one I know who called her by her given name. Even when he brought her here and introduced her, he did so as China, but himself, he called her Chloris," Sir Vernon said. "I expect Clive liked to do so because it gave him a sense of more intimate possession. He was not a jealous man, but he was very protective of China because she is so lovely and so naturally friendly that some men might misinterpret this as something a bit warmer.''

Morgan suspected that the age difference between them had something to do with it as well. He finished the last of the Canary, which was really too sweet for his taste, and put down the glass carefully before he spoke. He not only admired directness, he practiced it, but in his chosen career he had learned to gather his thoughts before he spoke. "Do you know of any reason why Lady Rawdon has chosen to remain in Macao rather than return to England now that Clive is dead?''

Sir Vernon shook his head. "I don't. I'm not in her confidence, but Sally might know of it. It isn't an unremitting love of the place, I can tell you that. Life for the English in China is not generally very comfortable, particularly here in Macao—I'll wager Amhurst has not found his post the plum that many back home regarded it to be.

"And it isn't as if China were raised here either and bore a sentimental attachment for the place. Her parents moved on to new missionary outposts ever few years or so. She was one of only a few spared when a fever swept their little colony a month or so before she met Clive. I expect their travels formed a bond of sorts between them. When he came to Macao, it was the first time he'd settled in any place for more than a few months at a time since he left England after his first wife died. But of course you know that.''

Morgan nodded abstractedly. He was now curious

to know more about China beyond simply wishing to meet Clive's elusive widow. He meant to get past her defenses, if he could, to see her as Clive must have done. "Do you think I have a chance of persuading her to return with me to England?"

Sir Vernon ran his finger around the rim of his glass. "Hard to say." He favored Morgan with a long, speculative look and then decided that direct speaking was in order. "Clive told me that his family didn't precisely welcome China with open arms. She's strong, but she's not insensitive. I think it hurt her quite a bit that she was judged sight unseen. That's the reason Clive didn't take her home to England, and it's the same reason China may not accept your offer of an escort."

Morgan gave a short laugh. "We aren't worth the effort to avoid us. I won't deny what you have said, but it is unfair to make it a blanket statement. Certain circumstances in my uncle's life led us to assume that he would never marry again, so naturally there was surprise when he did so, but I personally have tried to have no opinion at all until I come to know Lady Rawdon for myself."

Sir Vernon nodded. "Very wise. Appearances are not always what they seem. The very best of good fellows was Clive, but completely self-absorbed. The only person I ever knew to bring him completely outside of himself was China. Yes, he loved her. I don't doubt it. I think they were happy together," he added, at last answering Morgan's original question.

Another question hovered on Morgan's lips, but he left it unasked and the subject was turned for the time remaining until they were called to luncheon. He wanted to know from China herself if she had loved her husband. Whatever her answer, he thought he would know the truth of it, and that would very probably tell him as much as he needed to know about Chloris Rawdon.

4

CHINA WAS SCARCELY in a quake about her promised interview with Morgan the following morning, but as she went about her usual household tasks, spoke with her servants, and sat through morning calls with friends, her mind was constantly drifting to thoughts of what she would say to him or he to her.

Jack called, as he did most mornings, and did not seem as surprised as she that Morgan had descended upon them without further warning. He offered to stay with her when Morgan called, but China shook her head and gently declined his offer. "No. I have no way of knowing what he may wish to discuss about Clive or his family or even my inheritance. I am sure he would not wish to speak freely in front of any one else, and that would only mean putting it off to another time. I would as lief have it over and done with and then Wrexford will not have the least power to make me feel at a disadvantage."

"There isn't the least reason now for you to feel at a disadvantage," Reid informed her. "And if Wrexford means to quiz you about Clive or anything else, I should think you'd want a bit of support."

China smiled, but her tone was decisive. "No, Jack. You know me too well to think that I will shrink from any confrontation with Wrexford now that he has forced this meeting on me." She rose from her chair and held out her hand to him until he took the hint and stood reluctantly. "He should be here soon," she went on, linking her arm in Jack's as she firmly shepherded him toward the door. "Come back after luncheon, if you like, and I promise I'll tell you all about our interview."

At the door Jack turned to her and gently embraced her in a brotherly clasp. "I still wish you'd let me stay. If there is any dissembling to be done, you could not find a better hand at it than me," he said with a wry inflection. She shook her head and he sighed. "Very well. But I shall be back, and before luncheon, not after. If Wrexford does say something to upset you, you'll need a friend to talk to."

China smiled. "Now you are imagining the worst. I shall manage quite well, whatever the circumstances. I always do, you know."

"No one would ever make the mistake of calling you a shrinking violet," Jack said with a slight laugh that conveyed an intimate knowledge of her personality. "But don't overestimate your strength. Your friends are always here if you need us."

China was torn between exasperation and amusement at his concern, which could only serve to increase her own anxiousness. A glance at the tall clock that stood in the hall told her that the morning was fast waning. She had no wish to continue the discussion, which she knew could go on indefinitely, so she agreed demurely that she would call upon him or Sally should she feel the need, and after a few more like exchanges at last saw him out of the door.

Though China continued to keep herself occupied for the next hour or so, the time weighed heavily. She constantly found herself looking for a clock to tell her how much further the morning had advanced. She was in the main receiving salon at the front of the house which overlooked the wide carriage sweep and the high iron gates leading out to the street and for the third time in a quarter hour she got up from the writing desk, where she was ostensibly occupied writing a let-

ter to her aunt in Cornwall, and went to the window
to see if there was any sign of the earl. As she turned
away, disappointed again, she caught sight of her expression in a hanging mirror. She examined her reflection critically and though she looked quite lovely
dressed in a gauze morning dress the blue of a cloud-
less sky, she was not pleased with what she saw.

She disliked Jack and Sally's comments about her
concern over Morgan Wrexford's opinion, but she saw
clearly that they were right. Why on earth should she
be dressed in her finest morning dress, her golden hair
piled high in masses of shining ringlets looking as if
she were about to attend a Venetian breakfast at the
home of a fashionable London hostess, just to impress
and gain the approval of a man who, after all, was
nothing to her but a connection by marriage? It was
true, as Sally had said, that if the family meant to
contest Clive's will, it would not hurt to have one of
the Rawdons think well of her, but China realized that
in such a matter whether or not the earl found her
physically attractive was not likely to weigh very much
with him if he decided to support the other members
of his family.

China raised her chin as if she addressed Morgan
instead of her own reflection. There was not the least
need to impress the Earl of Wrexford. He would have
to take her as he found her or not at all. Her first
thought was to go to her room to remove the pins from
her carefully coifed hair and to put on her oldest cotton
day dress, but she smiled at herself for entertaining
the opposite extreme and in the end she simply returned to her writing in a far more relaxed state of
mind. When Morgan was finally announced about
three quarters of an hour later, China was able to greet
him with genuine equanimity.

"I hope I may be forgiven for coming to you so late
when I promised I would call first thing in the morning," he said as he bowed over her hand. He smiled

at her in the friendliest of fashions and there was an
admiring gleam in his eyes. Despite his belief that he
would find China to be a beauty, he had never supposed that he would find himself strongly attracted to
her, but it was so. He had not admitted to himself that
he had been infected by Amelia's belief that Chloris
Tennant had used some underhanded ploy to persuade
Sir Clive to marry her, but these doubts had risen to
the surface with the acknowledgment to himself that
China had probably not needed to use any such ruse.
She was so very lovely, and the intelligence, breeding,
and gentle nature which so clearly shone in her eyes
might have, in his opinion, enslaved any man she chose
to favor. If she had been set upon the town in the usual
fashion of young girls of good birth and breeding, she
would undeniably have caused a sensation.

China did not immediately reply to his handsome
apology. Her calm had not survived the first exchange
of greetings. The touch of his hand had seemed to
warm her in an astonishing manner and her heart began to beat a bit faster. Her feelings were similar to
his. The attraction she felt toward him was immediate
and strong and thoroughly disconcerting, causing her
to regard him fixedly without being aware of it.

Morgan saw at once, of course, that the degree of
attraction was mutual and it amused him and pleased
him as well, though his intentions toward her were still
of the most honorable. "Have I a smudge on my chin,
Lady Rawdon?" he asked, gently quizzing her.

This very naturally caused China to recollect herself
and to blush rosily. She was as given to directness as
he, but not above dissembling. "I beg your pardon,
my lord, if I have stared you out of countenance," she
said with her sunniest smile, determined not to give
herself away any further. "But you are so very like
Clive, you know. For a moment it seemed to me as if
he had come through the door again."

Morgan was not quite so pleased by this remark.

"Am I?" he said, with a faint lift to his brows. "I know our coloring is similar, but I have never heard the likeness much commented upon."

China said with apparent dismissal of the topic, "It is something in the expression, I believe. You need not apologize for your lateness," she said as if she hadn't given his visit a spare thought. "There was no set time for you to arrive."

Morgan permitted the change of subject. "Sir Vernon wished to show me some of the stock he is breeding to send home to enhance his own cattle, and I had no idea when I agreed to go with him immediately after breakfast that we would have to travel so far beyond Macao to the farm where they are kept." He followed China to the chair she indicated to him in a small conversational grouping near the doors leading to the garden.

China herself sat on a small sofa facing him. "It would be impossible for Sir Vernon to pursue his interest in breeding in Macao," she said conversationally, to give herself time regain her composure. "The Portuguese and the Chinese between them would make it impossible both physically and financially. Even as far out as the farm is in the countryside, there is always the risk that the stud will be confiscated and even the farmers punished for assisting an Englishman. The only reason anyone does so is because they are so poor that they consider it worth the risk for the sums that our countrymen are willing to pay."

"Quite," Morgan said thoughtfully. "I had heard, of course, that the English are resented in this region, and in fact to a degree in all of China, but I had no idea of the extent of it until I spoke with Sir Vernon yesterday. Even in the short time I have been here, I have seen some evidence of it myself. It can't be easy living here, or even comfortable."

"Not easy, no, but I wouldn't say uncomfortable. In any case, it is a very subjective matter. I am sure there are many places where life would be easier, but far more uncomfortable.''

He smiled. "Such as England?''

China had already had a taste of his directness the day before, so it didn't surprise her. "Yes. That is exactly what I meant. I do hope the only reason you have come to Macao was not to persuade me to return to England with you, my lord, for it is very unlikely that I shall do so.''

"But not impossible?''

She smiled and shrugged. Her innate honesty would not let her dissemble. "Unlikely,'' she repeated with firmness.

"That is the principal reason I have come,'' he acknowledged. "I fail to understand, Lady Rawdon, why you are so resistant to the idea. I am not suggesting that you never return to Macao, merely that you come with me to England to see to your inheritance. You know that Clive has made you guardian with me of both his son and youngest daughter.''

"Of course I do.'' Her tone was dry to the point of being caustic. "But since I am completely unknown to them, I think it would be presumptuous for me to interfere in their lives.''

"Interference and guidance are not synonymous. I think it was the latter that Clive had in mind.''

"I think the latter would be mistaken for the former in the circumstances,'' she responded wryly.

"A lack of any responsibility could also be taken for indifference.''

His expression was so impassive, she could not guess at what lay beneath it. The tone of his voice implied comment, not judgment, but it was impossible for China not to be defensive. "At least it may not be construed as hostility,'' she retorted.

He smiled, as if satisfied at the response he had solicited. "It might be.'' He saw a martial spark come into her eyes and his smile broadened. "By some,

Lady Rawdon, not by me. Come, let us call quits. One thing I have not come all this way for was to quarrel with you. I know you have not received the warm reception from all of our family that Clive hoped you would. There are extenuating circumstances though. You are familiar, I suppose, with Clive's history.''

China nodded. ''I understand that his children were much attached to their mother and it cannot have been easy for them to lose their father, in a manner of speaking, as well. But that is the past, the distant past, and nothing to do with me.''

Morgan shook his head. ''It is everything to do with you. Clive's eldest daughter, Amelia, was perhaps the most affected because she knew her parents best. Her way of dealing with her loss was to romanticize it. She turned her father into a tragic hero who was doomed to wander the world grieving for his lost love. I suppose it made her feel less abandoned and excused Clive for his neglect. When Clive married you, that image was shattered. It was time, I suppose, for Amelia to face reality in any case, but the abruptness of it—we none of us knew of your existence before we received Clive's letter telling us of your marriage—was like being doused with ice water for Amelia.''

China found his frankness both flattering and disturbing. She felt obliged to defend Clive, but as a child she had herself at times felt a burden to parents who had often seemed more interested in saving the souls of heathens than in nurturing her, and she could sympathize with the hurt Amelia must have felt for her father's neglect. ''Most of us romanticize our parents to some degree,'' she said levelly. ''It is a child's way of dealing with the foibles of adults.''

His gaze was assessing. China did not flinch from it. ''Perhaps if Clive had brought you to England before his death,'' he said in agreement, ''Amelia would have seen for herself that her image of her father was only a child's fantasy, but instead, the image continues, romanticized even further by his death.''

China smiled sardonically. ''I am cast as the designing female, I suppose. No doubt she feels I tricked her father into marriage with only a thought to his purse. I wonder she doesn't hold me responsible for his death in some way.''

There was a warning in her voice that Morgan caught at once and was surprised by. ''Not directly, but yes, I think she feels that if Clive had never married you, he would not have remained so long in Macao and might thus never have succumbed to a foreign infection.''

China rose from the sofa and walked away from Morgan in some agitation, causing him to wonder what sensitive spot he had touched. Had she nursed him in his final illness and did she fear that she had not been able to do enough for him? It spoke of a devotion he had not expected, but it was the likeliest explanation.

''Clive hated being ill above all things. Weakness of any sort was intolerable to him.'' She turned back toward him, her serenity hastily recovered. She wondered what devil had prompted her to bring up the very topic she would most have wished to avoid. ''I did what I could for him—when he'd let me,'' she said, unconsciously responding to his unspoken question. ''The best thing that can be said is that his illness was brief. He could not have borne a slow death.''

A silence fell between them and they gazed at each other across the span of half the room, two strangers bonded by a spurious intimacy of kinship by marriage. Neither spoke and neither looked away. Finally Morgan rose and walked over to China, coming so close to her that she had to raise her head to meet his eyes. Her heart did not again resume its rapid beat as it had when he had first come into the room, but she was very aware of his physical presence. Dispassionately, she did not seek to deny the attraction she felt toward him. In fact, she had the sudden wish that he would in some way touch her, and from the way his eyes rested almost caressingly on her for a long moment, she thought for a moment that he might, but he did not.

He nodded in agreement. "No, he could not have. Clive would have been ravaged by his own self-loathing as much as by any illness."

China marveled a little at his understanding of her late husband, but reminded herself that Clive had been his uncle and they were perhaps closer than she had realized. "In any case," she said, deliberately moving away from him to increase the distance between them, and feeling mildly ashamed of her prurient thoughts in the midst of such a conversation, "you must see that you cannot persuade me to return to England by appealing to my duty as guardian to Clive's children."

"You dislike the way you feel you have been pre-judged, China. I wish you would not consign all of the Rawdons to the devil in your turn."

A richly ornamented sliding door was open to the small garden, for the day was exceptionally warm for the season. She walked to the doorway to stand framed against the sunlit foliage, having no artful intent for the way that it enhanced her delicate beauty. "It is difficult to feel charity where none is reciprocated."

Morgan repressed a sigh. Whatever else his cousin's widow was, she was not biddable. He found himself admiring her spirit even while it exasperated him. "We really are not such a bad lot, you know," he said, coming up behind her to stand too close to her for her comfort once again. "I admit there are times when one or another of us may not always appear particularly congenial to the world, but more often than not it is a personal eccentricity rather than nastiness."

She turned slightly and glanced swiftly up at him, her skepticism plain in her expression. His smile in response was so wholehearted and so sweet that she nearly caught her breath at his physical beauty and the unwanted effect it was having on her. She turned away again and stepped into the garden, drawing her shawl about her against the cooler air of the outside.

Morgan followed her, falling into step beside her as she began walking down the path away from the house. "You didn't realize you were marrying into a family of eccentrics, I presume. How unjust of Clive not to have warned you! It is more than just Clive and me driven by the restlessness which is endemic to all Rawdons and Amelia's excess of sensibility and romanticism. Did he never mention our mutual uncle Thaddeus Rawdon?"

China was not certain if he was confiding in her or quizzing her. "No," she said a trifle coolly.

"He kept rats."

China was certain she had heard him wrong. "Cats?" she queried.

"No rats. River rats, to be more specific. Culled from the Thames. Couldn't keep a female servant in the house. And then there was Great-Aunt Elvira."

His voice was so even, so matter-of-fact, that she was becoming certain that he was roasting her. Even looking up at him, she saw nothing in his expression to suggest it, yet she knew it must be so. "What did she keep?" China asked with suspicious curiosity.

"Company with the Lord Mayor of London." A gurgle of laughter escaped China, and Morgan said, "That's better. Laughter suits you much better than hauteur. Great-Uncle Samuel wasn't laughing, however. When he discovered the Awful Truth, he felt obliged to challenge the Lord Mayor to a duel. His pistol, however, misfired and he had to stand and wait for the Lord Mayor's fire. He disgraced himself, I fear."

Though China was not certain she believed in the existence of either Great-Aunt Elivra or her cuckolded husband, she could not resist the obvious bait. "In what way?" she asked as deadpan as he.

"Fainted dead away. The Lord Mayor was forced to discharge his gun into air. But Great-Uncle Samuel had the best revenge."

Knowing what was expected of her by now, China said dutifully, "Did he?"

Morgan nodded gravely. "The Lord Mayor ended up with Great-Aunt Elvira."

"A termagant as well as an adulteress, no doubt."

"No doubt at all."

China could not keep back her bubbling laughter. "You are a complete hand, my lord," she admonished him.

"And not a bad fellow either, which you will see for yourself if you stop regarding me in the light of the enemy."

"Is that how you think I feel about you?" she asked. For the first time, she felt genuinely comfortable with him. She wondered if she were wise to let down her guard with him, but she could not help liking him.

He stopped and put his hand on her arm, touching her for the first time since he had taken her hand in greeting. "I give you no blame for your suspicions of me, but believe that I have come out of a genuine wish to make your acquaintance as well as to persuade you to return with me to England to your own best interest."

She smiled. "I may be a fool, but I think I do believe you."

A sound behind them made them turn together toward the house. Jack Reid was coming through the garden door, advancing toward them with a casual, but purposeful stride. She wondered briefly what Morgan thought of Jack's unannounced arrival, which spoke eloquently of their intimacy, and felt a momentary concern for his opinion which she instantly dismissed. Morgan had said he was not here to judge her and she would not, in any case, compromise her friendship

with Jack to prevent him from forming erroneous conclusions.

He did not do so, but he did note the easy familiarity
between China and Jack. It was not only the fact that
Reid obviously ran tame in China's house, but also the
easy intimacy that was between them which was pat-
ently of long standing. He might have assumed at once
that they were lovers, the thought certainly occurred
to him, but he found himself unwilling to believe the
obvious until he could do so with more certainty. That
in itself surprised him, for he was by nature a cynic,
particularly with regard to the relationships of men
and women.

China was not entirely pleased by Jack's arrival. She
and Morgan had begun to get on together quite famously and she was sorry to see their tête-à-tête brought
to an end. Unbidden, the thought of whether or not this
attraction would come to an even greater understanding
between them came to her to be dismissed instantly as
absurd. Morgan was Clive's nephew, the head of his
family; the attraction had an almost incestuous flavor
which simultaneously excited and repelled her.

She made Jack and Morgan known to each other and
saw the mutual assessment in each man's eyes. "I confess myself surprised, Lord Wrexford," Jack said in
his easy manner, "that you should come all this distance merely to persuade her to return to England to
see to her legacy."

"Are you?" Morgan said with an unreadable inflection. "Yet I have, and do not yet count the journey
wasted."

"What! Are you going to abandon your friends after
all, China?" Jack said with a surprised laugh. "Lord
Wrexford must possess a remarkable gift for persua-
sion, for I thought you quite set against it. Surely a
competent solicitor could attend to the matter without
the necessity of a tiresome journey, though it might be
in your best interest to employ someone other than

James, James and Landry. Not to call their integrity into question, you understand, but a firm employed by the Rawdons for generations might be said to have a quite natural bias.''

There was no discernible change in Morgan's tone of voice when he spoke, but even on so short an acquaintance, China recognized his annoyance in the way that his eyes became more hooded as if he wished to disguise the emotion. "I fear I do misunderstand you, Mr. Reid. I was not aware that Lady Rawdon stood in need of protection from her own family.''

He looked exactly what China as a child, before she had ever seen a titled person, had supposed an earl should look like, a bit haughty and remote. "I think we should go inside. It is quite a bit colder than I had supposed,'' she said without truth, hoping to deflect the conversation to safer topics. "It is nearly time for luncheon,'' she said, stepping into the room. "Will you join us, Lord Wrexford?'' she asked, though she hoped he would refuse. She could not imagine a more uncomfortable meal if she had to play conciliator for the whole of it.

"Thank you, Lady Rawdon,'' he said with an equal formality, yet giving her a brief, intimate smile that made him look very differently from the way that he had only a few moments before, "but I fear I must decline. Sir Vernon and Lady Weston are expecting me.''

"Perhaps another time,'' China said, returning his smile. China asked Jack a question about a horse he had recently acquired, hoping that he would take the hint and not return to their previous conversation, but it was in vain. As soon as he replied civilly to her question he turned to Morgan, "Was it perhaps only overcaution on the part of Mr. James, who wrote to China hinting that the validity of Clive's will might be in question?''

China could have throttled him for revealing to Morgan that she had had sufficient anxiety over the matter to discuss it with a friend. She herself had said nothing to Morgan, waiting to see if he gave it any mention, and she would have preferred, in any case, to have chosen the time to ask him plainly if the will was to be contested.

Morgan glanced at China before replying. "Did he?" he asked. "If so, I think he might have been said to be protecting Lady Rawdon's interests as a member of the Rawdon family as well as he does for any of the rest of us."

Jack's smile was cynical. "And if the will is contested? Who's interest will he protect then?"

"That is a question you would better put to Mr. James than to me, Mr. Reid," Morgan replied somewhat coolly.

It was a mild enough setdown, and China was grateful for it. She suspected that Morgan had a razor tongue when he wished to use it thus, and she did not want Jack to feel its lash for he only meant well, however much she disliked his interference. "And so I have," China said, hoping she showed no excessive concern. "I wrote to him and asked him plainly if that is what was intended." But since it was out in the open, she could not resist asking, "Is it?"

"I wish I could say to you that any such suggestion would be absurd, but in all truth I cannot," Morgan owned candidly. "My mother hinted in her last letter to me that there has been talk of it, though it is none of her doing." Though he did not say so, China had no doubt which of the Rawdons it would be who would wish to see her disinherited. "But I can also tell you that my mother has had it from James himself that the will is in perfect order and quite equitable. I wish you will not tease yourself on that head. Such an action would undoubtedly fail, and create the sort of scandal that we should all abhor."

China was relieved by his words, but not entirely sanguine that Amelia, if she was determined to believe that China had no right to her portion of the estate, would stop at creating scandal.

"What do you think of the will?" Jack asked Morgan

baldly, apparently not even considering that Morgan might think his interest in China's private affairs impertinent.

Whatever Morgan thought, he only said, "It is a matter of indifference to me. Clive was free to leave his property as he chose."

"Even though the whole of his estate would likely have gone to your cousins if Clive had not married China," Jack said, either not seeing or ignoring the imploring look that China cast him.

If Morgan's temper was being exacerbated by Jack's persistence, he controlled it admirably. "Or he might have left it to the Society to Preserve Seagulls," Morgan said with a faint smile. "It was entirely his own affair. We have made a beginning, Lady Rawdon," he said, turning to China and taking her hand. "I shall be here until the end of next month and I hope we may have the opportunity to know one another better whether or not I can persuade you to sail with me."

China expressed herself pleased that he meant to make so long a stay in Macao, though she was not yet certain it was sincere. "Then we may converse again another day, my lord. It is perhaps best if we do not approach too many fences at once."

Morgan's lips turned up slightly at this hunting reference. He supposed that it must come from Clive, for he doubted if China had ever been in on a chase in her life. "I hope I may see you tonight at the Fitchley-Gores'. I met Mrs. Fitchley-Gore last evening at the Westons' and she has been kind enough to include me in her invitation to Sir Vernon and Lady Weston to the party she has planned."

China felt slightly discomfitted at the mention of Mary Fitchley-Gore's name, wondering if she had given her the lie about taking luncheon with her the previous day. If so, Morgan did not put her to the blush.

"And perhaps we might ride together one morning as well," he continued. "Sir Vernon tells me that you do so most fine days."

China assured him that she would see him that evening and gave a vague acquiesence to his other suggestion as she walked him to the door herself, while Jack remained in the room. When she returned to her friend she was nearly in a temper with him and was controlling herself from speaking sharply to him only with difficulty. "Was it really necessary, Jack," she said as soon as she came into the room, "to behave as if you thought Wrexford had come with no other purpose than to oversee my ruin?"

"I didn't care for the way he was hovering over you when I entered the garden," Jack said plainly.

This was the last thing China had expected him to say to her, and a surprised laugh escaped her, evaporating her anger. "Dear heavens," she exclaimed. "Do you imagine he has designs on my person? I do not. You sound like a jealous lover, Jack."

"A concerned elder brother, rather," he corrected. "He is an attractive man, you are a recent widow and presumably vulnerable. You said yourself you knew of his reputation of being something of a rake. It is the oldest ploy in the world to disarm one's prey."

"Prey? Don't be absurd."

"You have not as much experience of the world as you think," Jack said, indeed sounding like a severe older brother. "You may have traveled more than most women of your age and station, but you lived perpetually in a closed missionary community which has virtually no relation at all to the sort of world Wrexford and his ilk people."

China made a face at him and rose to ring for a servant to have luncheon prepared for them. "You are putting me very much in mind of my father," she said, turning back toward him as she tugged at the bell pull. "It is as if you were describing Satan come to snatch my unwary soul from salvation."

"Perhaps I am."

China broke into a peal of laughter, her humor quite

restored by this flight into melodrama. "What nonsense you talk, Jack."

"Do I?" Jack said. "But I saw the way he was looking at you when I came into the garden."

China, strongly aware of the attraction between her and Morgan, and also what she felt to be the impropriety of it, said more coolly, "And in what manner was that? Like a hawk waiting to devour a fieldmouse?"

This made Jack laugh. "No. You would make a very poor sort of mouse. Don't fly into a pelter with me, China. It is only a friendly concern. With Clive gone, who else might you come to for protection, if not to me?"

China was regretting a little that Jack meant to stay for luncheon, for if he continued on in this vein she was certain to be quite out of charity with him. "I trust I do not need protection from Clive's nephew," she said acerbically. "Clive always spoke of him as a most honorable man."

She put a hand quite unconsciously to her temple and Jack was instantly solicitous. "Do you have the headache?" He laughed ruefully. "Did I give it to you?" He went over to her and took her hands in his. "I think I shall forgo luncheon today, China," he said as if he had read her thoughts. "Give my apologies to your cook. I wish I might see you tonight at the Fitchley-Gores', but I am promised to take dinner with Matt Carter. Perhaps you will be sufficiently amused tonight without me though," he could not resist adding.

China understood the remark, but would not acknowledge it. She assured him she would be bored to flinders without him present to share the evening's absurdities, but in fact, she did not give him another thought as soon as he had been shown out of the house.

5

THOUGH SHE WAS not consciously aware of it, China spent the rest of the day preparing for her next meeting with the Earl of Wrexford. After luncheon she tried on four different gowns before she was satisfied with what she would wear to the Fitchley-Gores' that evening, and even her jewelry and hair ornaments were chosen with more care than usual.

There would be no dancing, merely dinner, conversation, and cards. But China wished there could be—she had no doubt Morgan would ask her to stand up with him and there would be a perfectly legitimate excuse for her to feel his arms about her. It was this thought that came to her while Lucy was dressing her hair that forced her to acknowledge how much importance she placed on seeing him again that evening. Perhaps Jack was right and she did need to be on her guard, though the threat might be inward rather than outward. It was one thing to admit that an attraction existed between them and quite another to behave as if she meant to act upon it.

She recalled a stricture of her mother's that no properly bred young woman would permit herself to fall in love with a gentleman until he had declared himself. In this instance, particularly, it would be exceptionally stupid to do so. Because the Earl of Wrexford plainly admired her, because he had been kind to her instead of condemning, it did not mean that he held her in any warmer regard. Indeed, how could he? They were

barely acquainted. Yet her own thoughts remained recalcitrant.

China had selected a silk gown in a rich shade
of rose that did not wash out her delicate coloring the
way that a more insipid pink would have done. She stood
before her cheval glass and was pleased at the way the
silk caressed the rich curves of her body. The bodice
of the gown was not cut indecently low, but it flattered
her bosom quite nicely. She slowly ran her hands from
her waist over her hips and a realization struck her so
forcibly that she sat down rather quickly in the chair
behind her. She wanted Morgan Wrexford to caress
her so.

She looked up at herself in the mirror and saw that
her flush went down her throat to the curve of her
breasts. Unconsciously, she placed her fingers against
the faint swell just visible above the neckline of her
dress. A shiver of pleasure went through her as if it
were Morgan who had touched her and China looked
abruptly away from herself, embarrassed by her
thoughts. She was glad that Lucy had left her, for she
momentarily had no power to regain her composure.

She could not understand why she should feel this
way about Morgan. It could not be merely the resemblance to her late husband. Clive had been a loving,
affectionate man, a skilled and considerate lover who
had painstakingly taught her the wonder of her own
body and the delightful sensations that could arise in
it. She had cared for Clive, she had enjoyed their lovemaking, but she had never desired him—not like this.
And she had not yet spent a full hour in Morgan's
company. A small laugh escaped her at this thought,
finally dispelling her discomfiture. It was completely
absurd.

She contemplated remaining at home that evening
after all, but decided that being cowardly would serve
her no purpose. She could not avoid meeting him again
and it was certainly better to do so in company if she

was going to continue to have such disquieting thoughts about him.

China had been raised to a life of self-discipline and was well versed in the ability to keep her wants and needs in line with a more pragmatic reality. Having firmly called herself to order, she was able to meet him at the Fitchley-Gores' with no more than a faint fluttering of her pulse as he took her hand in his. She even maintained her aplomb when his intriguing green eyes smiled into hers with such warmth that she could not doubt that he felt as she did. But these fleeting transgressions against her self-control served to strengthen her and by mid-evening she was able to regard him quite unconcernedly as he sat across the room from her speaking with a very lovely Caroline Creely, who was flirting with him quite openly. She found fault with the easy way he responded to that lady, proving him to be the fickle rake he undoubtedly was, and she even decided that he was not after all quite so exceptional looking as she had thought at first sight.

Her scrutiny was noted by Mr. Dana Bovell, a distant connection of the Fitchley-Gores who had come to Macao about a year previously. He ostensibly was employed in some capacity by Mr. Creely in his importation interests, but Caroline Creely had commented to China in a dry manner once that her husband found Mr. Bovell not overly inclined to his duties and the merchant was only prevented from sending him to the devil out of respect for the Fitchley-Gores.

Bovell was commonly regarded by the charitable as something of a wastrel, by the uncharitable as an adventurer and soldier of fortune, but he was received by virtue of being a connection of the Fitchley-Gores and the ability to make himself pleasing when he chose. China could not like him, though he had a dry, often caustic sense of humor and was usually good company. He too frequently made her the object of his attentions and of late had occasionally applied his acerbic wit against her as if in retaliation for her lack of response to him. This did not overly concern China; if it meant that he had finally taken the hint that she had no intention of encouraging his pretensions, he was welcome to snipe at her with her perfect goodwill. His regard mattered to her not in the least.

With his black hair, deep blue eyes, and athletic form, he was in his way as physically attractive a man as was Morgan, but he had never made China's heart beat erratically and she had never felt the smallest desire to taste his lips on hers. She barely acknowledged him as he sat himself beside her on the arm of the overstuffed chair in which she sat sipping at an indifferent wine and listening to an equally indifferent rendition of a popular air being played on the pianoforte by Louise Richton, a fairly new arrival to Macao, who cast an envious look toward China as Dana joined her.

"Which is it, I wonder, that holds your interest so firmly?" he said in a lazy drawl, looking down at China through half-closed lids.

She looked up at him without concern, having no intention of going for the bait he cast to her. "Do you think it would be wise for Robert Creely to spend a bit less time in Canton?" she asked innocently. Morgan was not Caroline's only recent flirt, and China had heard whispers linking her name to Bovell's. But then, in their small closed society where there was little else to interest beyond the foibles of one's neighbors, a woman might smile one too many times at a man in one night and be accused of taking him as her lover.

Dana Bovell was no more easily hooked than was China. He smiled a smile as lazy as his voice. "I hope your nephew, or whatever it is Wrexford is to you, does not refine too much on the attention of a bored and lonely woman."

"I am sure he would not," she said dulcetly. "But

then, I do not know him very well. You might wish to pass on the caveat yourself, Mr. Bovell.''

He laughed softly. "Touché, Beauty." He stood and sat in the chair beside her which had just been vacated by Mr. Richton, who had gone to the pianoforte to assist his wife in a duet she was just beginning to play. "We have only just met tonight, but Wrexford seems a decent enough fellow to me, though I expect you may not think so.''

"Why should I not?" China said with surprise tinged with suspicion, wondering if Jack had discussed her private affairs with Bovell. They were friends of a sort by the circumstance of being the only men in the English community beneath the age of thirty.

"I merely suppose that he is come here to see for himself whether or not you have horns and a tail," Bovell said with a knowing smile. "He must be dashed curious to see what manner of woman his cousin married so late in life to come so far out of his way.''

"No doubt he felt it his duty to make my acquaintance," she said repressively.

"He is looking this way, and I think he means to join us." Bovell paused to observe the couple across from them for a few moments longer. "Yes. He is standing and taking her hand in his. She looks as if she wants him to hold it forever, but no, he has not even kissed it, merely a correct bow and now he is certainly turning this way. Poor Caro." He transferred his gaze to China. "Shall I stay and protect you, Lady Rawdon, or am I *de trop?*''

"De trop," she said without hesitation.

"Like Caro, I am destined to be the bridesmaid, I perceive." He gave a sigh of mock sorrow, rose, and bowed to her with a flourish. "If he toys with your affections as he has clearly done with poor Caroline's, Lady Rawdon, you need only signal your appeal across the room with your exquisite eyes and I shall be at your side on the instant.''

"That is a great comfort to me," she said dryly.

He laughed, and as Morgan came up to them he said, "Wrexford, this is no ordinary female. A friendly warning: If you abuse her sensibilities you shall have me to answer to, and others as well." He gave Morgan a brief nod of dismissal and turned abruptly and left them.

Morgan looked after him for a moment and then turned to China. "Now what the devil was that about?" he asked, mildly bemused.

China wished there was some heavy object at hand to cast after the retreating figure of Dana Bovell. "A private vendetta," she said with a welcoming smile. If Bovell had hoped to embarrass her before Morgan, he had failed. She was still in admirable control of her feelings toward the earl, and she did not think she had betrayed herself in the least to Bovell. It was merely a lure cast to see if she would rise to it.

But Morgan Wrexford was no fool. "Infringing on his territory, am I?" he asked baldly.

"If so, it exists only in his imagination," she said with complete indifference.

"Poor Mr. Bovell," he said, unconsciously echoing that man's thoughts about Caroline Creely. "In spite of the limitations of society here, Lady Rawdon, you have a loyal court of admirers."

"But I don't know that it is any great compliment," she said, smiling. "Society, as you say, is thin, and I am one of only two or three unattached females. It is another reason, I think, to remain where I am. In London, I should doubtless wither in the competition."

"No," he said with a definiteness that surprised her. "You would hold your own against any competition."

His words were flirtatious, but there was such a sincere expression in his eyes that China felt a faint flush brought on by the compliment. "What a pretty address you have, my lord," she said brightly. "I don't wonder at your reputation."

"What is my reputation, Lady Rawdon?" he asked with genuine curiosity as he took the chair Dana Bovell had vacated.

"Oh," she said, and paused as if she had to think to remember what she had been told. "Clive, I believe, said something once about your having broken your share of hearts."

He smiled and shook his head. "I don't think so. Certainly never intentionally. There is an old saying, Lady Rawdon. Believe half of what you see and none of what you hear."

"I hope you may subscribe to your own words, my lord," she said with a deliberate demureness that made him laugh again.

"Will you ride with me before breakfast tomorrow?"

"I ride very early in the morning," she said, hoping to discourage him. She needed more time to be certain of her control of her feelings for him before she wished to trust herself to an hour or so in his exclusive company.

"And I rise very early. We may start off at dawn if you like."

"Your curiosity to see the countryside must be quite intense, my lord."

"My curiosity about you is more so," he said, with that small upturning of his lips that was not quite a smile and which affected China quite against her will.

"You might satisfy that, if you wish, without the necessity of riding out in the half dark," she said in a flat tone designed to depress any further flirtation. "If you plan to be in Macao for a month, we shall doubtless meet any number of times before you leave."

"That is not how I wish to know you," he said, dropping his voice a little in pitch. "I wish to know you as Clive knew you."

China nearly gasped. The connotation was outrageous, but she would not give him the satisfaction of putting her out of countenance. "Do you imagine my public facade so different from the private?"

"Have you ever known it to be otherwise?"

"You, my lord, are a cynic," she said with a dry laugh. "Perhaps some morning we may ride together. Tomorrow I have an early engagement almost immediately after breakfast and I shall not be riding."

"The day after then?" he persisted.

China found herself both flattered and annoyed that he would not take the hint. "I am not yet certain of my plans that morning. Or the morning after that," she added hastily. "Perhaps by the end of the week or the beginning of the next."

"Or the morning that I sail?" he said, his smile growing. "I thought we were agreed, Lady Rawdon, that I am not an ogre or come to judge you. You have nothing to fear in me."

"Of course I am not afraid," China said crisply, and she thought to herself that she was far more afraid of herself than of him. She wished she had the ability to read him more effectively, but that, of course, could only come with time, and he had a way about him of making the most direct statements seem ambiguous that she could never be certain if she knew exactly what it was he was saying to her. Believe half of what you see and none of what you hear! China thought it delicious irony that he should have said those words to her.

"But it is quite your own fault if I do not have the time for you that you would wish," she said plainly. "I had no notion that you would be coming to Macao so soon, if at all, so I could scarcely plan for your visit. I am not in the habit, my lord, of spending my time idly."

"So I perceive," he said with a smile, not at all put out by the setdown. "I see that I shall just have to be persistent until you smile on me and grant me the favor of your time."

There was nothing in his tone to make China think he was being sarcastic, but the conversation was taking a turn that could well end up in daggers drawn, and she firmly turned it by asking him who had been to luncheon that afternoon at the Westons'. Morgan took her lead and after a few minutes more of conversation, he left her when Mr. Richton approached China to ask if she would play and sing for the company in her turn.

China did as she was bid, but only her considerable skill on the pianoforte saved her from making embarrassing errors, for her mind was far from the music she played. Her resolve about Morgan was undiminished, but her thoughts were once again in riot.

She had resisted the advances of all men except Clive since she had been old enough to attract the opposite sex, and never had she found it so difficult to do before. None had ever cut up her peace the way that the Earl of Wrexford did. And she could not even be certain that her feelings were reciprocated in quite the same way. If he were indeed a rake, it might be dalliance that he had in mind—or something worse. She was not a green girl to be easily seduced, whatever Jack might say about her lack of experience and supposed vulnerability. Yet she could not quite credit it that he meant to offer her any insult. In light of the relationship in which he stood to her, it would be most unprincipled for seduction to be his purpose, and Clive had never spoken of his nephew as being anything other than a man of honor. But Clive had known Morgan more through their correspondence than personal intimacy, and there might well be facets of the earl's character with which he could not have been acquainted.

It was a situation frought with pitfalls. Morgan might be genuinely attracted to her as she was to him and his intentions quite honorable; or he might be attempting to discover for himself if she was a woman of easy virtue who had duped his cousin into marriage. Even if he were sincere, he would be leaving Macao within the month. Unless she decided to go with him to England as he wished her to, she might well never see him again.

This was not a dilemma she had ever expected to face in her life; because they had never before been awakened, she had wondered if she possessed strong passions. Used to her well-ordered life, it was frustrating to her to have no answers at hand. The only solution that occurred to her was to avoid Morgan as much as possible and be glad that in a month's time the question of whether or not to live by proclivity or reason would be resolved of its own accord.

Morgan found China quite as disturbing as she found him. Possessed of considerably more experience in such matters than China, he had no difficulty recognizing and accepting the strong physical attraction he felt toward her. But like China, his concern was with whether or not to act upon it.

It was far more a matter of honor than of kinship or propriety that held him back. China was a woman alone in the world with a claim to his protection; what manner of man would he be if he abused that trust and seduced her for his own satisfaction? Yet it was still possible that she was not all she seemed. He still disliked admitting that he had in any way been prejudiced by Amelia's vituperation against her stepmother, but he could not quite banish the idea that China might not be quite the decorous widow she appeared. He had no concrete reason to doubt her virtue, but he had observed her naturally flirtatious nature toward many of the gentlemen in her set and supposed it possible that she might indulge in an occasional *affaire* with sufficient discretion to keep it from becoming widely known even in such a narrow society. It had already occurred to him that Jack Reid might be her lover, though her manner toward him was not openly flirtatious. That might, of course, be quite deliberate.

The temptation was, if anything, more powerful for him than it was for her. He had not the inclination for soul-searching that China possessed, but whether or not to put their attraction to each other to the test occupied his thoughts more than he would have expected it to do, and every time he saw China his resolve to let it lie lessened. He did not outwardly admit this to himself, but he knew, by the time he finally persuaded China to ride out with him in the Chinese countryside the following week, that the temptation was stronger than his power to resist it.

This happened far sooner than China intended. China actually had not ridden out for several mornings. On one or two occasions, as she had told Morgan, the press of other activities had made it impractical, but actually, her sole groom, who also served as a footman inside the house, had been suffering from influenza and was still not sufficiently recovered to accompany her on her rides, and to go out alone would have been foolhardy to the point of insanity. The hills surrounding Macao were not particularly dangerous or overrun with bandits during daylight hours, but an unprotected Englishwoman would have been considered fair game by many Chinese or Portuguese men and her person, if not her purse, might well be in jeopardy.

They had met every day since his arrival in Macao but always in company for even when he called at her house, he had always found China to be with some friend or other. China was coming to like him better and be easier in his company each time they met, and since Morgan was too much of a gentleman to continue his attempts at open flirtation publically, she was lulled into believing that the danger of losing her heart to him had passed.

When he repeated his request to ride out with her

one afternoon at the Westons', China, restless from the loss of her favorite exercise, impulsively agreed. They agreed to meet at a very early hour and China was already mounted and ready to greet Morgan when he arrived. She was as eager for the exercise as her mount, which sidled restlessly at the delay, and she was in ebullient spirits.

"You see, my lord, I do not keep you waiting," she said in a teasing fashion. "I don't think you believed me when I told you this was my usual hour to ride."

"True," he admitted without a blush. "Many women of my acquaintance consider early exercise quite out of the question if they are to complete a proper toilette."

"Are you suggesting that mine is incomplete?" she asked archly.

"You won't catch me out at that," he said, laughing. "You are as always a perfection of loveliness."

It was the first fulsome compliment he had paid her since the night they had spoken at the Fitchley-Gores' party, and China was startled by her reaction to it. It appeared that she had not yet grown as indifferent to him as she had supposed. She immediately lowered her head and pretended to concern herself with her stirrup leather. She wished her servant had been sufficiently recovered to go with them, but it was too late to concern herself with that now and in a few minutes they began down the drive.

"You are very wise to wear blue so often," he said, commenting on the deep-blue velvet habit that she wore. "It suits you better than any other color, I think."

China was determined not to be cast into confusion by his admiration. "Yes. Clive thought so too," she said very matter-of-factly. "It was his doing. When we were first married he took me in hand and ordered the whole of my wardrobe from England. I was a drab little creature before that. Grays and browns, I fear, are the fashion in missionary colonies.''

Morgan protested that she could never be considered drab however she clothed herself, but China ignored the compliment and set her horse off at a light canter down the still-empty street.

As soon as they were in open country, they let their horses out in a gallop to work out their fidgets. Finally they pulled up on a grassy knoll with a pretty panorama of fields and huts, the farmers and their men already beginning their long day of labor.

They gazed on this in silent companionship for some time before Morgan spoke. ''You ride very well, Lady Rawdon.''

She turned to him with a half smile. ''You sound surprised. Did you expect to find me mounted on a slug and clinging to the pommel?''

He returned her smile and shook his head. ''No. It is the degree of your skill which I am admiring. Your chestnut is obviously high-bred and has been fighting you for the bit since we began, but you keep him in check without effort.''

China inclined her head in acknowledgment of the compliment. ''My mother taught me to ride. Her grandfather used to hunt with the Quorn and her parents actually met on the hunting field. She and Papa chose to renounce the things of the world, but she never missed an opportunity to ride when someone was willing to mount her and she thought it a necessary part of my education. Papa,'' she added as an afterthought, ''was an indifferent horseman. Mama had such a poor opinion of such things that I sometimes wonder how Papa got past that to win her heart.''

This then was the explanation of her knowledge of hunting cant. It was both unexpected and quite charming. ''He probably wisely never let her see him mounted until he was sure of her,'' Morgan suggested with a knowing air.

China laughed. "Is that what you would have done?"

He nodded. "Most assuredly—if I had had to—and if your mother was anything like you. You must have had a most unusual childhood. I suppose late-in-life travelers like me always ask you fatuous questions about the places you have lived, but I pray you will humor me, Lady Rawdon; my interest is sincere."

It was a flattering speech and China was not immune to it. She complied, telling him of the varied cultures she had adapted to, the more interesting and less distasteful things she had witnessed, the triumphs and occasional disappointments of her parents in their mission. Morgan listened attentively and when China began to feel that she had almost embarrassingly monopolized their conversation she began to draw from him information on his career as a diplomat and she saw through his eyes another side of some of the worlds she had known—the side of the rich and the powerful. He did not aggrandize it but neither did he strip it of its glamour. He simply presented it matter-of-factly and China saw that it was not quite the fantasy world she had imagined as a child, living in conditions far from grand.

They had talked for so long that China lost track of time, but her mount, even after a good long gallop, was not content to be still indefinitely and he began to sidle restlessly beneath her again. "Perhaps we should be heading back to Macao. The sun is already high and my servants will begin to feel concerned if I am out too long. It isn't always safe, you know, to ride beyond the city."

"Bandits?"

"Sometimes. But mostly it is just the general hostility of the Mandarins and their men. I hate the restriction of taking a groom out with me as I usually do when I ride, but I know it is necessary."

"I hope I am at least as much protection as your

groom," he said with a smile. China was gathering up her reins but he put his hand over hers for a moment to stay her and nodded in the direction of a wooded area not far ahead of them. "Is there water there, do you know? Our horses will be lathered by the time we get back if we don't refresh them first."

It was not much of a detour and China agreed to it. They crossed to it at an easy canter and China led him to a small crystal-clear stream that sparkled in the sunlight, casting a cool green light about the copse in which it was situated.

"What a delightful spot," he said, pulling up before they had quite reached the stream to better view it. "And very English in character. This might be the wood at Ferris."

He dismounted and went over to China to assist her off her horse. China had not expected to dismount, but she made no objection. They led their horses to the stream and then stood beside them while they drank of the cool water.

China looked up at him and asked, "Do you miss Ferris?"

He seemed surprised by her question. "It is my home," he said simply.

China looked away from him, a wry smile touching her lips. "Yes, of course. I wasn't thinking to ask such a thing."

"Is that why you wish to stay here?" he asked his voice surprisingly gentle. "Is this home to you?"

China shook her head. There was a sudden knot of tears that caught in her throat and she didn't trust herself to speak for a moment. "It isn't that," she said truthfully. No place was home to her. She said abruptly, "You haven't yet asked me anything about Clive or our marriage. Why?"

"I knew you would tell me when you were ready to do so," he said quietly.

And China realized that he had known what she had

denied to herself. She needed to talk to him about Clive. He was either very wise or very clever. "I wasn't in love with him when I married him," she said baldly. She looked up to him again for his reaction, but there was none. He was staring into the water, his expression bland.

"I didn't suppose you were," he said without inflection.

China bristled instantly. "I won't deny that Clive came into my life at a most opportune moment, but I didn't marry him solely because he was a rich man."

Morgan turned to her. "There is no need to be defensive," he said with a slight smile. "I didn't suppose that either. Clive was a vital man who had no difficulty attracting women."

"He was," she agreed, and suddenly found she couldn't speak again.

Morgan took her hands in his and drew her near to him, but there was nothing in this to alarm her; he was plainly offering her comfort and nothing more. "You don't have to tell me if it is too painful for you to do so."

China shook her head. After a moment she had herself in control again. She told him virtually everything she felt she dared, from the day she and Clive had met in Kowloon until he had first become ill. She wasn't even aware that she was crying until Morgan raised a finger to her cheek and gently wiped away a new-fallen tear. Their eyes held and she felt instinctively that she had done the right thing to tell him the truth as far as she was able, and that he had understood without judgment, as he had promised.

He still held her hands in his, and slowly, almost as if he were giving her the opportunity to stop him if she wished, he drew her into an embrace. Her body was against his as she had imagined it would be in the brief fantasies she would not allow herself to indulge in. She could feel the hardness of his taut muscles against her, feel his suppressed strength. His eyes looked into hers in a penetrating way as if he sought an answer to an unspoken question. China could have pulled away from him; she felt no fear that he would try to force himself on her, but the proximity to this man that she frankly desired was more powerful than the urgings of her common sense. She wanted him to kiss her so intensely that her lips parted without her being aware of it.

His mouth came down on hers as gently as he had brought her into his arms. It was slow and very sweet. His tongue teased at her lips, her teeth, and found the warm, moist cavity within. She responded to him in a way she had never done with Clive. She pushed her body against him, aching to feel the hardness between his legs; proof that he desired her as much as she desired him. As if he read her mind, his hands slid from her waist to her buttocks and he pulled her tight against his loins. His lips left hers to travel in a burning trail to the hollow at the base of her throat. A gasp of sheer pleasure escaped her as she felt his tongue against her skin. She arched her back, raising her breasts which were already taut with anticipation.

He withdrew from her and gently undid the small buttons which with false chasteness covered the curves of her full breasts. He pushed down the lacy chemise and exposed her breasts to the air. He ran his fingers over the taut nipples of first one breast and then the other. "Dear God," he said on a breath, and took one of them in his mouth.

The sensation China felt traveled through her breast, down her spine, and into her thighs. She had to fight an urge to rip at her clothes so that he could touch her, taste her, everywhere. She had had no other lover than Clive, and Clive had been dead for more than a year. She might have blamed her wantonness on abstinence, but she knew it was more than that. She wanted this man, she wanted his body against hers and to experience the wonderful, ever-increasing arousal until they both exploded into pleasure. If he had laid her down on the grass at that moment, she knew she would have opened her thighs to him as freely as any whore on the strut in the Haymarket.

In spite of their closeness, she had always been shy about touching Clive, but China's need to know this man as intimately as possible was stronger than any shyness. She removed one hand from about his neck and moved it as slowly as he had caressed her, down his chest, his flat stomach. She didn't think about what she was doing, about what he would think of her; she was drowning in a sea of desire and not even attempting to rescue herself.

There was no doubt in either of their minds what the natural conclusion of this would be; like China, Morgan was choosing not to think, focusing entirely on desire and sensation. But they were saved, if that were the word for it, by a sound not far from them which penetrated to both of them in spite of their absorption.

Morgan raised his head. There was nothing to see, but it was plain the noises signaled the approach of other riders. They looked back at each other, the knowledge in their shared glance that their madness was at an end. Morgan reluctantly released her, cursing softly under his breath, and China hastily pulled up her chemise and bodice and redid the buttons while Morgan turned toward the horses to gather up the loose reins.

China felt a curious sense of loss, but also relief. Her heart still pounded in her ears, her flesh still glowed with sensation, but with physical separateness came the return of sanity. How could she have entertained, for even a moment, allowing this man, this stranger, to make her his irrevocably? There had been no words of love that brought them together, only a violent physical need.

He brought her horse to her and assisted her to mount, and China was glad of the activity, which naturally permitted her to place her attention elsewhere. She felt warmth in her face and across her breasts and knew she was flushed with mortification. By the time Morgan had mounted his horse beside her and gathered up his reins, she had her composure back and was able to reply to him that she was ready to begin their ride home. By tacit consent, neither said a word about what had just occurred between them.

They had not traveled far from the stream before they met up with Dana Bovell, Caroline Creely, and the Fitchley-Gores, who were riding in their direction, intending, as China and Morgan had, to refresh their horses before returning to Macao.

Dana Bovell spotted them first; China saw him looking at them in a hard way, doubtless noting that no groom accompanied them, but he said nothing to the others and it was Mary Fitchley-Gore who hailed them. "Have you been showing Lord Wrexford our pretty countryside, China?" Mary said as soon as they were close enough for conversation. "It is so picturesque, is it not, my lord? You should have told me of your plans and we might all have ridden together. We should have been a jolly party. We have only come into the wood for a bit of water for the horses; if you will wait for us we can go back together."

It was the last thing China wanted. Her composure was too fragile and the risk of maintaining it too great. Her eyes sought Morgan's involuntarily, signaling entreaty.

Morgan interpreted her glance correctly and said, "That would be delightful, Mrs. Fitchley-Gore, but I have an engagement this morning and we are already late heading back to Macao. I beg you will forgive me for preventing Lady Rawdon from joining you, but I fear I should lose my way if I returned alone."

"Oh, but we shan't be long," Caroline said, casting

Morgan a languishing look. "Only a few minutes and we mean to go back at once as well."

Morgan smiled at her with sufficient warmth for China to think that he meant to agree, but he said, "But if we go back with your party, Mrs. Creely, there will be too much to interest and distract to allow for haste."

"With only me for company Lord Wrexford is certain to make his appointment," China said with a dry inflection. Morgan cast her a surprised glance and she regretted the remark as soon as it was spoken. She saw Bovell too was looking her way and it made her uncomfortable, as if he had somehow guessed at what had just passed between her and Morgan, which she knew was only her own guilty fancy.

She met Bovell's eyes squarely and even managed to smile at him, though it took every ounce of self-possession she had to do so. His lips turned up in acknowledgment, but in China's imagination it was more of a leer than a smile. She turned away from him without haste or apparent concern.

She discovered she had lost pace with the conversation and caught the end of an invitation by Mary Fitchley-Gore to both of them to dine on the day following the next. China scarcely knew what she was agreeing to, but acknowledged that she was free on Thursday.

Morgan also accepted and Mary, clapping her hands like a pleased child, said, "And I shall ask the Westons and Jack as well. Perhaps we shall play lottery tickets or something equally silly and have a very comfortable evening with all of our friends. I know you must go, my lord," she said, holding out one gloved hand to Morgan. "We won't detain you, but we'll look forward to Thursday night."

Morgan took her hand and raised it to his lips, a smile in his eyes that brought a faint flush to Mary's cheeks and caused China to reflect that he was very practiced in the art of charming her sex. Finally they turned their horses, said last good-byes, and were off. China did not again look toward Dana Bovell, but she felt as if his eyes bored into her retreating back, though she knew it was far more likely her imagination than anything else.

They rode silently until they reached the end of the wood and then China let out her horse out in a full gallop without even bothering to wait to see if Morgan followed her. Her horse was flagging and she was herself out of breath from the wind rushing in her face. She gradually slowed her mount to a walk and then turned to find Morgan still beside her.

"Trying to lose me?" he asked with a quizzical smile.

China let her eyes rest on him briefly. She shook her head. "It has been nearly a sennight since I rode last. I enjoy a good gallop."

"Why were you so anxious to get away from your friends?" he asked without preamble. "Were you afraid they would guess what we were about?"

China thought she was used to his directness, but she was still unsettled by his bluntness. "It shouldn't have happened," she said, her mortification making her voice curt.

"Why not?"

China gave a short, surprised laugh. "Perhaps your previous conquests make you think it of no moment, my lord, but it is not so for me."

"I wish you would disabuse yourself of the notion that I am an unprincipled libertine," he said with mild complaint. "What happened was not by nefarious design, you know. It was quite natural, and unless I flatter myself, also mutual."

"We barely know each other," she said tartly, ignoring the last part of his remark, though it was certainly true.

He nodded, unconcerned. "Knowledge is a relative

thing. We have an understanding of each other that has nothing to do with length of acquaintance.''

There was a caressing note in his voice that made China's pulse rise a bit. ''Do we?''

''I thought so. There is a powerful attraction to each other which, I think, we both recognized almost at once. Is it so unnatural that as adults we should react to it in the way that we have?''

''Not unnatural if we were wild animals without reason,'' she said aridly.

He looked taken aback. ''I hope you think of it as more than that. I do.''

China felt a sense of elation, but she told herself it was still too soon to refine to much on his words. He might be telling her that he was falling in love with her as she was with him, but the enormity of it frightened her as much as it excited her and she was not yet ready to set her hopes too high.

''What I think, my lord,'' she said with a calm she was far from feeling, ''is that we have allowed this . . . this attraction to run away with us. We must remember in what relation we stand to each other.''

''The merest connection by marriage,'' he said, as if this very fact had not troubled him as well. Having given in to his inclinations, he was prepared to consign it to the devil. ''What has that to say to anything? Do you wish me to apologize for what happened by the stream? I could not be such a hypocrite to pretend that I wish it hadn't happened.''

''Well, I wish it had not,'' China said truthfully, setting her mount to a trot. She wanted something other from him than a sordid tumble in the grass, but she feared that her ready response to him might cause him to think of her as little more. The way to love was through the building of friendship and trust, not uncheckable passion.

Morgan kept pace with her and they continued in silence until the first houses were in sight, each absorbed in his own thoughts. "You are a beautiful woman, China," he said, using her sobriquet for the first time. "But it is not the physical which most attracts. I did think it my duty to make your acquaintance and to see if I could persuade you to return to England with me, but I also had a personal curiosity to satisfy. I wanted to see for myself what manner of woman had finally succeeded in capturing my elusive uncle." He slowed his horse to a walk again and placed his hand over hers on the reins, forcing her to do the same. "Now I know, and do not wonder at it."

"Am I to take that as a compliment?" she asked with a coolness at odds with the warmth growing again inside of her at his touch.

"Decidedly. I am offering you no insult, China," he assured her. "I am simply being honest and direct. I thought you preferred plain speaking."

China didn't reply because she didn't know what to say to him. She was not really offended; she was far more upset with herself than with him. Despite his reassurance, she was not convinced that he didn't believe her to be of easy virtue, and what could she expect after the wanton way she had behaved in his arms. He was man, after all, and a man might take his pleasures with impunity, but not so a woman. If the party of her friends had not happened by when they had, they would have made love on the grass by the edge of the stream. She had not the least doubt of it.

As if he were reading her thoughts, he said, "Don't assume of me what you imagine to be true of all men. I don't know what your experience of my sex has been, but I can guess the manner of moral teaching with which you were raised. We are not all ravishing monsters with no thought but to seduce and abandon."

"I am not so closed-minded. But neither am I ignorant of the ways of the world."

"Is that what it is?" he said. "Do you think I shall

think less of you for this days' work? You do me an injustice, China.''

China was beginning to find the ride interminable. Though they were on the outskirts of the city and already passing houses, it seemed to her as if she would never reach the safe haven of her own home. She needed time and solitude to sort out her thoughts. ''Perhaps I do,'' she conceded but without encouragement.

They rode in silence again until they turned into her street. ''At least admit that you do not dislike me,'' Morgan said.

''I do not dislike you,'' China said, looking up at him.

Morgan smiled in the way that never failed to raise her pulse. ''We have made a good beginning, China. I *should* regret what happened if I thought it would set us apart.''

All of his assurances were still not the words that China wished to hear from him. But she still dared to hope that she would yet hear them spoken. ''I should dislike that as well,'' she admitted.

''Then I am content.''

Understanding her need to let the matter rest, he then made a comment about a farming village through which they had passed, for which she was grateful. When they reached her house she did not ask him in for breakfast, although this had been her original intent. She did not wish to be tête-à-tête with him again so soon. It was less that she distrusted him than that she distrusted herself.

6

CHINA SENT HER excuses to Sally Weston that evening for dinner, deciding that she needed time to regain her self-command before she saw Morgan again. When she did so the following night at the Fitchley-Gores', she was pleased to find that she felt no awkwardness in his company. He was in excellent spirits, willing to please and at his most amusing, making comments with his dry wit that exactly appealed to her own. China found it quite easy to forget that there had ever been any constraint between them. His eyes when they rested on her held such a soft expression that she began to convince herself that she had been wrong to suppose that his intentions toward her had been less than honorable. Not every man was like Clive, ready to declare himself almost at once. Morgan would be in Macao for more than another fortnight, and by then her hopes might well be realized.

As for Morgan, beyond knowing that he enjoyed her company and desired her as a woman, his feelings about what had happened on their ride were a puzzle to him. When she responded to him with such eagerness, he supposed that she wished as much as he to sate their passion. It had not been a moment to pause and divine her character from this, but if their lovemaking had come to its natural conclusion, he very probably would have had thoughts to confirm China's fears. He enjoyed the company of women and had had a number of liaisons with like-minded women of the world, but he was no despoiler of innocence. If they had made love beside the stream, he would have supposed China to be one of their number and would have had no hesitation in embarking on an *affaire* with her for the duration of his visit to Macao. But China's mortification at her own behavior had seemed quite genuine. If he had wronged her, he was genuinely sorry for it, but, if anything, he desired her all the more. He found her completely enchanting, far more than merely desirable, but he was not yet ready to think beyond this.

What he was mostly aware of was regret that he would be leaving her in little more than a fortnight. His plans to sail from Kowloon the last week in January were already made and to put them off might lengthen his stay indefinitely, which he did not wish to do. The only solution he perceived was to succeed at what he had come to Macao to do, persuade China to return to England with him.

He did not think it wise to bring up the topic that night, but if he had, he might have received a more favorable response that he would have supposed; China herself had already begun to seriously entertain the thought of returning with him to England.

The party ended at an early hour, as was usual, but China was in ebullient spirits and not in the least wishing for her bed. Jack suggested that he might stop by for a bit of brandy before retiring and China was glad to have his company. When he first arrived, they spoke of general things, but when China poured a second glass for him he said in a too casual manner, "You appear to be on the best of terms with Wrexford. You rode out with him yesterday morning, did you not?"

China was a little surprised at first that he knew of their meeting, but then she realized that he must have heard of it from one of their friends who had met them in the wood. "Yes. And we go on quite famously." China sipped at the wine she preferred to strong spirits and smiled over the rim of her glass. "I wonder that I ever imagined he would be an ogre. He even told me that he thought me out of the common way and could understand why Clive had married me."

Jack's brows shot up. "Did he? Damme! So there is something to it after all," he added, more to himself.

China jumped on his words. "Something to what?" she said, so sharply that she knew she was giving herself away.

Jack shrugged with apparent unconcern. "Only a comment that Dana made to me tonight."

"Which was?" she demanded coolly.

"Don't comb my hair, China," Jack said with a laugh. "I am casting no aspersions. He said only what you have said, that you and Wrexford are getting on wonderfully well. But it was the way he said it, of course."

"Implying that it was something more, I suppose. That is very like him," she said with patent distaste. "No doubt he wishes to be spiteful because I did not care for the advances he had the impertinence to make toward me after Clive died."

" 'Heaven hath no rage like love to hatred turned . . . ,' " Jack quoted.

"Love had nothing at all to do with it," China said acerbically. "I am not even sure it was desire. More likely my fat purse."

"*Most* likely," Jack said with a cynical laugh.

China was furious with Dana Bovell for his insinuations, but she would not dignify or give them credence by letting her displeasure be known. She would continue to be no more than civil toward him, as she had been since the occasion when he had attempted to make love to her, but under no circumstances would she invite him again to her home even if she had the entire remainder of the English community at Macao in her drawing room.

China might have decided to confront Mr. Bovell if

she had known the extent of his perfidy, though. It was the day after the next when he and Morgan rode out again with Sir Vernon to view the progress of his stud, and while Sir Vernon spoke with the farmer who housed his cattle, Morgan and Bovell, who claimed an interest in the breeding of stock, went off on their own to the field to better view the animals firsthand.

When the topic of horses and bloodlines was finally exhausted, Bovell said, "I understand you sail from Kowloon at the end of the month. It is a pity your stay must be so short."

"I only meant this to be a brief visit on my way to England," Morgan replied. "The length of it has been determined by the sailing of the ship. I particularly wished for a merchant ship known to me which would take me to Lisbon or some other port from which I would be able to make a direct passage to England."

"I've thought myself of leaving Macao sometime soon," Bovell said as they began to walk back toward the buildings. "Conditions here are becoming increasingly unsettled and I think the time will soon come when most of us will either return home or find some other place in China to live that is more amenable."

"This open hostility puzzles me a little," Morgan confessed. "I know our countrymen have exploited China, as they have India and other places, but we have also put much back into the economy."

"Oh, it's the Portuguese, of course," Bovell replied. "We control most of the industry and exports in Canton, Kowloon, and other places and live here because of its convenience. They think, I suppose, that if they keep the animosity of the Chinese aroused against us, many of us will decide that the profits to be made won't outweigh the risk to our persons. Then the Portuguese could take over our already established businesses and reap the profits for themselves with a minimum of effort. They wouldn't even have to be the ones to fire a shot."

Morgan digested this and then said, "Then I wish all the more that I could persuade Lady Rawdon to return to England with me. Once I am gone, if matters do become worse, I shan't be able to help her, and even though I know she has friends, it is not a good thing for any woman to travel such a distance without protection."

Bovell nodded. "No. Even on the best ships the crews are usually a rough lot and not always completely controlled by the officers. But I think for the moment at least there is little chance of persuading Lady Rawdon to leave Macao."

"Why is that?"

Bovell shrugged in a casual manner. Too casual. Morgan was alert for his answer. "She has, as you say, many friends here. And other interests."

"Such as?"

"You are asking me to tell tales out of school, Wrexford," Bovell said with a laugh. "I have no wish to make you feel an outsider, but there are some things which are well known to our community but which it would be indiscreet to discuss with anyone else."

Morgan knew that Bovell wanted to be coaxed into indiscretion. Morgan's natural inclination was to not give him the satisfaction he sought, but his curiosity about China was greater. "But I am not just anyone else. I am a connection of Lady Rawdon's and my concern for her is sincere. Perhaps if I understood her reluctance to return with me, I would be better able to persuade her to do so, or at least feel content with leaving her behind."

"Perhaps," the other man agreed, and then fell into silence which Morgan made no attempt to breach. Finally he said, "She would not wish to leave here, as I've said, because of her friends. Particularly one friend."

"Sally Weston?" Morgan asked, though he was already starting to guess the track that Bovell was taking.

Bovell gave him a quick, assessing glance and then said succinctly, ''Reid.''

Morgan understood the insinuation. He said in a voice from which all emotion had been banished, ''Reid was Clive's closest friend, I understand. It is only natural that Lady Rawdon has turned to him for support since Clive's death.''

''Oh, yes,'' Bovell said blandly. ''They are the greatest of friends. Lady Rawdon has maintained the same degree of intimacy with Mr. Reid that she enjoyed when Sir Clive was alive to give them countenance.''

Morgan had a strong desire to plant a facer on the other man. It was clear that he wanted Morgan to believe that China and Jack Reid were lovers. It might even be true; Morgan found he didn't care to believe it, but acknowledged it nevertheless. There was no question that there was a marked degree of intimacy between them. But he set no store by the spiteful words of a man whose character he had assessed correctly within five minutes of acquaintance.

They had reached the farmhouse and were hailed by Sir Vernon. Morgan turned to the other man and said with a blandness to equal Bovell's, ''You greatly set my mind to rest. It is good that Lady Rawdon has someone here in addition to the Westons on whom she may rely if need be.''

Sir Vernon approached them, asking questions about their opinions of what they had seen, and the discussion was effectively at an end. Mr. Bovell was not deceived by Morgan's deliberate misunderstanding of his hints. He knew that what he had received at the earl's hands was a setdown, but he was not in the least perturbed by it. He knew that he had made his point with Morgan, and that was all he had meant to do.

His success was more complete than he knew. In spite of dismissing Bovell's words as malice, in the days that followed, Morgan discreetly watched China and Jack when they were together for some sign that they were

more than friends. He saw nothing. But he was too
much a man of the world to dismiss the possibility completely. Just because China had expressed mortification
at what had occurred between them, did not mean that
she did not have someone else for her lover. If China
had taken Jack Reid as her lover even while Clive lived,
they would by now be well practiced in public discretion and very unlikely to give each other away. He knew
of countless examples of such things among members
of the *ton,* most of whom married for position and convenience and then sought love in other quarters.

He really did not know how he intended to go on
with China. He did not continue to press her to return
with him to England, for he knew he would only set
up her back. But whenever the opportunity arose, he
presented her with a very attractive picture of the life
she might enjoy if she took her proper place in society,
and regaled her with pleasant anecdotes of various
memories of his family and the cheerful household at
Ferris Grange where he had been raised, for he sensed
that China felt the loss of her own parents and longed
for a sense of kinship and belonging. She made comments from time to time that gave him hope that this
tactic might prove successful.

It was what he wanted, what he had come to Macao to
accomplish, but his more personal feelings toward her
remained ambiguous. His pleasure in her company and
his desire to possess her continued unabated, but he had
no idea where it should lead. He was not of a nature to
readily imagine himself in love, but he knew that whatever
it was he felt toward China, it was stronger than he had
ever experienced before with any other woman. It was
also the reason that he took the trouble to see if he could
discover for himself if there was anything more than
friendship between China and Jack. He went at least as
far as to acknowledge that he did not want it to be true.

They spent a good deal of time in one another's company, far more than they might have if they had been

in England, for in such a narrow society there were not numerous activities and entertainments from which to pick and choose. Where one was, the other must also almost certainly be. Most of their time together was spent in company with others, and on the few occasions when they were alone, Morgan did not again attempt to make love to her. He did this in part because he knew she was still wary that he meant to seduce her if he could, and in part because he doubted the wisdom of giving in to his need for her when his other emotions concerning her were so unclear to him. But the attraction that had led to their few minutes of abandonment by the stream was as strong as ever; it was simply unacknowledged. Of that, he had no doubt at all.

Nor did China. As the days passed and their friendship grew, she knew herself to be in jeopardy again of letting her emotions run away with her sense. There had been impromptu dancing one evening at the Warings' and she had waltzed with Morgan. Feeling his arms about her even in a public embrace had filled her with a delicious inner warmth that reawakened her remembrance of that morning when she had abandoned herself in his arms. After this she found it increasingly difficult to keep these recollections from her conscious thoughts.

The devil of it was that she genuinely liked him. If she could have believed him to be a cold-hearted seducer who wanted to take his pleasure with her and be done with her, she could have put him quite firmly from her mind. But in spite of his reputation, of which she really knew nothing in fact, she could not think it, and refused to believe she was such a poor judge of character.

And she increasingly was coming to think that her feelings toward him were not unreciprocated. Morgan was too much of a gentleman to single her out for his attentions so particularly that it would occasion speculation and gossip, but he did not bother to disguise the obvious pleasure he took in her company, and the harmony between them was so complete that China began to feel as if she had known him all of her life rather than less than a month. And then there was that which she saw in his eyes from time to time, which was plainly more than merely admiration. He had not forgotten that morning when they had nearly made love by the stream any more than she had.

But the time remaining before Morgan would go out of her life, perhaps forever, was rapidly waning. In little more than a week he would leave for Kowloon, and from there sail for England. She recognized Morgan's purpose in speaking to her so often of England and his family, and it was not without effect. She had all but forgotten the fears that had plagued her before he had come to Macao that she would find returning to England a less than pleasant experience. Even A-melia's acknowledged hostility toward her faded from her thoughts along with her fears that Clive's will might be contested. But it was not this that made her think seriously of leaving Macao, it was because in doing so, she would not be parted from Morgan.

The decision, she knew, would soon have to be made, and yet she hesitated. Even if Morgan openly acknowledged his feelings for her, it would still not be easy for her to give up the only friends she had, the only real home she had ever known. A month was a very short time to truly know another person, whatever she might feel for him, and she was too practical by nature to really believe that the world was well lost for love. If she remained in Macao, she might be giving up her chance for happiness with Morgan, but on the other hand she might be making the gravest mistake of her life. It was a hard-fought battle between the urgings of her heart and her common sense, and she really had no idea which would yet win out.

7

THE MUCH-AWAITED return of Andrew Creely from Canton by his wife Caroline was not to go unmarked. Though Caroline had thoroughly enjoyed flirting with Morgan and would have set him up as her cicisbeo if he had permitted it, she had genuinely missed her husband, who had been forced to remain in Canton on business for more than two months. Caroline Creely also very much enjoyed a party. When it was definite that her husband was to be home in a few days' time, she began to plan an entertainment to mark the occasion and set her heart on having a ball, as much of the sort that she could have had at home in England as possible.

Her plans went smoothly, in spite of the short time she had to make them; only finding professional musicians presented a problem and finally through exorbitant bribery, which would likely dampen the enthusiasm of Mr. Creely when the bill for their services was presented, a small orchestra of Portuguese players from Macao was hired. It was a signal accomplishment, and in addition to the happiness of having her husband returned to her, Caroline had the additional satisfaction of knowing that she was envied and admired by her fellow hostesses, who had only dinner and the usual sort of rout and card parties to offer their friends for entertainment.

China was always happiest when in company, for she was naturally gregarious and really enjoyed being with people she liked. She was particularly pleased that Caro Creely had chosen a ball to celebrate her husband's return for she might expect once again to find herself in Morgan's embrace as they danced, their bodies moving in perfect rhythm to the strains of the music.

By this point she had abandoned lying to herself about wanting to be in his arms; now it was only a matter of degree. She was at a crossroads, and she knew it. The ball would take place exactly three days before Morgan was to leave them, and by then she must surely know if her future remained in Macao as Clive Rawdon's widow or in England as the Earl of Wrexford's wife.

China took luncheon with the Westons on the afternoon of the ball and all talk was of the evening's entertainment. When she met Morgan's eyes across the table, she knew that he was looking forward to it as much as she. She was astonished at the calm certainty she felt that this would be the night that he would finally speak the words she almost ached to hear. Then the decision would finally have to be made. She was in a state of excited anticipation that made her moods mercurial. One moment she was ebullient and the next almost dispirited.

Even Sally remarked on her humor when they were alone in her sitting room after luncheon discussing the gowns and accessories each meant to wear that evening. "I have never seen you quite so high-strung, China," Sally complained when China had flitted from her chair to the window to peer out at the garden and back to her chair again for at least the third time. "Whatever is the matter with you today?"

China had rarely had the luxury of a confidante. Jack was the closest thing to that sort of friend that she had known, but his earlier comments when they had discussed Morgan had made her feel that he would not understand her feelings. She felt herself to be quite close to Sally, but she had not said anything to her either about her feelings for Morgan, fearing that Sally would think her foolish for imagining herself in love with a man she had known for less than a month.

Yet in her keyed-up state, China was bursting with the need to discuss him and the likelihood that she would shortly be leaving Macao with someone and Sally was at hand. "What do you really think of Morgan Wrexford?" she asked abruptly.

Sally seemed startled by the question, which had no apparent connection with her own to China. "He is a very charming man, and as I said from the day he arrived, an exceptionally good-looking one as well."

"That isn't what I meant," China said, getting up again, this time to examine some porcelain figures on a table as if she had never seen them before. "What do you think of his character?"

"His character?" Sally's brow knit in puzzlement. "I suppose he is a man of character, if that is what you mean. He is a gentleman and always conducts himself just as he ought. But then we none of us know him very well, do we?"

"But there is much one may discern of a man on short acquaintance," China persisted.

"What do *you* think of him?" Sally asked shrewdly.

China shrugged with deliberate unconcern. "I like him very well, I suppose. He is certainly far from the stern judge come to condemn me that I imagined before he arrived. Morgan has always been very kind to me."

"Yes," Sally said slowly, trying to decide what she might read into China's words. "I think he likes you as well. Very much." She noted the use of the earl's given name, which made it obvious that there was an increased intimacy between them. In public they were more circumspect, and Sally wondered why. In spite of their short acquaintance, China and Morgan were connected by marriage and no one would wonder at if they chose to be on informal terms. This and China's carefully couched questions and answers made Sally quite naturally suspicious.

She had, in fact, noted them together on several occasions and had no doubt that there was an attraction between them, and she had no doubt that China was not just making conversation. It did occur to her that perhaps China had formed a tendre for the handsome earl, and though she did not blame her—Morgan was a man to make any woman's heart flutter—she did think it foolish.

She was perceptive enough to guess that China feared it foolish as well, and this made her hesitant to discuss it plainly. "Have you thought any further about returning with him to England?" she asked leadingly. "I know he leaves the day after tomorrow, but it is still not too late to change your mind."

"I don't know," China said with a sigh. "One minute I think that I do wish to go and the next that it would be foolish to make such a decision with haste."

"But you would not again be able to do so in the company of Lord Wrexford, if you wait to go some other time," Sally said. "I expect you would be much more comfortable having someone to make the journey with whom you could rely upon for protection. It is not the easiest thing for a woman to travel alone, particularly if she is young and pretty."

China laughed. "Do you think I shall be ravished at the first port, Sally? It is not really so dangerous, you know. I have done it before when I went to school in Bath and then returned to my parents, and I was much younger then."

"Yes," Sally agreed, "but you did not do so alone. Each time it was arranged for you to travel with someone at least known to your parents who was also making the journey. You would very likely have no one but Lucy for company if you do not choose to go now. If you get on so well with Wrexford, you will not only have his protection but a charming companion as well.''

''I suppose,'' China said noncommittally. It was obvious that Sally was beginning to guess at the import of their conversation, and China teetered on the edge of the decision whether to confide in her or to change the topic altogether.

Sally, growing impatient, decided to take the matter into her own hands. ''My dear, what is it? You are falling a little in love with Wrexford, are you not? Are you afraid that you shall lose your heart to him by the time you reach England?''

''Either that or my virtue,'' China said, turning from the window, a self-mocking smile on her face.

''It's like that, is it?'' Sally said, concern puckering her brow. ''Oh, dear! What shall I counsel you? I know I should tell you not to be too quick to run away with your emotions, for I fear that a man as handsome and charming as Wrexford must have broken any number of hearts. What of Wrexford? Does he return your regard?''

''I think so, but he has not spoken of it yet,'' China admitted. ''I have never felt so great an affinity with any man before, not even Clive. It is as if we each know what the other is thinking before we can speak. When we are together it is almost as if there were no one else in the room.''

''A sad case,'' Sally said with a small sigh, and then smiled encouragingly. ''Well, there is no need to imagine the worst either. Perhaps Wrexford does feel as you do. You know that it is generally not as easy for a man to acknowledge his feelings as it is for our sex. If you really believe that there is a chance of it, then the foolish thing might be to allow him to leave Macao alone. I don't really think you need fear that he will take advantage of you. He is a man of honor, if I am any judge of character.''

''And I am the daughter of missionaries,'' China

said with a dry smile. "And yet . . ." She broke off, not quite willing to admit how eager she was to abandon the virtue she claimed a concern for.

"And yet you want him to make love to you," Sally supplied, understanding more than China knew. "You are a normal young woman with normal desires, and you have been alone for more than a year since Clive died, but I hope you will not let your heart run away with your sense." She got up and went to stand beside China at the window.

"I hope so too," China said, taking her friend's hand. "I think I wish I did not have to make up my mind what is best to do so quickly."

"Dearest China," Sally said, returning the pressure of her hand, "I can only tell you that I for one see no blame in your wishing to be with Lord Wrexford. But only you can search your heart and decide what is right for you."

China knew that this was true. It was something that her dearest friend did not reproach her for her longings, but Sally could not make a decision for her, though at the moment she wished it could be that simple.

By the time China dressed for the ball, her spirits had risen again and she was inclined to think that if Morgan declared himself in the smallest way she would be ready to pack for the journey to England in a trice, trusting to Sir Vernon and Sally Weston to settle her affairs in Macao. She had chosen an ivory silk gown with a gauze overdress shot with gold threads that made her hair shine like new-minted guineas and her skin glow like fine porcelain. It was the most fashionably cut gown she possessed, revealing the curves of her voluptuous figure to perfection.

Though she did no acknowledge it openly, there was no doubt in her mind that she dressed for Morgan. But he was not the only man present that evening to appreciate the extra care she had taken, and she was surrounded by an eager court from almost the moment she entered Caroline Creely's ballroom.

This was not the Marriage Mart of the *ton* and there was a considerable dearth of eligible men, but most of the married men of her acquaintance were not adverse to a bit of flirtation with the beautiful young widow and she was sought eagerly by most of them to stand up with her and several vied for the honor of leading her in to supper, which made her wonder if she would find a spare moment for the sort of conversation she longed for with Morgan.

In England, even in the provinces, the waltz had become so commonplace as to raise scarcely an eyebrow except from the highest sticklers, but abroad, it was still considered a bit daring. Mrs. Creely, determined to be in the forefront of fashion, instructed her players to essay no fewer than three waltzes for her ball. China danced the first of these with Andrew Creely, while Morgan led Caroline onto the floor. Andrew Creely, despite the fact that he made no pretense as many others did that he was anything but a merchant, had really very good connections in the *ton,* and he and Caroline had moved in tonnish circles in London before Andrew had decided that he preferred to make his own fortune rather than wait for someone to die for it. He was a polished performer on the dance floor and made just the sort of light, flirtatious conversation appropriate to the intimate and exhilarating dance. But China responded to him more from practice than pleasure.

China surreptitiously watched Caroline make play with her fine eyes while she danced with Morgan, who was quite obviously taking more enjoyment from his flirtation with his hostess than China did with her host. An accomplished flirt herself, China knew very well that flirtation was far more pleasant a pastime than any serious wish for it to lead to anything more, but she could not quite help the pang of jealousy she felt watching Morgan look down at Caroline as if she were his sole delight. She wished he might have asked her to stand up with him for the first waltz, but banished the thought immediately. As the highest ranking personage in the room, he had behaved most properly asking his hostess to honor him with the dance, just as Andrew Creely had paid her rank a similar compliment. She and Morgan had exchanged no more than a few words after the dinner to which they had been invited before the ball began, but the admiration she had perceived so plainly in his eyes had once again heightened her sense of anticipation that she might end the night knowing at last the extent of his regard for her.

The musicians were not terribly good, but everyone was in a festive mood, more than willing to be pleased, and scarcely seemed to notice. Only Mr. Bovell made a comment to China, when he led her into the cotillion immediately following the waltz, that they should have to particularly mind their steps since they could expect little support from the music.

China stood up with Mr. Bovell because she could think of no excuse that would not sound churlish, but she wanted no part of his company, and found it an effort to be even civil to him. They made only inconsequential conversation during their dance but when it was ended, he unobtrusively drew her a little away from the others, talking to her earnestly on some subject which held no interest for her and to which she scarcely gave her attention. She was actually making up excuses in her mind to be rid of him when he mentioned Morgan's name and finally gained her attention.

"It is a pity that Lord Wrexford must leave us so soon," he said. "We have all been very well entertained since his arrival; having a nobleman of his consequence in our society seems to have greatly inspired our hostesses. I suppose when he leaves we shall go back to a quieter mode of life. No doubt, some of us shall be sorrier than others to see him go.''

There was a sneering note in his voice and China wished she might slap the impudent smile from his face, but she said with only a hint of coldness behind her well-bred civility, ''I shall certainly be sorry for it. I have long wished to meet Clive's family and it was very gracious of Lord Wrexford to come so out of his way to visit me. I have enjoyed sharing my memories of Clive with Lord Wrexford.''

''What?'' demanded Bovell in apparent astonishment. ''Is that all you can say for one of the most celebrated rakes of the *ton?* I am sure he would feel quite dashed if he knew you were so impervious to his charm that you thought of him in no other light than as your late husband's nephew.''

His tone was so insinuating that it was plain to China that he meant to lure her into making a rejoinder that would give him fuel for his viperish tongue. ''I think it would be exactly what Lord Wrexford would expect of me,'' she said coldly. She was about to excuse herself without apology when Morgan came up behind her, briefly touching her arm above the elbow as if in warning, making China wonder how much he had overheard.

''What should I expect?'' he asked conversationally.

''That I should share my memories of Clive with you,'' China said with a smile that excluded Mr. Bovell.

''But of course,'' Morgan replied. ''I have considered myself honored by your confidences. Do you know, Bovell,'' he said at his blandest, ''I believe Lady Weston is searching for you. I think you had asked her to stand up with you for the next set.''

Bovell looked blank for a moment, not remembering any such thing, but he did not deny it. He politely bowed over China's hand, thanked her formally for their dance, and left them.

"I hope I didn't interrupt," Morgan said casually. "I had the impression that he was making a pest of himself, but I might have been wrong."

"On the contrary, you are perceptive," China said, laughter in her eyes. "He was trying, I believe, to make me betray myself into indiscretion."

"So have I," Morgan said outrageously. "With no better success."

It was the first time he had spoken to her so since that morning when she had gone well beyond indiscretion with him, and also the first time he had even hinted at what lay between them. China felt her heart begin to beat a little faster, but she would not allow herself to be shy of him. "Have you?" she said with remarkable composure. "I should have thought it was Caroline with whom you courted indiscretion. Andrew's return has been most timely for the good of her reputation."

"Do you dislike my attentions in that quarter?" he said quizzingly.

China turned a little away from him. "No. Why should I? It cannot matter to me who Caroline might chose to set up as her flirt. The novelty of a new face among us has its attractions."

"Cat," he said affectionately, pleased by this display of jealousy. Like China, he was very conscious of how little time remained of his stay in Macao. Uncertainties still plagued him, but he was increasingly aware of how little he wished to give up her society. "Are you really so indifferent to me?" he asked, surprising himself with the question.

"I like you very well, my lord," she said, as lightly as she could manage.

"A glowing encomium," he said, laughing. "I am quite unmanned. I thought we had progressed well beyond such formality."

"If you are trying to put me to the blush," China

said severely, "you will find yourself as far out as Dana Bovell."

"And as well served for my vanity, no doubt," he responded amiably. "Do you think we might contrive to slip away for a bit of private conversation without quite tarnishing our reputations? I have something I wish to say to you."

China's heart now began to hammer in earnest. She certainly had no wish to discourage him, but neither did she want him to suppose that she would engage in any further dalliance with him, if that were his intent. "Something you cannot say to me here?"

"Something I would rather not say to you here," he said. "I do not wish to be interrupted. Fred Waring has been looking this way for the past ten minutes and no doubt wishes to solicit your hand for the next dance."

"If he observes us leaving this room together, he shall probably wonder what it is you have been soliciting me for," China said tartly.

Morgan only smiled. "There is an empty anteroom next to the card room. Meet me there. I think you can manage to avoid Waring's avid eye for five minutes to accomplish your escape."

China did not reply immediately, and he said with a note of challenge in his voice, "Are you afraid to be alone with me, China?"

China refused to let him put her out of countenance. "I don't think so," she said ingenuously. "Have I cause to be?"

His smile was equally guileless. "None in the least. In five minutes, then?"

China agreed, as she had always meant to do, but having done so her emotions were in a turmoil. Excitement, fear of disappointment, uncertainty, and self-satisfaction all gathered together in a tumble inside her breast. But she would not fail him; she had to know what he would say to her. It might prove to be something quite unexceptionable, but she didn't really believe that. His attentive manner toward her of late, the caressing note in his voice when he spoke to her, and the strength of the attraction between them which remained unabated, convinced her all the more that her intuition, which told her that he would at last make his feeling for her plain, was to be relied upon.

China had walked over to speak with Louise Richton and Mrs. Waring and did not see Morgan leave the room. She knew that to slip out herself in a furtive fashion would probably not go undetected, so she gracefully ended her conversation with these ladies and proceeded toward the door into the hall in an unhurried manner, pausing to speak with several of her friends along the way. The second waltz had just begun and the dance was so popular that even most of the stragglers near the door left to take part in it and the hall itself was completely empty.

China entered the anteroom quite calmly, as if assignations were commonplace to her, pushing the door closed behind her but not permitting it to quite shut.

Morgan was staring into the hearth in a brooding fashion, one hand resting negligently on the mantel, but he straightened and turned when he heard her enter. "I was beginning to fear that Waring had entrapped you after all."

"I did not wish it to look as if I were in any haste to leave the room," she said. "Particularly if anyone had noticed you going into the hall."

Morgan smiled at her caution, but made no comment. "I leave for Kowloon the day after tomorrow," he said without preamble.

"I know."

"Do you sail with me?"

China was a little startled by the abruptness of the question, and did not know how to answer him. Practically, she knew her answer should be no, but if he had couched his query differently, she was still not certain she would not be ready to do so. "It is rather late to be making preparations for such a voyage," she said evasively.

"Not if you only mean to visit," he said, damping her hopes that he meant to make her a more permanent proposal. "You need only pack what you will for the journey and give instructions to your household until you return."

China did not want her disappointment to show. In spite of the confusion of her feelings, she had not thought it would affect her quite so much. "I own I have thought quite seriously of it," she said, her voice as unconcerned as she could make it, "but I think it would be best to wait until I can settle my affairs more permanently here. I do not mean to remain in Macao indefinitely."

China had come only halfway into the room, and he walked over to her. "Agents could be employed to do that if you decided to make your home in England." He laid his fingers against her cheek and traced the edge of her face to gently cup her chin in his hand. "Come with me, China. Not because it is your duty to Clive's children or to see to your inheritance."

"Why then?" she asked, almost breathless, her pulses pounding at his touch.

"I don't want to leave with you still here, and I must. Come with me that we might be together." He bent his face to hers to kiss her, softly, but very erotically. China's arousal was instantaneous and without control. Morgan's arms moved about her waist and she lifted her own arms about his neck. The kiss deepened very gradually and grew steadily in intensity until it seemed to China that they had been kissing for hours and would never stop.

Morgan certainly didn't want to stop, but he was cognizant of their surroundings and the fact that they could be stumbled upon by other guests at any moment. He released her a little only to gather her close again in another moment, unwilling to relinquish the softness of her body against his or the sweet taste of her lips. He wanted her so badly that if it would not have been madness to do so, he would have brought their lovemaking to its natural conclusion then and there.

China's senses were swimming as well. Only one thing had any meaning for her at that moment, and that was the molten touch of his hands and his mouth on hers. Her resistance to him had seemed only to fuel her desire for him and this time she would not repulse his advances. With the words he had spoken, all of her doubts had fallen magically away, and she knew now what she supposed she must have known all along: She would go with him to England.

But her need for reassurance was not yet abated. "Do you really so wish it?"

"Don't you?" he asked, sounding a bit anxious.

China could not deny it. She looked into his green eyes and the last of her disquiet was put to rest. "Yes, but it seems like folly to do so in such a mad-dash fashion."

"Let us be fools for love, then," he said, placing a quick, gentle kiss on her forehead. "Enchantress! I think I must have kidnapped you if you had said no. I no longer wonder what it was that made Clive fall in love with you. If it is a spell you cast, I am quite willingly enslaved."

He hugged her to him very tightly, more in the excess of his finally acknowledged feelings than in passion this time. He had had no idea that he would declare himself to her this night, but when it had seemed to him that she did not mean to leave Macao, he knew how important to him it was that she go with him. If this were not love, he had no idea what else he might call it. He only knew, beyond doubt, that China had become necessary to his happiness.

They began to make love again and it was soon obvious that their control over their desire was fragile. With all of her hopes realized, China did not deny to herself that she wished for the consummation of their love as much as he did. She wished with all of her heart that they were any place but here in a house full of people where there was no chance of their having more than these few minutes alone.

Morgan, as if reading her thoughts, said, "I wish we might find some more private place to be alone, but the others must be missing us by now in so small a company."

China did not take him to task for presumption; her response to him had been too complete. It was impossible that he could not know that she wanted him as much as he wanted her. "We could go to my house." She could hardly believe she had said such a thing to him. "I could say that I have the headache and leave, and you might find an excuse to give to Vernon and Sally."

He looked at her so steadily and for such a long moment that China feared she had said the wrong thing, that her forwardness had disappointed him. But her anxieties were unfounded. He kissed her lightly and fleetingly. "Are you certain?" He laughed softly. "I'm not certain I won't find the door firmly barred to me when I arrive."

China shook her head, consigning her conscience, fueled by years of her parents' harping on the sins of the flesh, to perdition. "I'm certain," she said, very quietly but firmly.

"Very well," he said, and mitigated the coolness of the expression by kissing her one last time. "Give it a little time before you leave. Just before or just after supper would be best. You needn't say anything else to me. I'll know when you've gone, and I'll follow you at a suitable interval."

At first China thought that after supper would be best. Full of food and wine, everyone would be too caught up in their revels to note particularly that both she and Morgan were gone from the ball. But she found the next hour of waiting—even though she spent the time fully occupied in dancing and conversation—almost unendurable. She told herself that if she waited until after supper it might be late enough that Sally, who was not particularly fond of late hours, would suggest leaving also, and perhaps even insist on coming to her house to see to it that she took a bit of laudanum for her headache and went straight to bed. It had happened before.

When the last set was forming before supper, she sought out Sally, who was just about to take the dance floor with Mr. Richton, and made her excuses.

"Oh, my dear! How dreadful!" Sally said with concern, making China feel a bit guilty for lying to her. "Tonight of all nights to be taken with one of your headaches. Do you wish me to come with you?"

"No," China said without emphasis to avoid suspicion, which in her present state of mind she feared would be likely. "It isn't that bad yet, which is why I wish to leave now. I think if I go home and straight to bed I may avoid it altogether and spare myself lying on my bed all the day tomorrow. I'll find Caroline and give her my excuses, and then call for my chair."

"Be sure to take an extra footman with you," Sally admonished. "I'm sure our entertainment tonight is well enough known in Macao and who knows if footpads might not be lurking about hoping to come across castaway guests who will not be able to put up a great deal of fight."

China promised and quickly went to find her hostess before Caroline could take her place on the dance floor.

8

IT WAS REALLY remarkably simple, she reflected, when she entered her house to be greeted by her butler Dosset and sent him directly to bed, assuring him that she had no further need for the services of any of her staff that evening. He did not appear to find anything in the least odd about her early return, and the last hurdle was crossed when she peeked out of her bed-chamber door to find the house in complete darkness and stillness. she had never before given any thought to what was necessary to conducting an affair of the heart, but everything had gone so smoothly and well that she decided that she had wasted a great deal of anxiety for no purpose.

She did not undress, but lit a bed candle and went into her sitting room, which faced the street, putting it on a table near the window so that he would see that the house was not in complete uninviting darkness, and waited not with anxiety but with anticipation. It was not really very long before she saw that shadowy figure of a man approaching. She hastened at once down the darkened hall and stairs, her heart finally beginning to thud as she waited at the door to open it for him as he approached. She had a momentary fear that it might not be him after all but one of the foot-pads Sally had warned against and that she might be putting herself in danger, but she carefully drew open the door to a slit so that she might be certain it was he. She heard the faint scrape of the iron gates in front of the house, which she had deliberately left unlocked, and she drew open the door a bit more. In the almost nonexistent light of a new moon, she could still see the whiteness of his shirt front. When he mounted the last step and stood before her, she caught at her breath. This beautiful man who stood before her loved her and would, in a very short time, be her lover in the fullest sense of the word.

He closed the door quietly behind him. He took her in his arms at once and kissed her tenderly and lingeringly. "Do you know," he said very softly into her ear, "I was afraid you would change your mind and bar the door to me."

"No," she said in a breathy voice, already aroused from his touch, "I admit I am a little afraid, but I want to make love with you."

"There's no need to be afraid," he said, and kissed her again.

As they stood in the pitchdark hall, their kissing took on increased fervor and neither wished to stop long enough to mount the stairs. But at last he released her. "This is your last chance to show me the door," he said with a soft laugh.

China shook her head and took his hand, leading him up the stairs. The connecting door to her sitting room was open and the faint glow from the bedcandle still lit in that room was the only light. China let him draw her near to him again and kissed him fervently while he slowly undid the small buttons at the back of her gown. He slipped the lowcut bodice from her shoulders and pulled the giving silk over her hips so that it fell in a soft cloud about her feet. She stood before him in only her chemise and petticoats, her heart pounding, but her uncertainties banished.

He shrugged himself out of his form-fitting coat and undressed without haste. Her eyes were becoming quite used to the darkness, and even in the faint candlelight she could see how well-formed his body was.

He was hard and lean and muscular and she ached to feel his bare skin against hers.

In another moment he obliged, removing her chemise and petticoats and gathering her against him. Her flesh was so warm and pliant and her full breasts crushed against his chest aroused him to such a degree that he hoped the control of his passions he wished to have would not escape him, for he intended this night to be memorable for them both.

He laid her on the bed and covered her body with his own for a moment, foreshadowing the possession that would soon be his. He lay beside her, exploring her mouth with his tongue, luring her to an equal response as her own desire matched his. He took one firm, round breast in his mouth, teasing the hard nipple with his tongue and teeth as he guided her hand between his legs and parted her thighs with his own.

China gasped when he touched her, and her legs spread apart as if of their own volition. The measurable degree of her arousal was obvious by her wetness and readiness for him, but he had no intention of rushing matters.

China had not touched any man intimately except for Clive, and she marveled anew at the warmth and firmness of the shaft she held in her hand as she gently caressed him in return. She felt as if every inch of her body were prickling with longing and this, of course, was the source of her need. It was important to her that she give him as much pleasure as he gave her, and though it was not a thing that she had done with Clive, she found she wanted to taste as well as touch him. Doubt of what he would think of her if she did such a brazen thing held her back, but only for a few minutes. When she could bear it no longer, she sat up and bent over him, taking him in her mouth.

She was astonished that giving him pleasure could increase her own, but it was so. The sweet sensations generated by his touch intensified and became focused and then spread out again in an explosion of pleasure that was no longer localized but seemed to involve every part of her body.

He lay her down again and then entered her, and she was surprised again that instead of dissipating, the sensations again became so strong that she knew she would have pleasure again and very quickly. It happened almost without warning and was so powerful that she could not help crying aloud. Even in the midst of this she could feel that he too was feeling the same wonderful pleasure and they subsided into peace simultaneously.

They lay side by side for a very long time, silent, but still kissing occasionally and touching each other, reluctant to entirely put an end to their union. Slowly this escalated and the fervor was renewed and brought to the same wonderful conclusion. China had always enjoyed her lovemaking with Clive, but it had never been like this, so intensely satisfying that even sated, she yearned for it to go on endlessly.

Eventually they drifted into a light sleep. The candle in the sitting room had long since guttered, but faint light was seeping into the room from the windows, the drapes of which were still drawn open, before Morgan stirred. He sat up, awakening China, who caught at his arm as if to keep him from leaving.

He bent down again and kissed her lightly. "I wish I didn't have to leave you, beauty, but you know I must."

"I know," she said quietly. "Do you think Vernon and Sally have missed you?"

"Possibly, but when I left I went out with Joseph Pickering and Matthew Carter, and Pickering, who was a bit castaway, providently—and rather loudly—invited us to his house for something a bit stronger then 'dashed champagne.' If they think anything at all, it is probably that I am still there too foxed to make my way home."

China smiled and reached up to touch his face. "Will they? I have never seen you drink very much."

"Every man has his day," he said with a laugh, and gently took her hand from his cheek, kissed the palm of it, and got out of bed and began to dress.

As China lay in bed watching him, she had an unexpected sense of abandonment. It was inappropriate because she knew that he would return to her as soon as he could and on the very next day she would leave Macao in his company to sail to England with him. Yet the feeling was there and she had to restrain herself to keep from getting out of bed and holding on to him as if she were afraid to let him out of her sight.

She shook off the feeling but did get out of bed, and found a wrapper to cover herself with, though she did not feel in the least shy being naked before him. It was impossible for him to stay with her any longer. As it was, now that it was becoming light, the risk of his being seen leaving her house was greatly increased. Her servants were decent enough people, but she could imagine how quickly the news would spread throughout their ranks that he had spent the night with her. And from there it was the work of hours before all of their employers knew it as well. If they were to be married, it should not matter, but she had been raised too strictly to forgo at least the outward proprieties.

So she watched him dress without comment, letting her thoughts wander over their future together, wondering if they would be married romantically at sea by the captain of the ship or wait and have a proper wedding in England. She smiled to herself at the thought of what the other Rawdons would think if another of their number married her out of hand and presented them with the *fait accompli*.

When he was dressed, before they left the room, he took her in his arms again and in the space of moments, the heat of their mutual passion returned. If there had been any way to preserve China's reputation in doing so, he would have undressed again and taken her back to bed, happily remaining there with her for the rest of the day. Her response told him that she was as reluctant as he to bring their night of love to an end.

"God, I don't want to leave you," he said into her ear, holding her tight against him. He kissed her again and then put her firmly away from him, saying with a smile. "Perhaps I had better see myself to the door. If we take leave again downstairs, we shall probably still be there and caught in a compromising position by your housemaid when she begins her chores."

China agreed, not for that reason, but because she did not want to witness the finality of the door closing behind him, putting the final period to their wonderful night. He kissed her lightly again, not touching her this time, as if he dared not, and finally left her. China was tempted to run to the window to see a last glimpse of him as he went down the street, but she closed the door and leaned against it, letting the memories of all that had happened between them wash over her.

She went back to bed, determined to sleep at least for a few hours. After the ball, it would be assumed by Lucy that she would not wish to rise too early. But her sleep was fitful at best, for she replayed in her thoughts every moment of the time that she had been with Morgan. It was after eleven when Lucy finally came in to bring her water and her morning tea, and even though she had had so little rest, China got out of bed feeling quite well and even refreshed.

China went through her day with the appearance of her usual composure, priding herself that no one could guess that she had spent the night before behaving like a wanton in bed with a man she had not known a full month before. It gave her a secret pleasure to hug this knowledge to herself while betraying it to no one. She

began her preparations for leaving Macao as soon as
she had had her breakfast. The first person she told
was her maid Lucy, who was stunned, but who was
quite happy to agree to return to England with her
mistress. In spite of the high wages, she had had quite
enough of this outlandish, hostile place.

China then assembled the rest of her staff, informed
them of her intention, assuring them that she would
see to it that they continued to be paid until they found
other situations—which would scarcely be difficult with
the shortage of their calling—and asked if they would
remain until her house was closed up and sold. Sir
Clive and Lady Rawdon had been an excellent master
and mistress, and their servitors were sorry to have
lost them both in such a short space of time, but all
wished her well, and a few privately thought that it
was only right that a lady of her quality should finally
take her proper place in the world.

China's next chore was to call on the Westons to beg
Sir Vernon to see to her affairs in her absence. She had
no doubt at all of his response, but she knew that both
he and Sally would be saddened to see her leave, and
Sally, certainly, would know the real cause of her going. They would be happy for her, but it would be a
mixed leavetaking, for she would miss them quite
dreadfully as well. She hoped she might see Morgan
as well when she called, for she longed for the sight
of him again, as if he had not just left her only a few
hours earlier.

But Morgan was not at home. China was disappointed, but quickly forgot her chagrin as she listened
to the exclamations of surprise and delight from the
Westons and answered their many questions. In spite
of having confided in Sally, China was circumspect
about Morgan. She said nothing of his pledge of love
to her the previous night, but her glowing features and
exuberant smile told Sally, at least, all she needed to
know. Sir Vernon declared himself very happy to be

of assistance to her and in the space of an hour, much was settled, setting China's mind to rest that her interests would be well looked after.

China decided against calling on any of her other friends. She knew they would stare when she told them that she had decided to leave Macao on such short notice, and she had no time to spare for tedious explanations. She regretted that her own indecision had made haste so necessary that she could not take a proper leave of them all, but it couldn't be helped. There was much that she personally needed to see to before she could be ready to leave with Morgan on the following day.

Jack called, as she had supposed he would, shortly after luncheon, and took her news with surprisingly little comment, merely wishing her every happiness and remarking that he, too, had begun to think seriously of returning to his home in Sussex. "I wonder if they will kill the fatted pig, if I do," he said in his inconsequential way.

Though she tried not to think negatively, it bothered China that Morgan, when he had left her, had said nothing about seeing her the following day, though she had naturally assumed it. She had not cared to inquire too closely where he might have gone when she had visited the Westons, not wishing to appear too anxious to see him, but now she wished she had. The morning waned, the afternoon came and went, and she had had no word at all from him.

Absurd anxieties began to plague her. It was unthinkable that he had had a change of heart toward her in so short a space of time or that he had said all that he had to her with no other intent than breaking down her guard so that her seduction might be accomplished. Yet, as she had felt intuitively the day before that they would at last acknowledge their love for each other, she had an uneasiness now that something unpleasant awaited her. She remembered her feelings

when he had risen from her bed that morning and felt
a small frisson in her spine.

She would not give in to her disquiet, however, and
kept herself well occupied, choosing what she would
take with her and directing Lucy in her packing. The
time passed more quickly than she would have thought
possible and it was after five when Lucy reminded her
that she had yet to give instructions to Cook about
dinner and did she intend to dine at home. China had
no other engagement for the evening—everyone was
recuperating from their night of gay dissipation—and
she ordered dinner for seven, hoping that perhaps
Morgan would come to her by then and remain and
dine with her.

When she heard the peal of the front bell from her
sitting room, her heart leapt, so certain was she that
it must be Morgan at last. She wanted to run out to
the top of the stairs to greet him, but she took herself
in hand so not to appear foolishly eager. She heard the
heavy masculine tread on the stair and could not resist
turning to stare at her half-closed door to see him the
moment he came into the room.

But it was not Morgan; it was Jack. China schooled
her features not to fall in disappointment, but even so
Jack must have seen something because he said, ''It's
just me, dearest. Since you are to leave us so soon, I
came to see if you would take dinner with me tonight.
It will likely be our last chance for any time together
before you go.''

China felt a guilty start. Before Morgan had come
to Macao, she had spent much of her time with Jack,
but since there had been so many parties of late and
so many other things to occupy her, they had scarcely
spent a single night in their old occupation of dinner
and pleasant conversation. ''I have just ordered dinner,'' she told him. ''Stay here with me and we may
have a comfortable coze afterward.'' If Morgan should
call now, it might look a bit singular that she dined

with Jack alone, but he knew of their close friendship and this did not particularly concern her.

"Unorder it," Jack said. "I have already directed my cook to make all your favorite dishes as a parting gift."

She felt quite reprehensible, but his consideration gave her no pleasure. She did not at all wish to be from home that evening. But she could not be unkind enough to tell him so, and so she summoned up an enthusiasm she was far from feeling and agreed to dine with him at his house.

Jack was delighted and settled himself in a comfortable chair to wait for her while she dressed. When she returned to him, she found he had had sherry brought for them as he informed her that they would not dine until eight and was in no hurry to leave for his lodgings, she was glad enough for the opportunity to remain a little longer at home.

This time he asked her a number of questions about her plans when she returned to England. She had not confided in him any more than she had in Sally about what had occurred between her and Morgan the previous night, but Jack was too shrewd not to guess it on his own and when he asked her point-blank about it, she admitted that she hoped to be married to Morgan as soon as they might decently do so when they reached England.

He nodded at her news, as it confirmed his assumption. "I must admit I am both surprised and not surprised at it. I think you've had a tendre for the fellow since he got here, but he didn't strike me as the sort of man to fall head over heels in love on such a short acquaintance, though one never knows."

"I thank you," China said caustically. "I am clearly a silly widgeon whom you quite accept would lose her heart so easily."

Jack smiled. "Your sex is notorious for its willingness to cast its cap over the windmill," he said provocatively, and at her outraged gasp, deftly turned the subject, saying, "Did you note the ostrich feathers that Juliet Waring had adorning her hair last night? Must have found them lying about in some old trunk. She looked a perfect quiz, didn't she?"

China was glad enough to change the topic to light gossip and a rehash of the events of the night before. The next hour passed quickly and for the first time that day she had not thought of Morgan. It was well after seven before she recalled him again, and though she did not wish to admit it, China knew she had quite given up hope that Morgan meant to call on her or make any attempt to see her that day. Perhaps he was busy with his own preparations for leaving, but he might at the least have sent her some note, or so she thought, though perhaps he had no idea of the anxiety his silence was engendering in her breast.

When Jack at last suggested that they had best be getting along to his lodgings before his cook despaired of them, she made no demure. It was becoming increasingly unlikely that she would see Morgan again now before tomorrow.

Morgan spent his day in perfect equanimity. He felt neither anxiety nor doubt, because he had no cause for it. He felt quite happily secure of China and it did not so much as occur to him that *she* might have had a change of heart since that morning. And he had every intention of seeing her before the day was out. He spent his morning in the company of Andrew Creely, who wished to discuss conditions in India with Morgan, as he was planning on expanding his business interests there, and in the afternoon Morgan went out with Sir Vernon to the farm to view the progress of a recent foal. Sir Vernon was in his glory with his horses and an appreciative and well-informed audience, and the few hours they spent at the farm advanced into remaining for an early dinner prepared by the farmer's wife.

It was early evening by the time they finally made preparation to leave and the arrival of the farmer's son with the news that he had passed a large group of mounted men on the road back to Macao caused further delay. It might, of course, mean nothing, but Sir Vernon sharing the concern of his neighbors about the increasing hostility of the Mandarins toward the hated English traders, insisted on returning to the farmhouse to discuss with the farmer alternate safer routes back to Macao.

Morgan privately thought that sticking to the main road was likely to be a safer course than riding cross-country, where they were surely an easier prey for ambush. But he knew that his knowledge of the area and the Chinese was far inferior to the older man's and he made no comment in the discussion that ensued, though the continued delay chafed at him. The farmer's son added his might and even offered to accompany them at least to the outskirts of Macao, but both his mother, who was terrified for his safety, and Sir Vernon, who had no wish to have any repercussion visited on the farmer and his family if it were known that they were assisting Englishmen, finally dissuaded him from that course.

As it was, because the area beyond the main road was unfamiliar to him, Sir Vernon found it necessary to go over their proposed route several times to ascertain that there would be no likelihood of their losing their way, which could be very dangerous indeed if they ended up wandering about unfamiliar country aimlessly. By the time they left the farmhouse a considerable while later, Morgan was barely able to contain his impatience to be back in Macao. They did not lose their way, as Morgan more than half expected they would, and nor did they encounter any other horsemen, but their route was circuitous and time-consuming and it was after eight when they finally reached the Westons' house.

He knew it would not look well for him to call on China alone in the evening, but everyone must soon know now that she was returning to England with him, so he did not refine too much on it. He had no real doubt of finding her at home, for Sally Weston had remarked earlier that this was the first evening in many that they could not claim a single engagement. But fate was not kind.

When Dosset opened the door to him at a bit before nine, he thought he detected both surprise and a bit of suspicion in the man's expression before it was carefully schooled to impassivity. As if it were two o'clock in the afternoon and the most natural thing imaginable, Morgan asked for China.

"Her ladyship's not at home," said the carefully disinterested voice of the servant.

This was the one prospect that had not occurred to Morgan, and he found himself a little taken aback by it. He cursed himself for not ascertaining from Lady Weston if she knew what China's plans might be for the evening. Or from China herself, for that matter. He was aware that he had said nothing to her about when he would see her that day, but then he had supposed that he would be able to go to her far earlier and it had not seemed of any importance at the time. "That's a great pity," he said, letting his voice slip into an indifferent, fashionable drawl. "I had something I particularly wished to discuss with her tonight, since I shall be occupied tomorrow making ready to leave for Kowloon in the afternoon. Do you know where I might find Lady Rawdon tonight?"

The servant, who was a more a man of all work than a proper butler, nearly shrugged before he realized his inappropriateness of this and turned the gesture into one of straightening his shoulders. "Couldn't say for certain, my lord. Her ladyship left in the company of

Mr. Reid, and they might have been visitin' any of their friends for dinner. Didn't say specifically.''

Morgan didn't think the man was putting him off. It was just his misfortune that circumstances had played against him. She might be anywhere—with the Fitchley-Gores or the Creelys or the Warings or half a dozen other places. He certainly couldn't go uninvited from house to house seeking her out, so there was really nothing for it but for him to accept his defeat with good grace and return to the Westons'.

He spent the remainder of the evening quietly playing three-handed whist with the Westons, giving no evidence that he was disappointed in his plans or wished for any company other than theirs. He played well, but automatically. His mind was on China and where she might be and what she would think that she had heard nothing from him that day. He had not even discussed with her the time they would be leaving for Kowloon, and finally it occurred to him that she might be a bit anxious and very likely annoyed at his carelessness of her feelings.

9

IT WAS NEARLY midnight when Sally Weston retired to bed and Morgan and Sir Vernon sat up a scarce half hour longer over glasses of brandy. Morgan was far from tired despite the excursions of the day, but he deferred to his host's wish to retire and went to his bedchamber. He undressed partway, dismissing Gilley when he had removed his coat and neckcloth and exchanged his shoes for slippers. He always traveled with a few of his favorite books, for he could never be certain of coming across something to entertain him in such exotic parts of the world. He selected an account of life in the court of Henry VII by Wallington and settled himself to read until sleep overtook him.

He did not recall actually falling asleep in the comfortable chair in which he was settled, but when he awoke with a start the reading lamp was low and about to go out and a search for his watch revealed that it was quarter past the hour of two. At first he was not certain what had jolted him awake, but then a sound, something like a shriek muffled into a moan, made him realize that it had been a scream. As his consciousness cleared, he became aware of other sounds, distant shouts, another far-away scream, and an occasional sharp crack that was almost certainly gunfire.

He was into his coat and pulling on his boots before he took the time to analyze what must be occurring and he flung open the door to his room and ran into the dark hallway and down the stairs without stopping to think what it was he meant to do. He met Gilley, who was coming to awaken him, at the foot of the stair, and he followed his valet into the drawing room. He arrived there to find Sir Vernon and his wife together with their servants huddled together around a single branch of candles. A housemaid was sobbing quietly, occasionally giving vent to a louder cry, such as the one that he had heard earlier, and Sally was trying desperately to convince her to be calm. The curtains were drawn tight and the light was the farthest from the windows that it could be, as if a fear that someone seeing it from the outside might expose them to danger.

As indeed it might, Morgan thought grimly. He was completely awake now and his faculties in perfect order. The sounds from outside were still sufficiently distant for him to think that whatever the danger was, it was not yet imminent. It was a raid on the community, he supposed, whether by bandits, the armed men of the local Mandarins, barely indistinguishable from the former, or even the envious Portuguese. It hardly mattered. He left the drawing room without speaking and went into the adjoining room to peer out a window and saw nothing outside but darkness and greenery and an ominous glow to the east. It was the direction in which China's house was situated.

All at once he was convinced of her danger and he went back to the drawing room. "I suppose we should not be surprised," Sir Vernon said to him, his mouth a tight line. "But I did not think it would come to this."

"They mean to murder us all," said the housekeeper in a voice of gloom, and started the maid to weeping louder and more gustily.

Sally called them both to order, quite futilely, and Sir Vernon instructed his manservant to see if he could grope his way about in the dark to find something restorative in the cellar, since he and Morgan had finished the decanter kept in that room before they had gone to bed.

As the man left, Morgan said tersely to Sir Vernon. "I'm going to see how Lady Rawdon fares and bring her and her household back with me."

"Oh, China! How could I have forgotten her?" said Sally, her voice nearly a wail, showing that for all her outward calm, she too was very near to hysteria. "She must be terrified out of her wits. Please go to her at once, Lord Wrexford, and make her come back with you whatever she may say. I shan't have a moment of peace until she is under this roof."

Morgan privately agreed and, barely listening to the cautions of his hosts for his safety, he let himself quietly out of the house. It had begun to rain in a teeming way; just in the space of running to the gates he felt wet through. The rain made the darkness of the night gray, but destroyed visibility. He could scarcely see the houses he passed as he ran down the street in the direction of China's house. Others must have been awakened as he and the Westons had been by the commotion, but like the Westons, their houses presented a dark, blank front as if no life stirred in the silent street.

The ominous noises to the east continued. There was still the occasional cry or shriek, and the babble of loud voices had became louder as he approached in that direction. There were thankfully, no further sounds of gunfire. Morgan moved stealthily as he moved into that section, staying close to houses and walls and trusting no shadow. He spied several men running, but never near enough for him to recognize them as friend or foe, but he went on his way unaccosted. It seemed to him an eternity before he reached China's house, and his relief was great when he saw that her house appeared unmolested. It was very near, though, to others that had been, and in addition to the sounds he had heard since awakening was added that of weeping women fairly nearby and somewhere a child bawled lustily.

China's house was as dark as the Westons' had been, and at first he regarded this as a good sign until he stepped up to the door and found it half open. His heart felt as if it had dropped into his stomach. If she were harmed, he would never forgive himself for having given up seeing her so easily last night. If he had been with her when all this began, she would now be safe away from here. Where she might actually be at this moment, he did not stop to think. He pushed open the door, for the first time heedless of his own danger, and went into the house.

There was no sound at all. The house was not as large as the Westons' and it did not take Morgan very long to search every room and even the servants' quarters. The house appeared completely empty. Returning to the ground floor from the upper regions, Morgan stood for a moment irresolute. Then he heard, or imagined he heard, a sound coming from the stairs leading to the kitchen. He cursed himself for having dashed out of the Westons' without arming himself first, and ducked into the shadows of the hall. He had not long to wait before the door into the hall opened and a man stepped into the hall with as much caution as Morgan had used. Morgan let him advance a bit further and then came at him from behind, pinning him in an armlock that took the other off guard and rendered him helpless.

"Don't kill me, for the love of God," the man pleaded in perfect English. It was clearly one of China's servants and not a straying marauder.

"I don't intend to," Morgan responded, and released the man partway to make his hold on him less painful. "Where is your mistress?"

"My lord? Is it you, then?" Dosset shook his head. "I don't know no more than when you called before.

She left with Mr. Reid, like I said. They didn't say what they were about, and they haven't come back.''

"Lady Rawdon hasn't returned since early this evening?'' he asked, surprised into speaking his thought aloud. He let free his hold on the man's arm and Dosset stepped away, unconsciously rubbing his arm, for Morgan's touch had been none too gentle.

"No, my lord,'' he said, residual fear making his tone obsequious. "When she is out with Mr. Reid, we have standing instructions to leave the gate on the latch for her and a lamp on in the hall and go to bed. Mr. Reid sees her home, I suppose, and sees that she gets in all right.''

Morgan digested this without comment. "Where are the others? Downstairs?''

The butler shook his head. "When the shoutin' and shootin' started, they fled like rats off a sinking ship. I tried to tell them that they were likely safer here than out in the streets, but everyone seemed to think they were a goin' to be murdered in their beds.''

"But you have seen no violence here? Did you know the door was ajar when I arrived?''

The servant's eyes widened at this information. "Was it now? I wondered how you got in. The last damn fool out the door didn't even have the sense to shut it, I reckon. I was stayin' belowstairs thinin' that if they started throwin' rocks or shootin' guns, I'd be better off where nothin' could reach me through no window.''

"Whatever has happened, I think it is mostly over now. Your fellows should come straggling back if they weren't fools enough to run in the wrong direction. If Lady Rawdon is with Mr. Reid, she is doubtless well,'' he added without expression. "You may tell her I called to assure myself of her welfare when she returns.''

Dosset agreed that he would and Morgan let himself out of the house. He had implied that he meant to return home, but he had no intention of it. He was not yet completely sure of China's safety, but there was no harm in alarming the already frightened servant. She might have gone with Reid to visit the Warings or another of their friends who lived in the area where the disturbance had taken place. But surely, she should not have still been out when the trouble started.

He left the house and went back into the rain which still fell steadily but not quite as heavily as before. He stood on the bottom step oblivious of the rain and he heard the door latch firmly behind him. There were no longer any sounds of shouting or weeping, only the teeming of the rain. It seemed unnaturally still to Morgan.

He very much feared he might find China at Reid's lodgings, which was a strange emotion to have in the circumstances. Reid's rooms were in a house not far from the Westons' and it was likely that China would be as safe there as she would with the Westons. But he did not much like the grim thoughts that assailed him at this prospect. He would not rest until he knew for himself where she was to be found and that she was well.

He felt other curious emotions as he swiftly made his way to the house in which Reid lodged on the ground and first floors. A part of him did want to find China there, for then there would be no question of her safety, but another part of him could not help hoping Reid had merely escorted to the home of some other friend, where, the hour becoming late, she had been persuaded to stay the night. He had refused to entertain Dana Bovell's dark hints that China's relationship to Reid was rather more than just friendship, but now he could not but recall them.

The hour was so far advanced that there could be virtually no question of China's visit to Reid's house being merely a social visit. Standing in the rain, scarcely noticing how wet through he was becoming, he remembered well the passion, equal to his, she had displayed during their lovemaking. He naturally had no idea what manner of skill his uncle had possessed as a lover, but there was no doubt that China knew well the art of pleasing a man in bed. He had only delighted in it at the moment of experiencing their mutual pleasure, but now he wondered if it stemmed from a practice greater than he had supposed. If Reid were China's lover, then she had played him for a fool. Yet, still, he did not want to believe it. He finally stepped into the street, pausing only to pull the gates shut behind him.

Morgan began his way down the street with the same careful furtiveness that had brought him to China's house. Even though all appeared quiet now, a bit of incaution could literally be life-threatening. He did not turn in the direction of the Westons'. He had no intention of leaving China tonight in the sole company of Reid and his servants.

Reid lived in a small narrow house at the end of a street, set a little further apart from its neighbors than most of the other houses in the area. On the ground floor he had only two rooms, a consulting room and a surgery. Even if Reid had not the right to the title doctor, he was treated and accepted as such and received ''patients'' who came to him for advice or more practical help in those rooms.

Unlike most of the other houses, there was light to be seen in one window of Reid's house. The ground floor was dark, but on the first floor, it was evident that not everyone slept or cowered in fear in a dark corner. Not certain if he would be answered, but determined to gain entry by some means, Morgan went directly to the front door and rapped the knocker firmly. He was forced to do so several times before finally he heard the sound of a window being drawn up above him and he stepped back down the front stairs to look up.

A head, backlighted and made unrecognizable, peered down at him from a first-floor window. ''What the devil do you want?'' said a voice gruffly and in accents somewhat artificially refined. It was clearly not Reid who spoke.

"Let me in, man," Morgan said to him in a voice of command that was rarely gainsaid. "It's Wrexford. Is your master at home?"

The head was pulled in abruptly, as if the man were pulled form behind, and Reid himself appeared at the window. "Is it the Westons? Is anyone injured? I didn't think the trouble had come this far, but there was such confusion that I could not be certain."

Morgan ignored his questions. "Is Lady Rawdon with you?" he demanded.

Reid's head came up a little, indicating his surprise. He made no reply, and Morgan said, "I am come from Sally Weston," he said. "She is afraid for Lady Rawdon and has charged me to bring her to her."

There was still a long pause before Reid spoke. "Lady Rawdon is safe."

"I'll take her to the Westons'," Morgan repeated, in a voice meant to brook no objection. He was well aware of his disadvantage outside of the house and in the street. He could scarcely storm the house and re-move her forcibly, but he had no intention of leaving until she was in his company, whatever that required.

But Jack Reid was not to be bullied. "She is safe," he repeated. "Certainly safer than if you took her back through the streets to the Westons'."

"Have you asked Lady Rawdon what she wishes? Tell her that Sally Weston is most distraught about her welfare."

Reid looked down at him without comment for a long moment, the backlighting hiding his features and his expression. Then he withdrew from the window and out of sight of it. Such a long time passed that Morgan wondered if he would just be ignored. From somewhere to the east of him he heard a sound of gunfire again, a suppressed scream, and then quiet.

Perhaps it was still not over and what Reid had said might well be true. Even if this area were relatively safe, he still had to get China to the Westons' house, and if bandits were moving in to see what looting might be had, the danger was still very real.

Finally it was China herself who come to the window. "Are the Westons safe? It has been hard at times to tell just where the gunfire and noise have been coming from."

"They are safe," Morgan replied without inflection. "The trouble seems confined to the east part of town thus far. But Lady Weston has made me promise to bring you to her. She won't rest until she has you with her and knows you are unharmed."

China did not respond. Even unable to see her features clearly, he knew that she hesitated, perhaps out of fear or even embarrassment. She could not have wanted him to find her like this any more than he was pleased to have done so. Finally she said, "I was afraid to go back to my house and meant to stay here tonight, but it would be better, I suppose, to go to Sally."

Morgan heard Reid's voice behind China, speaking in an argumentative tone. Doubtless he was trying to persuade her against leaving. China moved away from the window and though it was not shut again, no other head appeared in the opening and he waited on the steps, half wondering if he was on a fool's errand. He would wait, though.

Sooner than he expected, he heard the sounds of the bolts being drawn back on the door and it opened revealing China and Jack Reid, their figures silhouetted against the light of a lamp that had been lit in the hall. China said something Morgan could not hear to Reid, embraced him briefly, and then stepped out of the house. Morgan felt as if he had been delivered a leveler; it had wanted only that. Reid did not follow her, nor did he speak even a word of greeting to Morgan.

Morgan watched China descend the stairs to him

without comment or expression. "We shall have to move quickly and keep to the shadows as much as possible," he said in a voice without any discernible emotion. "Even if the worst is over, there will doubtless be looters still about looking for easy prey."

Jack finally came out upon the steps, extending his hand with a small, but lethal looking pistol in it to Morgan. "If you are unarmed, take this. I think China is mad to leave this house, but I shall be easier in my mind if I know you have this for protection."

Morgan wanted to tell him in no uncertain terms what he might do with his pistol, but the advice was too practical to ignore. He took it from Jack, ungraciously not even offering a word of thanks. He did not, at the moment, trust himself to speak civilly to the other man.

Though China knew Morgan must wonder at finding her with Jack, not knowing about the evil seed which Dana Bovell had planted in his mind, it did not occur to her that he would make any iniquitous assumptions about them. She and Jack had lingered over dinner until nearly ten and then had played chess for a while before sitting comfortably in quiet conversation. At about midnight, China had thought it best to leave—she still had much to do before leaving Macao the next day and she had not even any idea at what hour that might be—but Jack, reminding her that this would be their last night together, persuaded her to remain a bit longer.

China had permitted him to pour her a glass of wine and had made herself comfortable, curled into a corner of a small sofa in his sitting room. She really had no idea just when she had fallen asleep, but she had little memory from the time she had accepted a second glass of wine until Jack had shaken her awake not more than an hour ago, when he too had been awakened by the ruckus in the streets. She was not so naive that she could not imagine the possible construction that might be put on her spending the night with Jack, but she had given her heart as well as her body to Morgan, so that he must know he was the one man she wished to be with, and there was no reason, in her mind, for him to doubt her.

Their flight to the Westons' was accomplished almost in silence, which was only broken on occasion when Morgan advised her to watch her step or to move closer to him as he moved swiftly but stealthily through the streets. It only took a few minutes to reach the Westons' house, but the journey, made in anxiety, seemed far longer to China.

Morgan took China not to the front door, but to a servants' entrance on the side near the back of the house. The house was so dark and so incredibly still that China felt an irrational fear rise in her that, entering it, they would find everyone gone or robbed and beaten or worse.

But at Morgan's swift rapping, the door drew open and they slipped through a crack barely wide enough to admit them into the house. The servant did not take them to the drawing room, where Morgan had left the Westons, but down to the kitchen and there, the scene made eerie and unreal by the flickering of only two or three kitchen candles, sat the entire Weston household, masters and servants, side by side, drawn together in fear. There was a strong smell of tallow mixed with staler odors of cooking which was quickly replaced by a delicate violent scent when Sally came to China and drew her into her arms for a fierce embrace.

"Oh, my love, I have been so frightened for you," she said, releasing China and holding her at arm's length as if to examine her for any possible injury. "Thank God Wrexford found you at home safe and unmolested."

China's eyes went to Morgan's, waiting for him to contradict this assumption, but he surprised her, saying blandly, "When I reached Lady Rawdon's house I could actually see as well as hear people running and shouting only a few houses away, but her house had not been touched.''

"Yet," Sally said with a shiver. "Dear God, what is happening? I know we are resented here, but I never thought it would come to this.''

"I had some fear of it," Sir Vernon said ominously. "But it didn't seem to me that anything like this would happen so quickly and so violently. With all the shooting and screaming, it must be a sure thing that some have been injured, maybe even killed. Reid will have his work cut out for him when the dust settles. I only hope he can cope with it, for all our sakes.''

Again, China's eyes sought Morgan's, and again they met. His expression was not unpleasant, but it was stony and unresponsive. "I am sure Mr. Reid will do the best he can," he said evenly.

Morgan was standing by the kitchen hearth which, kept always lit but banked, gave off a glow so feeble it contributed almost no light to the room. China thought the flickering light of the candles, which cast shadows and hollows on his face, made him seem almost sinister. She turned away and sat down at the wide wooden table next to Mrs. Haggerty, the Westons' cook-housekeeper, and said nothing. Exhaustion born of fear swept over her in a wave.

Morgan was speaking quietly with Sir Vernon and Gilley, discussing the watch they meant to keep for the night. Sally, seeing her friend leaning wearily on the table, went over to her and said, "I think you should try to get some sleep. Your danger was more real than ours and must have been very trying. Mrs. Haggerty has a settle in her sitting room and I am sure she would not mind if you lay down upon it for a few hours.''

Mrs. Haggerty agreed readily to this and China, too weary to expostulate, allowed herself to be led into the cozy room off the kitchen that was the housekeeper's private domain. She had been genuinely afraid when the tumult had started, in spite of Jack's protection, but now, though the danger might not yet be over, she felt no fear at all. She lay down on the settle and did not even notice the harness of the wood. Within the space of moments she was asleep.

10

THE FOLLOWING MORNING was bright and sunny and cheerful, and China, to her astonishment, awoke in a large comfortable bed in one of the bed-chambers upstairs. She had no recollection of getting there, either by her own power or by being carried. There was a fire in the hearth, and Sally's own maid was standing by the wash table pouring hot water from a can into the basin.

"Good morning, my lady," she said, her tone so sunny that if China had been in her own bed at home she might have thought she had imagined the night before. "It was the devil's own night last night, but the birds are singing this morning."

China could not but agree, but as she dressed she had an odd feeling of unreality. She went downstairs as quickly as her toilette could be completed and found the Westons and Morgan in the breakfast room. The men were still conversing in low tones and Sally was leafing through an old edition of the *Lady's Magazine* which a friend from London had sent to her a few months before. "I gave Mitzi instructions to let you sleep," she said to China as the latter seated herself at the table. "I wonder you did not bring Lucy with you last night."

"Lady Rawdon's servants had fled by the time I arrived," Morgan interjected. "There was only Dosset left to protect the house."

"That is infamous," Sally said, outraged. "For even

your maid to abandon you out of fear of her own skin is unpardonable.''

"Most behavior that took place last night by people maddened with fear must be pardoned,'' Morgan said. "I found Lady Rawdon well, and that is all that matters.''

Once again, his words led to the assumption that he had found China in her home, making her wonder why he was so intent on creating that false impression. Morgan glanced up at China and she sent him a questioning look, but he did not respond, merely looking again to the old newspaper he was skimming through.

"Perhaps it is only the sunshine after the rain of last night,'' China said, "but I have had the most disconcerting feeling since I awoke that last night was no more than a dreadful nightmare.''

"It was that,'' Sir Vernon agreed, breaking off what he was saying to Morgan to address China. "But a very real one. There are three dead that I know of,'' he added in a flat tone, "and many more have been injured. One or two houses were razed and a great many ransacked and robbed.''

It was a very minor consolation to learn that the dead were little known to anyone at the table and not any friends or acquaintances, but it was no less horrid and tragic for that. China feared the answer but had to ask if there was any news of her house or servants.

It was Morgan who answered her. "Since we left last night,'' he said, continuing the subterfuge, "we have had no word, but all is quiet now and it is safe to go into the streets again. Whenever you are ready after you have eaten, we will go to your house and see for ourselves how it has fared.''

China had little appetite but forced herself to drink the strong black coffee that Sally pressed on her and she nibbled at a bit of toast without managing to eat very much of it. Her impatience to know what had happened to her home overwhelming her, she finally announced that she was ready to leave as soon as Morgan wished. He agreed to go at once and taking no more time than to accept the loan of a bonnet to go with the morning dress Sally had insisted that she wear, China left the Westons' in Morgan's company.

It seemed odd to China, and troubled her, that Morgan seemed determined to speak of nothing but commonplaces as they walked to her house. His manner to her could not be described precisely as cool, but his voice held none of the usual warmth that she was accustomed to hearing when he usually addressed her. She wanted to ask him why he had not come to her the day before, but his manner was so distant that she did not feel comfortable doing so. She could not understand the change in him; surely there was no reason for him to be vexed with her, and very likely it was just his response to the dreadful events of the early morning hours. Yet she felt that it was something more than that, and something, moreover, to do with her. She remembered her feelings the day before that something unpleasant awaited her and perhaps it was not horror of the raid on the English community after all.

When they arrived at her house she recoiled in shock and all thought of Morgan's odd humor was banished. Every window that faced the street was broken and the front door, imposing as it was, hung crazily from one hinge. Before Morgan could prevent it, China began to run toward the house, oblivious to his call that she might yet find danger lurking in the house.

But the house was completely empty. Inside, the destruction was as bad as the outside. Furniture, draperies, paintings, anything that could be smashed or slashed was in ruin, strewn about the floor. China stood as if paralyzed in the doorway of what had been her elegant drawing room when Morgan finally caught her up. She turned and looked at him with eyes wide with horror.

Morgan put his arms around her and drew her against him. She submitted to his embrace, though she had not meant to give in to any weakness. After a few moments of just enjoying the feeling of comfort and protection in his arms, she moved away from him. "How could anyone be so horribly destructive?" she said with dismayed astonishment.

"Those who value life cheaply are not likely to balk at destroying inanimate things," he said with flat practicality as he went back into the hall and into the room that had been Clive's study. Here the destruction was even greater, if possible, with even the books not just thrown from their shelves but ripped to shreds, the pieces of paper in odd shapes and sizes settling on the once beautiful carpet like a fall of dirty snow.

It was on viewing this room which both she and Clive had so loved that her composure deserted her. She placed her hands over her face as if to block out the sight of it and began to silently weep.

Morgan watched her with something like dismay. The hardness he was determined to feel toward her softened in spite of himself. However much she had duped him before, he did not think this was an act. She had admitted to him that she had not been in love with Clive, but she clearly was not without any feeling for his memory. He moved to embrace her again. China twisted her body in his arms and lay her head against his chest, sobbing as if her heart had been broken. In spite of his determination to distance himself from her, he could not deny her the comfort she sought. He brought her tight against him and caressed her gently, murmuring comfortingly against her ear.

Despising himself for his weakness, he could not help being stirred by the feel of her soft yielding body against his own, the scent of her as intoxicating as ever. Almost abruptly, he drew back from her.

But China didn't notice the deliberateness of his movement. The storm of tears was abating, and she turned to look again at the room. She picked her way over the rubble and, bending, she extricated a curiously wrought, heavy gold and onyx object which had been lying half-covered by the shreds of paper. She held it up to Morgan for his inspection as if it were a prize she had just won in some game of chance.

"Clive brought this from South America," she said in a deadened tone. "It is said to represent some ancient god."

Mechanically, Morgan reached out his hand to stroke the smooth surface of the object she held in her hand. "Keep it," he said almost gruffly. "It may be the only thing you salvage from this place."

China looked up at him with eyes so blank that he wondered if the shock had disordered her senses. Her abrupt question, incongruous as it seemed at the moment, put him equally off balance. "Why didn't you call on me yesterday?"

"I did," he said in a tone as flat as hers. "I had prior engagements most of the day and returned much later than I intended. I came here as soon as I could, but you were not at home."

China thought she detected a note of reproach in his voice and felt the injustice of it. "It was after seven when I left. I had given you up," she said with a trace of her usual spirit. "Didn't Dosset tell you where I had gone?"

Morgan did not really wish for this conversation; he did not want to descend into anger and recriminations. "Merely that you were out in the company of Jack Reid," he said tersely.

"Then you knew where I might be found."

"No. I had no idea you had gone to Reid's lodgings," he said with as little inflection as he could manage. "But even if I had known, I couldn't have followed you there."

"Why not?"

He looked at her face, with its every appearance of

innocence, for a long moment. Obviously, she meant to brazen it out. He had no intention of playing her game. "What excuse might I have given? It would have looked most singular. It is strange that none of your staff have come back," he said, abruptly turning the subject. "Even Dosset must have left before the house was ransacked." A grisly thought occurred to him. He drew her farther into the ruined room and settled her on a small sofa that had once been upholstered in rich brown leather but which now was ripped almost beyond recognition. "Stay here for a moment. I'll search the house and see what else is to be found."

"I want to come with you," China said, rising, but he pushed her down again. "I know you are intrepid, but it may be far worse than you imagine."

His hand was on her shoulder, but China shrugged him off. "I doubt that it could be. I'm coming with you."

Her voice abided no argument and he made none, allowing her to follow him when he went back into the hall. The entire house was in the same state as the drawing room and study. In China's bedchamber her wardrobes had been emptied and even the portmanteaus so careful packed the day before had been pried open. The beautiful dresses and gowns that Clive had gone through so much trouble to have made for her were torn beyond repair. Even her scent and few cosmetics had been smashed and the room reeked with the odors that in the amounts intended were alluring but in concentration were nauseating. China did not even attempt to enter the room to salvage anything, she merely observed from the doorway as she had in the drawing room, and then, squaring her shoulders, turned away from the destruction.

The last place that Morgan led her was down the stairs to the basement, where the butler had been when Morgan first had come to the house to find China. He had no reason to suppose the man had not escaped unharmed, but the possibility that he had suffered a fate similar to the contents of the house had to be faced, and he would have much preferred it if he could have convinced China to remain upstairs while he investigated on his own. To his relief, the basement was as empty as the upper floors and there was no sign of any injury or bloodshed. He was relieved to find nothing, and his shoulders relaxed visibly, making China guess what he had feared to find.

"I must find my servants," she said quietly behind him.

"We shall. I'll take you back to the Westons' and then I'll go out again and make inquiries. Your maid and some others may guess that you would go to the Westons' and seek you out there."

China was used to her independence and of taking care of matters for herself, however unpleasant this might at times be. Her chin came up, but it was more than independence that made her say, "It is my responsibility to reassemble my household. I thank you, Morgan, but I shall inquire myself for my servants. I must know for myself that they are well." From his behavior since he had taken her from Jack's house it was clear to her that something had occurred to make him feel differently toward her than he had professed the night they had spent together. It was also clear that he did not intend to discuss it with her—for now at least. All manner of wretched thoughts assailed her, but she banished them for the present. It would be a long journey to England on the confined quarters of the merchant ship and she was certain to discover soon enough the cause of it.

For the first time, Morgan smiled. "Very well," he said, and saw the flicker of surprise in her eyes. "If you want my assistance, I shall be available."

"You are to leave today for Kowloon," she said pointedly.

He turned and looked at her for a long moment before speaking. "*We* leave for Kowloon," he said. "Or have you changed your mind again?"

Was there a faint sneer in his voice? She could not be certain. "I am not sure that I should go now. It would be asking a great deal of Vernon to set all of this to rights for me." But this was not the only reason she now had doubts about her decision to go with him.

He waved his arm at the mess and destruction in which they stood. "There is very little that I perceive worth salvaging. Now there is even less for you here than there was before. And who is to say this sort of thing will not continue. China is a hostile place for Englishmen, even outside of Macao."

China laughed suddenly, but not with mirth. "I don't even have to worry about packing now, do I?" she said with bitter irony. She walked out of the kitchen and up the service stairs without answering him.

Morgan followed and they went back out into the street. After what he had seen the night before he had felt some regret that he had succeeded in persuading her to leave with him, but now, perversely, he was determined that she not change her mind. It occurred to him that her excuse for demuring might have more to do with her meeting with her lover the previous night than the one she had given him. "I doubt there is anything of value left in the house that has not been stolen or destroyed, but when we find your maid, it might be best to have her go over your things in case some jewelry was missed in the looting."

China made no reply, but she walked beside him without leaning on his arm for support. Where they should have turned to go to the Westons', she continued straight and Morgan knew where she was headed. If it had been safe he would have left her; he supposed she might prefer to be alone. But when they reached Reid's house, she made no attempt to enter, merely satisfying herself that it appeared not to have been damaged, at least from the outside. There was a great deal of activity about the house, as people seemed to be hurrying in and out of it. "Doctor" Reid was obviously as busy as Sir Vernon had predicted he would be.

China came to a halt when the house was in sight but still at some distance. "I had dinner with Jack last night to take my leave of him," she said in a low voice, almost as if she were just speaking her thoughts and not addressing Morgan at all. "He has been a very good friend to me, particularly since Clive died. He persuaded me to take more wine with him after we had played chess for a while, and I fell asleep on the sofa in his sitting room. He didn't wake me until the shouting and the shooting started. I wish he had not let me sleep, though he meant well. I should have been home when the trouble started. I had no idea it would be a night I should never forget."

China had no idea why she told Morgan this. He had asked her for no explanation, and she still did not suppose that he assumed Jack to be her lover. But the words spilled out almost of their own volition. She turned and looked at him, but his eyes were as expressionless as green agate.

Their eyes held and Morgan made no reply. Her words washed over him without affecting him for good or for bad. Vulnerable was not a word he would have used to describe her; she was a strong and independent woman, but she looked very young to him at this moment, and as beautiful and fragile as fine porcelain. A china doll, he thought, though he did not know that this was what Clive used to call her. He put his fingers against her face for a moment and bent and kissed her very lightly, heedless of who might see them.

China could not explain it to herself, but this act, though it should have reassured her, made sudden tears well in her eyes and spill down her cheeks.

"Please go to Sally and let me find out what has happened to your household," he said, more gently than he had yet to speak to her that day. "I don't want to strip you of your independence, but it will be faster and easier for me to do so. There is no question of our leaving for Kowloon today, but we must be gone by tomorrow or we may miss our ship.''

China hesitated and then nodded, wiping her tears with her gloved hand as her composure returned to her. She allowed him to lead her in the direction of the Westons'. When he addressed her again it was to comment on the ship that was to take them to England, whose captain he had known for several years. The remark was unexceptional in itself, but it was spoken in a far warmer and more natural tone of voice than he had used before. She was not sure what his kiss and the change from coolness to warmth meant, but at this moment, with her emotions in tumult, she did not want to analyze it. He left her with Sally to go back into the streets to gather what news he could of her servants.

Sally was horrified by what China told her of the destruction they had seen, not only in her own house but in many that they passed, and they had not even gone into the portion of town where the worst of the trouble had taken place.

China expressed her doubts to Sally about leaving them with such chaos to see to after she was gone, but Sally assured her that Vernon would not shrink from a task more onerous than he had supposed. ''We shall both miss you dreadfully, of course, but I think it is right that you should go, China. This may have been a climax of events, or it may only be the beginning,'' she said, unconsciously echoing Morgan. ''Even Vernon was saying last night that we have to think of what our future will be here in Macao. I don't think he will wish to leave China entirely, but we may have to go somewhere else. It is barbarous that the Chinese will not allow any English to live in Canton except for the traders at certain times of the year. Kowloon, perhaps. I don't know, but I begin to think that we shall all have to go from here or be forever in fear for our safety.

You have nothing to keep you here, and your future happiness lies in England, not here.''

China, though she had shared her doubts and desires with her friend, had said nothing about the night she had spent with Morgan, though it was possible that Sally had noted his absence from the house that evening and made her own assumptions. ''Perhaps,'' she agreed with a wry smile, thinking that she had doubts there now as well.

So it was once again a settled thing by the time Morgan returned to the house with China's maid Lucy and a few of the other servants in tow. Lucy fell on her mistress's neck, weeping voluably and declaring that when she had gone back to the house earlier in the morning and found it in such shambles she had feared her mistress kidnapped or worse.

Sally broke up this affecting reunion by reminding China that since all of her clothes had been destroyed, she would need something other than the dress she had borrowed that morning and the silk gown she had worn the night before to take on the voyage. ''The Rawdons will think you a perfect quiz if you arrive in ragged finery,'' she said, laughing, and China realized it was the first time she had heard anyone do so that day. Sally insisted that her own wardrobe was at China's disposal, and they went up to her dressing room, bringing Lucy with them. In a short space of time they had selected a few dresses that Lucy felt would need little alteration to more perfectly fit her mistress.

''Oh my lady, it is so sad,'' she said mournfully. ''All your beautiful dresses destroyed and your jewels taken by barbarians who will probably know no better than to feed them to the pigs.''

China was sure the ''barbarians'' had more sense than that, but she agreed it was a shame. She didn't really feel that way, though. In a curious way, she almost felt as if a burden had been lifted from her. The house she and Clive had lived in had at times seemed empty to her since he had died and now, with all of their things destroyed, it was a shell and nothing more. She had put the curio she had found in the study in her reticule and she had that to remember Clive by. She felt no compunction at all leaving the house.

The rest of the day was spent in these last-minute preparations, and they sat down to a quiet dinner that evening, China choosing to retire early for the journey on the morrow. Morgan remained with Sir Vernon in his study, preferring company to solitude that night.

China drank warm milk to assist her sleep and supposed that this and the emotionally exhausting day she had had must make her fall into slumber at once, but it was not so. Her body was tired, but her mind had a life of its own, her thoughts hopping about in a grasshopper fashion. Mostly, though, she thought of Morgan. His manner toward her had been distinctly unloverlike except for when he had kissed her in the street, and even then it had been a kiss devoid of passion. It was as if that night before last had not happened. It was not alluded to by either of them by word or glance.

In light of all that had occurred, it would be absurd for either of them to be thinking of such things at this moment, but it troubled her, nevertheless, adding to her already growing concern about the change in his manner toward her. She could not believe he had had a change of heart so quickly, and she had the frightening thought, banished as soon as it occurred, that he had not meant the things he had said to her. Jack was right in saying that she knew nothing of the men of Morgan's world. It might well be the stock-in-trade of the practiced rake, however dastardly it was, to tell a woman what she most wished to hear if it would win him her bed. Instead, she made herself think of what lay ahead of her in England, but in her tired state, even these thoughts dwelled more upon the possibly unpleasant. Finally, after lying awake far after she had gotten into bed, she fell into a weary sleep.

11

THE FOLLOWING MORNING, Sir Vernon was concerned that her house be secured and the men of the house, including the servants, went there to board it up to keep out further intruders until the debris could be gone through and sorted out. China insisted on going back with her maid; if there was anything of her own to be salvaged, she wanted to know it for herself. As it was, there was very little. A pearl set that Clive had given her when he had begun paying her his addresses, some underthings in a drawer that had escaped notice, and just one dress that had not been torn to rags—ironically, the blue morning dress she had worn the day she had gone to visit Sally out of restlessness and had first become acquainted with Morgan Wrexford.

The morning was far advanced by the time Sir Vernon's traveling carriage arrived at the front door ready to take Morgan and China and their servitors to Kowloon. Even if China had wished to do so, there was no time to say good-bye to her other friends, who were doubtless busy setting their own affairs to rights after the chaos that had befallen them. China left notes and messages with Sally for all, but the hardest to write was to Jack. She had not seen him again since she had left his house with Morgan. She knew that his work must be occupying his every minute and had not wished to call to interrupt him, and she had not expected him to call on her. It saddened her to think that

it might be years before she saw him again, for though
he talked of returning to England from time to time,
she knew he had left under a cloud after having a great
row with his family, and that this had hurt him far
more than he admitted. His elder brother had died the
year before, making him now his father's heir, but still
he put off going back and might never do so.

The place where Morgan, through the agent of his
valet, had arranged for them to stay in Kowloon was
more of a house letting out rooms than an inn, but it
was comfortable enough for one night, and the simple
supper they were served—in community, with their
servants eating beside them—was good and ample. In
deference to their status, a small room off the main
chamber was set aside for them after dinner, where
they were served rice wine and almond cakes in relative privacy. China was not entirely certain she wished
for privacy with Morgan. His manner toward her was
no longer cool as it had been the day before, but still
it was not what she would have expected after what
they had shared together.

Her pride would not permit her to show him that she
even noted this difference and she, too, made no reference to the declarations of love they had made to
each other, or the physical confirmation of it they had
shared. But as the evening progressed and the second
bottle of rice wine was produced, Morgan's manner
became far easier and warmer toward her, and China
was only too willing once again to excuse his earlier
distance as the result of all that happened in the last
two days.

The merchant ship captained by Morgan's friend,
Gilley had ascertained, had indeed docked the day before last and was nearly fully provisioned, expecting
to leave on the first tide the following morning. Morgan suggested they retire for the night, since they were
to go to the docks at a fairly early hour, and China

made no demure but allowed him to escort her to her room, which adjoined his.

At the landing it seemed the most natural thing for him to take her in his arms and she went to him without hesitation. His kiss was deep and lingering and China felt the tension she had scarcely acknowledged begin to seep from her as she relaxed into his embrace, all her fears vanishing on the instant. Nothing had changed between them after all.

But it had. Morgan made love to China against his better judgment. The easier manner between them and the rice wine had mellowed his resolve, formed when he had found her with Jack Reid, to repudiate all of his feelings for her. It was impossible for him to be with her without being affected by her both emotionally and physically. He had not even let himself consider her simple explanation for why she had still been with Reid when he had found her that night, but now he found himself wanting to believe it. There had been many women in his life, but none who had moved him as China had done. She stimulated his mind as well as his senses. He wanted to make love to her again as much to reassure himself as out of any physical desire. It was as if possessing her again would convince him that he had been mistaken about her and Reid.

With her firm but pliant body molded tightly against his, with her lips meeting his in an equal passion, it was easy for Morgan to dismiss his doubts as it was for China to abandon her pride and fears. Lost in the pleasures of their embrace and hidden in the shadows with no light save that from below, there was no thought of time passing or the possibility of interruption. If either noted the sounds of arrival of another traveler, they did not heed them.

"Come to bed, Beauty," Morgan said huskily into her ear, and China was only too willing to follow him, but hasty footsteps ascending the stairs made her halt and look to see who was coming up them. She withdrew from him a little to do so.

To China's astonishment, the new arrival was Jack Reid. Morgan saw him too and released her at once. When Jack saw China, he ran up the last stairs and immediately took her in a fierce embrace which China was too surprised to resist.

"I couldn't believe it when Sally sent me your note telling me that you were leaving today," Jack said, a bit breathless with his exertions. "I thought you must not leave at once after what had happened or I should have come to you yesterday or this morning. I couldn't let you go without even a proper farewell."

China felt a return of her guilt that she had not made the effort to see Jack before she had gone. "I would have gone to you, but I knew how busy you must be with so many people injured. I thought I would be in the way."

"Dear God! How could you think it!" he said with clear reproach.

"I think Lady Rawdon believed she acted in your best interests," Morgan said coolly, causing Jack to turn and note him for the first time.

"Wrexford, I know you wished China to return to England with your escort," Jack said, "but in the circumstances, with everything in Macao in chaos, I think she must wish to see to her affairs herself rather than leave them in the hands of others."

"Apparently she does not agree," Morgan said, the coolness replaced by a tone of cold steel.

Jack ignored him. He turned back to China, still with his hands gently clutching her arms. "China, come back with me to Macao. Sally is talking now of going back to England in a few months if matters do not improve, and you may leave with her then if you are still of the same mind."

There was a silence and China felt that both men were waiting for her response. "I don't think my decision was unconsidered,'' she said evenly. "What happened the night before last has altered nothing. I trust Vernon to see to everything, which he has agreed to do. Since all that I had has been destroyed, there is nothing to keep me in Macao any longer.''

"Not even the friends who love you?'' Jack asked, sounding wounded.

China was surprised by his words. He had not tried to persuade her against leaving when she had dined with him that night, but he had made suspiciously few comments about her decision and perhaps he had intended to do so before she left, only becoming distracted from doing so by all that had happened. "I hope my friends in Macao will remain my friends even though I return to England,'' China said gently, not wishing to hurt Jack. "I hope you have not traveled this distance just to try to persuade me to stay, Jack. There must be many who need you in Macao.''

Before Reid could respond, Morgan said with a definitely dry inflection, "If you will excuse me, I find the journey has wearied me and I am going to bed.'' He sketched China a brief, quite formal nod of good night and went into the room allotted to him, leaving China alone with Jack on the landing.

China found herself both perplexed and dismayed at Morgan's retreat, but perhaps it was no more than tact. He could scarcely expect her to follow him to his room in front of Jack, and he might reasonably suppose that she would not wish to abandon her friend when Jack had taken such trouble to take his leave of her. She moved a little away from Jack so that he released her and then, taking his arm, she suggested they return downstairs to the parlor she and Morgan had just quitted.

They were brought glasses of the rice wine that she had enjoyed with Morgan, but Jack ignored his glass and took one of China's hands across the table. "Do you really wish to leave in this hurley-burley fashion,

China?'' he demanded. "You told me only a month ago that you had no intention of returning to England. I can't believe you were so easily persuaded by Wrexford to change your mind.''

China's supposition was confirmed by his words. "You knew the night before last that I meant to go,'' she said patiently.

"But I no more than half believed it. I know you believe yourself in love with Wrexford, but, dear lord, you can scarcely know the man on such short acquaintance. But I thought that when you had had a bit more time to reflect on it, you would realize that marriage to a virtual stranger was not a thing to contract with haste.''

"I *am* in love with Morgan,'' China said firmly, suppressing her annoyance at his doubt of her sense.

"Are you equally certain that he is in love with you?'' Jack persisted.

China wanted to give an indignant affirmative to his question, but something prevented her. She said instead, "Are you suggesting that he has only pretended to be to lure me back to England with him?'' She laughed at the absurdity of it. "It can't have mattered to him *that* much.''

"Perhaps he has another purpose,'' Jack said, releasing her hands and picking up his glass.

"Such as?'' China said with noticeable coolness.

"You know what his reputation is,'' he said, his tone almost careless. "It will be a long voyage in close quarters.''

"And he has hopes that we may become lovers,'' China finished for him, smiling to herself as she wondered what Jack would think if she told him that this was already an accomplished fact. "We are to be married, Jack,'' she said, and even as the words were spoken, she realized for the first time that Morgan, though he had told her he loved her, had never mentioned marriage. It was she who had assumed that they would be wed when they returned to England. The thought made her feel cold inside, and inspired an anger she did not wish to feel toward Jack for making her doubts return to her.

Jack looked at her for a long moment and then sighed. "As you say," he said without further comment on the subject. "But you might still be married to Wrexford if you do not go at once but remain and go with Sally and Vernon if they decide to leave as well."

"And if they do not decide to go?" she said, barely curbing her impatience. "Then I must travel by myself, which I own, I do not at all wish to do. Why are you so determined to convince me to stay?"

"I care too much for you to want you to do anything you will regret."

"I shan't regret this," China said rigidly.

"Have you forgotten about the other Rawdons?"

"Of course not," she said, this time so shortly that she sounded curt.

"What do you think they will have to say when you greet them and then in the next breath announce your betrothal to Wrexford? If they were shocked and displeased by your marriage to Clive, how do you imagine they will take it that you have appeared to have ensnared yet another Rawdon?"

China, had, of course, thought of this that morning while she had watched Morgan dress to leave her, but she had not let it weigh with her. She did not intend to do so now. "They may be unpleasant about it, but it will affect nothing."

"Not with you, perhaps. What can their opinions matter to you, after all? But it may be different with Wrexford."

China rose abruptly. She had been pleased and touched that Jack had cared enough to come all the way to Kowloon to say good-bye to her, but now she wished he had not. "This is a pointless discussion,

Jack, and it is likely to lead to us parting as less than friends. I know you are only concerned for my welfare, but trust me to know what is best for me."

Jack at last saw that she was offended, and sighed. "I'm the last one to point the finger of wrath at you, you know that. But I could not be easy in my mind letting you go without at least making a push to convince you to think on this thing before it is irrevocable." He picked up his glass again, tilted it back sharply, and drained the contents in one swallow. "God, I'm worn to the bone. I rode here, fearing that if I took a carriage, I'd miss you before you sailed. Very well, China. I'll be your friend even when I think I may be making a mistake letting you go without any further argument. Just remember that you can always come back here if that is what you wish. Don't let Wrexford or anyone convince you to stay in England if everything isn't as you hoped."

"If the trouble continues, you may none of you continue in Macao," China pointed out.

"Oh, I expect our race is too intrepid to be routed completely," he said with a short laugh. "But I am no hero. If it becomes bad enough, I'll sail to safer shores. You know I have been thinking on it myself since Harry died." His voice sobered. "Wherever I am, China—and I promise to always keep you apprised of my wanderings should I decide to go elsewhere than England—there will be a home and a friend for you there."

China reached for his hand and squeezed it eloquently. She thought if she spoke the words might stick in her suddenly constricted throat. Jack was the truest friend she had known in her life, and she felt suddenly very guilty for wishing him at the devil because he was worried about her future.

"You must be as weary as I am," Jack said. "Go up to bed, China. I'll get someone to find me a bed for the night here. I think perhaps I won't stay tomorrow to see you sail. I might not keep to my promise not to try to persuade you against it again in the morning light.''

China gave him no argument. Tears started in her eyes as she realized that this was the last time she would see him for perhaps a very long time. They embraced and hugged each other for several minutes before he kissed her lightly and let her go. China went up to her room without looking back, knowing that that was what she must do from now on.

Morgan was still awake when he heard China come up the stairs—the thin walls made the smallest sound from the remotest parts of the house penetrate to every corner. Several minutes after that he heard a man's steps ascending. They stopped on the landing and then a door opened and closed. He had no idea which room Jack Reid had entered. Morgan turned on his side, a position he favored for sleeping, and refused to let his mind linger on any possibilities.

The next morning dawned sunny and clear with a good breeze but not strong enough to make the sea choppy. China stood on the dock beside Morgan and Lucy and for the first time in three days her spirits were light and her expectations hopeful. With her usual good humor restored, China gave no thought to the doubts Jack's words had engendered in her or any difficulties she might face when they arrived at their destination. She felt her blood stir with a sense of impending adventure.

Lucy was too happy to be going home again to be in anything but good humor and Morgan, too, seemed determined to be at his most agreeable. Not even the sight of the rather small and fragile looking frigate, a merchantman carrying spices and silks back to England, that was to convey them so far made China have any last-minute doubts.

China had been up with the sun and downstairs shortly after Morgan. He had greeted her pleasantly and made no mention of Jack's visit the night before other than to tell her that Jack had left for Macao after taking a light breakfast. China responded to this by saying that she and Jack had said their good-byes to each other the night before.

Morgan cast her a swift, slanting glance. "Reid is a good friend to give himself so much trouble," he said at his blandest, a characteristic manner when he kept his thoughts to himself.

China had the feeling from these words and Morgan's behavior the night before that he had not been best pleased by Jack's show of devotion to her, but she did not want to put a negative interpretation on this and spoil her feelings of ebullience, so she made no further comment and let him turn the subject to the voyage they would embark upon before the morning was out.

12

IT WAS NOT a rough crossing, though they did run into at one or two squalls that were fearsome for a short time, but quickly blew over. The harmony between Morgan and China lasted a good part of the journey as well. What finally wore away at China's good spirits was Morgan's return to a more distant manner toward her. They continued on the friendliest terms, spending much of their time together, but he made no further attempt to make love to her again and all physical contact between them was kept to a minimum. In the month he had been in Macao, she had never noted any tendency in him toward moodiness, and when she attempted to breach the span he erected between them, she found him unresponsive.

China was hurt by this, wondering if Jack were right about her being too quick to fall in love with a man she knew so little of, but it had not been an emotion she had had the power to control. Once again she sought for excuses for his puzzling behavior. The captain of the ship, Mr. Wraxton, was a very congenial man. It turned out that he had also known Clive from a time he had spent in the West Indies when Clive had lived there, and he expressed himself very pleased to welcome China to his domain. Perhaps Morgan did not wish there to be any chance that the true relation in which they stood to each other would be guessed at by Captain Wraxton or the officers of his ship. China was not his wife, or even officially his betrothed. It might be nothing more than a concern for her reputation, she reasoned, though she knew in her heart that it was a thin justification. It might explain his unwillingness to show his affection for her during the day when they might be observed, but in the deep of the night when they were undisturbed in their cabins, it was not a convincing excuse for him not to seek her out.

But he came neither next nor nigh her, as the saying was, and the inner hurt began to eat away at the outer humor. They had been at sea for more than a sennight and they dined most nights with Captain Wraxton and Mr. Hatfield, his mate, and afterward, when these men abandoned conviviality to see to the numerous things that needed attending to before they sought their beds for the night, China and Morgan would play piquet or walk about the deck, sometimes engaged in a lively discussion and at others, merely enjoying the night, the stars, and the salt spray, with conversation desultory at best.

It was on one of these latter nights that the harmony between them was completely shattered. Though China talked frequently of her life in Macao and her friends there, she had made only occasional mention of Jack, though not in any conscious intent. But this night he was much on her mind, and she spoke her thoughts aloud.

They generally kept to the edges of the boat to keep out of the way of the sailors going about their duties and Morgan leaned against the starboard rail looking out at the sea rising and falling in gentle swells. China was standing a little behind him, but she moved over beside him and he looked up at her and smiled. "You are an excellent sailor, China. I know we have had better weather than we might have expected at this season, but even during the squalls you have never lost your appetite."

China smiled at this. "Do you imagine it a compli-

ment to inform a lady that she has a good appetite, my
lord?'' she asked quizzingly.

"I certainly meant it as a compliment.''

"Jack always says that I have the strongest constitution of any female he has ever met,'' she said with
a short laugh. "He meant it as a compliment also,
though delicacy is, I am told, much admired in my
sex. I am never sick, you know. Even Mama and Papa
at times succumbed to a local complaint during our
travels, but I never did. Jack thinks it is because I was
exposed to every sort of thing from the time I was a
babe.''

"Perhaps he is right.''

"Oh, I think he is. Jack doesn't make statements
that are uninformed. Even though there were circumstance that did not permit him to finish his schooling
to qualify for his medical degree, he is as knowledge-
able as any doctor with the title that I have ever known.
In fact, I think he has the finest understanding of any
man I have ever met.''

"A considerable compliment indeed,'' Morgan responded with a caustic inflection.

"I know it is selfish of me to wish him to leave
Macao when so many rely on him there, but I hope he
will decide to make up his quarrel with his parents
and return to England,'' she said with a faint wistfulness. "I shall miss him very much, I know. For a
moment, when I saw him coming up the stairs at Kowloon, I thought that that was why he had come, and I
was very glad of it.''

Morgan said nothing to this. He turned again to stare
out at the endless horizon.

"I think if Jack does come back to England one day
and does not wish to return to his family,'' she went
on, heedless of the fact that her words gave no pleasure to her listener, "I shall see to it that he has what
he needs to return to university for his degree. What

is the point of being rich if one can't give to the friends one loves best?''

"Indeed," he said with a dryness she could not mistake. "Perhaps if you had told him of your ambition in his aid, you might have persuaded him to come with us."

For the first time China began to wonder if he were a little jealous of her closeness to Jack. It pleased rather than concerned her. It was the first sign he had given her since the night before they had left Kowloon that his feelings for her remained unchanged. If he were jealous, it would even explain his odd behavior that night, retiring when Jack arrived in what she could only call a huff. This thought led to another that was closer to the truth. He might even suppose that she had deeper feelings for Jack, though what impediment he might imagine there could have been to their marrying after Clive had died, if they had loved each other, she could not guess. The absurdity of it amused her and her spirits were once again buoyant. "Jack would not be swayed by such a thing," she said to tease him a little. "His character is too noble for that. His feelings for me have nothing to do with my fortune. It is a purer love than that."

Morgan continued to look out over the sea, but at these words he turned to her abruptly. He could not believe that she was speaking to him so openly about her lover. He wondered if she had drunk more of the wine they had had with their dinner than he had noted. "Are you in love with Jack Reid?" he said as if the words were torn from him. He had not meant to betray his feelings to her, but he could not prevent himself from speaking the question in is mind.

China saw that she had upset him, and though her intention had been to startle a response from him, she had no wish to hurt him. "No," she said, smiling and shaking her head slowly. She placed one hand against his neck. If he would not come to her, whatever the reason, she would go to him. "I am in love with you."

She lifted her face to his and kissed him, not caring if Captain Wraxton himself observed them. For a moment his lips were unresponsive, but then he put his hand on her waist and drew her against him, kissing her with all the fervor she could have hoped for. Their lips and tongues teased at each other, their bodies clung together as tightly as if they wished to meld into one. China felt a heady mixture of pleasure and triumph. Whatever it was that had been troubling him since the night of the raid on Macao, once they had reestablished the intimacy they had shared the night before that, she was confident that she would be able to discover the cause of it and bring an end to any discord between them.

"Come to bed," she said, echoing his words to her in Kowloon, but this time there would be no interruption.

He released her with obvious reluctance, pulling her back to him for one more quick kiss before he followed her into the Great Cabin and her stateroom. If China were bent on proving herself a wanton to him, she could not have played the part better. She played the aggressor in a way that the mere thought of would have put her to the blush before she had given her heart to him.

She lit just sufficient candles in her stateroom to give them light but still have it soft enough to enhance her seductive mood. She undressed for him slowly for his delight and insisted on undressing him herself with equal slowness, pausing to kiss and caress each part of his flesh that she exposed, honing their passions to a fine point. When they lay down on her bed they made love with a fevered urgency that culminated in an eruption of pleasure that left them both breathless and spent.

They lay quietly in each other's arms in the flickering

candlelight. The movement of the ship beneath them made her narrow bed seem as if it were being gently rocked by an unseen hand, lulling them both into a languorous drowsiness. But China did not want to fall asleep just yet. She stretched liquidly, like a cat, enjoying the supple sensuousness of her body.

Morgan stirred beside her, caressing the sloping curve of her waist and hip. He had not meant for this to happen between them again, but once it had begun he thought it foolish to deny himself the pleasure of this woman whom he desired so much in spite of the blow she had dealt him. He didn't believe the words of love she had spoken to him—what could they be but false and uttered to palliate her conscience? He was not a man who would complaisantly share his mistress with another, but Reid was in Macao, and soon they would be in England. With proper discretion they might enjoy an *affaire* that would bring no harm and much pleasure to them both. Now that he was awakened to the truth of her character, he thought he should have no difficulty letting his emotions run away with him again.

China turned in his arms to face him, kissing his forehead, the tip of his nose and his lips. "Do you think anyone saw us kissing on the deck?' she asked, but without concern.

"Unless the crew were suddenly struck blind, I should say so," he responded.

China laughed, a self-satisfied sound; a cat purring after having her cream. "It doesn't matter now, though, does it?" she said, confident, not asking for reassurance.

"I suppose not," Morgan agreed, lifting himself into a semi-sitting position against the pillows. "None of the watch that might have seen us is likely to have any connection with the society in which we move and even if Wraxton learns of it through them, he is not a man to indulge in gossip. But when we are in England, we shall have to be more discreet.''

China felt a quickening within her that had nothing to do with pleasure. ''What need have we of discretion then?'' she asked.

Morgan understood her. He had, of course, intended marriage when he had admitted his love for her in Macao, but now there could be no question of that. ''In addition to the consideration of your reputation, we must think of the relation in which we stand to each other. If it were suspected that we were lovers, it would be damned awkward, especially within the family.''

China felt as if cold hands clutched at her spine. She raised herself up as if to better see him that she might discover in his expression that she had misunderstood him. He looked down at her, a faint smile playing on his lips, his eyes admiring the full swell of her breasts as she moved. ''They shall know it soon enough,'' she said, her voice almost pleading with him to confirm her rapidly dissolving belief that they should be married when they reached England.

''Not if we are discreet,'' he replied, evaporating her hopes completely.

China turned and swung herself out of the bed, bending to pick up her chemise as she did so. Her mind felt curiously blank and she pulled the fine lawn undergarment over her mechanically, not wanting to feel the vulnerability of her nakedness. Then she turned back to him and said savagely, ''You wish me to be your mistress.''

''Isn't that what you are now?'' he said, with a smile that made her hate him for a moment.

China was shocked beyond anger. It was as if he wished deliberately to insult her. ''Then you never meant it when you told me you loved me?'' she said, sounding perplexed rather than incriminating.

"Oh, I suppose I did. After a fashion." He got up and began to dress.

China watched him with a dull fascination. "Was it just to seduce me?" she said when he was nearly finished.

He paused in the act of buttoning his waistcoat. "Let us have done with protestations of innocence, China," he said sardonically. He had not wished to quarrel with her, but the pain that he had born and repressed, pretending to himself that she had no power to wound him, welled to the surface making him want to wound her in turn. "It puzzled me at first," he said, "what attraction could keep you in Macao after Clive's death. It could not be merely a dislike of leaving your friends; one who has spent her life living in one place and then the next must be quite used to starting anew in a strange environment. In my chosen profession I have learned that patience is often its own reward. So many unanswered questions are made known if only one bides ones time. Had you begun to tire of your lover, or did you see in me a better prospect for your future comfort?"

If he had slapped her, he could not have dealt her a fiercer blow. "Is it the fashion in England to speak in riddles, my lord?" she said, as anger at last began to come to her defense. "You are my lover."

"One of them."

Morgan's reflexes were excellent, but China moved so swiftly that she caught him off guard and delivered a resounding slap to his face. He responded instinctively and grasped both of her wrists in a hold that was far from gentle. China scarcely noticed his roughness, her palm stung so, and with satisfaction she imagined how his cheek where the blow had landed must feel. Their eyes met in a furious glare from which neither flinched. "You forget yourself, madam," he said in icy fury. "A home truth is difficult to accept, I suppose."

"I told you the truth."

"On which occasion?" he asked with contempt.

"On every occasion." She was becoming aware that he was deliberately hurting her. Tears started to her eyes, but not from any physical pain. "If you mean Jack, he is not, nor ever has been, my lover."

"Just one of your best loved friends," he said mockingly. "Don't bother to gammon me, Lady Rawdon." He made the formal use of her title an insult. "It matters not to me what bed you chose to lie in before, but now that you bear my stamp, if you wish this to continue, you will not play me false. I have an intense dislike of being made a fool."

He released her so abruptly that China stumbled backward a step. It was difficult for her to control her voice to keep the tears that threatened to choke her from being made obvious, but she managed it. "I suppose you also think like Amelia that I seduced and tricked Clive into marrying me and changing his will in my favor." Her anger making her reckless, she added bitingly, "I wonder you don't accuse me of poisoning Clive or smothering him with a pillow to realize my wicked designs."

"Did you?" Morgan said with an unpleasant smile.

China caught at her breath, realizing what she had said and equally appalled at his response. Her fragile self-control dissolved and she knew she could not speak again without sobbing. She turned away from him so that he might not see the struggle taking place in her, and in a few moments she heard him leave the stateroom. She cast herself on the bed where so short a time ago she had thought her happiness secure, and cried so uncontrollably that Lucy heard her and came to see what was amiss and found her inconsolable until her weeping finally wore out of its own accord.

Morgan did not go to his stateroom but returned to the deck, going to the rail again, needing the salt air and spray to cool his rage. After a time he rested his face in his hands. He stayed in this position for a considerable while.

China might have been craven and taken her breakfast in her room, but she was already angry with herself for shedding so many tears for a man who had proven himself not worth her grief, and would not permit herself this further indulgence. She would face Morgan Wrexford and prove to him the character of which she was made.

Her misery expended, she was amazed at the calm that came over her. It was not that all feeling for him had died with their bitter exchanges; there was a dull ache within her that only time could hope to heal. Neither did she hate him, even after his horrible reading of her character.

So this was what he thought of her. He claimed that he had not prejudged her, but he was only too willing to believe the worst of her. Whether he acknowledged it or not, his mind had been tainted against her before he had ever set foot in Macao. Of this she was certain.

Lying awake in her bed after Lucy had left her, China played over and over again in her mind virtually every exchange that had taken place between them since the night they had first made love, and his behavior from the time when he had found her with Jack, which had puzzled her so much, was now made plain. He had supposed that she had been spending the night with Jack as her lover—and the very night after she had declared her love verbally and physically for him. She *would* be worthy of the title doxy if that were true.

If only he had given her some hint of what he had thought, she might have convinced him of the absurdity of it, but instead, she had continued blithely ignorant of his suspicions, and every word she had spoken of Jack, every scene he had witnessed between them, had fed the poison in his mind. Had Morgan meant any of the things he had said to her the night of the Creelys' ball or was she deceiving herself that he had ever really cared for her?

Her thoughts continued in this vein the next morning, and she came to the conclusion that if he had loved her, she had hurt him, however unintentionally, just as he had hurt her. Yet she was not ready to forgive him for the hard things he had said to her, even if she now had some understanding of why he had done so. He had confronted her with nothing before he had made his judgment of her, given her no opportunity to speak in her own defense. Even if she wished to explain it all to him now, to try to make him believe that she and Jack had never been more than friends, she doubted very much that he would listen to her. And she would not beg him for a hearing; her pride forbade it.

She sat down to breakfast with Morgan and Captain Wraxton, her eyes still a little swollen and red, but otherwise she contrived to behave in quite her usual manner. Morgan was quieter than usual but he gave no other indication that anything untoward had occurred between them the previous night.

At this point, China was still too angry and hurt to discuss what lay between them, even if he should broach the subject. But unless she chose to spend the day and night in her own stateroom, she could not avoid his company. When she went out on the deck again to enjoy the sunshine and the brisk morning air, Morgan followed her and fell in step beside her. Neither spoke for some minutes, but China found nothing constraining in the silence. At the moment it mattered not to her whether he walked beside her or left her again without a word.

When they had made almost a full circuit of the ship, she paused at the bow, to squint out over the sea, dazzling like a million floating diamonds in the bright sun, as if she might see the destination for which they were headed. Morgan lightly touched her arm to gain her attention and she turned to look up at him. "Forgive me, China," he said but without any great show of contrition. "I should never have spoken to you as I did last night."

"No, you should not have," she said, as calm as she felt and as cool as the breeze which whipped fine golden tendrils about her face.

"It would be best, I think, if we were to forget our quarrel and all that has gone before," Morgan said, his voice as unemotional as hers. "It is not as if we could go our separate ways entirely when we leave this ship, and we would do well to begin again."

China had not expected him to have any great change of heart since he had left her last night, but his impersonal manner stung her nevertheless. "How separate our lives shall be in England remains to be seen," she said, matching his tone. "But you need have no fear that I shall wish to remember anything that has occurred between us, or embarrass either of us by any mention of it."

Her coolness had an odd effect on him. When he had lashed out at her the night before, he had wanted to hurt her, to pay her back for the manner in which he believed she had abused his affections. The pain he had seen in her eyes, her barely controlled tears, had not moved him. But her calm dignity and pride made him feel the reprehensibleness of his behavior. He suddenly wished that he might take her in his arms again and beg her to absolve him. The thought startled him as much as if it had been some aberration of his nature, and he pushed it from his mind with a savage firmness.

"Then I expect we shall jog along together tolerably well," he said almost indifferently to hide his unexpected and unwanted feelings.

China regarded him for a silent moment, the expression in her eyes near to contempt. Then she turned and walked to the Great Cabin, not heeding whether he followed her again or not.

The remainder of the journey was uneventful. No great storms were encountered on the sea and no further storms erupted between China and Morgan. For a few days they remained cool and punctilious toward each other, but time and propinquity soon brought that to an end, and by the time they reached Portsmouth, they were once again on fairly easy terms. It was not that anything changed between them since the night they had made love in her stateroom, but each was aware of the sense of coming to terms with each other, and there was an enjoyment in each other's company which neither sought to deny. But it was as if an invisible line were drawn between them which neither dared cross. For all their friendliness with each other, there was a wariness as well, and China was very glad when they arrived in Portsmouth a full two days earlier than Captain Wraxton had predicted.

She surprised Morgan when they reached the port by announcing that she did not intend to go with him directly to Hertfordshire, but to her mother's family in Cornwall. "They can't be expecting you," Morgan said, expressing his surprise at her decision.

"No," China agreed. "But I have not seen my Aunt Cynthia since I was at school in Bath, and I have had frequent letters from her begging me to visit her whenever I should return to England. I don't really fear for my welcome."

"But my mother will be very disappointed when she hears you have come back with me and have not come to Ferris," he said, not caring for this turn in their plans which he had considered set. "It will look odd if you do not."

"How could it?" China said. "Neither Lady Wrexford nor anyone else has the least idea that I have come to England, so they cannot be expecting me."

"But once I tell them you are here, they will wonder of it."

"Is there anything wonderful in my wishing to go to my own family first?" China said with a bit of asperity. She did not suppose it mattered to him where she chose to go, and she cared nothing for appearances. The Rawdons had not precisely welcomed her to their bosom and she saw no reason to pay them any particular deference. After the way matters had fallen out between her and Morgan, she was not particularly anxious to please him, or for that matter, to continue in his company. By the strength of her will, fed by her pride, she had deadened all feeling toward him, but it was by effort, and she wanted to be away from him for a time so that a more natural healing process might have a chance to occur.

"If you mean to go to Ferris, you may say that my arrival will be a little delayed," China continued. "I may even visit my cousin, Lord Calabrae, with whom I spent some time when I was last in England, and I shall certainly wish to go to London to see Mr. James and to have clothes made."

"At that rate, it will be a month before you come to Hertfordshire," he said. "Come with me now, for only a sennight or so if you wish it, and then I'll escort you wherever you choose to go first."

But China refused to be persuaded. "No," she said, shaking her head firmly, "I have quite made up my mind to going into Cornwall first. I imagine I *shall* be at least a month delayed, but since everyone has waited nearly three years to make my acquaintance, it seems a small enough time to postpone the meeting."

Morgan saw that she was not to be dissuaded from her intentions and gave up the attempt. He was not sure what he thought of it, but guessed correctly that she wished to distance herself a bit both from him and his family and to assert her independence. In fairness, he could not blame her, but it was a damned nuisance.

It would look odd and perhaps give rise to questions he might find discomfitting to answer. For far from the first time, he cursed himself for having had so little sense or self-control in his dealings with China simply because he had let himself be overwhelmed by a physical attraction, which was what he had set his mind to convince himself that his feelings for China had been.

China found herself not nearly as anxious to visit her mother's family unannounced as she had led Morgan to believe, but she did indeed receive a warm welcome from the Rydens when she reached their home in Cornwall in a post chaise she had hired in Portsmouth. They made much of her and were clearly delighted that she intended to remain fixed in England for an indefinite time, if not permanently. China's aunt, though her gentility was as unquestionable as her breeding, did not move in the first circles of society, but she knew that as Lady Rawdon, China would certainly be expected to do so. Cynthia Ryden knew which modistes and maunta-makers were the most fashionable and she offered to go up to London with her niece to see to it that China was turned out properly for the position she was to take in the world.

China was grateful for this as well as for the happy welcome she received, for she knew she really had no idea how to go on. She also wrote to her father's cousin, Lord Calabrae, in Northumberland, apprising him of her arrival and stating the hope that they might meet soon, and on the very day that she and her aunt were to leave Cornwall for London, she received a gratifying reply from his lordship informing her that he, too, meant to journey to the metropolis within a month or so and would look forward to calling upon her as soon as she had settled in town and was ready to receive visitors. All of this helped very much to remove China's feeling of strangeness in a new country, and she was very glad that she had made the decision not to go directly to Ferris Grange. She was beginning to feel established in her own right and would be able to face the Rawdons with far greater equanimity than if she had gone to them feeling like a poor relation hoping for their acceptance.

She also received a very warm letter from the dowager Lady Wrexford, expressing disappointment that their meeting was put off for a time and the hope that this would be as short as possible, and also polite letters expressing similar sentiments from Amery and Annabelle. From Amelia, there was no word at all, and China found this mildly upsetting, or at least a bit foreboding, though she supposed it was no more than she should have expected.

When she arrived in town and she and her aunt were established at The Star, a fashionable hotel in Henrietta Street, she paid her first visit to Mr. James, who was most gracious and who, in his cautious way, assured her that there appeared to be no difficulty with Clive's will or her inheritance. He advanced her a very generous sum for her immediate needs, insisted that all tradesmen's bills be sent directly to him until such time as she wished to go over her own accounts, and offered to see to the arrangements necessary to have Rawdon House opened and staffed for her as soon as was possible so that she could leave the hotel and be in her own home.

With all of these necessary details seen to, China threw herself quite happily into an exhaustive round of shopping for her clothes and for a number of household items which she deemed immediately necessary after her inspection of Rawdon House on the day after her arrival. She made appropriate replies to all of the Rawdons, informed the dowager and Morgan of her intention to open Rawdon House and remain fixed there for a few more weeks at the least, and congratulated herself on having made a very good start on her new life.

13

MORGAN DID NOT have as pleasing a time of it on his arrival at Ferris Grange as China was having in Cornwall and London. His mother, in her mild way, managed nevertheless to castigate him quite severely for his inability to convince China to come with him to Hertfordshire.

"You really should have insisted, my dear Morgan," she said on the morning after his arrival as they sat over late coffee in the morning room. "How shall it look to the world that Clive's widow did not choose to come to us at once?"

"It shall look as if she preferred to go to her own family first," he replied patiently, though it was an argument that had been gone through thoroughly on the previous night and one he had hoped was exhausted. "It is hardly remarkable for a widow to seek the comfort of her own kin."

"If she were recently bereaved, perhaps," Lady Wrexford said, not conceding the point. "But Clive has been dead for over a year and she is a Rawdon now. There has been some whispering, you know, that we have not been as accepting of Clive's wife as we might have been, and I would as lief put a period to it at once now that she is here. It was hardly a grand match, but there is nothing wrong with her breeding and the only objection we might have been expected to have was that she was unknown to us when Clive married her."

"Whose fault is that?" Morgan said with a sardonic smile.

His mother sighed. "I know. But you know how headstrong Amelia can be, and I fear she has written her displeasure to one or two of her closest friends who doubtless passed this interesting information to one or two of their closest friends. You know how these things get about."

"She has also made her displeasure, as you phrase it, known to Lady Rawdon, so I really do not think it wonderful that China felt she would find a greater welcome with the Rydens than she would with us. I am sure she does not mean to cut us, Mama, so there is no need to be in a pucker. When she is ready she will come to Ferris, or we shall meet her in London before that."

"China?" said Lady Wrexford, sounding puzzled. It was the first time she had heard China's sobriquet.

"It is how Lady Rawdon is called by her friends," Morgan explained, inwardly wondering if it was wise to betray their intimacy. He decided he was being overly defensive.

"China! How outlandish! Because she lived there?"

"Because her parents had a penchant for all things Chinese. It suits her," he said shortly. "Do you mean to go up to town at all for the Season?" he said to change the topic.

"It is most vexing, but Amelia has flatly refused to do so," the dowager said on another sigh. "Rawdon House has not been open since Clive was last here for her comeout just before he left for China and she has always stayed with us at Wrexford House since then, but now she claims that since her father's house is no longer her own, she has no home in town and would as lief remain in the country."

"I don't suppose the fact that Purdham is still at Longview has anything to do with her recalcitrance," Morgan suggest dryly.

Lady Wrexford spread her hands ineffectually. "What am I to do about that, Morgan? He is Margaret's brother, and we have known the Purdhams all of our lives. I don't like the connection overmuch myself, for I think she might do much better than a younger son of a marquess if she would only make a push to encourage some of the young men she has met in town, but she is so shy and serious that she did not take, and she has her heart set on Prentice. Amelia will be of age soon enough to make her own choice," she added with a sigh, for she knew the matter was quite out of their hands even if Morgan should object, which he had when she had informed him the night before that Amelia was desirous of marrying Lord Prentice Purdham. "I know nothing really wrong of Prentice other than that he is considered a bit fast and is known to be expensive, but it is not fair to judge a man on the excesses of his youth. Amelia will be in possession of an extensive fortune when she comes of age, and if she chooses to bestow it on a man of unequal means, I really do not see what we can do about it."

"I might do something about it," Morgan said crisply. "That extensive fortune, as you phrase it, is not hers to expend before she is five and twenty if she marries without my consent. But I wish it might not come to that. I have no desire to figure as the wicked guardian. I wish you might have dissuaded Purdham from fixing her interest in the first place."

A martial light sprang into his mother's eyes. "And how was I to accomplish that?" she said in an injured voice. "I did attempt to give him the hint, and Amelia as well, but I was ignored. Amelia might have listened to Amery if he had warned her against him, but Amery thinks Prentice a capital fellow and would not be likely to interfere in his elder sister's affairs in any case. And you," she said, making her home point, "were not much better than Amelia's own father. Always junketing about the world as if you had no responsibilities other than to your own pleasures.''

Since it was his diplomatic career that had caused Morgan to absent himself so much from England, rather than personal preference as in the late Sir Clive's case, it was perhaps an unfair comparison, but Morgan did not shrink from the criticism. ''The knot is not tied yet,'' he said flatly, ''and won't be until Amelia comes of age in October. I made that quite clear to her last night. She didn't like it, but for all of her occasional impetuousness, she won't go running off to Gretna with Purdham, not with so little time before she is her own mistress. Until then, we need not consider her marriage to him a settled thing. And who knows, Purdham may improve on acquaintance. As you say, what I know of him stems mostly from his salad days, and my reading of his character may not be a true one.''

''I hope you may be right,'' his mother said. ''I could wish he were more like Margaret or his brother Walter, who is so steady, but it is no easy thing for a younger son to live a fashionable life on merely an allowance, and all he has of his own is a legacy from his mother, who still enjoys excellent health. I can see how he might find himself running into debt without really meaning to.''

Morgan thought, but did not say, that these excuses did not account for Lord Prentice Purdham's penchant for gaming hells, high flyers, and tastes well beyond his means. But there was no cause yet to condemn him as a libertine or a hardened gamester, and what he knew of him were old *on-dits*. ''Well, it augurs a poor business sense, if not less desirable propensities,'' he said. ''I am willing to reserve judgment of him until we become reacquainted, though. I understand Amery intends to go up to town for the Season, even if it means taking lodgings.''

''Yes,'' his mother replied, a troubled frown creasing her brow. "Though I admit I should be a bit anxious if he did so. It is not that I do not trust Amery not to fall into scrapes if he is on his own in town, but he is at the age where he is quite convinced that he is up to snuff, but of course he is not. I wish Amelia were not so adamant about remaining at Ferris, though. I should feel equally anxious leaving her here alone with only the servants to look after her, for I know Annabelle would wish to come with me, and then Miss Hopper must accompany us as well."

"Of the two, I prefer that you remain here with Amelia, if it comes to it," Morgan said. "I don't much like the idea of leaving her here alone with Purdham in the neighborhood with only Hoppy for chaperone. Amery is less of a concern to me. It is to be expected that he will find some way to make a cake of himself before he reaches his majority—we all do. But I don't believe there is any vice in the boy. I own I am not pleased that he has been sent down from Magdalen for that silly prank he pulled of setting frogs loose in the chapel, but it was only a boy's stunt to puff himself off before his fellows. We spoke this morning and he has promised me that next term he will attend more to his studies than to seeing what he may do to set the dons on their ears. He meant it, I think, and there is no harm in letting him on a loose rein until then."

"I hope you may be right." The dowager sighed. "It is just that I have not been best pleased by some of the friends he made when we were in town last fall for the Little Season."

"Such as?"

"Martin Ramsgate, for one."

"Isn't he a friend of Purdham's? I know I have been out of touch with much of the news of the town, but I have never heard anything to his discredit."

"There was a bit of *on-dit* last Season," said his mother. "He is said to have an unfortunate taste for

deep play and that his father had to pay rather stag-
gering debts to keep him from landing in the Fleet."

"Did Amery frequent the hells when he was in
town?"

"I suppose, though I did not ask," his mother admitted. "All the young men do, I think. It is most
fashionable. But if Amery had debts, I presume he was
able to meet them, for he did not apply to me for any
funds beyond his allowance."

"That is one thing I would not tolerate," Morgan
said adamantly. "I have no objection to settling any
of the usual sort of debt that a boy his age may fall
into, but I won't let him squander his inheritance in
gaming hells."

"Oh, no! I am sure Amery would not," Alyce said
hastily. "I only meant that I wish he would make
friends with young men more his age, who are less
intent on cutting a dash. You must not mind me, Morgan. You know that I worry over the least thing. It was
so with you when you were first on the town, too, you
know."

Morgan smiled reminiscently. "You thought I should
end up marrying my first opera dancer, did you not?"
he asked, most indelicately.

But Alyce, for all her quiet gentleness, was never
missish. "It was not that one so much as Lady Mars-
den," she said baldly.

"Ah, yes," he said, struck by the memory which
he had not recalled in some time. "The Fatal Widow.
How does she fare?"

"She has married Sir William Bovery. It was the
on-dit of last Season. I wonder you did not hear of it."

"Perhaps my friends were being discreet in light of
my former connection there," he said provocatively.

"You do not still care for her?" Alyce said with
concern. "It must have been all of eight years ago."

"I was not in love with her then, if that is what you
mean."

"You were quite besotted," his mother insisted.

Morgan laughed. "No. Or at least, not to the point that you needed to have the least concern that I would one day present her to you as your future daughter-in-law."

"Have you never been in love, Morgan?" Alyce asked curiously.

The question startled him. "At least a dozen times, I expect," he said with deliberate lightness. "Are you of a romantical nature, Mama? I never suspected. You were never given to pouring over the latest novels from the lending library."

"No. I don't think I am, really," Alyce said with a smile that was sweetly sad. "But I did love your father, you know. I hope that you shall be equally fortunate to be in love when you marry, Morgan."

Morgan found he was not comfortable with the turn the conversation was taking and was glad when they were interrupted by the arrival of Amelia, who came in to the room to tell her aunt that she was going driving with Lord Prentice, who followed her into the room with such easy familiarity that it was obvious to Morgan that he was quite used to running tame at Ferris.

Amelia's manner when he made himself reacquainted with Lord Prentice was wary, but Morgan was careful to be at his most civil to Purdham, engaging him in light conversation for several minutes before Amelia, impatient to be off, reminded her "betrothed" that he had left his horses standing in the cold, and they departed.

Morgan's interview with Amelia the night before, when she had told him of her wish to marry Lord Prentice, had been a bit stormy. She actually had said very little when Morgan had informed her of China's arrival in England, though her lack of response to the news was telling of her dislike of it in itself. She was glad that China had not come with Morgan to Ferris

at once, and confided in her brother that she would
have considered it a piece of presumptuousness if Lady
Rawdon had descended upon them expecting them to
take her to their bosom without qualification.

"I don't see it that way," Amery was unwise enough
to say. "But since you do, you should put it to her
credit that she had the breeding not to be presumptuous." His sister glared at him so furiously for this
remark that he quickly changed the topic before she
could mount her hobby horse of animadversions on
their father's unknown widow.

But to her cousin she had said nothing at all about
China, knowing that she would likely receive short
shrift for her remarks. Instead, she was very full of
her own activities since Morgan had last been in England, and most of these involved in some way time
she had spent in the company of Lord Prentice Purdham.

"Pren has just acquired the most spanking bit of
cattle for his phaeton," she had informed him at the
end of her recital. "They were a part of Chesterly's
breakdown and he got them for a third of their worth.
Wait until you see them, Morgan. He will be calling
tomorrow to take me for a drive and you must come
out with me to admire them. He really has the most
excellent taste."

"What I recall of Chesterly's taste in cattle does not
encourage me," Morgan said dampeningly. "All show
and no go."

"I suppose that is what you think of Prentice as
well," Amelia said, becoming instantly defensive.
"Aunt Alyce has been writing to you, I imagine, and
filling you with stupid gossip."

"Actually, Mama has been very reticent on the subject of your attachment to Prentice," Morgan replied
in his mother's defense. "I had no notion it had come
to the point of betrothal until she told me so this afternoon. And any opinion I may have of Prentice is

based on a lifetime acquaintance, not second-hand gossip. I think, in the circumstances, it would be best if you put off any announcement of a betrothal until September, when you are of age.''

"But why should we not announce our betrothal at once?'' she demanded with angry surprise. "Aunt Alyce has said we may do so as soon as you returned and gave us your approval, though what that signifies when I shall be of age by October, when we plan to marry and you shall no longer be my guardian, I have no idea.''

"But you are not yet of age and I am still your guardian for now,'' Morgan reminded her with more gentleness than he was feeling. It was plain that Amelia was expecting no objections, and would not take well to any he might make. He regretted the possibility of a scene, but he would not give his unqualified approval when he felt he could not honestly do so. "Perhaps you forget that I still have control of your fortune until you are five and twenty, unless you marry with my consent.''

Amelia's eyes went round with disbelief. They were sitting in the bookroom after dinner, where Morgan had requested her to attend him so that they might discuss her attachment to Lord Prentice. Amelia rose from the wide leather chair in which she sat and went over to the hearth where a fire burned furiously against a night so cold that not even a house as well-constructed as Ferris could keep it from penetrating its walls. She was sensibly dressed in a long-sleeved, high-necked gown that was obviously expensively made, but which Morgan privately thought showed little style. Even so, she had a warm shawl wrapped about her, which she pulled closer about her as she stood before the fire. "Do you disapprove of the match?'' she asked without turning to him, her tone unreadable.

"I don't know yet,'' Morgan said with sincerity.

"What objection could there be?'' Amelia cried,

abandoning her dignified pose as she turned to him. "We have all of us known Prentice all of our lives. His sister Margaret is my closest friend and all of the Purdhams have been very nearly family to us."

"I know that Prentice has something of a reputation that I cannot quite like and—"

Amelia cut him short. "I know that he was not a pattern card youth and that he got into a few scrapes in his salad days," she said defensively. "But that was years ago, and you have not even been in England very much since then, so what would you know of anything?"

"I know that I do not intend to pass judgment on Prentice either way until I have come to know him better," Morgan said patiently. "I have not said you may not marry him, Amy. I know that you may please yourself on that head in a few months and tell me to go to the devil if I do not like it. I shall have control of your inheritance then, not your person. All that I am asking you to do for now is put off announcing your betrothal until it is your own decision to make."

"And if you do not approve of my marrying Prentice by then?" she demanded frostily.

"Then we shall see."

"I cannot believe it!" she said with angry astonishment. "You, who would not hear a word against Papa's marriage to That Woman of whom none of us knew the least thing, would cast a rub in the way of my marrying a man you have known since our cradle days?"

Morgan was till tired from the journey from Portsmouth, which had been made in an icy rain over abominable roads, and he was in no humor for histrionics. "Calm yourself, Amy," he advised with an edge to his voice. "I have not said I mean to cast the least rub in your way, so don't go borrowing trouble. And, I remind you, now that Lady Rawdon is in England and will soon be with us, you had best get used to the idea that she is your stepmother, whether you like that fact or not.

You had best get into the habit of speaking of her with proper respect. She is your guardian as well as I, as I am sure you are aware, and I could not in good conscience give you my permission to announce your betrothal, even if I would, without her equal consent.''

Amelia opened her mouth to speak and then shut it as if she recognized that she was about to do herself more harm than good by clashing with her cousin. When she did speak again, it was with more temperance. ''Actually, Prentice said that perhaps it might be best to wait until I had gained my majority. He is as eager to be wed as I, but he knows that I am not my own mistress yet, and knowing that I feel as I do toward Th—Lady Rawdon, he did not wish me to be put in the uncomfortable position of needing her consent. It is I who think the delay unnecessary. That should prove to you, if nothing else does, that Prentice has a very proper regard for my feelings.''

Morgan thought that at the very least it showed that Purdham was shrewd. He did not really have a need to ingratiate himself with Amelia's guardians, with her so close to being of age, but their approval, even if grudging, would be more comfortable than a marriage made in the teeth of familial opposition, and it was also very likely that Purdham knew of the restrictions on Amelia's control of her money if she should marry without proper consent.

He made no remark to this, but said instead, ''Whatever your feelings, Amy, you would still be wise to court Lady Rawdon's kindness rather than her enmity. If you set up her back, she may not be likely to look with favor on your wish to marry someone unknown to her and may withhold her consent. Then it would not matter what I think of it—we must both agree, you know.''

Amelia nearly gasped with outrage. ''She would not dare! Who is she to judge my choice of a husband after the way she has behaved?''

"In what way is that?" Morgan said with dangerous softness.

Amelia went over to him and said furiously, "You have actually met her. I can't believe she has managed to pull the wool over your eyes, Morgan; you are too knowing to be fooled."

"I have found Lady Rawdon to be very pleasant and well-bred," he said levelly. His personal feelings about China were kept to himself. "If you are hoping to meet a harpy to have your prejudices confirmed, you will be sadly mistaken."

"I intend to forgo that pleasure," Amelia said frigidly. "If she comes to Ferris I shall leave at once for Cedar Hill."

"Thereby proving yourself to be as ill-bred as you are determined to believe Lady Rawdon to be," Morgan replied sardonically.

Angry tears stung at Amelia's eyes. "I can see there is no point talking to you, Morgan. She has obviously seduced you as she did my father."

Amelia touched a far more tender spot than she could have imagined. "Don't talk fustian," Morgan said tersely, rising. "If you don't show a bit more conduct, Amy, you will quickly convince me that you are neither mature enough nor settled enough to be thinking of marriage to anyone."

"I will marry Prentice whatever you or anyone else may say," Amelia said on a sob, stamping her foot like an angry child. "You used to be very kind and understanding, but since that woman came into our lives she has poisoned everything. I wish you had both stayed away for good." Her tears could no longer be held and she fled the room, crying gustily all the way to her bedchamber.

Morgan sat down again and finally gave vent to an audible sigh. The last thing he had wished to do was quarrel with his cousin. It had been his intent to speak to her calmly and rationally about both her betrothal and her unreasonable prejudice against China. But her headstrong manner had irritated him and his gift for diplomacy had deserted him. He had handled her badly and he was more vexed with himself than her for having so little control of his tongue.

He was also stung by Amelia's parting shot. It had been too close a hit. He certainly did not for a moment think that China was responsible for their quarrel, but he was aware of a subtle change in himself since he had met her. He was more introspective than was his wont, for one thing, and perhaps a little inclined to impatience. What had passed between them had affected him more than he cared to admit.

His offer of carte blanche to her aboard the ship had been impulsive; he had meant to bring an end to their physical intimacy after he had found her with Jack Reid. The offer had been intentionally insulting, but if she had accepted it—as he had half-convinced himself by then her character would permit her to do—he would have continued their relationship as lovers at least until the powerful physical response she evoked in him had lessened, which he was certain it would in time. Instead, she had reacted to his offer with hurt and humiliation. And she had cried. He had not expected that, nor the cool dignity with which she had faced him on the following morning. His belief that she had duped him with false words of love while continuing her connection with Reid remained unchanged, but not with quite the certainty he had felt on that night.

He knew now the wisdom of the philosophy that it was unwise to engage in amours too close to home, but it was done and could not be undone, and China was a Rawdon and now in England, a fixed part of their lives. He rose again and went to the cupboard and poured himself a glass of cognac from a crystal decanter, which he drank off with more haste than prudence. It was the finest French cognac, meant to be savored, but it seared his throat like a self-inflicted punishment for his sins.

He knew that losing his patience with Amelia had

made matters worse rather than better, and he wondered if even his skills as a diplomat, belatedly applied, would be able to mend matters before China was finally among them.

But his abilities were never put to the test. Amelia appeared to have realized—or Lord Prentice had convinced her—that she was doing herself no service by belligerent insistence that she would flout the approval of her guardians, and she was in determinedly cheerful spirits for the next several days. She did not herself make any further reference to her stepmother, and whenever the subject came up she maintained a careful silence, doubtless deciding to say nothing at all if she could say nothing good.

Quite unexpectedly, she came down to breakfast one morning at the end of the following week and asked Morgan if he would care to ride with her. "Prentice and I usually ride in the mornings, but he is gone to visit friends in Cambridge today and I should hate to give up my exercise."

"You might take a groom," Morgan suggested blandly at this somewhat back-handed invitation.

"I would rather ride with you," Amelia said a bit diffidently, not certain that he did not mean to snub her. A bit of reflection and discussions with her betrothed *had* served to make her see that her overly defensive manner worked only to her detriment. Beside this, she regarded Morgan more in the light of an elder brother than a cousin, and truly did care for his good opinion.

Whatever her feelings, Prentice had pointed out to her, she would have to receive her stepmother eventually, and would only look foolish if she did not. For Morgan's sake, if for no other reason, she would muster up what civility she could manage toward China. Since her hope to contest her father's will had been firmly dashed by both Mr. James and Morgan, there was nothing to be gained by open hostility, and perhaps much to lose. She might say that she cared nothing for China's approval of her proposed marriage to Lord Prentice, but she did not wish to suffer the indignity of being granted an allowance instead of having full control of her own finances, which she grudgingly admitted was within China's power to effect. Though she loved Prentice, she was not blind to the fact that he was expensive, and she did not need him to point out to her—which he did, nevertheless—that they could never hope to live in any sort of style on their mutual allowances.

Gathering about her the tatters of her dignity, Amelia was prepared to set Morgan's mind at rest about the eventual meeting between her and China. She wasted little time in doing so, begging his pardon for having let her feelings get the better of her sense that afternoon in the bookroom. "It was the surprise of learning that she has come to England so unexpectedly, I think. But I quite see that it is in the best interests of us all to have harmony among us. I promise you, I shan't make any uncomfortable scenes when we do meet."

Morgan smiled, wondering if her resolve would actually outlive this meeting. "You should have ample time to prepare yourself for its actual occurrence," he said. "I had a letter from Lady Rawdon only this morning informing me that she had decided to go up to town in a few days and plans to be fixed there for some time while she sees to her wardrobe and a number of other matters. Perhaps she is not overeager for the occasion herself."

"I suppose I can't blame her," Amelia said, surprising Morgan with the admission. "I know I have not accorded her any welcome. Amery and Annabelle have both written to her, but I would not. I shall do so as soon as I know her direction in town."

"It is likely to be Rawdon House," Morgan said with a slow, sidelong glance to ascertain her reaction.

Amelia did not swallow this with ease, but swallow it she did. "Then I shall direct my letter there," she said, keeping control of her voice, which was threatening to quaver. "I wonder if it would be a good idea if we went to London ourselves,'' she added musingly. ''Should you object to opening Wrexford House? I know after all of your travels you might not wish to find yourself thrust into the hectic pace of the Season, but it might even be a good thing if Lady Rawdon and I were to meet in town rather than here.''

Morgan wondered a little at this, for it was because of Amelia that his mother remained fixed at Ferris, though she pined for her friends and the gaieties of the Season which was just getting underway in town. He might have commented on this sudden change of mind, but thought it politic to let it pass. ''If you like. I know that Amery intends to leave for town in a week or so and I don't think Mama would object to the change. But you know, Amelia, it will look most odd if you stay with us at Wrexford House instead of going to Rawdon House, which is your home.''

''It is not,'' Amelia said with a caustic note she could not prevent from showing in her voice. ''You forget that Papa has left Rawdon House to his wife.''

''I think you forget that, like it or not, Lady Rawdon is your stepmother,'' he said gently, not wishing to begin their quarrel again. ''Of course you may stay at Wrexford House if that is what you prefer, but it will cause talk.''

Amelia digested this. Actually, Amelia's change of mind about going to London had little to do with China. Lord Prentice had informed her the previous evening at a dinner party at a neighbor's which they had all attended, that he was planning to visit the metropolis himself shortly instead of remaining at Longview for the spring, as he had originally said he intended. She did not want to say anything to Morgan that might make him suspect this, or put her at outs with him again. ''I see the point of what you are saying,'' she conceded, ''but if I could go with you and Aunt Alyce to Wrexford House first, until I have actually met Lady Rawdon and see how we get on, I might be persuaded to remove to

Rawdon House in a few days or so, if she should wish it. She might not, you know.''

Morgan knew that it was possible that China might not wish it. Though they had parted on friendly terms, she had her own reasons for wishing to keep them all at a distance, which was apparent in her choice to go her own way as soon as they had reached the shores of Portsmouth. Yet he had the conviction, which surprised him, that China would do everything that was proper toward her stepchildren, even if doing so went against what she truly wished to do.

He did not admit it to himself openly, but he was anxious to see how she got on for himself. She was in his thoughts more than he liked and when he had received her letter informing him that she would be going to London and meant to remain there for a period of time, he had had the thought that he might ride up to London himself for a few days to attend to some business of his own. He had spent only a day or two there to report to his superiors when he had parted from China, and there were a number of matters that needed his attention after his long absence from England.

When they returned to the house and sought out Lady Wrexford, she greeted the news that Amelia had agreed to go to London for the Season with pleasure and without question. It was quickly agreed that they would leave as soon as Morgan had made arrangements to have Wrexford House opened for them and fulfilled a number of commitments he had made regarding the business of the estate; very likely by the end of the following week or the beginning of the one after that. Morgan went to his study to draft a letter to China to tell her their plans, and he could not help wondering as his pen scratched against the elegant foolscap what her reaction would be on receiving his information.

14

SINCE MORGAN'S LETTER had been directed to China in Cornwall, where he had supposed her fixed for a few days yet when he had written it, it had to be forwarded to her at The Star and she did not receive it until only a few days before the time that Morgan had told her they expected to arrive in town. China was completely unprepared for his news; she had had it in her head that she would finally meet the other Rawdons on her own terms when she felt comfortably enough settled in town to make the journey to Ferris. Reflection, though, made her realize that this had been an unrealistic hope. It was the beginning of the Season in town and much of the polite world was already in residence, enjoying every sort of fashionable entertainment that inventive hostesses could imagine and effect.

China lived outside of that world yet, and though she constantly happened upon members of the *ton* going to and from their various parties and excursions, she did not really think of herself as belonging to their world. Yet the first circles of society was the world that Clive had been born to and to which all of the Rawdons naturally belonged. As Clive's widow, she had a right to take her place in it. She felt no trepidation about this for her own sake, but if the Rawdons were cool toward her, this would certainly be transmitted to their friends, if only tacitly, and she might find herself not accepted in spite of her rank.

China, who had lived quietly most of her life, did not think this mattered very much to her, but that same afternoon, when her carriage passed the gates of Hyde Park during the hour for fashionable promenade, China found herself gazing a bit wistfully at the exquisitely attired men and women, walking, riding, and driving, and all seemingly known to each other. Quite suddenly, she knew that it did matter to her after all. For the first time in her life, she wanted to cut a dash.

Instead of returning to Henrietta Street as she had planned, she had the coachman of the carriage she had hired for her stay in London take her to Rawdon House, where a number of servants hired with her approval by Mr. James were already making the effort to get the house in order again.

China had meant to stay at the hotel and only open Rawdon House for her residence when she had returned from her supposed visit to Hertfordshire, but when she arrived at the house she asked her new housekeeper, Mrs. Barrett, to wait upon her and informed that startled lady that the most pressing needs of making the house habitable must be seen to at once for she intended to remove from her hotel not later than Saturday morning. Since she could not meet her "family" on her own terms, she would not allow herself to feel at any disadvantage when they came to her. She felt she would have done so if she were still putting up at a hotel like a visitor instead of as Lady Rawdon of Rawdon House and Myerly Hall. They would find her established in her own home and ready to receive them.

Her aunt was surprised at her sudden decision and equally surprised China by deciding not to make the move with her but to return to Cornwall. "It is really better for you if I do not stay, my dear," Mrs. Ryden said gently when China begged her to reconsider her decision. "I am very happy that you are come to live in England at last and I hope we shall see one another frequently, but I only came to town with you to bear you countenance and to introduce you to the fashionable shops and modistes. Your wardrobe is nearly complete now and you will be in your own home, not an impersonal hotel where it would look odd for you to be unchaperoned.''

"But that is nonsense, Aunt Cynthia,'' China protested, surprised at the feeling that she needed her aunt to support her. "I have greatly enjoyed our time together and I still need you to bear me company when I face the dragons.''

Mrs. Ryden smiled. China had confided in her a little of her doubts about meeting the remainder of Clive's family. "So have I enjoyed it, but it is time for me to go. My dear Roger has been most patient, but I have noted a tendency in his most recent letters to make remarks about things that do not seem to go quite right in my absence. It is nonsense, of course, but it shows that he misses me, for which I am grateful. As I said, it is better that I go for your sake as well. You wouldn't wish to make the impression of hiding behind my skirts when you meet Sir Clive's family,'' she added shrewdly. "It would be an entirely false impression, in any case, for you are one of the most intrepid young women that I have ever met.''

China did not reply at once and Cynthia Ryden added a bit uncertainly, "You are not concerned about making the acquaintance of Clive's children, are you, my dear?''

At these words, it was China who laughed at herself. Whatever they might think of her, even Amelia, she was equal to facing it. "No. You are right,'' she said taking her aunt's hand and squeezing it affectionately. "I should make the worst sort of impression if I seemed timid when meeting them. I am not, really. It is just anxiety, I suppose, for Clive's sake, that we should all get on from the start.''

"And why should you not?" her aunt asked with surprise. "To know you, my dear, is to love you."

China was grateful for her aunt's encouragement, but she doubted it would be as simple as that, no matter how the Rawdons were variously disposed to think of her.

Mrs. Ryden returned to Cornwall on Friday and China removed to Rawdon House to personally supervise its immediate refurbishing the same afternoon. There was much to be done which could not be accomplished in only a few days, such as new hangings for the windows and the recovering of some furniture and replacement of other pieces, but China contented herself with making the house presentable for the arrival of the Rawdons and knew the rest would come with time, as would her own feelings of security in her new role as stepmother.

On the following morning, China sent word to Wrexford House to await the arrival of the Rawdons, that she was in residence at Rawdon House and would be pleased to see any one of the family that should wish to call as soon as they had arrived and were over the fatigue of their journey. She did not really expect anyone to visit her the same day that they came to London, but she had just finished dinner on Monday evening and was in the bookroom discovering with delight that Clive had kept an excellent library when Barrett, her butler and husband to her very efficient housekeeper, announced the arrival of Lord Wrexford and Sir Amery Rawdon.

The unexpectedness of their visit permitted China no time for trepidation at meeting Amery, and she went to the saloon where Barrett had placed them with unruffled equanimity. When she entered, her eyes sought Morgan's at once and he smiled encouragingly. She thought she saw in his eyes for the barest second some other emotion, though she could not be certain what it was, but it was gone so quickly she supposed she might have imagined it.

Both men rose, and Morgan came up to her and took her hand, his smile warm. "Lady Rawdon, China, permit me to make known to you Amery Rawdon, your stepson."

China liked Amery on sight. His smile was engaging and lit his light green-gray eyes. He was not as like his father as she had imagined he would be—Morgan had more of the look of Clive than he did—but she could find some resemblance there, and she felt a sudden warm emotion that this attractive young man who stood before her, looking a little as if he might be doubting his welcome, was actually her late husband's son, of whom he had spoken often and with affection. She felt instinctively that she would come to care for Amery in his own right.

Amery bowed over her hand in his turn with the assumption of gravity, but his fetching smile quickly returned. "I am not quite certain how I should address you," he admitted. "I suppose in propriety it should be as Mama, but I am not certain you would care for that."

China laughed lightly, feeling completely at ease. Time appeared to have changed her usual reaction to Morgan, as well. She had felt not the smallest increase in her pulse when he had taken her hand. "No, I don't think I should," she agreed. There was really no great difference in their ages, and they both recognized the absurdity of this address. "Please call me China. All of my friends do so."

China rang for Barrett and ordered Madeira. When it had been brought and they were comfortably seated, Morgan made apologies for his mother and the Rawdon sisters, claiming that they were quite weary from the journey and would call upon China in the morning. China accepted his excuses without question, though she wondered at the veracity of them. But she pushed her doubts aside, reminding herself that she had not expected even Morgan to call upon her so quickly.

"Oh, Belle would have come with us right enough," Amery said ingenuously, confirming China's suspicions. "But Mama thought it not proper for her to do so without her and Amy, and Amy said she had the headache as soon as we came through the door and went right up to her room."

If Morgan wished to send him a quelling glance, he refrained from doing so, and turned the subject by asking China a question about her family in Cornwall. At first, conversation was limited to this sort of exchange, the polite conversation of strangers coming to know one another better. But gradually, as Amery and China became more comfortable with each other, their conversation became more lively and soon Amery was confiding in China that he hoped to purchase a bang-up-to-the-mark racing curricle he had seen at the long holiday before he had been sent down from university, and his hope of finding a matched team worthy of the vehicle. He was quite pleased that China appeared to have considerable knowledge on the subject of horse-flesh and that she did not question his expensive purchase, though she might have done so, since she controlled his purse strings as much as did Morgan.

China for her part found his openness and youthful enthusiasm engaging and she quite saw how a young man just setting upon his career as a man of fashion would wish to cut a dash. She would not have cast a damper on his pleasure if it had meant opening her own coffers to cover any deficiencies in his allowance. In short, they were quickly in perfect charity with each other.

Morgan spoke little, only when addressed or to essay some comment, knowing it was best to let stepmother and stepson find their own level with each other. But the pleasure of this felicitous interview was diminished a bit for China when Amery finally brought up his sister's name, commenting acidly, "Amy wanted me to take Purdham with me to Tattersall's when I go there, but he wouldn't know a plow horse from a thoroughbred without someone to point it out to him, though he's a dashed good fellow in every other way."

"Who is Purdham, pray?" China asked with a puzzled smile. "Not one of your grooms, surely, if he cannot distinguish good conformation."

Amery gave a bark of laughter. "No, he's not a groom. He is Lord Prentice Purdham, the son of the Marquess of Varden, whose estate marches with Ferris, and he and Amy are betrothed."

This time Morgan did cast a quick look in Amery's direction as if to silence him, and China guessed he was not pleased by this turn in the conversation. Morgan had said nothing to her about an attachment between Amelia and any man, but then it might be recent and he might not have known of it before returning to England.

If this were so, then she wondered how Amelia's betrothal had been sanctioned. Though she had told him that she did not mean to interfere in the lives of her stepchildren, feeling that she truly had no right to do so whatever Clive's will might say, she knew from the reading of Clive's will that no marriage could take place before Amelia was five and twenty without the consent of her guardians if she were to have the control of her fortune and she wondered, feeling mildly piqued, if Morgan had given that consent when he had returned to Ferris without consulting her. It dulled the warm feeling of acceptance she had felt on making Amery's acquaintance and reminded her again that she was still an outsider in this family, whatever the legalities of her situation.

"I had no notion that your sister was betrothed," she said, keeping her voice even to betray no inner thoughts. "It is of recent date, I gather."

"It is not yet a settled thing," Morgan answered for his cousin. "Amelia is still under age and must obtain the consent of her guardians to marry for several years yet in any case."

China felt mildly appeased at these words. She thought she heard a note of wariness in Morgan's voice and perhaps a bit of warning for his cousin. She saw Amery cast Morgan a quick, uncertain glance, and she guessed that there had been some discussion, not all of it pleasant, on this topic. She also saw clearly that they had closed ranks against her and did not mean to share any of this with her. It increased her feeling of separateness. "I shall look forward to making Lord Prentice's acquaintance as well as Amelia's," she said, with a smile that she was required to force.

It was not long after that that the gentlemen rose and took their leave of her. As Amery quitted the room, Morgan paused for a moment and then took both of China's hands in his and looked down at her with such patent admiration that China felt her color begin to rise. "I thought you exceptionally lovely in Macao," he said, his voice a silky and very alluring drawl. "I had no idea that it would be possible for you to become even more beautiful. You are looking remarkably well, China. I trust this means that England suits you."

China now realized that her quick assumption that Morgan no longer had the power to affect her was mistaken. But at the least, she had herself in control of the emotions that he so easily engendered in her. "It certainly means that English fashions suit me," she said with her easy laughter, showing no sign of her feelings. "Beyond visiting shops and a bit of sightseeing with my aunt, I really have not done very much to acclimate myself in London, but I am so used to pulling up roots in one place and planting them again in another that I always find myself at home fairly quickly.

Once I begin to go out a bit and meet new people, I shall be feeling that I have lived here all of my life."

"I hope so," Morgan said, smiling. He released her hands and picked up his hat, gloves, and cane from the table by the door. "We shall remedy your solitude shortly. My mother has an acquaintance which must embrace most of the Upper Ten Thousand, and you will soon find yourself knowing more people than you had ever cared to. She did want to come with us tonight, you know," he added as if he had read her doubts about his excuses. "But Amy is a poor traveler—obviously she didn't inherit that penchant from her father—and Mama was feeling peaked as well, so I insisted that they wait until tomorrow. I hope you do not mind."

Once again China's quicksilver emotions changed and she felt only admiration for Morgan's concern for his mother and cousin, putting aside all thought of any intended slight. Morgan took a step nearer her before taking her hand in his again in leave-taking, and for a moment she thought he was going to kiss her, but his bow was correct and formal.

China had wondered what she would feel when she next saw Morgan and she had to admit to herself that having done so she still did not know. He could set her pulses racing, there had never been any doubt of that, and he would probably always do so, but she had no idea if she was sorry or glad that any hope of a warmer relationship between them was at an end. At least she had maintained her composure and was now certain that she would continue to do so.

She had half-supposed that Morgan would accompany his mother and cousins the next day to set everyone at ease, but it was only Lady Wrexford and Clive's daughters who were announced on the following morning a little before noon. China had herself attended services at St. George's and supposed a similar purpose had delayed their call. It proved to be correct, though Lady Wrexford, both from her good heart and excellent breeding, apologized to China for the delay.

"Annabelle in particular was so anxious to meet you that she tried to persuade me to forgo church this morning, but I reminded her that you are a daughter of a clergyman and assured her that you would not wish her to do so."

"And that it would make a better impression than haste, as well," Annabelle said with an irrepressible peeping of her dimples.

China saw at once that the younger girl was very like her brother, not only in appearance but in personality as well. Everything about her was sunny, from her quick smile to her bright, wide-open green eyes, the same shade as Morgan's. Even at sixteen, it was apparent that she was destined to be an accredited beauty and outshine all the other young girls who made their comeout the same Season that she was presented to the polite world.

Amelia, who had yet to speak beyond a rather quiet exchange of greetings, appeared almost a changeling compared to her siblings. For one thing, she was the one who was most like Clive in features, but she had not the rich auburn hair of the Rawdons, or their expressive green eyes. Her hair was a light honey brown and might have been to her advantage had it not been dressed with such simplicity, in what China quickly castigated herself for thinking of as housemaid's braids, that it did nothing to improve her rather mild prettiness. There was also a contrasting subdued quality about her which China could not yet be certain was because of the girl's disapproval of her or simply a characteristic of her nature. If it were the latter, China ceased to be surprised that Amelia was in her third Season and still unmarried—if not unattached. Her face gave the impression that it preferred somber lines to cheerful ones, and there was a faint air of hauteur about her that might have been only a cover for shyness.

Their early conversation took much the same turn as the evening before with Amery as they sought to become acquainted. Amelia, though she displayed no open hostility toward her stepmother, spoke scarcely at all, sipping at her lemonade and refusing the little seed cakes that China's cook had made up for the occasion. As if to make up for her charge's taciturnity, Lady Wrexford chattered almost inanely about the amusements of town and the people she hoped to introduce to China in the very near future.

"I can see, Lady Rawdon," she said with clear approval, "that you have spent your time in town well, visiting the fashionable modistes. Surely that dress was made by Madame Celeste. Her style is unmistakable, you know, and everyone who wishes to be in the forefront of fashion has their dresses and gowns made by her."

"I prefer Mrs. O'Reilly," Amelia said in a flat tone, breaking her silence. "I would rather dress for myself than the the opinion of others."

The implied criticism was unmistakable, but China refused to let the girl put her out of countenance, though a tart rejoinder sprang into her thoughts. The pale blue cotton day dress that Amelia wore enhanced neither her figure nor her rather pale coloring. "Fashionable aspirations are not to everyone's taste," China said sweetly, and then wished she had not. Amelia turned a gaze on her that for the first time hinted at her true feelings, and China knew she would not appease the enmity the girl was determined to feel toward her by letting herself be baited into caustic rejoinders. It would only serve to convince Amelia that her opinion was correct.

Lady Wrexford, with her usual peacemaking skills, said, "I think you have both chosen exactly right for your personal styles. You, Lady Rawdon, would not appear half so to-advantage in Mrs. O'Reilly's conservative designs, while Amelia's gentle prettiness is more suited to it. I declare,'' she added, quickly changing the topic, ''I have never seen the woodwork and furniture glow so. You must have had an army of servants in to set everything so to rights in the house so quickly.''

''Lady Rawdon certainly possesses the means to do so if she wishes,'' Amelia said with such an acid inflection that she evoked a frown from her gentle aunt.

But China had herself in hand and she merely said, ''I wish you will call me China, Amelia, and you and Annabelle as well,'' China added, turning again to Lady Wrexford. ''I am glad that you have noticed my efforts, for I did wish this house to seem to you as it was when Clive still lived.''

''You mean to make some changes, I suppose,'' Lady Wrexford said, casting a critical eye about the room. ''I have always thought those dark blue velvet draperies spoiled the effect of this room, which is otherwise quite cheerful.''

''So do I,'' China said with a soft laugh. She saw Amelia's head come up sharply at Lady Wrexford's mention of changing the house and waited for the expected criticism, but his time Amelia held her tongue.

''Are we to come here to live with you, China?'' Annabelle asked artlessly, not pleasing anyone else in the room by her remark, precipitate as it was.

China said what could only be expected of her. ''Of course, if you wish it. This is your home as well as mine.'' She cast a quick, almost challenging glance at Amelia, but the girl maintained her former silence, not even looking up from the glass of lemonade she held clasped in both hands in her lap.

''Oh, I think I should like it very well,'' the younger girl replied ingenuously. ''You are so very pretty and so very nice, not at all a wicked stepmother like in the books from Hookham's Lending Library.'' Then, realizing what she had said, she blushed rosily.

China merely smiled at her naiveté and Lady Wrexford rose to leave, saying, ''Well, that is a matter that can be decided a bit later, when your stepmother has had time to become more settled. Will you dine with us at Wrexford House tomorrow, China? Afterward, we had planned to go to a musicale at the home of another member of the family you have yet to meet, Dorothea Crestin, who is also anxious to make your acquaintance. I think the two of you should get on very well, for you are of an age. Thea is a delightful creature, full of a great deal of prattle at times, but really quite clever and charming. I hope you will be friends.''

''I hope so, too,'' China said as she also rose. She missed Sally quite a bit more than she had expected to and very much would have liked to have someone to whom she could talk more confidentially. She liked Lady Wrexford quite as much as she did Annabelle and Amery, but she was aware of that lady's awkward position, and until Amelia could be brought at the least to accept China, she thought that Lady Wrexford would find the role of confidante uncomfortable.

China graciously accepted the invitation to dinner, and saw her guests to the door, and when they were gone she let out her breath as if she had been holding it. The interview had not proven as difficult as it might have been, but it confirmed China's belief that it would be no easy thing to overcome Amelia's determination to dislike her and made her wonder if she should even take the trouble to try. It was plain that Annabelle and Amery were already disposed to like her and she thought that it might be better for her peace to be content with that. But her pride would not let it go. Perhaps Amelia could not be convinced to like her, but China was determined that at the least she would gain the girl's respect.

China dressed with extraordinary care the following

evening. At first she thought to wear the most conservative of her new gowns to show Amelia that she was not a slave to the latest kick of fashion, but decided against this course, choosing instead a silk gown in a rich blue shade that made her eyes almost luminous in their blue beauty. It would not do for her to bring herself to Amelia's level, but she must make Amelia accept her as she was once they came to know each other better. Nothing else would do for China.

She had hired a fashionable coiffeur to give her hair a more stylish cut, and Lucy had proven herself quite adept at copying the dressings that he had taught to her on his visit. Tonight China wore her hair à la Greque, a classical but very feminine design that suited her rich golden tresses and brought out her features to perfection. The reflection that gazed back at China as she stood before the cheval glass in her dressing room was so exquisite and fashionable that China laughed with delight and felt an excited anticipation like a young girl in her first Season, which other than the fact that she was six and twenty was, of course, exactly what she was.

It was obvious that her mirror had not lied the moment she stepped into the small saloon where the Rawdons awaited her before dinner. Amery came up to her at once and, advancing beyond a correct bow over her hand, clasped her in a quick embrace and lightly kissed her cheek. "Dash it, China," he said with open admiration, "you'll put the noses of all of our Accredited Beauties out of joint once you're out on the town. Every blood and pink in town will be vying to lead you into the dance, and the unsuccessful ones will write silly poems to your fine eyes."

Lady Wrexford admonished Avery for his candor, begging him to spare China's blushes, but China, with the confirmation that she looked her best, laughed delightedly and thanked him. "Though I hope you may not turn my head."

"Then they will term you inaccessible rather than incomparable," Morgan said, coming up to her and saluting her in the more correct way. "It might be preferable, for there will be rakes and fortune hunters among their number without question."

"I thank you, my lord," China said with mock coolness. "It reassures me to know that my purse will be sought as well as my person." But she took no affront at his words, for it was clear in his eyes as they rested on her in a lingering way that he shared his cousin's opinion of her loveliness.

When Morgan stood aside, another gentleman was revealed behind him whom China had not previously met. "Since Wrexford and Rawdon have stolen a march on me by already having your acquaintance, I shan't wait to be properly introduced but shall present myself." He took her hand and raised it to his lips, actually touching them against it, though this custom had been abandoned a full generation before. "I am Prentice Purdham, a very old friend of the family, and I hope your friend now as well."

His manner was openly flirtatious, and the way that he looked at her disturbed China far more than the admiration she had seen in the expressions of either Amery and Morgan. There was something in the manner in which he gazed on her that was too familiar and made her feel suddenly as if her gown were too daringly cut for propriety. He also held her hand in his a fraction longer than was proper and, glancing to his right, China saw Amelia looking at her with such a stony expression that she almost felt for a moment that she had done something to encourage Lord Prentice's attentions.

China deliberately turned away from him and made a remark to Lady Wrexford about how elegant she found Wrexford House and her hopes that Rawdon House would one day be as fine.

"Lady Rawdon does not find that Papa's house as it

is meets her taste,'' Amelia remarked in an overloud voice to a woman standing beside her who China, turning in her direction, noticed for the first time.

Morgan, following her gaze, said, ''Forgive me Margaret. I did not mean to neglect you in the introductions. China, this is Lady Margaret Purdham, Prentice's sister.''

The awkward moment passed and China took the other woman's hand, though she only held out two fingers for China to clasp. Margaret Purdham's gaze was not precisely critical, but it was so steadily assessing that China might have felt uncomfortable if she had let herself be. China saw at once that this must be a friend and confidante of Amelia's and she would find no easy welcome there either. But China had the gift of regalness as well when she chose, though it was not really her nature, and she inclined her head with just the right degree of polite disinterest and echoed the other girl's insincere wish that they might become friends. Prentice, coming to stand beside China again, said heartily that he had no doubt of it, and dinner was fortunately announced at precisely that moment.

Unfortunately, China found herself seated beside Purdham for dinner, and his attentions were as continuous as they were unwanted. China did her best to maintain her conversation with Amery, seated to her right, but Prentice constantly interrupted her with comments or questions, nearly always followed by some overly flattering remark. Amelia sat opposite her, and though she was too well-bred to openly follow her betrothed's conversation with China, China knew there was little she missed, and sighed inwardly, knowing this would not make her task of winning Amelia's acceptance any easier.

China wanted to give Prentice a heavy setdown that could not be misconstrued, but this was hardly the time or place for it. When dinner was over, she could scarcely recall what she had eaten, so absorbed was she in trying to ward off the young man's attentions. She rose with alacrity when Lady Wrexford did so, and hoped the gentlemen would not be in too great a hurry to join the ladies in the drawing room.

This room proved as elegant as the saloon and gave China a very good opinion of Morgan's and his mother's tastes. She said as much to her hostess, which clearly pleased the older woman.

"I look forward to seeing what you will do with Rawdon House," the dowager commented. "Clive was so seldom in England since Eugenia died that it has remained virtually untouched since that time, though he did replace one or two pieces of furniture that were hopelessly out of date when he was here for Amelia's come-out."

At these words, China found herself glancing across the room where the three younger women sat chatting in a lively manner. Amelia had made it plain that she did not approve of China's plan to make changes, but China had no intention of winning her recalcitrant stepdaughter's approval by bowing to her criticisms. It was her house now, and though she was willing to make it a home for the younger Rawdons, she did not intend to be influenced by an sentimentality for the way it had been in their mother's time.

As if reading her thoughts, Lady Wrexford said, "You mustn't mind Amelia's little comments. I am sure she would agree that the house needs refurbishing, but doesn't care to admit it. She was very attached to her mother, you know."

The men came into the room at this moment, far sooner than China would have liked, and she was glad she had chosen the chair next to Lady Wrexford's and not the small sofa at the other side of it, giving Prentice leave to sit beside her. She quickly turned her attention back to the dowager to avoid catching his eye. "I was pleased that Annabelle would like to come to live at Rawdon House, but I am not certain that

Amelia would care for the notion. I won't force the issue, but I would have liked very much to have had Amery and Annabelle with me. Clive might have left the house to me in his will, but I continue to think of it as theirs as well."

It was Morgan who approached them first, and he was in time to overhear her comments. "I see no reason why that cannot be arranged if they wish it. Amelia may please herself," he said, electing to sit on the sofa at the other side of his mother.

"You don't think it would look odd if they came to me and Amelia did not?" China asked, addressing him.

"It will look odd for her, not for you," Morgan replied, clearly unconcerned. "It is commonly known that Amelia has idealized her mother and was bound to resent anyone set in her place. People will judge you for yourself and not Amelia's unreasonable attitude toward her father's remarriage."

China sighed, and spoke her thoughts aloud. "I wish that Clive and I had come here while he still lived. It would have made matters much easier, I think."

A mistiness came into Lady Wrexford's eyes. "I don't wish to press you too soon, but I hope you won't find it too painful to tell me about Clive's last years and even his illness at some time when you feel comfortable doing so. I admit that there were moments when I cursed him for following his own inclinations after Eugenia's death rather than remaining to see to his responsibilities, but I really was terribly fond of him and there are times when I can't bear to think that I shall never see him again."

China felt a catch in her own throat at these words. She had not been in love with Clive, but she had cared very much for him and at times she felt the same. She met Morgan's eyes, but his were so expressionless that she could not guess at his thoughts. "Of course, if you wish it. Perhaps you could visit me tomorrow, or the next day if that is more convenient, and we shall spend as much time as you wish discussing Clive. I would like it, I think. There really has been no one to whom I could speak about him who knew him so well in Macao. And perhaps you can tell me about his life before he left England. He didn't speak of it over-much.''

It was arranged for the following day, and Lady Wrexford excused herself to remind everyone that they had best be getting ready to leave for Lady Crestin's musicale. Morgan moved over to his mother's vacated chair beside China. ''Thank you,'' he said quietly. ''It will please Mama very much.''

''I want to do it,'' China said with a smile. ''I like her very much, you know.''

Morgan responded with a smile of his own. ''I hoped that you would. And you have clearly made conquests of both Annabelle and Amery. Don't let Amelia spoil that for you. Eventually she will become used to the idea that you are Lady Rawdon and her attitude will change. She can be difficult at times and perhaps she does not compare well with Amery and Annabelle, who have the gift of making themselves liked quite easily, but she is intelligent and good-hearted in most ways. It is just on this one topic that she lets her emotions rule her judgment.''

Though there was nothing in his tone to betray it, China sensed that Morgan was not as fond of Amelia himself as he was of his other two cousins, and she felt a sudden unexpected wave of pity for the girl. Amelia was pretty enough, but even at sixteen Annabelle outshone her both in looks and in personality. Good-hearted or not, China felt that Amelia was someone most people would find it difficult to like easily. In some ways fate had not been particularly kind to Amelia Rawdon, and China determined to remember this in her future dealings with her stepdaughter.

"Do you truly wish to have Clive's children with you at Rawdon House?" Morgan asked, breaking into her thoughts.

"Yes, I think I do," China answered, and realized that she meant it. She would even make Amelia welcome if she chose to live with her.

"Then leave matters to me," he said, and rose and offered her his arm to lead her downstairs to the awaiting carriages.

China rode in the Wrexford carriage with Morgan, his mother, and Amery to Crestin House, while Amelia went with the Purdhams in their carriage, though there was an awkward moment when Prentice attempted to insist that China ride with him and his sister. It was not made easier by Annabelle's saying, "I should think you would want Amelia with you, Prentice." But it served to stop Purdham from persisting, and China gratefully allowed Morgan to hand her into his carriage.

China was aware of an uncomfortable quivering in her stomach as they entered the trim Georgian townhouse belonging to Sir Archibald and Lady Crestin. But this was more from excitement than nervousness, for she loved being in company and greatly anticipated making the acquaintance of Lady Wrexford's friends. Her only unreasonable fear was that they might mark her as a provincial the moment they set eyes upon her. As if Morgan sensed her concern, he surreptitiously squeezed her hand as they mounted the stairs together and when she looked up at him gave her such an encouraging smile that she once again felt at ease.

It was remarkable to her that there could be such understanding and empathy between them and yet he could not feel for her as she did for him. She had all but convinced herself that she had been cured of her love for him, but in her heart she knew it had not been that simple to overcome her feelings. Yet he behaved now as if he had never told her he loved her—or had never even been her lover, for that matter. That must be sophistication, she thought wryly, and wondered if she would ever attain such a state. She wondered if she would even wish to.

China had the will to please and be pleased, and the result of this was that everyone who met her that night came away from the party thinking that China was as charming and agreeable as she was beautiful. Several of the gentlemen paid her extravagant compliments and such was the pleasantness of her personality that not one of the women present found her nose put out of joint by the attention China received from the men. Only Amelia and Lady Margaret kept themselves a little apart from China, and China, thoroughly enjoying herself, neither noticed nor cared.

She answered a great many questions, some bordering on impertinent, about her background, her marriage to Clive, and her life in Macao, but she sensed that these were posed from genuine interest and she took no offense. It was not just the pleasant company that made the night a success for China, there was also the music. A string quartet played exquisite compositions by Mozart, Hayden, and other great composers, and the focus of the evening was on a young pianist who was being much lionized in the *ton* that season as the latest musical genius.

China loved music, but her life had given her limited exposure to fine works performed by superb musicians, and she was delighted and thrilled by the performances of both the quartet and the pianist. If this were a sample of what life would be like in England, she knew she would have no cause to regret her decision to leave Macao. She did not forget the potential difficulties that Amelia's hostility might yet cause her, or the unhappiness that her relationship with Morgan had caused her and her need to be on guard about her feelings for him, but her spirits for now were buoyant and her hopes high.

Both by deft maneuvering and the fact that there were so many others who vied for her attention, she managed to avoid Prentice for most of the evening, but she would look up from time to time and find his eyes on her. She had had the feeling from the moment she met him that he was perhaps a bit foxed, and she hoped that it was the wine making him indiscreet and that he would not continue such a blatant show of his interest, which she found embarrassing, and force her to give him the setdown he deserved. Scorning his attentions might cause her as much difficulty as allowing them to continue.

When the pianist finished playing, a woman's voice beside her said, "I see you have an appreciation for the compositions of Beethoven. There are those that think his works too modern, but there is so much emotion in all that he writes that I cannot help being affected by it."

"I have heard of his music, of course," China said, turning and finding Lady Crestin next to her, "but it is the first I have heard it played. I think it is wonderful."

"So do I." Dorothea Crestin astonished China by then saying abruptly, "I see that Prentice has been making a cake of himself staring at you all night. I saw you casting him a wary glance once or twice. You are concerned because of Amelia, but I assure you his attention is not as flattering as you might think. Lord Prentice is, as they say, in the petticoat line, and he is forever setting up flirts right under Amelia's nose. He must have a marvelous gift for convincing her that he loves her above all others; she usually does not seem to mind."

"I think she would mind very much in this case," China said dryly.

Thea laughed. "The wicked stepmother." She saw the sharp look that China sent her, and laughed again. "Oh, you mustn't mind my knowing all the Rawdons' darkest secrets. I am a cousin, you know, and Amelia is wont to pour out her opinions to anyone she feels comfortable with if one will listen with a bit of attention. Poor girl, I think she is lonely sometimes.''

''She does not seem very comfortable tonight,'' China said musingly, ''though she must be at the least acquainted with everyone here.''

''She hasn't your ease in making friends, that is for certain,'' Thea said, confirming China's assumption. ''This will be her fourth Season, you know. She did not take, and her shyness, which sometimes causes her to seem abrupt and taciturn, put off even most of the fortune hunters. I think she wants nothing more than to retire to some quiet country estate and bear Prentice a quiverful of brats.'' Thea paused for effect. ''Not, mind you, that he will be there with her overmuch. Just enough to keep her breeding and happy. I don't wonder that she's jealous of you. You are so very lovely and you have the gift of charming everyone you meet. Even if you had not committed the unpardonable sin of captivating Clive, she would have probably disliked you on sight.''

China saw what Lady Wrexford had meant about Thea's prattle, but China did not mind her impertinence. She was obviously a very good-natured person and her directness was not meant to give offense. China gave her a warm smile. ''I can see it would be pointless to dissemble with you, Lady Crestin. I admit that when I first came here I was in something of a quake about Amelia, for she never has made any secret of her dislike of my marriage to Clive, even to her father in the letters she wrote. But I am beginning to understand it a little better and I hope that Amelia and I shall at least come to terms. I do not yet set my sights on the improbable hope of friendship.''

''Very wise,'' Thea said, nodding. ''And I wish you will call me Thea and permit me to call you China. I heard Lady Wrexford address you so, and I think it is an unusual and very pretty form of address—and in the circumstances, very appropriate.''

"I would like that very much," China replied. "Only Clive has ever called me Chloris—and my parents when I had misbehaved," she added, dimpling.

Thea laughed and said it was the same for her, and the two young women clearly found much to be in charity with with one another. When China mentioned an appointment the following day for fittings with Madame Celeste, Thea recalled a similar engagement and they agreed to meet for ices at Gunter's beforehand the next afternoon.

15

CHINA RETURNED HOME that night very much in spirits and over the next few days she found her new life in England so very much to her liking that she could hardly recall her earlier concerns that had made her put off leaving Macao so long. In addition to her growing friendship with Thea Crestin and the renewal of her acquaintance with Lord Calabrae, she added many other new acquaintances, attending parties and other entertainments most evenings in company with Lady Wrexford and Amelia. Though the latter remained cool toward China, she kept any stronger feelings of dislike to herself, and China regarded this as something to congratulate herself for.

It was a fortnight after the Rawdons had arrived in London that Morgan called upon China to inform her that the younger Rawdons would be coming to live with her before the end of the week if she still wished it.

China found herself surprised by this, for it had not been mentioned again since the night she had first dined at Wrexford House. This must have shown in her expression, for Morgan said, *"Do* you still wish it?"

"Yes, of course," China said hastily, and added expressionlessly, "Does Amelia come as well?"

"Yes," Morgan said, and waited for a response. In spite of what she had told him, he had not been certain of her sincerity. She might have made the offer because she thought it was expected of her. If so, it was a bit late to regret the gesture.

But China evinced no hint of regret. She was still optimistic that Amelia could be brought to see that her prejudice was unreasonable. She said quite easily, "Then I shall have Mrs. Barrett prepare three bed-chambers. Do you know which rooms were their own? I should like them to be as comfortable as possible."

Morgan agreed to speak to Mrs. Barrett about this and when the housekeeper came to them and was finally dismissed, Morgan got up to take his leave. This was the first Morgan had sought her out in private, though they had been together in company almost every day since his arrival in town, and though he had made it clear to China by his behavior toward her that their relationship was to be the formal one of two people related by marriage there was something in the way he looked at her that was like a caress that made it impossible for hope to die completely in her.

They had danced more than once at the various parties and balls they had attended and when they touched it had been the same as it was in Macao, as if an erotic current had passed between them. China was trying very hard to forget, as he seemed to have done, that they had been lovers, but at such moments she almost ached to be in his arms again, however foolish she knew such feelings to be. She could not believe that he felt nothing when the desire within her was so strong, but he wanted her as his mistress not his wife, and apparently he accepted her refusal of his offer as final and with complete sangfroid.

They spoke for a few more minutes of common-places while Morgan retrieved his hat, gloves, and cane from a table by the door. Then he asked with apparent concern, "Are you happy here, China?"

"Why yes," China said, a little surprised. "Do I seem not to be?"

"No," he admitted with a smile. "It has seemed to

me that you are getting on famously, but you are too well-bred to show any unhappiness in company. I admit to a twinge of conscience now and again for insisting that you come to England. If you were unhappy, the burden should be mine.''

''Actually it would be my own,'' China said, laughing. ''I have told you that I am used to being uprooted. If I were unhappy it would be quite my own fault. But I am not. In fact, I am enjoying myself quite a great deal.''

''Yes,'' he said, and added dryly, ''Last night at Mrs. Ponsonby's I gave up hope of having even a word with you, so surrounded were you by your court. You are a beautiful woman, China, and a very rich one as well. You have not had a lot of experience of society and should have a care to its pitfalls.''

There was a note of censure in his voice that made China's pleasure in his concern for her evaporate. ''Such as?'' she queried with no discernible change in her tone.

Morgan hesitated for a moment and then said, ''Most of the men who have been honoring you with their attentions are unexceptionable, but there are one or two whom you have been encouraging who will not add to you consequence.''

China almost gasped aloud at this pompous speech, but she said sweetly, ''Really? You must instruct me, my lord. Who might these gentlemen be?''

''Lord Peter Fairchilde and Mr. Collingswood for two,'' he replied, not appearing to have discerned her pique. ''They are both gazetted fortune hunters and libertines who have barely escaped social ostracism.''

China appeared to muse on this for a moment. ''Yet I have met them in the most unexceptionable drawing rooms. Is there anyone else to whom you object?''

Morgan smiled. ''I see you would like to comb my hair for my well-meant advice. It is no more than that,

China. I have no right to object to anyone you might chose to be acquainted with.''

"No you don't," China agreed, still keeping her voice level. "I should regard your opinion though. You have something of the reputation of a rake yourself, my lord, so I suppose you should easily recognize a member of your own fraternity. I have learned to my regret that if one is unseasoned, one is all too easily seduced.''

China wished she might have bitten back her words, spoken in anger, as soon as she had said them. She had meant to play the game as well as he, never referring to what had happened between them, behaving as if it had not occurred. She saw his expression change.

"Is that what you think it was?" he said, an edge to his voice.

At least it was in the open again. China felt a sense of relief almost equal to her foreboding. "Wasn't it?" she said, keeping her tone deliberately light. "I thought you made that clear to me. I suppose I should be flattered that having attained your goal you still wanted me, even supposing that I already had a lover in Jack Reid.''

"I think we have already had this discussion," he said frigidly. "You made it obvious that you found my offer much less than flattering. I think we should leave it at that.''

"I should be very happy to, my lord," China replied, letting her anger at last become blatant. "If you refrain from questioning my conduct, I shall not comment on yours.''

"As you wish, madam," he said stonily, and turned and left her.

China could have wept with vexation as she stared at the door he had closed behind him. The last thing she had wanted was open enmity between them, but her wretched tongue had gotten the better of her. It had been too forlorn a hope that he would be moved

by her indignation to apologize for having misread her;
his opinion that she was of easy virtue was obviously
unchanged. And why should it be? She had permitted
him to make love to her with little more than a fortnight's acquaintance and he believed she was Jack's
mistress. The irony of it made her laugh, albeit bitterly. Now it was likely that she would have more than
Amelia's hostility to contend with.

The young Rawdons arrived in state two days later.
The elegant Wrexford town carriage brought them to
Mount Street and it was followed by a more service-
able baggage cart so laden that China was astonished
that three young people who meant to reside in town
for less than another three months could have brought
so much with them. But as Annabelle explained as she
entered the house and hugged China happily, "We
have brought all our earthly belongings with us, dear
China. This is to be our home now."

"You may not know what you have got yourself in
for, Stepmama," Amery said, grinning behind her.
"It's a good thing we're getting a bit long in the tooth
and you probably won't have us on your hands forever,
or you might regret your generosity."

China laughingly assured him that she had no fear
of it, and looked up to see Amelia coming through the
door with Miss Hopper, Annabelle's governess. Amelia's expression contrasted sharply with whose of her
brother and sister. Her features were set, with no hint
of a smile or of pleasure, and she immediately looked
about the hall in a critical way, though China had done
nothing yet to alter that part of the house except remove a massive marble table that had resided against
the side of the stairs, narrowing the hall and creating
a navagational hazard.

As if reading her thoughts, Amery said, "I see you
got rid of that wretched Italian table. Grandpère

brought it back with him from the Grand Tour and
Papa always called it a cursed nuisance.''

"How would you know what Papa called it,''
Amelia said sharply. ''You were just a babe when Papa
left, and I doubt he confided his tastes to you.''

"Well, Aunt Alyce said he hated it,'' Amery said
defensively, his smile evaporating. "I remember running down the stairs once when we were here with
Papa and banging my head against the dashed thing. I
think he said something of the sort then.''

It was not a propituous beginning, but it was Annabelle's ingenuousness that dispelled any discomfort
again. "You must have been very small, Amery, to
bang your head on a table,'' she said giggling. "I don't
recall it at all, not even when we came to visit you,
China, but if it was ugly, I am glad it is gone. Are we
to have luncheon soon?''

Wondering if conversations like this were going to
become commonplace now, China sighed inwardly,
but smiled at the younger girl. "Very soon. But first
you must go up to your rooms and unpack so that you
feel really at home.''

Mrs. Barrett led the procession upstairs. Amelia's
room was reached first. China had been very careful
to change nothing at all in that room, merely having
the hangings taken down, carefully cleaned, and re-
hung and turning the room out for a thorough clean-
ing. But Amelia gave no evidence of either pleasure
or displeasure. She went into the bedchamber calling
to her maid, who had arrived with the baggage, to find
her headache powders. She did not even give Mrs.
Barrett the opportunity to show her the smaller room
beside it which China had allotted to her as a dressing/
sitting room.

Amery's was next, and here China had allowed herself a little license to make the boy's bedchamber more
suitable for a grown man. Amery declared himself

pleased and, placing a brief kiss on China's cheek, disappeared into it.

Annabelle had been the easiest for China to provide for. The last time she had lived in this house, four years ago, she had been still a child and had been placed in the nursery. China saw at once that this would not do for her now, and had had the room across the hall from the schoolroom at the end of the hall made up for her. Here China had indulged herself, giving to Annabelle all the accouterments she had dreamed about having in a room of her own when she had lain awake at night in the plain room she had shared with three other girls at her school in Bath. The hangings were not the heavier silk, damask, or velvet sort favored by adults, but of the finest Indian muslin. Sunlight poured into the room accentuating the light feel the muslin gave it, making it not only a very pretty room, but light and cheerful in feeling as well. Annabelle actually clapped her hands in delight.

"Oh, it is perfect, is it not, Hoppy," she said, almost running about the room to peer into every corner. "I shall not even mind having to set stitches in the afternoon if we may do so in those chairs by the window." She turned to China and said prettily, "Thank you, China. It is everything I could have wished it to be, though I did not think of it before."

As usual, Annabelle's ebullience made up for Amelia's taciturnity and China knew that for now that would have to be enough for her. The next few days fell out as China expected they would, peaceful enough as the young Rawdons acclimated themselves to their new surroundings and always cheerful whenever she was in company with Amery or Annabelle. Amelia was always civil to her, but when China sought to appease her by asking her for household advice, Amelia rudely rebuffed her, saying that China was now mistress of the house and must please herself, and China found for the first time that she had difficulty keeping her temper intact with the girl. Even if the hostility was not open, it was always there like an underlying cancer which eventually began to make itself manifest in other ways.

There were several occasions when China entered a room to find Amelia in conversation with her brother or sister and the moment she joined them all conversation ceased and an uncomfortable silence enveloped them. There was little doubt in China's mind that she was the topic under discussion and that from Amelia's point of view, at least, it was not favorable, but China refused to be cowed. China invariably made some light comment, which was gratefully returned in kind by Annabelle or Amery, but gradually there was an increasing constraint in the conversation whenever Amelia was present that seemed to affect even Annabelle's usually sunny nature.

Morgan had called the day after his cousins had arrived at Rawdon House to see how they were settled, and though his manner was a trifle cool, he made no reference to their argument. China made a point of being at her most charming with him, and in a day or so he had thawed to take up again his usual easy manner with her. China told herself that she was happy with this state of affairs between them, but she could not deny the feelings of dissatisfaction that always surfaced after they had met.

She finally forced herself to examine these feelings one evening when she accompanied Amelia and Lady Wrexford to Almack's. Lady Margaret and Lord Prentice were also present, as was, more surprisingly, Morgan. He had commented caustically on this bastion of the Marriage Mart in her hearing, disparaging the way that each Season's crop of young girls was put on display for the highest bidders like slaves at a Mideastern auction, as he had phrased it. This was China's third visit to Almack's since Lady Wrexford had procured her one of the coveted vouchers, and the first time that Morgan had put in an appearance. It was also the first time that she had seen Lady Margaret grace the assembly rooms, and though she did not register this connection consciously at first, by the end of the evening, she wondered if this were the reason for Morgan's attendance.

Morgan spent only a few minutes with China and his mother when he first came into the rooms and he did not even ask China to stand up with him. But China noted that he danced with Margaret twice and several times she happened to note him in conversation with her. Once or twice since coming to Rawdon House, Amelia had made an oblique comment about her cousin and Lady Margaret, which might have been interpreted to mean that there was an understanding of sorts between them, and even Prentice, on one of the rare occasions when he had called to see Amelia and China had not been quick enough to make an escape, had hinted to her something about there being more than one possible connection between their families. China had not particularly regarded their comments, for she had never noted anything loverlike in Morgan's behavior toward Lady Margaret, but as she became wiser in the ways of the society in which she now lived, she realized that love might very well have nothing at all to do with Morgan's choice of a wife. He had claimed, however briefly, to be in love with China, but he had offered her carte blanche, not the honor of his name. In the eyes of the world, China had also learned, marriage to her by a man of Morgan's consequence, with her unpretentious claims to gentility and odd upbringing, would be considered far more of a mésalliance than marriage to Lady Margaret Purdham, the daughter of the marquess whose lineage might be traced to royalty and whose rearing was properly conventional for her class.

China, as usual, did not want for partners, but she found she was not really in a humor for flirtation that night and she begged Mr. Johns, to whom she was promised for a country dance, to release her from her promise so that she might sit with her friend Lady Crestin, who had seated herself in the area set aside for chaperones on her arrival with her niece whom she was sponsoring that Season.

Thea was very pretty, if not the beauty that China was, and popular with the gentlemen, and would not have wanted for partners, but she rarely danced, confiding to China that she really did not care for it. "It is a sad deficiency in my accomplishments, I know," she said, sounding far from unhappy about it, "but I have never been proficient at executing the movements and always feel quite ungainly on the floor. I gave it up after Archie and I were married—recalled all the things that I am good at and stopped making excuses for myself. It was an enormous relief."

China, who was just a bit tired after a day that had included a Venetian breakfast given by Lady Sefton and an afternoon ride with several of her new friends to view the gardens at Richmond, sat down beside her on the sofa and said quizzingly, "Don't you miss the flirtation that goes with the exercise just a bit?"

"Not at all," Thea said without hesitation. "If my flirts want my company, they must come to me. If they do not, then the ones with whom they favor their attentions are welcome to them."

"Very easily said by one who already has a very attentive husband."

Thea smiled a little smugly. "I do admit that after six years of marriage, I have nothing to complain of. Are you hanging out for a husband, China?" she added curiously.

"No," China said, letting her eyes travel over the dancers taking their places in the set that was forming. "But," she said, her eyes showing a trace of self-mocking laughter, "it is foolish not to be open to the possibilities. I think I must have a latent romantic

streak after all, though Clive always said I was the
most practical woman he had ever met.''

"Why should that preclude romance? Do you have
anyone in mind?''

China shook her head, but her eyes came to rest on
Morgan, who was again in conversation with Lady
Margaret not many yards from them. Thea followed
her gaze and said with great casualness, "There are
those that wonder that Lady Margaret has never thrown
her cap over the windmill. She is not precisely pretty,
but most would agree that she is quite attractive in her
way. She has not wanted for suitors. Perhaps now that
Wrexford is returned we shall see if there is any truth
to the rumors about an understanding between them.''

China was startled by her own reaction to these
words. An unexpected frisson went through her. There
was no reason why she should feel any reaction at all;
she had been thinking much the same herself that evening. But hearing the words from Thea's lips somehow
gave the possibility more credence. It was absurd for it
to matter to her whom he did finally choose as his wife.
But the feeling was there and she did not deny it.

"Do you think them suited?" she asked Thea, careful not to betray that feeling in her tone.

"By birth, perfectly,'' Thea replied after a moment of
consideration. "By temperament, too, probably. Morgan
is more of a social creature than Lady Margaret, I think,
but he has a serious side to his character and would probably prefer a conventional bride like Lady Margaret who
will dutifully bear his children and make an excellent hostess. They say that his work for the Foreign Office was so
highly commended that he may be considered for a Cabinet post in the not very distant future.'' She watched her
friend as she spoke, but China gave none of her thoughts
away, and Thea wondered if she had mistaken the look
she had seen come into China's eyes when they had first
rested on Morgan and Lady Margaret.

When China returned home that evening, she lay

awake for a considerable while, for the first time since their quarrel on board the ship letting her thoughts retrace everything that had passed between her and Morgan since the afternoon she had met him at Sally Weston's house in Macao, and trying to understand her reaction both to seeing him with Margaret that night and to Thea's comments about the possibility that he might make Margaret his wife.

She rarely practiced self-deception and she did not do so now. She began to realize that her vague feelings of dissatisfaction were a result of her own ambiguity about him. There had been no such ambiguity in Macao since the first time he had taken her in his arms by the stream. She had known then that the attraction was more for her than merely physical and she had not resisted letting herself fall in love with him. But then her only experience of men of the world had been Clive, who had unquestionably been in love with her, and because of the obviousness of Morgan's equal interest in her and his desire for her, which she had assumed was the manifestation of her reciprocated feelings, she had not thought to doubt that he felt exactly as she did.

Her bubble of happiness had burst quickly enough. His neglect of her on the very next day after they had made love, his manner toward her and quick judgment of her when he had found her with Jack that night, had made it clear that he was not as besotted as she had been. She recalled, with a slight feeling of shame, how she had tried to explain her relationship with Jack, but Morgan had not listened, or not cared. For those brief moments in his arms again the last time they had made love, she had dared to put her fears aside and suppose she had imagined his changed manner toward her, but all hope had died when he had made it plain to her that it was a sexual liaison he wished for and nothing more.

China was more than hurt, she was very angry— with him for using her and betraying her hopes and with herself for being so foolish as to have those hopes in the first place. And now, having been in society for less than a month, China saw just how foolish she had been. Any one of the men who paid her extravagant compliments night after night would have gladly bedded her if she had indicated a similar interest, but with the exception of one or two who she knew had as much an eye to her purse as her person, there was not one who had yet to indicate an interest in a more permanent and respectable relationship.

She heard the *on-dits* about a number of widows and matrons who were assumed to have lovers, and learned quickly that as long as one was reasonably discreet, such affairs were not only tolerated, they were condoned. She did not subscribe to the excessive morality of her parents, but their beliefs were more ingrained in her than she had realized, for she found herself shocked by this blasé attitude toward infidelity and immorality. Since this was the world to which Morgan belonged, it was not really wonderful that he had supposed that she would accept his offer to make her his mistress. She was fair-minded enough to understand that in a society where arranged and politically expedient marriages were the norm, with no thought to desire, never mind love, such behavior and self-justification for it were inevitable. But she could not deny her own background either. She could never reconcile herself to accept their mores even if it meant that she remained alone for the remainder of her life. This was an extremely lowering thought and tears started at her eyes, which she blinked away angrily.

Understanding and acceptance were not the same thing. It was one thing for her to accept Morgan's rejection of the love she had offered him when she knew him unattached elsewhere—perhaps in her mind she had not really abandoned the unlikely hope that he would one day feel for her as she did for him—but to know that he contemplated marriage to someone else enhanced her humiliation and pain. She wished for the first time since she had arrived in England that she had not come, or at the least that she might leave and go somewhere where she did not have to see Morgan day after day and be constantly reminded of her shattered dreams and have to pretend that he was nothing more to her than the nephew of her late husband. For some time she toyed with the idea of touring the capitals of Europe, as she had once told Morgan she might choose to do, as she restlessly turned one way and another in a futile attempt to find a comfort that eluded her.

It was a pointless fantasy and she knew it. If nothing else, her nomadic life had taught her that the difficulties of one's life followed one wherever one went, for such things were dependent on oneself and not on a place. It would be a form of defeat to leave England now, in any case. Amelia would doubtless feel she had routed her, and Annabelle and Amery would probably feel disappointed that she had offered them a home and then vanished on her own pursuits in a way that they were all too familiar with from their father's behavior after the death of their mother.

She would stay, then, but at the cost of her own heartache. Time heals, and China supposed it would; most of the time she was able to keep her feelings for Morgan very sensibly in control. These were only occasionally inflamed to leave her with the dull ache of a longing she could not satisfy and this night, seeing Morgan with Lady Margaret, hearing Thea tell her that the world apparently expected them to make a match of it, was one of those times. It would pass, but there would be other times as well, she had no doubt of it, and this was what she was in dread of. It was in fretting over this and wondering what she might do to prevent herself further heartache that she finally fell into a sleep that was leaden from her overtiredness.

16

DESPITE HER POOR SLEEP, China awoke early when the birds were first calling and the first rays of dawn were seeking entrance through small cracks in the imperfectly closed draperies. She did not feel heavy with sleep as she had supposed she would, but curiously light and in excellent spirits. She sat up in bed wondering what had caused this change from her unhappiness of the night before, and after a few moments a small smile curved her pretty lips. She remembered that just before the mists of sleep had overtaken her, she had at last decided on a course of action.

With her new resolve to buoy her spirits, she wondered how it had come about that she had become so meek and missish. Another lesson she had learned from her life, so unlike that of most gently bred young women, was self-dependency. She had lived in native villages and in quarters too primitive to be imagined by most of the women she had met in England. She had born indignities and deprivation with equanimity, she had overcome poverty and great loss. Yet she had been willing to accept her present unhappiness without a murmur, entrenching herself in self-pity. If she did not make at least a push to put matters right again, how could she expect anything else?

She got out of bed and went over to the window, drawing the draperies and letting the sunlight flood into the room and over her as she stood before the window in her nightshift. Its warmth made her feel strong, and she lifted her face to the sun like a flower. She laughed aloud, and the sound of her own voice startled her into silence. She smiled at her own foolishness and opened the curtains as well and then the window, leaning over the sill to look down at the garden. It was not yet in full flower, but already very pretty and inviting, the dew, which had not yet been dried by the sun, sparkling with caught rays. If she had been on the ground floor she would have climbed over the sill and gone into the garden heedless of her deshabille to enjoy its fragrances as well as its visual beauty.

Morgan was not indifferent to her, even if he did not have the sort of regard for her that she wished he might have, and there had been an empathy between them since the day they had met that had nothing to do with the physical attraction which had so overpowered all else between them. That had been a mistake, she saw now. For her, it had been an expression of her growing love for him; for him, the gratification of his desires, and doubtless it had caused him to regard her in the same light as the widows and matrons that she herself scorned for their easy virtue. It would be no easy thing to correct the false impression she had given, to re-establish the rapport which might have led to her hopes being fulfilled, but if she didn't try, then she might as well resign herself to heart-sighings and self-pity. She was reasonably certain that Morgan liked her, she knew he desired her, was it so impossible after all that he could come to love her? She would never know if she retired from the field and let Lady Margaret carry the day.

She was not certain she knew how to make a man fall in love with her. Her parents had protected her from the advances of men when they were alive, at school she had lived in a convent-like atmosphere, and Clive had declared to her that he had fallen in love with her on sight with no effort at all on her part. But if she did not know precisely how to go about making Morgan fall in love with her, she knew that continuing to behave as if he were no more to her than a connection by marriage, or worse, quarreling, would accomplish the reverse. She was guilty, as he had complained, of encouraging the gentlemen he had named to flirtation, enjoying the exercise for its own sake. But with the one man whose attention she truly desired, she was always most proper and correct. It was defensive, of course, to salve her pride, but it effectively brought to an end any further hope of intimacy between them.

China knew she must begin again with Morgan; if she did not do so now, it might well be that her hopes would be forever dashed by the announcement of his betrothal to Lady Margaret. He did not have the feelings for that lady that he had for her—China was certain of it. She did not again mean to be foolish enough to take him to her bed; inflaming a man's passion was no sure means of enslaving his heart. But she would remind him in subtle ways of the power of that attraction he felt toward her, and by being agreeable and lightly flirtatious when they were together, she would see to it that he always took pleasure in her company. One way or the other, he would want her again as he had in Macao, and this time it would be as it should have been then, as his wife.

If he did not, then China knew she was setting herself up for perhaps a pain far greater than that she had felt before, but if she did not make the push for her own happiness she would live the rest of her life with the scarred and tender spot he had touched in her heart, wondering if she had failed in her one heart's desire only for the want of a little risk and resolve.

It was too early to go down to breakfast, but China was too exuberant for further sleep. She dressed herself in a soft green cotton morning dress and finally did go out into the garden, happier with her thoughts for company than she had been in months.

It was not a particularly large garden, but the sun was far higher in the sky when China finally had her fill of wandering about it. Her light slippers and the hem of her gown were damp from the dew and she was intending to return to her room to change before coming to the breakfast room when the sounds of voices coming from the morning room caught her attention. It was a man and woman speaking and the discussion they were having was obviously heated.

The woman's voice was unquestionably Amelia's, but the man was not Amery. At first China thought it must be Morgan, for she could not imagine who else would call at so early an hour, but though he spoke more quietly than Amelia, the timbre of his voice was wrong for it to be Morgan. Curiosity and the feeling that as a proper chaperone she should know who it was who was closeted alone with her stepdaughter, made China gently push open the door, which was ajar, and step into the room. It was Prentice who was with Amelia and he was still dressed in evening clothes and looking a bit disheveled.

They were so intent on their discussion that neither noticed China. "It is not fair to say so to me, Prentice," Amelia was saying, sounding more hurt than angry. "I am not my own mistress yet and shall not be for another six months. You know I would marry you tomorrow if I could, and then everything I have would be yours. But Morgan thinks it would be best not to even announce our betrothal until I am of age and I do not like to make a scene when there is so little time to wait."

"*If* what you have is yours when you are of age," Prentice said gloomily. "Wrexford took the trouble to mention to me that he could choose to control your fortune until you are five and twenty. Maybe he

thought it would put me off. Thinks I'm a dashed fortune hunter or something, I suppose.''

China, hearing Prentice's remarks, thought that he
seemed more concerned about the potential that
Amelia would be deprived of the use of her fortune
for another four years than for the fact that they could
not immediately announce their betrothal, which
hardly surprised her. Lord Prentice's continued attentions toward her, a little more circumspect after that
first occasion, continued whenever her care to avoid
him slipped, and she doubted seriously that he held
her stepdaughter in any real affection. She was about
to make her presence known to them when Amelia's
next words arrested her.

"Surely not," Amelia said. "It is probably the work
of That Woman. It would not surprise me to learn that
she is a hypocrite as well. We all know why she married Papa. It is probably not enough for her that she
has robbed us of our rightful share of Papa's estate;
she wishes to control my money as well as long as she
can.''

China felt an angry flush stain her cheeks. Torn between the desire to rush into the room and angrily defend herself and flee before she lost her temper and said
things that would make the breach between her and her
stepdaughter even greater, she chose the half course of
stepping away from the door, still unnoticed, and back
into the garden where she stood against the wall of the
house until she regained her composure. Unfortunately,
with the door open their voices were still clear and what
she heard further did not improve her temper.

"Shouldn't say those things, Amy," Prentice said
soothingly. It was not to his advantage to have their
discussion turned away while Amelia embarked on her
favorite topic of animadversions to her stepmother.
"Even if it's true, Lady Rawdon is no harpy. Her
breeding is unexceptionable and she is well liked.
People will start saying that it is you who cared more

for your father's money than his happiness," he added unwisely.

"Prentice," Amelia said with a wounded cry. "You defend *her* to me? Though I should not be surprised, I suppose," she added bitterly. "I have seen the shameless way she makes up to you. It is not enough for her, I suppose, that she stole my father's affections from me; now she must have you as well."

"Nonsense," Prentice said quickly. "I don't care a fig about Lady Rawdon, and this digression isn't solving anything for me. I still must find a way to come up with two thousand pounds today to pay Antrop. He tried to make a cursed fool of me at Watier's last night by implying that I would not be able to redeem my vowels from him right away. I should have called the bastard out," he said heatedly, as the memory of his humiliation returned to him.

"Why don't you ask Lady Rawdon for it?" Amelia said sweetly. "I am sure she would consider it a trifling payment for the satisfaction of being able to assist you and knowing I could not."

China did not want to hear any more, and neither did she wish the argument to continue possibly to be overheard by any servants. She retreated quietly away from the house and then returned, making sure that this time her approach would be heard. She came to the open doorway and stopped, looking in with apparent surprise. "Lord Prentice? I had no notion you had called," she said with a smile as she entered the room. She allowed her eyes to travel over his evening clothes, enjoying his discomfort as she did so. "I have been in the garden, so perhaps Barrett could not find me."

"Prentice called to speak with me," Amelia said coldly.

"No doubt," China said with just a hint of dryness, and added with another smile as false as the first, "But Barrett should know to send for me or Miss Hopper as well. It is not as if you are officially betrothed . . .

yet.'' There was the faintest of pauses before she spoke the last word.

China saw a spark of rage come into the younger girl's eyes and thought that she would finally be goaded into making her hostility manifest, but Amelia dropped her eyes and said, almost mumbling, ''It is a private matter, and Prentice asked to speak to me alone.''

''Oh?'' China said with a fine show of innocent curiosity.

In spite of Amelia's presence, Prentice's smile to China was warm, as were his eyes. ''It is a trifling matter. You are quite right, Lady Rawdon, I have behaved improperly. Please don't chastise your butler on my account. I was insistent that I did not wish you to be disturbed at so early an hour.'' He gave a soft, self-deprecating laugh. ''You can see I am not precisely dressed to be making morning calls. A friend is to be married in a few days and I'm afraid our revels continued past the dawn.''

''Then you must be exhausted and wishing for your bed,'' said China, and turned to Amelia again. ''Have you broken your fast yet, Amelia? I know you have promised to take Annabelle shopping this morning and you would not wish to disappoint her by making her wait.'' She then took her leave of them to go to the breakfast room, giving up the notion of changing her dress. She knew that Amelia would feel constrained to join her, whatever it would cost the girl to swallow her ire, and China's goal of ending her tête-à-tête with Purdham was accomplished.

When Amelia did come into the breakfast room several minutes later, Annabelle was already seated at table happily chattering about visiting Grafton House, which was not a fashionable emporium, but which had the virtue of offering many bargains. China was careful not to let show in her manner that she had any cause to be upset with Amelia. She was actually more troubled than angry by now. Nothing she had overheard Amelia say had surprised her, but it showed that any progress she might have hoped she was making with her stepdaughter was mistaken. Amelia's dislike and resentment were clearly as strong as ever. China did not know what else she might do to mitigate this and that was what disturbed her the most, for she did not wish to continue indefinitely treading on eggshells.

By the time she finished her breakfast, however, she had had a thought which hoped might turn her unhappy situation to advantage in more ways than one. When Amery had left for his own pursuits and Amelia and Annabelle on their shopping expedition, she went to the morning room and sat down at her writing desk which faced the window overlooking the garden. She carefully mended a pen before she began to write, but then sat several minutes thoughtfully tapping the feathered end against her cheek while she sought for just the right words for her missive. Satisfied at last, she wrote out a short note, signed and sealed it, and after giving it to a footman to deliver personally, returned at last to her room to change, this time into her prettiest sprigged muslin morning dress, letting down her hair and tying it back with only a blue ribbon the color of her eyes.

Her wait was not of long duration. China was back in the morning room, this time penning longer letters to Sally Weston and Mary Fitchley-Gore, when Morgan was announced.

"I was about to go out when I had your note, but thought I had best come at once. I hope nothing is amiss," he said as he greeted her, but his tone was light, so China supposed him to be in good humor.

"Did I alarm you?" China said with a smile as he sat beside her on the small sofa across from the writing desk. "There is nothing precisely wrong, but since we are joint guardians of Clive's children, I thought that there were a few matters we might discuss. I had no idea that living in England would mean having one's time so thoroughly accounted for," she added with a short laugh. "I had to send my regrets to Mrs. Beameth this morning begging her to forgive me for not attending her waltzing party so that I might finally catch up with my correspondence. I have already had a letter from Sally Weston and I have not yet found the time to reply."

Though there was no reproach in her voice, Morgan felt it. He had not called at Rawdon House since their quarrel, though their relations were again cordial. He had discovered that day that China still held the power to stir his emotions too greatly, for good or for bad, and he thought it best to avoid occasions for private conversation until he had a better control of his emotions where she was concerned. "I should have taken the trouble to call myself to see how you have been getting on," he said with a faint note of apology, though China had asked for none. "It is all too easy to let the demands of the Season become overwhelming," he added, grateful for the easy excuse her words had given him.

China laughed. "Well, now we have made our excuses to each other, and may see to our obligations."

"I hope you don't think of our charges as obligations," he said, smiling, "but I don't think you do, do you?"

"No," China agreed. "Annabelle and Amery bring me far more pleasure than obligation. They have both shown me an affection and acceptance that is far greater than I'd dared to hope for. I am not so much older than they are, but my life at their age was very different. They are both so full of liveliness that I feel as if I am being given the opportunity to relive those years in a much lighter way, and I am grateful for it. I am enjoying myself quite thoroughly."

"I think you have been very good for both Annabelle and Amery as well," he said. "I don't doubt they were happy living with my mother, but now they

are coming to feel that they have a home of their own
and I can see already the change this has wrought in
them for the better. Annabelle is livelier than ever and
Amery has gained a self-confidence he didn't possess
a month ago.''

China was delighted by his encomiums. It was a
more propitious beginning than she had even hoped
for. ''I hope I am the cause of it,'' China said with a
swift smile. ''I own I am sometimes concerned about
Amery, he is so set on cutting a dash and is out so
much with his friends that I scarcely set eyes on him
except at meals and when we are in company together,
but he seems very content with our arrangement. And
Annabelle is ever a source of delight to me. I want
very much for them to be happy here with me.''

''They are.'' He paused, and added, ''Don't worry
too much about Amery. He is just testing his wings. I
hope you are not fretting about Amelia, either. That
will take time, you know.''

''And I am impatient,'' she said with a soft laugh.
''I know. But it is not only that she does not try—she
will not even let me do so.'' China sighed. ''It is unreasonable, I suppose, to want everything at once. I
do hope Amelia will be happy when she is married to
Lord Prentice. I think if she found personal content-
ment, she might finally get over the hurt of her father's
abandonment.''

''She might, if Prentice is the right man for her.
You are no more sanguine on that point than I am,''
he said plainly.

''No,'' China admitted, ''I am not.''

''It doesn't help that Purdham makes his attraction
to you plain for all to see, including Amelia.''

He spoke in a level voice, but China cast him a swift
glance. She saw no censure in his expression and felt
relief. ''I wish he would not,'' she said in a heartfelt
manner. ''I have given him the hint as best I can with-

out delivering a crushing snub, but he refuses to understand me.''

"It may take that," Morgan informed her. "He is the sort who enjoys the chase as much as the conquest, and he will not give up the challenge too easily.''

The purpose of China's note to Morgan asking him to call was more than just to attempt to reestablish the intimacy they had once known. She did wish to discuss Amelia's proposed nuptials with him and she had been undecided how much to confide in him of her eavesdropping earlier in the morning. Given the underlying dryness in his tone when he spoke of Purdham, she felt she might be candid.

"Prentice called on Amelia this morning before breakfast," she said cautiously. "I was in the garden and overheard them talking as I was coming into the house.''

Morgan frowned slightly. "Indeed? Purdham isn't usually one to leave his rooms before noon. He belongs to a set that considers any earlier hour to be up and about as barbaric.''

"He had not yet been to bed, I gather," China said a trifle caustically. Morgan's brows rose in question and she went on, "I openly confess to eavesdropping, though I did not mean to at first. I am not certain, for I heard only a portion of their conversation, but I believe he has need of money for a debt of honor and he thought that Amelia might be able to assist him.''

Morgan's expression changed subtley. The frown was gone and there was a slight upturning of his lips, but it was not in humor. "Did he? I confess myself unsurprised. I acquit him of being a hardened gamester, but deep play is very much in fashion and Purdham is always in the fashion. It is an expensive way of life. Do you think him a suitable husband for Amelia?''

China was startled by his question. "I should ask you that," she said frankly. "You have known him most of your life, and I have only just met him.''

Morgan laughed, this time clearly amused. "A very judicious response. You would do well in the diplomatic corps. But I want your opinion. An indifferent observer is often the better one."

China did not hesitate. "No. It is not just that he appears to me to be expensive, as you say, or that he pays far too much attention to other women, but I do not feel that he has any real regard for Amelia other than an offhanded sort, more like an older brother than a suitor. She, on the other hand, is clearly besotted with him. I fear this will pass when she is faced with the realities of marriage, and I doubt she will be very happy."

Morgan rose and went over to the French doors open onto the sunny garden. "My sentiments precisely," he said, and smiled. "Do you think we should forbid the bans?"

China went over to him and and returned his smile. "Heaven forbid! She would believe it entirely my doing, and I should be damned eternally as the wicked stepmother."

"It would avail nothing," he reminded her. "After October the best we could do would be to prevent Amelia from receiving her inheritance for another four years. I thought that might answer, but I doubt it. It is a very large fortune, and with his own lack of fortune and somewhat dubious reputation, Purdham is not likely to be welcomed with open arms by any other families with well-dowered daughters. He may even suppose that we would dislike seeing Amelia's husband in River Tick and cough up the dibs any time he might outrun the bailiff. He's probably right."

"Then what are we to do?"

Morgan shrugged. "Nothing except rue our impotence, I suppose." He saw China's dubious expression and laughed softly, reaching to cup her chin in one hand, the first flirtatious gesture he had made toward her in some time. "Yes, I know you think me very poor-spirited, but if you think on it, you will see I am right."

"I suppose," China admitted reluctantly. There was something in the way that he looked at her that made her heart begin to beat a little faster. She knew she had made the right choice of topics to begin again with him, for their guardianship of Clive's children formed a bond between them that would serve her purpose better now than the heat of their mutual passion had done. "But I wish Amelia could be brought to be a bit more objective about Prentice. She can be very set in her opinions," China added dryly.

"As you well know," Morgan said, letting his hand drop away from her face. "I should have said pig-headed, myself. Some claim it is a family trait. The Rawdons are not easily dislodged from their beliefs. I had best be on my way," he said after another moment. "I am promised to Lord Dudley for luncheon and I have to see James in the city on a small matter beforehand. Don't fret yourself about Amelia, China. She is beyond either your influence or mine. Concentrate on Annabelle and Amery, if you wish. They like and admire you, and a deal of good may be done there."

They were standing very close together, and China could feel the pull of attraction between them so strongly that she almost felt as if he would take her in his arms at any moment. She moved away from him deliberately. It was too soon to reawaken the physical desire between them. That had clearly been a mistake. Too much, too soon. If there was to be any hope of a lasting attachment between them, it must be built upon mutual regard and trust, not the urgings of lust. "And so we come full circle to the start of our discussion," she said lightly. She held out her hand to him. "I shall try, Morgan. It does hearten me to know that you think well of my influence on Amery and Annabelle."

"I never doubted it," Morgan said, surprising her. He took her hand and held it in his for a moment

before releasing her. "I promise to attend to my portion of our shared responsibilities more assiduously in
the future. We shall be very proper guardians and discuss our charges at unexceptional intervals from now
on," he added with a smile, and then left her.

China thought she had made a very good beginning
and was pleased. Her pleasure continued during the following fortnight, for it was unquestionable that Morgan
sought out her company with far greater frequency again
and they certainly did not spend all of their time together discussing the young Rawdons. Though they had
enjoyed many intimate discussions in Macao learning
about their individual lives and their pasts, those times
had always been overshadowed by their intense physical
attraction to each other. China did not attempt to deny
the current she felt pass between them still whenever
they touched, but she kept these feelings in check, allowing herself to be mildly flirtatious with him when
the situation warranted it, but always keeping him at
just the right distance to keep their friendship growing
but to prevent any recurrance of the passion that had
once flared between them. And from the amount of
time he chose to spend in her company, the way that he
responded to her with an equally flirtatious manner, she
felt gratification for the course she was taking. If they
were ever to be lovers again in the way that she wished,
she knew that first they had to be truly friends.

China did not forget about the rumored match between Morgan and Lady Margaret, and without seeming to, she managed to observe them whenever they
were together. But if Morgan did have intentions toward Lady Margaret, she was more certain than ever
that love played no part in them, and she was heart-
ened. If and until it was a settled thing between them,
she had no reason to despair.

17

It was at about this time that China had her second letter from Sally Weston, and in it she mentioned that several of their acquaintances from Macao were about to embark for England. There had been no trouble in Macao of the magnitude of the first uprising, but several Englishmen unwise enough to go about the countryside unattended or to go out into the streets after dark had been attacked, robbed, and beaten and for many the lure of fortunes to be made in the East was not sufficient to make up for the threat to their personal safety. The Watsons and the Creelys were both making plans to leave in a week's time, and Jack Reid was to accompany them.

China, returning to the first page, sought the date of the letter and discovered that it had been written at about the time that she and her aunt had first arrived in London. This should means that her friends from Macao should be arriving in England shortly if they had left as planned, and China regarded this with mixed feelings.

She had missed Jack every bit as much as she had missed Sally, but this would not be a propitious time for him to come to London, and she hoped that he planned to visit his family in Sussex for a bit before coming to town. It was not likely that he would move in the circles to which her marriage had given her an easy entrée, but he would certainly call upon her and she would not dream of denying his friendship because she feared that Morgan would draw his own conclusions about the resumption of it. But it was inconvenient at just this moment, when her progress with Morgan had again raised her hopes.

There was no word from Jack, or the Watsons or Creelys for that matter, as another week passed, though China supposed they should have no great difficulty in learning her direction, and she supposed that either something had delayed their arrival or that they had none of them come to London when first arriving in England. It was already May, and all of the *ton* were making plans to leave town in another month either to go to Brighton or some other fashionable resort or to return to their country seats.

Lady Wrexford wished to return to Ferris Grange with Annabelle, but the Purdhams had hired a house in Brighton for the Season there and Amelia very naturally wished to go there as well to be near her betrothed and his sister. Lady Wrexford and Morgan as well thought it improper for her to accept an invitation from Lady Margaret since she would be under the same roof as her Prentice and Amelia was in high dudgeon for two days after hearing this dictum.

It was after this that Amelia finally began to thaw in her manner toward her stepmother, but her frequent references to the pleasures of Brighton and how certain she was that China would enjoy a month or two by the sea made her intent transparent, and China reflected dryly to herself that while Amelia had condemned her for hypocrisy, she was not above practicising it herself to serve her ends.

China was not put off the idea of going to Brighton by this, though. Amery also was partial to the scheme and China, who was truly enjoying her foray into polite society, found it attractive as well. But her principal reason for entertaining the idea despite Lady Wrexford's opposition to it was that she was not at all eager to spend the summer at Ferris Grange *en famille* with a

pouting Amelia. The seal was set on the matter when
Morgan announced that he had taken lodgings in Brighton, at least for the month of July. China had no intention of allowing him this time in the company of Lady
Margaret while she was miles away communing with
nature by herself and dealing with Amelia's sulks.

China wondered if Morgan would frown upon her
wish to rent a house in Brighton, since Amelia would
certainly spent a great deal of her time in company with
Lord Prentice, but he seemed pleased by her decision
and even offered to journey to the sea village himself to
find something suitable—no easy task so late in the Season—for her to rent. It was while he was gone on this
errand with Amery, whom he had persuaded to accompany him, that China was paid a call by Dana Bovell.
She was surprised when Barrett brought Bovell's card
to her in the library while she was reading a new novel
she had brought home from Hookham's the previous
day. Sally had made no mention of Bovell's intent to
return to England in her letter, but she was not displeased to see him in spite of the fact that she did not
particularly like him, because he was sure to have news
for her of all her friends in Macao.

Barrett showed Bovell into the library where China
awaited him and he greeted her with an ardor out of
line with their previous acquaintance. He brought her
hand to his lips with a flourish that was so theatrical
that China was forced to hide a smile at the absurdity
of it. "My dear China, your beauty has never been
more apparent. You are a veritable English rose. I can
see I needn't ask if the air of our motherland suits you.
You fairly glow with vitality."

"Thank you, Mr. Bovell," China said with pointed
formality. He had only dared address her with familiarity a few times in Macao, when he had been a bit
foxed at some party or other, and she had not cared
to give him a setdown in company with their friends.
But she meant to set him at a proper distance at once

for fear that he would become encroaching. "I find living here very pleasing indeed. Have you just come from China? I had a letter from Lady Weston a fortnight ago and she told me that several of our friends had decided to return to England shortly after I left."

"I have been here since Saturday last," he said, seating himself without being asked, and clearly in the attitude of one who does not doubt his welcome. "I journeyed on a merchantman with the Watsons and Jack Reid, but several others also were making arrangements to leave within the month. Even Weston, who has declared that he won't let himself be driven away, was not so adamant in his stand by the time I left. It is an uncomfortable situation at best, and possibly dangerous, as you have cause to know. I shouldn't be at all surprised if all of our set find ourselves reunited here in England before the year is out."

China doubted privately if Bovell would find the inclusion in their society that he assumed. He was not liked overmuch and Sally had once described him frankly as a *chevalier de fortune* and her husband even more frankly as a Captain Sharp. It was not likely that he would find an easy acceptance outside of the limited society of Macao. "Did Jack go to his family in Sussex? I have had no word of him, so I presume he has not come to London."

Bovell stated that he believed that was Jack Reid's intent, and the next half hour was spent pleasantly enough in a discussion of their mutual friends and acquaintances and all that had occurred in Macao since China had left. It was nearing the time for luncheon, and though China had no engagement, she did not wish to encourage Bovell by asking him to join her for the meal. He had already stayed beyond the correct amount of time for a civil visit of one who was no more than an acquaintance and China was beginning to feel she would have to give him the hint to bring their conversation to an end when Amery came rushing into the room with Morgan in tow.

"We found a capital house, China," Amery said without ceremony. "It's right on the Steine, which might be a bit noisy, but we shall be excellently situated. It's a barn of a place and I've been trying to persuade Wrexford to give up his lodgings and stay with us. You are both guardians to me and Amelia, and we're all related, so I don't see any inpropriety in it."

His boyish enthusiasm came to an abrupt halt as he finally noted Dana Bovell, who rose for the introduction. China made Bovell known to Amery, who in his exuberant humor greeted him heartily. Morgan did the same in a more subdued manner.

Bovell did not excuse himself on the arrival of Morgan and Amery, as most well-bred people would have done, but appeared to regard it as an excuse to extend his stay, immediately engaging Morgan in conversation about conditions in Macao and the East in general. Morgan responded politely but without any notable encouragement. He glanced at China, read in her expression that she found her guest tiresome, and said, very nearly interrupting the other man, "I know you will excuse us, Mr. Bovell. I did not presume to hire the house in Brighton for Lady Rawdon without gaining her approval first and there is some urgency in our need to discuss the matter if we are not to lose it to another lessor."

This was more than a hint and could not be ignored, and Dana Bovell at last took his leave of them. When he had gone, Amery possessed himself of the chair that Bovell had sat in and said, "He seems a very good sort of fellow. You must be glad to see one of your old friends, China. Did anyone else leave China with him?"

"Mr. Bovell mentioned a few others who made the journey," China replied vaguely, "but I gather they have gone to their families and have not yet come to town. Tell me about the house. If you think it at all suitable, we should make a decision about it at once.''

They discussed the matter for a quarter hour and finally came to the conclusion that China would make an offer for the rental of the house at once through Mr. James. Amery was delighted and offered to go immediately to the city to Mr. James's office as his stepmother's emissary.

"I can see I have made the popular decision," China said with a dry smile when Amery left them. "Even Amelia has come close to appearing friendly toward me since I said that I would consider going to Brighton."

"Is that what you truly wish to do?" Morgan asked with mild concern. "You needn't put yourself out to please either Amelia or Amery."

"No, I think I am going to Brighton as much for myself as for them," China said truthfully. "When I was at Miss Grayson's Academy, several of the other girls would go to Brighton with their families for the summer and would return with such delightful tales of the Pavilion, walks along the Steine, and the fantastic bathing machines, that I have always wished to go there myself."

"But you may do so next season if you would wish to go to Ferris instead now. You must feel at least a bit worn at times from all that has occurred in the past few months."

China smiled dryly. "I thank you, my lord, for thinking me such a poor creature. You know that it is quite a common thing for a missionary's daughter to be forever adapting to strange new societies. It is simply a matter of adjusting to the customs of the natives."

Morgan took her hands in his and squeezed them gently. "And you have done so with ease and grace, China."

His voice was so warm that China felt her heart beat faster. "I suppose it would be improper for you to stay with us in Brighton?" she asked with a wistfulness she did not attempt to hide.

"I wish I might," he said with sincerity. "If Mama were with us, it might just pass muster, but with your beauty and my reputation, we should still have half the harpies in the *ton* looking at us askance.''

''They would do so now, if they saw you holding my hands in this way,'' she informed him.

He glanced down at their entwined hands as if he had been unaware of the contact, but he did not release her. Instead, he drew her nearer him. As always, his feelings toward China were so ambiguous that he was not aware he was going to kiss until he bent his head and did so. He felt a slight hesitation in her, a brief withdrawal, and then her lips became pliant against his. He had not intended this. Like China, he felt that giving in to their strong physical attraction as they had in Macao had been a grevious mistake, and after the night they had made love on the ship, he had not intended it to occur again.

Since they had come to England, his feelings for her had yet again been undergoing a subtle change. It was impossible for him to put her from his mind when they were so often together, and he could not deny how much he enjoyed being in her company; far more so than with any other female of his acquaintance. He genuinely liked China and did not want to believe that she was a well-bred doxy who had married Clive for his fortune, taken Clive's closest friend for her lover, and made love with himself for her own advantage. But neither could he resolve in his mind a belief in her complete innocence. When he watched China flirting with one or another of the gentlemen who made no secret of their admiration for her, he found he did not like the dark thoughts that came to him, or his reaction to them. But he had not the least cause to believe that she had taken any one of these men for her lover and he was a little ashamed of himself for his readiness to suspect that she might have. It was a quandary to him that he could tell himself that he didn't give a damn what she did as long as she did not make scandal for the family, but yet the thought of any one of those men touching her in any way more intimate than to lead her into the dance made him feel as if he had been gutted.

His desire for her remained unabated, but like China he kept it in check. Despite his feelings for her, which he could not help, he thought it was best to let matters lie. But the spark between them was too bright and too volatile. It lay dormant for a time, but ignited all too easily, as it did now.

His arousal was instantaneous. It was as it had been that day at the stream in Macao—a petal-soft kiss that blossomed quickly into full-blown passion. He could feel her breasts pressed tight against his chest and his hands caressed her as if seeking to know every contour of her body. He pulled her tight against his loins as if he could magically banish their clothing and penetrate her at once as he wished to. The taste of her mouth and her tongue was intoxicating, her scent made him ache to bury his face in her soft and yielding breasts. He was very near to forgetting that it was the middle of the morning and that they were in the library in Rawdon House where they might be interrupted by servants or one of the young Rawdons at any moment. A wide sofa was invitingly near at hand and he was about to scoop her into his arms and carry her there when he felt her begin to pull away from him, her hands moving against his chest to push him away.

"We must not do this, Morgan," China said breathlessly.

Morgan's response was to tighten his embrace and cover her mouth with his again, stifling her protests. China wanted to bring their loving to completion as much as he did, but she did not dare give in to her desire.

In a way, her ambitions had finally been realized. The charade that they were no more than connections by marriage was at an end. But a declaration of passion was no more a declaration of love now than it had been in Macao or Kowloon. It was love for her, and until and unless she knew it was the same for him, she did not dare to settle for less. This time she submitted to his kiss for no more than a moment before she pushed against him so sharply that he had no choice but to release her.

He stood looking at her for a long moment. There was something intense in his expression that gave her a quick prickle of fear, as if she thought he meant to ignore her refusal and take her against her will. But then the corners of his mouth turned up slightly and he said, ''No, we must not.'' Yet he gathered her into his arms again, gently embracing her so that her fear evaporated. ''Whether we will or not, China, we cannot deny our attraction to each other.''

''No,'' she agreed, and waited. She knew the words she wanted to hear him speak, but she would not lead him.

His smile turned wry. ''The pretense is absurd and I suspect will always be short-lived,'' he said, speaking his thoughts aloud.

''Then what are we to do?'' she asked quietly. ''I will not be your mistress, Morgan.''

''You made that quite clear before,'' he said a bit dryly, and finally released her and walked over to a sideboard where he extracted a decanter of brandy and a glass, filled it a quarter way, and drank it down with reckless haste. He turned toward her again and said as much to his own astonishment as hers, ''What if I asked you to marry me?''

China took in her breath silently. ''Are you?''

Morgan laughed suddenly but without humor, and put the stopper back in the decanter with a sharpness that made the crystal ring. ''I don't know,'' he said, with more honesty than tact. ''I had not thought of marriage.''

''Thank you, my lord,'' China said caustically, her suspense and her hope dissolving together. ''Then your question to me was purely rhetorical. Or perhaps you thought you must go that length this time if you are to overcome my resistance.''

''No,'' he said fairly sharply. He had no idea what

had made him speak those words, but they could not be taken back. When he had first realized in Macao that he was falling in love with her, it had been the natural thing for him to wish her to be his wife, but the blow of finding her with Jack Reid had banished all thought of this from his mind and he had never consciously entertained the idea again. Yet from somewhere within him, the desire to possess her completely again had emerged quite without his volition. It was so unexpected that he did not know if he had meant the words or not. "I have never in my life wanted a woman as I want you, China. And it is not entirely physical desire. You have come to mean much more to me than that."

It was very nearly a declaration of love, but not quite. She did not believe he had meant to offend her; it was obvious that he had confused himself by his near proposal. But she felt stung by his words nevertheless. She could not help feeling that he stopped short of admitting a love for her because he did not think her good enough to be his wife. "You would seem to be in a quandary, my lord," she said coolly. "Perhaps you should have sought to know your own mind better before speaking to me."

He laughed a little uncertainly. "I wish you would not call me 'my lord' when you are annoyed with me. It makes me feel like a chastened schoolboy."

China smiled reluctantly, but her tone was unchanged. "I don't think you mean to insult me, but you make *me* feel like a demimondaine attempting to rise above her station."

"Good lord," he said with amazement, and a little pique as well. "You are being overly sensitive, China. It is no such thing."

China did not mean to argue with him again, but this half-declaration was more hurtful to her than his offer to make her his mistress. It was the object of her dearest desire within reach, but not quite, and the frustration of it made her bitter. "Isn't it?" she said frigidly. "Am I to be flattered that you speak of marriage to me and then in the next breath tell me that you don't know if you meant it at all? Why speak of it then? Do you imagine that I shall become your mistress after all in the hope that it may lead to more? If I do marry again, it will be to a man who holds me in a better regard than you appear to do."

He saw that he had genuinely offended her and knew that his own confusion had caused him to speak more plainly than he should have. "I have not handled this matter with much grace, have I?" he said ruefully.

"No you have not," China agreed roundly, and moved away from him in agitation. "But *I* have been thinking of marriage of late. Sir Henry Portmer has asked me to be his wife." She had not meant to tell him of the offer one of her admirers had made to her only the night before. The gentleman had been in his cups and had declared himself after she had repulsed for the dozenth time his attempts to lead her into romantic seclusion. She had not seriously entertained his offer for a moment, but she wanted something to throw back at Morgan for his carelessness of her feelings.

"Portmer," he said with a mixture of astonishment and contempt. "You can't be serious."

"Why not?" she demanded, turning back to him.

"For one thing, he is twenty years your senior, at the least, and for another, he is a member of York's dissolute set with nothing to recommend him but his fortune," he said brutally. "If you are looking to marry to advantage again, you may do better than that."

"Is that what you think it is?"

"What else could it be," he said, letting his anger show. "You can't expect me to believe that you have any affection for a man of his stamp."

"Why should I not form a regard for a man who has consistently treated me with kindness and openly

declared his love for me?'' she demanded in a deliberately taunting tone.

The contrast was not lost on Morgan, and it was
more stinging than he cared to acknowledge. He gave
a brief snort of laughter which said plainly what he
thought of her question. ''Many men bandy about the
word *love* to their purpose.''

''You do not think it possible he may hold me in
genuine regard?'' she asked dulcetly.

''No. He wants to bed you, and for an old court
card like Portmer, marriage would be his only hope
of success.''

China felt slapped by his brutal frankness. ''I should
trust you to know. That is your dilemma as well, is it
not? But you are still hedging your bets, hoping the
attraction I feel toward you will win the day without
anything more than a half-hearted hint at something
more.''

It was not the truth, but he was upset enough to
respond to her accusation this time. ''China, that is
not what I meant,'' he said in a tone that was far from
conciliatory.

''I know what you meant,'' China said furiously. ''I
thank you for the honor you have nearly done me, but
I fear I must decline your less than flattering hints at
an offer of marriage.''

''You are deliberately misunderstanding me,'' he
said coldly. ''I know I have not spoken with any noticeable address, but I only meant to be honest with
you.''

''Then be honest with yourself,'' China recommended tartly. ''I acquit you of deceiving me in Macao; then I deceived myself. I know only too well what
it is you want of me now, and throwing me the sop of
hinting at deeper feelings changes nothing.''

He said nothing for at least a minute. They faced each
other like opponents rather than lovers. ''And this is what
you think of me,'' he said with a quietness in contrast to

their previous heat, but the ice in his tone bespoke his anger as clear as any heat. "I thank you, madame, for making yourself so plain. No doubt it will resolve matters for me as well. I wish you well of Portmer," he added with a sardonic inflection, and walked out of the room without any further word of leavetaking.

China walked mechanically to the sideboard and replaced the decanter. She picked up the glass he had used, looked at it unseeingly, and realized that her hand was shaking slightly. She put it down again and walked to the window which faced the street. There was no sight of Morgan, but she had not expected to see him. Her activity was a means of delaying the painful thoughts that she knew would quickly flood in upon her.

She had no idea why she had deliberately provoked another quarrel with him. She did not even want to think of the consequences of it. He had hurt her—whether or not he had meant to—but she had always known that that was the risk she was taking when she set her heart on making him fall in love with her. But she had not supposed that it would hurt quite so much, worse than it had even when he had so insulted her on board the ship. To be so near to her goal and have it snatched away from her by his equivocation was more than she could bear.

She very much feared that this quarrel would be their last. Perhaps he was sincere in suggesting that he was beginning to care for her, but she did want him to love her reluctantly, and she realized now that it was not really possible to make someone love you if they could not. It had been folly from the start. If she could not have Morgan on her terms, then she told herself she was far better off ending any hopes at all. It was the only sensible thing to do, but she felt so wretchedly hollow inside that she could take no pride in her practicality.

18

CHINA'S HOPEFUL BELIEF that she had touched her depths and matters could only improve for her proved to be premature. It was a matter of pride to her that no one should guess at her unhappiness and she would have no part of languishing airs or self-imposed isolation. She went to the Ponsonbys' that same night and continued to go into company with the appearance of her usual good humor intact. It took a considerable exercise of her will to maintain this facade, though, and when she finally returned at night to the quiet and privacy of her own apartments, she felt a weariness that she had not previously known from her revels. It was a blessing, though, for she fell easily into sleep rather than lying awake with her thoughts to torment her.

She did not see Morgan again that night and on the day following their quarrel, Lady Wrexford told her that he had gone to Ferris that morning to attend to some business there, causing China to wonder if he had done so deliberately to avoid her.

Her life at Rawdon House, at least, appeared to be going very smoothly. Annabelle was disappointed that she was not to remove to Brighton with her brother and sister, but it was not in her nature to fret or pout and she was quickly resigned to it. Since she was still too young to go out in company as she wished she might, she confided in China that she supposed she would become bored with the resort and was as well off returning to Ferris to be with her friends in the neighborhood. Amelia was still in spirits about going to Brighton to be with Prentice and her coolness toward China had abated considerably.

China knew a little concern for Amery, for he spent less time going to proper parties with China and Lady Wrexford and more and more of his time with his friends in town going to places like Cribbs' Parlour, the Argyll Rooms, and various fashionable gaming hells. This was nothing in itself, for many young men so sported themselves, but there were nights when he came home so thoroughly castaway that he could scarcely mount the stairs without the assistance of Barrett or his valet and others when he did not return to Mount Street until mid-morning looking disheveled and rather disreputable.

China did not wish to be interfering, so she held her tongue for the most part, but on at least one occasion she attempted to speak to him about it. Amery had laughed rather sheepishly and admitted that he had been a bit hey-go-mad of late, but he assured her that he was not falling into the clutches of irretrievable vice and was simply enjoying a lark, and promised that when they went to Ferris after Brighton, he would settle down and prepare for the next term at Magdalen. His manner was so easy and sincere, so little defensive, that China felt her concern assuaged for the moment. Even Morgan, after all, appeared to feel that it was no more than the behavior of a healthy young man of spirit seeking to establish his manhood.

China knew that among those Amery styled as his friends was Dana Bovell, for she had seen him in company with Amery several times. That Mr. Bovell had been taken up by Lord Prentice's set of which Amery was a part was apparent also. Even Amelia had appeared to take a liking to Bovell, and more than once he was included in some excursion the young people embarked upon. Only Lady Wrexford appeared to regard him in the same light as China did, though she always treated him with civility. She remarked to China once that though Mr. Bovell seemed personable enough, she thought him a bit encroaching. China did not disagree. She did not invite him to her house for any of the small, quiet entertainments she provided for a few friends, nor did she encourage him to call. He seemed to take the hint and did not come to Rawdon House even to see Amery or Amelia, which he might have done unless China chose to forbid him the house, which she would not have cared to do. She did not want his friendship, but neither did she want his outright enmity.

China's assumption that Bovell would not find an easy entrée to the circles in which she moved proved correct, but at large entertainments where personable young men were at a premium, he was occasionally in attendance. Thea noted her coolness toward Mr. Bovell and commented on it, supposing that China ought to have been pleased to have an acquaintance in town that she had known in China. China chose not to confide in her about Bovell's presumptuousness and treachery toward her, but her offhand response to Thea's remarks created more speculation in her friend's mind than the simple truth might have done. Others too noticed how firmly China kept Mr. Bovell at a distance and it made his acceptance into exclusive circles far less likely than it might have been if China had received him as a friend.

In spite of her coolness toward him, Dana Bovell continued to pay her more attention than she wished, and Lord Prentice also appeared to be completely impervious to her hints that she found his company less than desirable. Sir Henry, Lord Peter, Mr. Collingswood, and others continued to pay her court, but she met no one who sparked her interest in the least, and in her dispirited moments she felt as if she were doomed to attract only men toward whom she felt not the smallest return of regard.

The one bright spot in this lowering week was the arrival in town of Jack Reid. He came to her at once, still in his traveling clothes, apologizing for not stopping first to change into clothes more suitable for visiting, saying that his eagerness to see her again had made him not wish to delay any longer. China was so very glad to see him that if he had been as dirty as a chimney sweep, she would have hugged him just as fervently as she did when he was shown into her sitting room.

"I know I should have written to you," Jack said with self-reproach as he settled beside her on a sofa. "But you know that I am a wretched correspondent and hate to write."

"I don't think I have ever beheld you with a pen in your hand," China agreed with a laugh. "Did you descend upon your family unannounced as well?"

"Yes," he admitted, smiling, "and my poor mother had a fit of the vapors. It appears she had a dream about me being on a ship in a storm only the night before, and she thought I was my own ghost come to confirm her worst fears."

"But they must be even more delighted than I am to have you here in England," said China.

"Yes, I think so. 'Dear John, come home. All is forgiven.' " His accompanying laugh was self-mocking. "With Harry dead and my younger sister married and gone to Wiltshire to live with her husband, I am no longer the black sheep but the returned prodigal. It is only a small estate, but my father's health has been failing of late and he is very glad to have me return to take up my responsibilities. He once thought my ambitions in medicine just another proof of my perverse nature, but the first night I returned I made him a posset to help ease his gout and he has learned firsthand the usefulness of my knowledge."

"Do you settle in Sussex, then?"

"I think so. I suppose I always knew that I should one day."

China laughed. "It would seem that we are all of us come back to take up our preordained fates."

Jack agreed, and they spent a full hour discussing their experiences since they had last met and what news he could give her of their friends still in China. China's eyes sparkled with recalled pleasure as she recounted her meetings and growing closeness with Amery, Annabelle, Alyce Wrexford, and Thea Crestin. She spoke of the many parties she had attended, her plans to renovate Rawdon House, her hopes to visit Nottinghamshire and the small estate she had inherited from Clive there before coming to town again for the Little Season in October, her desire to see the Pavilion and other anticipated delights of Brighton, and many other such things, but she made little mention of Amelia or Morgan and said nothing at all of the things that had occurred to mar her pleasure.

Jack refrained from questioning her about these things, supposing that if the marriage she had assumed would take place between her and the earl were in the making, or if she had found her fears that Clive's eldest daughter would not accept her groundless, she would have been eager to tell him of it. But China herself was very aware of the omission and when they had talked themselves to a standstill on other topics, she knew she could no longer avoid admitting that her happiness since arriving in England was not complete.

The few months separation that were between them and the fact that Jack had been right when he had tried to convince her that she was setting her hopes too high, made her diffident of discussing with him the more intimate details of these things, but she did admit to him that she and Morgan were not to be married.

"I suppose you discovered you should not suit after all," Jack said blandly in reply to this information.

China's smile was a bit acid. "I should like it better if you just said 'I told you so.' "

"All right," Jack replied with a short laugh. "I told you so. I suppose he offered you carte blanche instead."

China disliked his perceptiveness, but she did not shy away from the truth. "Something like that," she acknowledged.

"The devil take Wrexford!"

"No," she said levelly, "the mistake was mine. Because I had come to care for Morgan, I assumed he must feel the same. I know you did try to warn me, Jack, but I did not wish to listen."

"It must make it deuced awkward for you now."

China shook her head. "Not generally. We have come to terms." This was true enough. After their last argument, there could be no doubt that each knew where the other stood.

Jack looked alarmed. "China, you have not . . ."

"Become his mistress," she interposed. "No, Jack. I have not." She might have added that Morgan had made a similar assumption about her relationship with Jack, but she did not wish to face the inevitable discussion that would follow this revelation. "I think I have monopolized our conversation quite enough," she said with a deliberate lightness. "You must tell me more of your plans now that you are in England."

Jack knew that she merely wished to turn the subject and he readily obliged, guessing that China would find any discussion of what had happened between her and Morgan too hurtful just yet. If she wished to tell him, she would do so in her own time.

China was genuinely sorry to learn that Jack only intended to remain a fortnight or so in London while he conducted some business for his father. She expressed her regret and made him promise to call whenever he found the time to do so. "We go to Brighton at the end of the month," she told him, "and after that to Hertfordshire, but I do not mean to let us grow apart because of the distance. Even if you will not write to me, I promise to be a faithful correspondent and you must visit me whenever you may.''

Jack readily agreed, and also accepted an invitation to a rout party to be held at Rawdon House at the beginning of the following week. As he was leaving, Thea arrived, and China was pleased to make her new friend known to Jack. When he left her he kissed her lightly at the door before descending the stairs, and as China turned back to the room where Thea awaited her, she saw the speculative look in her friend's eyes. ''Don't begin imagining things, Thea,'' she said sternly. ''Jack is an old friend and nothing more.''

''But a very dear friend, it would appear,'' Thea remarked with an air of innocence. ''If you don't want anyone to be imagining it is more, you should reserve your signs of affection for each other for more private moments.''

China felt slightly exasperated at this mild reproach, though she knew Thea meant well. ''Not you too, Thea. I begin to think I must behave like a nun if I am not to incur censure in every quarter. I need only smile at a man, it would seem, for everyone to think he is my lover.''

''Well, you did more than smile at Mr. Reid,'' Thea pointed out, settling herself comfortably in an overstuffed chair. ''It is because you are so beautiful, my dear. If you were fat or plain, you might have as many male friends as you chose and nothing would be thought of it. Does Wrexford return in time for your party? You will want to have a particular care in showing your preference for Mr. Reid when he is about. Gentlemen are always lamentably suspicious of one's 'old' friends if they are of the opposite sex.''

''Whatever do you mean?'' China asked more sharply than she intended. ''Morgan met Jack in Macao, of course. He is well aware of our friendship and

it hardly matters in any case what he might think of
it.''

"No?" Thea said, her skepticism plain. China had
not confided in her her feelings for Morgan, but Thea
was an astute woman, particularly in ferreting out a
romantic interest among her friends, and she had noted
numerous little signs between them of their mutual
attraction. "I thought that perhaps you were engaged
in cutting out the redoubtable Lady Margaret, but perhaps I am mistaken.''

China was dismayed that she had been so transparent and wondered if others of her acquaintance were
engaged in similar speculation. It was a notion she
knew she must dispel. "I like Morgan very well," she
said, "and enjoy his company. But he is just my
nephew by marriage and you must not be imagining
that it is more than that.''

"Really? And yet I thought—" She broke off
abruptly. China's words brought her to the conclusion
that something had definitely occurred to bring to an
end to what she had come to regard as a promising
romance. Instinct told her that the carefree manner
that China had been affecting of late was a mask for
deeper feelings. Now the earl's sudden departure from
town was more readily explained. It was obvious that
China did not wish to confide in her, and she had too
much regard for both China and Morgan to pry merely
to satisfy her own curiosity.

Thea shrugged as if to turn the matter off lightly. "I
don't think there will be much joy for Lady Margaret
in any case, in spite of Amelia's hints to the contrary.
Attractive gentlemen like Wrexford know only too well
the effect they have on our sex and often amuse themselves at our expense. Some of us are fortunate enough
to know better than to refine too much upon it." Then
obligingly she turned the subject, saying, "Alyce told
me you have engaged Trumble to decorate your rooms
in spring blossoms for your rout party. Didn't you find

him the most amusing little man? I had him do my
ballroom last year to celebrate Archie's and my fifth
anniversary, and learned far more about horticulture
than I ever wished to know.''

China gratefully seized upon this topic, though she
was not deceived that her friend had not guessed more
than she would have wished about her and Morgan. A
part of her wanted very much to pour out her hurt and
disturbed thoughts about Morgan, but she had become
used to keeping her own counsel, and her wounded
heart and pride made her appear too ridiculous in her
own eyes to admit that despite her proclaimed beauty
and attractiveness to men, she had not the power to
attach the one man who had captured her own heart.
It was at moments like this that she most missed Sally
Weston. To her alone might she have unburdened herself.

The preparations for her rout took up a considerable
amount of her time and energy for the next few days,
and her spirits rose in a corresponding ratio to her
receding thoughts of Morgan and her own unhappiness. She awoke the morning of the party feeling better than she had in a considerable time and marveled
at her own power of recuperation. She had known that
she would grow less troubled with time, but she had not
expected it so soon. It made her wonder if she could
have been quite as in love with Morgan as she had
imagined. If he decided to remain at Ferris for the rest
of the Season and did not go to Brighton as planned
either, she would have been very glad of it.

China put as much care into her appearance that
night as she had to the preparations for her party. She
chose a gown in an icy blue shade with a silver gauze
overdress that was in the latest kick of fashion, quite
daringly cut and cunningly designed to caress her in
seductive folds with every movement.

To her surprise and pleasure, for the first time
Amelia sought her advice on her dress for the party.
Amelia had disdained China's fashionable flair and had

never once paid her any compliment on her appearance, but on the night of the party she came to China's room as Lucy was putting the finishing touches to China's hair, placing delicate blooms among China's high-piled curls to complement the floral decor of the saloons in which the revels would be held.

Amelia's gown was a similar shade of blue but made in a more modest fashion as befitted her age and unmarried state. Her gown did not lack style, but its cut was too unimaginative to do her the justice it might have done. She regarded China without envy, though, and when China finally dismissed Lucy, she asked a bit diffidently if China might suggest some manner of accessory to complement her dress.

"Prentice made a remark the other night," Amelia admitted, "that he would be glad when we are married and I might dress in a less insipid manner."

China had no doubt that the young man's careless remark had wounded Amelia and wondered that Amelia had not chosen to respond to it with more spirit than she appeared to have done. She privately agreed with Prentice, though she deplored his want of tact, but if it had the result of bringing Amelia to her for advice, then she would choose to be grateful to him.

China regarded her stepdaughter critically for a moment and then opened a drawer in her dressing table, searching through several lengths of ribbon until she found the one she sought, and then she went to the chest where her jewel case was kept and selected a simple, delicately wrought pendant and earrings of sapphires and tiny diamonds. She rang for Lucy again, and when the maid appeared she was requested to re-coif the younger girl's hair, threading the ribbon through her hair, while China removed the insipid string of pearls from about Amelia's neck.

Amelia was not blessed with natural curls as China was, but the application of a curling iron, and Lucy's considerable skill with dressing hair, quickly transformed the severe and unbecoming pinned-up braids in which Amelia usually dressed her hair into a softer style that was suited to her age and yet gave her an air of greater sophistication. The barest amount of rouge was applied to Amelia's cheeks and her lashes delicately darkened with kohl. The sapphires and diamonds glowed against her petal-white breast and her unremarkable appearance was subtly transformed. Amelia would never be a beauty as China was, but in her quieter way she was quite lovely, and the happy sparkle in her eyes as she viewed herself in the mirror hung above China's dressing table enhanced the improvement considerably.

The smile she turned on China was the most genuine that China had yet to receive from her. "Thank you, China," she said. "I know that Prentice will be pleased."

China returned her smile and said a bit dryly, "I hope that *you* are pleased. You should dress to your own satisfaction and let Prentice look to himself."

Amelia did not appear to take affront at the implied criticism of her beloved Prentice. "I only wish him to be proud of me. His father has decided that Prentice might be suited to a career in politics, for he thinks he is too idle. He means to put him up for a seat in his gift later in the year when it is expected to become vacant. If I am to entertain important personages after we are married, I know I must do my best to be a credit to Prentice."

China thought Amelia's retiring nature ill-suited to the role of political hostess, but she made no comment and they went down together to greet their guests who would shortly be arriving for dinner before the party began.

China did not expect to see Morgan at her table, though he had been one of the select few invited to dine, but she found that despite the moderation in her feelings toward him, she felt a faint stab of disappointment that he did not appear. The dinner was a complete success, with all present in excellent spirits, and China regarded it as a good omen for the remainder of the evening.

As guests for the rout party began to arrive, Lady Wrexford received them in company with China, Amery, and Amelia, for which China was grateful. The presence of the older woman, far more experienced than she at entertaining, helped to put her at her ease, for this was the most lavish party she had planned since coming to England. The only thing that marred her pleasure was the arrival of Lord Prentice, who had been invited to dinner but had declined pleading a previous engagement, in the company of Dana Bovell, who had not been sent a card. It was apparent to China at once that Prentice was a bit foxed and she was vexed that he had taken it upon himself to bring an uninvited guest, particularly Dana Bovell. But Amelia greeted both men with obvious pleasure, not seeming to notice Prentice's inebriated condition, and if Lady Wrexford disapproved of Prentice's and Bovell's presumption, she was too well-bred to give any sign of it. China, too, had no choice but to make Bovell welcome, though she privately wished him at Jerico. Jack was one of the last to arrive and his presence, at least, helped to dispel her annoyance.

The secret of successful entertainment, Lady Wrexford had advised China, was good food, good wine, and good company, and China had provided all three in abundance. She moved about the three saloons thrown open to accommodate her guests attending to each one and gracefully accepting their compliments. Supper was announced at midnight and very few of her guests had left to attend other revels; it was plain that all were enjoying themselves, and China felt a decided sense of self-congratulation.

China felt too exuberant to have much appetite and she merely picked at the excellent food Sir Henry had

insistently procured for her before excusing herself to
have a word with the musicians in the first saloon
whom she had hired to play a soft background accom-
paniment to the conversation of her guests. She then
journeyed belowstairs to compliment her chef and his
staff for the excellent supper, and it was on her return
to her guests that she passed an antechamber in which
a number of tables had been set up for card playing
for those who preferred it to conversation, and she
heard her name called softly.

She did not at first recognize the voice and she entered the room to find Prentice quite alone, since the
players who had peopled the room earlier were still
discussing their supper. He came up to her at once and
drew her farther into the room. "My compliments,
fair lady," he said warmly. "You have acquitted yourself admirably as a hostess. In the future you will find
cards for whatever entertainment you choose to give
avidly sought after."

"Thank you, Prentice," China said, discreetly
withdrawing her hand from his. "I think the evening
has gone very well. But I had best return to the supper
room before my neglect of my guests quite spoils the
impression I have made thus far."

As if he hadn't heard her, he closed the distance
between them, coming to stand close enough to her to
make her uncomfortable. "It is not just your gift of
pleasing your guests that delights, China. Your beauty
tonight is dazzling. I think you have managed to be-
witch every man present. If you were to bestow your
fair hand on a man with political ambitions, I have no
doubt he would find himself prime minister in short
order."

China did not take pleasure in his fulsome compliments. Given what Amelia had said to her of his new
ambitions, she had the uneasy feeling that he was
speaking of himself. "I should imagine it would take
more than a flair for social gatherings and an attractive

wife to make any man's career," she said in a flat way, hoping he would take the hint.

"But both are very necessary accouterments in our society," he replied. "I shall be standing for Parliament soon, and it is a matter that has become of some importance to me."

There was an overbrightness in his eyes that made her believe that his inebriated condition had worsened rather than improved. She suspected unhappily that in entering the room she had stepped into exactly the situation she had been taking considerable effort to avoid. His words and the caressing note in his voice told her that he was about to attempt to make love to her and she hoped to deflect this by reminding him of his supposed attachment to Amelia. "No doubt Amelia will prove herself to be all that you would wish in that respect. She is young and still inexperienced, but she will learn quickly all she must do to help you advance your career."

"I have been wondering if she will find herself suited to the role," he said, as if musing on the idea. "She does not really enjoy company as you and I do. I think she prefers a quieter style of life."

"You knew that when you asked her to be your wife," China reminded him a shade tartly, and moved away from him nearer to the door. "It is a bit late to be changing horses in midstream."

To her dismay he followed her and slipped a constraining arm about her waist. "China," he said in an avid voice, his face very near to hers and nearly overpowering her with the scent of strong spirits, "Don't pretend to misunderstand me. I know you feel you must be circumspect because of my attachment to Amelia, but don't pretend you are indifferent to me. I have known since the night we met that something passed between us that could not be denied. I have been fighting it as well, but I know now that I was sadly mistaken in my regard for Amelia. There is affection, certainly, but it is as toward a sister. I should never have deceived myself that it was anything warmer.''

China listened in amazement to his brazenness. ''Then you should communicate your change of heart to Amelia, not to me,'' she recommended. She reached to remove his arm, but he put his other hand behind her head, and forced her lips to his. She would not lower herself to struggle in his embrace but let him kiss her without according him the smallest degree of response. ''I think you forget yourself, my lord,'' she said icily as his lips left hers. ''Your assumption of my return of your feelings is entirely false. I tolerate you as Amelia's friend alone.''

He ignored her, planting burning kisses on her ear and throat, and China felt a faint stab of alarm. She could not imagine that he would attempt to ravish her in her own home when it was full of guests, but if he was quite castaway he might let his passion run away with his common sense. She inched her fingers between them, realizing that words would not suffice to free her from his unwanted embrace. Before she could push him away, the sound of someone entering the room made her turn to see Amelia standing near the door, her expression one of astonished horror.

Summoning her strength, China at last freed herself. It was only then that Prentice became aware of Amelia's presence, and if she had been a disinterested observer, China would have found his patent dismay comical. ''Amelia, it is not what it seems,'' he said with a slight slur to his words.

''How could you do such a thing,'' Amelia said, her voice strained with threatened tears.

It took China a moment to realize that it was herself and not Prentice that Amelia addressed. China's composure was too ruffled to permit of her usual tact. She was not only upset by what she had just undergone, she was furious that this semipublic display of his impudence had been discovered by Amelia, who clearly was prepared to put all blame on China for her betrothed's betrayal of her affections. "Don't be foolish," she said sharply to Amelia. "You must have seen that I was trying to free myself. I would scarcely welcome the advances of a man who would make love to me while all but betrothed to another."

"You may think me a fool, but I am not," Amelia said hotly, her voice catching on a sob. "I have always known you for what you are since the day Papa wrote to us to tell us that he had married you. Your pretense to be sweet and unaffected may convince others, but I know just how common you are. Dana has told me how everyone in Macao laughed up their sleeves at poor Papa while you cuckolded him with his closest friend, and you have even had the brazenness to bring that man here to Papa's house. I suppose no number of conquests are enough for you, you must even play the slut with the man you know to be promised to me."

Prentice said nothing, moving a little away from them, quite willing to let China bear the brunt of censure for his reprehensible behavior. China cast him a look of such contempt that he had the grace to color. China's own color had drained at the vile epithets which her stepdaughter spat out at her. "I have not thus far presumed to question your choice, Amelia, but you are certainly a fool if you do not know this . . . man for what he is. He has been attempting to make love to me from the day we were introduced, and only succeeded as far as he has by catching me off guard tonight. If it is not me, it will surely be some other woman who captures his fancy, and if you marry him you will find yourself humiliated time and again."

"I won't listen to your lies," Amelia said shrilly. "Prentice loves me and has always been devoted to me before you came here. Because I have not spoken does not mean I have not seen the way you have been making up to him. He is a man and could not remain unaffected by your deliberate design to gain his attention.''

"His devotion is to your fortune, not to you," China said plainly.

Amelia put her hands to her ears as if to block China's words. "You are a common whore," she said histrionically. "You disgrace the name of Rawdon."

China was too livid herself to think clearly. The advances she had thought only earlier that evening to have made in her relationship with her stepdaughter had clearly been no more than on the surface. No amount of balm applied in a calmer moment would erase this scene from either of their minds. It was the deadening of her hopes that fueled her anger into a hostility to match Amelia's. Without thinking, she slapped the girl smartly across the face. A brief, shocked silence followed before Amelia finally dissolved into tears. Horrified at what she had done, though she did not think the action undeserved, she turned and boxed Lord Prentice's ears for good measure, for he was the cause of the destruction of her peace. China turned on her heel to leave the room and nearly collided with Morgan who was entering, closing the door behind him.

"What the devil is going on?" he said in a stern voice. "There are people in the hall returning from supper and you can be heard quite clearly."

None of the three occupants in the room replied to him and from China's furious glare, the fact that her hair and dress were slightly disarranged, the sheepish appearance of Purdham, and Amelia's hysterical weeping, he formed his own, fairly accurate assumption of what it was he had interrupted. He met China's eyes and then passed on to look at Purdham as if observing a particularly disagreeable insect. That gentleman did not meet his eyes, but pushed past him without ceremony and left the room. Morgan smiled grimly, but made no comment. He turned his attention to Amelia, who had cast herself into a chair and was weeping with abandon.

"Whatever it is that has occurred to overset you, Amelia, have the countenance to save your vapors for the privacy of your own chamber," he said with a notable lack of sympathy. "We have guests in the house and if you do not wish to make scandal, you had best compose yourself."

His matter-of-factness instead of affronting Amelia made her pause in her weeping and rise to cast herself against his chest. "It is That Woman's fault. She is a witch. She destroyed Papa's life. He should probably still be alive today if not for her. Now she will take Prentice from me if she can. She will ruin us all if we let her."

He put his arms about Amelia while she wept more quietly against his shirtfront. He looked up at China over the girl's head, but his expression was unreadable. China did not flinch from his gaze. If he wanted to believe Amelia's hysterical accusations, he was welcome to do so; she would not stoop to an unnecessary defense. It would doubtless only confirm what he was only too ready to believe of her on his own. As upset as Amelia, though not given to histrionics, she was past caring at that moment.

"If you do not calm yourself, poppet," he said more gently to Amelia, "you shall complete your ruin. You would not wish to wash our dirty linen in public. We shall remain here for a bit until you can do so, and China will return to her guests to inform anyone interested that you have been taken of a violent headache and have retired for the night to your rooms."

He glanced at China again and she thought she saw a faint smile in his eyes that she had no idea how to read. She did exactly as he suggested, leaving the room without having spoken a word.

All of China's considerable reserves were put to the

test for the remainder of the evening. All the happiness she had felt at the success of her party had vanished. She still smiled and conversed with her guests with admirable composure, but she could not wait for the time when the last of them was shown to the door.

It was also plain to her that the evening would be remembered for more than her skill as a hostess. Though she made the excuses that Morgan had provided for her, there were those who knew or guessed that some untoward event had occurred within the family and she had no doubt that whispered gossip had already begun.

Lady Wrexford, beyond looking at her in a questioning manner when she returned to the principal saloon, made no attempt to discover what had occurred until the party was at an end. Morgan did not appear again, and China supposed he remained with Amelia to soothe her and perhaps prevent her from giving in to her emotions and behaving in a way that would overset their careful attempt to quell as much talk as they could. She had no idea when Morgan had arrived; he had not been in the supper room when she had left it, and how many others knew of his presence in the house she had no idea.

Prentice appeared to have left, but Dana Bovell, for all that he was uninvited, remained conversing with her legitimate guests with an effrontery which would have amazed her if she had not come to believe that there was no degree of arrogance which that man could not attain. Though she had not responded to what Amelia had claimed Bovell had said of her, she had not forgotten it, and she doubted her command of herself to ask him to leave without creating another scene. She avoided so much as acknowledging his presence, but as a number of people began to leave at last, he came up to her to take his leave with an impudent smile.

"You did not expect to see me tonight, I suppose,

fair lady,'' he said. ''But I knew I might impose upon our previous acquaintance and that you should not object.''

China knew he was casting it up to her that he had managed to spend the evening in her rooms, drinking her champagne, eating the excellent supper she had provided, and all without her approbation. ''I should not have expected to see anyone who did not receive a card of invitation from me tonight,'' she said baldly, too vexed for civility.

But Bovell laughed. He was clearly enjoying her discomfiture. ''I thought perhaps it had gone astray,'' he said mildly. ''I know you as too well-bred and kindhearted to forget an old friend. But perhaps I am mistaken?''

''You are mistaken,'' she snapped, her eyes flashing her annoyance. Lady Jane Southby and her daughter were about to leave and were speaking with Alyce and would soon pass on to her. If they should overhear China's exchanges with Dana Bovell, there would be even more cause for gossip over the breakfast cups.

''Then perhaps I am not mistaken in another assumption,'' he said, and waited for her reply.

But there was none. China regarded him stonily, hoping that her lack of response would speed him on his way.

He sighed as if in great sorrow. ''I don't know why it is you should wish to see me excluded from your circle of friends, Lady Rawdon, but it appears to me to be so. I have ever been an admirer of yours and a faithful friend.'' He paused to add significance to his next words. ''But your success, if I may term it such, has been incomplete. I think you may find other members of your family more kindly disposed toward me.''

''I doubt a man of your character, if *I* may term it as such,'' China said in a sardonic voice that was almost a whisper to prevent it from carrying, ''may be a friend or give fidelity to anyone. You have certainly not done so toward me. If you are brazen enough to presume upon your acquaintance with Sir Amery or Miss Rawdon to insinuate yourself in this house again, I shall have you removed forcibly if necessary.''

Lady Jane was upon them as she finished this speech, which even in her anger she knew was likely unwise, and she turned her back on him pointedly to receive that lady's expressed gratitude for her hospitality. She held Lady Jane and her daughter in conversation longer than necessary, until she was certain that Bovell had at last left her house. She wished she might have held her tongue, for she knew the degree of spite of which he was capable, but the events of the night had robbed her of her usual control on her temper.

China had no taste for strong spirits, but she did not hesitate to accept Amery's offer to join him in the library for a glass of brandy when the last guest had finally departed. He, too, of course, was aware that something portentous had happened and, casting a critical eye over his stepmother, he decided she needed something of a more medicinal nature than champagne punch to soothe her before she sought her bed.

Lady Wrexford also remained and went with them to library where China was finally forced to give a somewhat expurgated account of the events that had occurred in the card room. Lady Wrexford was indignant on both Amelia's and China's behalf, but Amery was no more ready to believe the worst of his childhood friend than Amelia had been. ''I know Pren behaved like a dashed bounder tonight,'' he said placatingly, ''but he was pretty well up in the trees when he arrived. He usually doesn't drink so much at dinner, but the wine was excellent and he said that Lodder gave them cognac he had just received from France after dinner and he overdid it a bit. I daresay tomorrow he will be feeling worse from having made such a cake of himself than he does from the effects of the alcohol.''

"I don't think alcohol is an adequate excuse for the way that Prentice conducted himself tonight," Lady Wrexford stated in her mild way. "We have all noticed that he has been much taken by China since he met her, and it does not surprise me in the least that he dared to assume she would welcome his advances. Lord Prentice Purdham thinks rather too much of himself, if you ask me."

"But I am sure he never meant to offer China any insult," Amery said staunchly. "The Purdhams have been friends of ours forever."

China wondered what that had to say to anything, but she only said, "Whether he intended it or not, he has caused a great deal of trouble this night. Amelia was most distraught and will not allow that it was not entirely my fault." She sighed. "I might have hoped that my wretched experience could have been turned to good advantage if she had been willing to admit to herself that her lover is faithless, but she is determined to think that I encouraged his advances."

"Amelia was no doubt speaking out of her distress," Amery said, apparently willing to overlook even his knowledge of Amelia's prejudice against China to smooth the matter over. "When she has had a bit of rest and time to think, she will realize that it was just the result of Prentice being jug-bitten."

The look China gave to Amery was far more eloquent than words could have been to express her opinion of this likelihood. His eyes dropped away from hers and he quickly downed the remainder of the amber liquid in his glass. "Well, it is done in any event," he said briskly, "and we shall have to make the best of it." He went first to Lady Wrexford and then to China, kissing each lightly and advising them not to let what had happened disturb their rest.

"Aren't you going up to bed, Amery?" Lady Wrexford said, a troubled look in her eyes.

"No. I promised a few friends that I would make

an appearance at an inn we frequent in the city after the party." He smiled disarmingly at the dowager. "Don't fret, Aunt Alyce. I shall be back before the birds begin to sing, and won't need Barrett to see me up the stairs tonight, I promise you."

Lady Wrexford made no further comment as she rose to leave. But China sensed her continued concern. "Amery is right, you know. We must not tease ourselves about him. He has assured me that he is just enjoying himself until he must return to school. Not even Morgan believes that he will fall into any serious scrapes."

Lady Wrexford squeezed China's hand with gratitude for her comforting words before releasing it to pick up her reticule from the table in the hall. "I know you are right, but I have not yet gotten over the habit of worrying myself about the children even though they are quite grown. He was a very mischievous child, but he was never willfully bad, just getting into the sort of trouble I suppose all boys must as they grow. Heaven knows," she added with a sigh, "we have had enough to concern us for one night without Amery."

A sudden thought occurred to China. "Where is Morgan? He never returned to the company. He surely can't still be with Amelia."

"I suspect he preferred to slip out again unnoticed once he had turned her over to her maid for comfort," the dowager suggested. "He must have arrived only minutes before the fuss began, and not many people even knew of it. I did not myself until you told me. I thought him still at Ferris when I left Wrexford House."

"Why should he make a point of coming," China said, more to herself than to Lady Wrexford, "when he likely had traveled all day and had only just arrived in town, only to leave again without a word?"

Lady Wrexford clearly found no mystery in her son's behavior. "Perhaps he thought his sudden appearance so late would only occasion more talk after what had happened.''

China allowed the matter to drop. Privately, she suspected it was something more than that. He had probably left to avoid her after what he had witnessed. He would put the worst construction on it, she had no doubt, and give at least some credence to Amelia's vituperation; she could not doubt that after their last argument. She was aware again of the gnawing hollow feeling when she thought of him, which had only just left her completely that same morning—or rather yesterday morning, since Wednesday was now advanced. Resolutely, she pushed all thought of Morgan from her mind, a surprisingly easy task in her weariness. There was not very much either of them might have said or done to make the breach between them any worse, so what did it matter after all.

19

CHINA'S WEARINESS was more emotional than physical and she awoke fairly early the next morning in spite of the late hour she had sought her bed, feeling better than she would have thought possible. It was a glorious June morning and even the usually noisome air of the city smelt fresh and sweet. China decided it was too lovely a day to spend either in bed or in the morning room setting stitches. She rang for Lucy to have her habit set out and her favorite gelding saddled and brought to her from the mews.

Only Annabelle was in the breakfast room when China came downstairs, and for once China would not heed her pleas to be taken along for the ride. China did not want a comfortable saunter in the park but to gallop full out once she had gone beyond the promenade. Seeing that China did not mean to relent, Annabelle gave it up and China left only in the company of her groom.

China chose Green Park over Hyde Park because it was less likely that she would meet any acquaintance there at this early hour. As soon as she dared, China called to her groom to follow her as best he could and let her horse out to enjoy the exhilaration of headlong flight. Even away from the main promenade, she knew her behavior would be condemned as hoydenish if she were observed, but she was not, and she returned to the promenade at a sedate trot.

She had not gone far when she met with Jack, who

was in company with two of his acquaintances whom he made known to her at once. The four stood talking commonplaces for several minutes when they were approached by another lone horseman who proved to be Morgan. China knew that he rode some mornings in the park, for she had ridden with him on several occasions, but she had had no thought that she might meet him this morning.

Whatever he might choose to read into finding her with Jack, he greeted Jack with every appearance of pleasure and a bit of surprise, since he had not known of that man's return to England until then. "I think you have made the wise choice," Morgan said when apprised of Jack's intent to take up his responsibilities in Sussex. "I have made the same one myself. Conditions in the East are fast making it fit only for merchants who think the gain worth the risk and soldiers who court it for the love of danger."

Jack agreed with this sentiment and, turning to China, asked if she had done with her ride and wished to be escorted back to Rawdon House.

China had intended to go home, but something in the way that Morgan was regarding her made her hesitate. She supposed he must wish to speak with her about what had occurred the previous night, and though she doubted she would take any pleasure in the discussion, she found she very much wanted to know what he would say to her. "I think I shall ride for a bit longer," she said to Jack, and was bold enough to add, addressing Morgan, "Do you just begin your exercise, my lord? Perhaps you will accompany me."

She thought Morgan's smile to her a bit sardonic, but his tone was pleasant enough. "It would be my delight."

Jack and his friends left them and China and Morgan remained where they were, watching them depart until they were out of sight. Morgan maneuvered his horse beside hers and said in an undertone, "Dismiss your groom. I want a private word with you."

He did not sound angry or upset, so she risked quizzing him. "Would you wish me to be guilty of impropriety, my lord? I thought you were concerned for my reputation."

He made her a brief smile, acknowledging the hit. "I deserve that, I suppose," he said dryly. "I don't want an audience for what I wish to say to you."

"You quite frighten me. Perhaps I should have accepted Jack's offer," she said provocatively, wondering what response it would elicit.

But Morgan refused to rise to the bait. "Humor me, China," he implored.

Wondering if she would regret it, China did as he asked and they started at a walk along the way she had just come. China waited patiently for him to speak, but he rode beside her in silence for several minutes.

"You are strangely silent for one who claims to have something to say," she said chidingly when she could wait no longer for him to begin.

His response gave her no satisfaction. "There is a path just beyond that oak tree," he said, pointing with his crop, and urged his horse to a trot, forcing her to follow his suit.

He led her through a thick overgrowth of trees to a clearing in which was a small and quite charming pond. It very naturally brought back to China the morning in Macao when they had ridden out to the stream, which discomfitted her.

At the edge of the clearing he dismounted and put his hand out to China to help her to do the same. She made no protest. By tacit consent they walked toward the pond.

"I had a long talk with Amelia after you left us," he said at last.

"I suppose she told you what happened," China said warily, wondering if he had believed Amelia's version of events.

"She told me she found you in Prentice's arms."

"She found me struggling to be free of them," China said tartly.

"Yes," he said, surprising her, "that was the impression I had when I came into the room. Don't look so surprised," he advised, smiling. "I don't automatically think the worst of you, whatever you may think. I know what Prentice is, even if Amelia is willfully blind to his faults."

"I do wonder at it," she said frankly. "You leapt to the assumption that Jack Reid was my lover on less evidence than that."

He did not respond to this provocative remark. "I think you should know something else that Amelia said to me," he said instead. "If it were just she involved, I would put it down to her resentment of you and say nothing, but it is more than that."

His tone was level, but China felt a sudden gripping inside of her, knowing that what he was about to say would be more than just the usual vituperation she had come to expect from her stepdaughter. "Nothing Amelia could find to say against me would surprise me," she said bitterly. "She was determined to hate me before we even met."

"I think this may." He paused for a moment before speaking again, as if seeking the best way to begin. "Bovell has not found an easy acceptance with many of our acquaintances since he has come to England. I think he thought he might trade on his acquaintance with you to do so."

China stared at him, astonished at his words. It was as if he had overheard her brief exchange with Bovell the night before, though that was not possible. Though this sounded like a diversion, China assumed it was not. "Yes," she agreed, some of her annoyance of the previous night showing in her voice. "I did not send him a card for last night, but he persuaded Prentice to bring him uninvited. He had the arrogance to inti-

mate quite openly that he thought I wished to see him
deliberately excluded from polite circles.''

"Bovell has been spending a deal of time in company with Purdham. He has found a niche of sorts with
some of the wilder bucks. I doubt any voiced resentment of you would be heeded in most quarters, but he
has said things—to your discredit—to Purdham which
Purdham has repeated to Amelia.''

"Which she is only too ready to hear," China interrupted. "Gossip from Macao about me and Jack, I
suppose.''

"Yes, but there is more.''

He paused again and China felt a faint chill, though
the day was warm. She thought she knew what he was
about to say, and her fears were realized.

"I don't believe he has made any outright accusations—that is no doubt Amelia's embellishment—but he
has implied that Clive's death was not what it seemed.''

China felt as if her heart had stopped for a moment.
"In what way?" she asked, and was surprised that her
voice was so steady.

"Bovell has said that Clive had not appeared to be
ill only a few days before his death.''

"He had been feeling unwell for some time," China
said with perfect truth. "His horror of illness or weakness made him determined to give no sign of it and he
managed to deceive even me for a time. The night
before he died it became apparent just how sick he
really was, but he refused to permit me to send for
Jack. He became so upset when I insisted that I thought
it best to humor him at least for another day. By then
it was too late.''

Her voice caught on her last words and she turned
away from him. Morgan placed his hand on her arm
in a comforting way. "You don't have to convince me
that Clive could be pigheaded about such things. Once
when he was visiting Ferris, he came down with influenza and shut himself in his room with only his valet

to attend him until he was better. I am afraid there is still more,'' he said with surprising gentleness. ''If I didn't think it would be to your disadvantage not to know the worst, I would keep it to myself.''

China's eyes stung with unshed tears. She could not turn again and look at him, for she knew she would begin to cry if she did. ''I want to know,'' she said brusquely.

''Bovell also implies that there are questions about the manner in which Clive's death was reported. He has said that no one was known to have viewed the body except you and Jack Reid, and that it was on Reid's word alone that Clive's death was accepted as the result of some unknown infection.''

China's desire to weep was evaporated by a sudden searing anger. ''You need not say more,'' she said with icy control. ''Since Jack is supposed to have been my lover, he doubtless abetted me in murdering my husband to gain his fortune.''

''I think that is what he implies,'' Morgan said quietly. ''I'm afraid it is what Amelia infers.''

''You were wrong, Morgan,'' China said, turning to him, her eyes bright with fury, ''I am not surprised. Is it what you also infer?'' she asked bluntly.

''I would not be telling you this if I did.''

China covered her face with her hands and Morgan enfolded her in a comforting, but avuncular, embrace. After last night she had not supposed that matters could be worse, and now she knew that thought as folly. This was far worse than she had feared. There was a seductiveness in Morgan's embrace that had nothing to do with desire and for a brief moment she was nearly persuaded to tell him the complete truth about Clive's illness and death. But her sense prevailed over her emotions. If matters had fallen out differently with Morgan, she might have trusted him—she had been tempted to do so more than once when they were in Macao. Whatever he might say about not believing the worst of her, she feared that when he learned she had been less than frank with him he would have the doubts which he now claimed not to possess.

"Amelia wanted to leave Rawdon House last night," Morgan said, breaking into her thoughts. "I persuaded her against it, which you may not thank me for, but it is for the best. We have no way of knowing if Bovell has whispered his poison into any other ears, and an open breach between you and Amelia would be given the worst possible construction if he has."

"Dear lord," China said, raising her head. "I feel as if I am about to face the tumbrel."

"We have no guillotine in England," Morgan said with a faint smile. "I knew this would disturb you very much, but it is not as black as it seems. I think I managed to convince Amelia before I left last night that she was allowing her imagination and her prejudice against you to run away with her. There will be a great deal of strain between you for a time, no doubt, but you must jog along with her as best you can for appearance's sake. I thought it only fair for you to know what you are up against."

It felt so comfortable and natural to have the support of his arms about her that she had a momentary wish that they might remain this way forever. But she knew it was self-deception to imagine that he meant anything more than to offer her a sort of comfort after he had so disrupted her peace. He would do the same for Amelia or Annabelle. She did not for a moment suppose he had forgotten the things they had last said to each other any more than she had. No doubt, his concern was for the potential scandal that might be caused by this and it had made him put aside his personal feelings. Knowing she might never again enjoy this physical closeness to him, she did not want it to end too quickly, but perversely, as if to punish herself for her self-indulgence, she did so, moving away from the circle of his arms.

"Forgive me, China," he said, and China was non-plussed. It was the last thing she had expected.

China raised her head. "For which offense?" she asked him, her manner ascerbic.

"All of them. You have not plighted your troth to Portmer?"

She almost had forgotten that she had told him of that dubious offer. She shook her head and said gravely, "No. We should not suit. I have decided I should be satisfied with what I have and need not marry to advantage again."

"You mean to cast all of my sins up to me, I see," he said on a sigh. "I suppose I cannot blame you."

"No."

"I have had time to regret the things that I said to you the last time we met. I have never wished to quarrel with you, but we do so nevertheless."

"Then perhaps it is best if we do not meet very often," China suggested, giving him no encouragement. She thought she had been successful in setting her mind against him and she did not want soft words from him now to tempt her. It was for the best if they were to mend their fences yet again, for appearance's sake if nothing else, but she didn't want to give him the power to wound her again.

"I don't want that."

She looked at him with feigned surprise. "Have you finally discovered, then, what it is you do want?"

"I think so."

"Still hedging your bets, my lord," she said a shade caustically, and walked to the edge of the pond so that the water at the low bank nearly lapped at her shoes.

"No. I want you to be my wife, China."

She had thought these the words she had most wanted to hear spoken by him, but she felt strangely unmoved. "I thought you did not wish for a wife," she said, turning to him.

"I went to Ferris intending to put a physical as well

as an emotional distance between us, but it wouldn't answer." He placed cool fingers against her warm cheek. "It was as well that I did so, though. It made me aware of how necessary you are to my happiness. Try as I might, I could not put you from my mind. I want you, China, as I have never wanted any woman before in my life."

He had said everything that she could have wished except that he loved her. "Your proposal sounds rather like the one you accused Sir Henry of making to me. You cannot bed me so you will wed me."

"Do you wish to misunderstand me, China," he asked dryly, "or merely to pay me out? I want to make love to you again more than you could imagine, but it is far more than that."

"Is it?" she asked with great seriousness.

"Dear lord," he said, goaded. "What more do you wish me to say?"

"That you love me, perhaps," she said very quietly.

"Why else would I wish to marry you?" he said a shade crossly.

"You do not sound like a man in love," she informed him.

"At this moment I want to shake you as much as I want to kiss you. As charming as your capriciousness can be at times, it is very vexing as well."

China said nothing, merely meeting his gaze steadily. He laughed and gathered her into his arms again. "I love you, China. With all of my heart. Marry me, my darling girl, please."

China let him kiss her then, and they were so occupied for a considerable time. Yet she did not give herself over to the happiness that should have been hers. Even telling her that he loved her proved not to be enough for her. They were both quite breathless when he finally released her.

Smiling at her, with his own happiness apparent, Morgan kissed her lightly again and they began to retrace their steps to the edge of the clearing where their horses grazed. "You know you still have not given me your answer," he said, quizzing her.

"I know," she responded, her tone so grave that he stopped and she did the same. "Do you still believe that I married Clive for what I thought I should gain?" she demanded.

"China . . ."

"And think that Jack Reid was my lover before and after Clive's death?"

"I think you have punished me sufficiently for one day," he said with teasing reproach, not willing to believe that her response to him could be negative. "Cry quits, beauty. My own past is scarcely without blemish. What does it matter?"

"And you still wish to marry me, in spite of thinking me an adventuress and adultress?"

"I didn't say that I thought that," he said with a bit of tartness.

"You didn't say that you did not." She turned and went to gather up her horse's reins.

"China, if we are to play games, I wish you will tell me the rules. I have no intention of quarreling with you again."

"There is no quarrel." She turned to him and her voice when she spoke sounded weary. "I know the honor you do me, Morgan, but I can't marry you."

She was about to lead her horse to a tree stump so that she might remount, but he caught the reins just below the bit. "China, have I been presumptuous? Are you telling me you don't return my regard?"

China was astonished at her own calm and no less astonished that she had refused his offer. It was what she had dreamed of and fantasized about since the first week of their acquaintance, when she realized that in Morgan Wrexford she had met the first man ever to stir her heart. She supposed her determination to put aside her hopes had succeeded only too well. She loved him, she wanted him, but not if he doubted her. She would always know, no matter how hard she tried to put it from her mind, that Morgan believed that she had schemed to marry Clive and had cuckolded him, even if he was willing to forgive and forget her past. And that doubt of her would likely fester for him as well. She recalled only too well the comments he had made to her about her flirtatious nature and what he had called her encouragement of every rake and libertine in town. True, he had spoken in anger, but if she married Morgan and he did not completely trust her, she might well spend the remainder of her life attempting to be circumspect and weighing her every word to other men for fear that he would suspect she was playing him false as he believed she had played Clive false. It would eventually destroy their love for each other, she had no doubt of it.

"It isn't that," she said coolly. "Will you assist me, Morgan, or let me mount myself? I wish to return to Mount Street."

His expression was mildly stunned. He really had had no doubt of her answer and was well paid out for his vanity. Mechanically, he helped her into the saddle, but he recaptured the reins before she could gather them up. "China, I don't give a damn about anything that happened before we met. I think you did come to love Clive in a fashion and you said yourself you were not in love with him when you married him. What does it signify now? If I love you and you are in love with me, there is nothing else to consider."

"What of Jack?"

"What of him?" Morgan asked, and China felt there was at least a trace of suspicion in his tone, confirming her belief that she was doing the right thing, however painful.

"He is my friend. He settles now in England and we shall continue to meet. Will you wonder each time we do if it is as lovers as well?"

"Not if you assure me there is nothing between you now."

China smiled sadly at the last word. "I assured you before that there never has been anything between Jack and me but friendship, but you do not believe it."

"I told you the past doesn't matter."

"It matters to me." She slipped her fingers through the reins, gently tugging them from his grasp.

He rested his head against her thigh for a moment, and that single act affected her more than anything he had said. She wanted to touch his head and retract everything she had said, but the moment passed and he raised his head, the supplicant look gone from his eyes.

"I won't beg you, China," he said without emotion. "If this is what you wish, so be it." He stepped back from her.

China wanted to speak but her voice caught in her throat. She thought it was just as well, for she did not know what she would say to him. She applied her whip to her horse and rode away from him, back down the narrow lane that had led them to the clearing.

This time she was not as successful at keeping her thoughts at bay. One moment she castigated herself as the worst sort of fool for spurning her chance to be with the man she loved, and the next she was equally certain that happiness with a man who could not completely trust her would have been illusionary at best.

The only solution, she quickly discovered, was to keep herself occupied as much as possible and to fall into bed too weary to think. Over the next two days she accepted every invitation that came to her. She did not see Morgan again until the following night at the opera, which she attended with Sir Henry Portmer and Thea. He was in a box across from hers with friends only slightly known to China. He did not appear to notice her before the curtain came up and China would not permit herself the bittersweet pleasure of looking at him while he was absorbed in the music and gave her full attention to the stage as well.

But Morgan had seen her and at the first interval he came to their box for a brief visit. They exchanged little more than greetings, and conversation was general until he left them. It was not as difficult a meeting as China had feared, and she knew she had better accustom herself to being in his company again, since it was a thing she could not avoid.

After the opera they attended a party at Mrs. Addleson's and China finally returned home in the small hours of the morning as ready for her bed as she could wish to be. She arrived simultaneously with Amelia, who had been out that evening with Lady Margaret. She bade Amelia good night as she started up the stair but received no reply. It did not surprise her. Amelia had not spoken to her except when absolutely required to in front of others since the night of the rout party.

China was beginning to regret her decision to go to Brighton, but it was already made, the house was rented, and she was determined to do her best to take pleasure in her visit to the resort. One thing she had decided on was that she would not go to Ferris at the end of August as originally planned. She had yet to see the estate in Nottinghamshire which she had inherited from Clive, and she would use her excuse of wishing to view it to beg off from her promise to spend the remainder of the summer with the Rawdons. She thought that if it were habitable enough, she would not return to town for the Little Season either, but remain at Myerly at least until the holidays, when she could not in civility refuse Lady Wrexford's invitation to take Christmas with them. By that time she would surely have regained her peace and be able to meet with Morgan in perfect equanimity and Amelia would be wed to Prentice and living with him and the Purdhams at Longview.

These were her thoughts and her firm intentions until Friday when she attended a rather small gathering at Thea's. She went in company with Lady Wrexford, Amelia having chosen, as she had since the rout party, to avoid her company as much as possible. Amelia was present, though, having come with Lady Margaret, as was Prentice, who had been very circumspect whenever they had met since the night he had attempted to make love to her, and he spoke to her only when there were others about and Amelia could not take exception to it. Morgan was not present, though Thea had mentioned that she had sent him a card, and neither was Amery. Taken as she was with her own problems and out of Rawdon House for a good part of each day and night, she had not given much thought to her stepson, but in a dim way it did occur to her that she had seen little of her stepson since he had left her and his aunt in the bookroom the night of her party.

China had had no premonition of disaster for the evening; in the simple law of averages, she would have thought it unlikely since she had brooked so much to cut up her peace of late. Everyone present was fairly well known to her and liked by her and the start of the evening was very pleasurable. Unthinkingly, she addressed a light comment to Amelia as they stood in conversation in a small group of friends. Instead of replying, Amelia cast her a look of pure venom and abruptly walked away.

China might only have been vexed at her rudeness if a sudden silence had not descended on the group. China saw that their eyes were upon her and realized that the silence was a shocked one. Amelia had given the cut direct to her own stepmother. To her chagrin, China felt her color deepen and it seemed to her that no one wished to catch her eyes. A friend of Thea's, Isabel Bantry, then made some comment to Lord Hugerson and the moment passed, but China's humiliation did not. For the remainder of the evening she imagined that everyone was speaking in whispers that ceased as she approached, and she was very glad of it when Lady Wrexford, claiming tiredness, suggested that they leave.

The carriage drive to Mount Street was passed nearly

in silence until they were only a short distance from
Rawdon House. Then Lady Wrexford, who had been
screwing up her courage to do so for some time, finally spoke. "I fear I have not made a very good job
of raising Clive's children for him," she said with a
weary sigh. "Annabelle is a dear child, of course, but
then she is very like her mother in character. I blame
myself for what happened tonight."

"That is absurd," China said, the lowering of her
feelings reflected in her voice. She had said nothing
of Amelia's deliberate snub to Lady Wrexford, and
Lady Wrexford had not been present when it occurred,
so it was obvious that her fears that the incident had
been discussed among the company were confirmed.
"Amelia's lack of breeding is quite deliberate. She is
willful and single-minded, and I have frankly abandoned any hope of proving to her that I am not what
she believes me to be."

"I had hopes of it too," Lady Wrexford admitted
with a sigh. "Perhaps when she is finally wed to Prentice she will come to see things differently."

"I doubt it," China said with a short laugh. "She
will forever be thinking that I wish to take her husband
away from her, as she imagines I did her father. It
doesn't signify. If it had not been Prentice who caused
the breach between us, it would have been something
else. She wishes to hate me."

"Oh dear," Lady Wrexford said, distressed.
"Surely, it is not as strong as that."

China did not bother to make her a reply and merely
kissed the older woman's cheek in leavetaking as the
carriage came to a stop in front of Rawdon House.
China did not ring for Lucy but undressed herself,
preferring the solitude. As she sat at her dressing table
brushing out her hair, she completely revised her recently made plans. Going to Brighton now was out of
the question, as was going to Ferris, and she intended
to send word to Mr. James in the morning that he

should pay off the lease and inform the owner of the house that he might let it to someone else. She disliked disappointing Amery, who had no part in all that had occurred, but it could not be helped. He could go to Ferris or share Morgan's lodgings or do whatever else he wished. China intended to begin packing in the morning to go to Myerly. Amelia and Annabelle would have to return to Wrexford House, and Amery would probably choose to do the same. The Barretts could remain behind to close up the house.

She had not changed her mind in the morning, but she did not have the heart to say anything to Annabelle, who shared her breakfast full of happy chatter. She would tell Annabelle and Amery together later in the day, for she meant to begin her journey on the morrow. She would have to inform Lady Wrexford before the end of the day as well, and Amelia could be told the happy news that she no longer had to bear her stepmother's company by that lady, for China had no intention of seeking her out. Amery had not joined them by the time their breakfast was done, but that was not very surprising since he had not done so in several days. China felt a guilty start that she had given so little of her attention or thoughts to anything but her own problems of late, and she asked Annabelle if she knew if Amery were still abed.

Annabelle looked a little surprised. "I have not seen Amery since Thursday. I thought he must be gone to visit friends. He would not think to mention it to me, but you must know."

China did not like to admit that she did not. "He has been out much of late with his friends," she said slowly, as she tried to recall the last time she had spoken to her stepson. It was really reprehensible of her not to have taken note of his absence from Rawdon House, and equally reprehensible of Amery not to have let her know if he meant to be away for a day or so. She did not really think, though, that this was the case.

She did not intend to discuss Amery with his sister,

fearing to alarm her, but she was somewhat alarmed herself. It had been very convenient for her to accept Morgan's judgment that Amery was mature enough not to fall into any serious scrape, but in reality he was only twenty and little more than a boy. She had certainly fallen down on the trust handed over to her by Lady Wrexford when Clive's children had come to live with her, and she knew she must amend this before she left for Myerly. She was not very much acquainted with Amery's valet, Hopkins, but she would have a word with Barrett, who she knew would be discreet, and see if he had any inkling of Amery's present activities as soon as she had finished her breakfast.

She did so within a quarter-hour and left the interview with her butler much troubled. According to the servant, Amery had not been home since he had stopped in to change his clothes before going out Thursday evening. He had no idea where Amery was to be found at the moment, but since Sir Amery was occasionally given to spending the night with friends after his revels, it had not been particularly remarked even in the servants' quarters. China thanked him, displaying none of her growing concern, and resolved to speak to Hopkins after all, to get the names of Amery's friends in the hope of making discreet inquiries in case he did not put in an appearance in Mount Street soon. She supposed that she might have sought out Lord Prentice or Dana Bovell to discover news of Amery, but she shrank from either course unless it proved absolutely necessary.

She decided to give Amery until after luncheon to return to Mount Street and then went to the writing desk in the morning room to pen a brief note to Jack Reid.

20

JACK RESPONDED to her summons at once, arriving at Mount Street within the half hour. "My dear, China," he said as he kissed her in greeting, "I expected to find you in the midst of some great calamity when I received your note. I thought fashionable women of the *ton* did not rise from their beds before noon for anything less."

She smiled at his quizzing. "The habits of a lifetime are difficult to change. I find it easier to do with less sleep. But I do find myself in a situation that is not at all comfortable, and I wish you to help me if you will."

Jack assured her that he was hers to command and she told him at once that Morgan had told her that Dana Bovell had begun to spread his poison against her as he had in Macao. "He knew exactly which ears would be most receptive to him," she said. "He knew that through Prentice he would reach Amelia, and her feelings toward me are so little secret that he must have easily learned that she would welcome anything to my discredit."

Jack leaned forward in his chair, resting his hands on the knobby head of his walking stick. He frowned slightly. "No doubt," he agreed. "But I don't know that it should upset you unduly. It is vastly unpleasant, of course, but Bovell is even more of a hanger-on here in England than he was in Macao where there were not enough of us to be overly particular in our company. I have seen for myself in the little bit that I have gone into company that you are very well liked, China. Beyond Amelia, is anyone likely to pay him any heed?''

China smiled a little for his naiveté. "As you say, Jack, you do not have much taste for polite society,'' she said dryly. "In Macao, there was the usual sort of harmless gossip that exists in any society, but here it is virtually a way of life for some people. They are vipers and care not whom they bite. Not the best liked or the richest and most powerful are safe from the lash of their tongues. The latter may sometimes escape the consequences, the remainder of us are condemned. I do not intend to cooperate in my ruin, if that is what it is to be. It is not just for myself that I have a care; I would not wish to bring injury to Clive's family, most of whom have been very good to me, and nor would I wish to serve Clive's memory so shabbily.''

Jack's brow puckered in perplexity. "What do you mean? What are you scheming, China?''

"Nothing. I have decided against going to Brighton after all. I am going to Myerly. Tomorrow, if possible, though I may have to put it off a day or so,'' she added, thinking of the obligation she felt to see to it that Amery was not in some sort of scrape.

"Running away?'' he said with obvious surprise. "That isn't like you. And if anything, it may make matters worse. If Bovell has told anyone else of his suspicions, it may well seem that you fled because you are guilty.''

"And it may also serve to bring speculation to a halt. Out of sight, out of mind. For all that I have been accepted by the *ton,* I am really an outsider, made one of them solely through my marriage to one of their own. I would be of far greater interest to them if I were the daughter of Sir Something or Lord Whatever. The harpies will move on to fatter prey. Besides,'' she added, seeing his skepticism, "it is not unnatural for me to wish to visit my property in Nottinghamshire, which I have never seen.''

"In a rather precipitate manner, don't you think?" he said with a touch of waspishness. "This is nonsense, China. You told me that you were enjoying your life again and looking forward to the season in Brighton. Why the devil should you go off on this mad start just because the possibility exists that you may have to face a bit of gossip brought on by a man most people would not even credit?''

China sighed. "It is more than that." She told him of the scene Amelia had created only the night before. "It is more than the humiliation of having been cut dead by my own stepdaughter, it is the way that people looked at me afterward, or rather the way they did *not* look at me. This time it was only embarrassment that made them avoid my eyes; it will be something else next time.''

Jack pondered on this for a few moments, absently tapping his stick against the chair. "I can see that an incident like that would upset you, but I still think you are making a mistake running off and leaving that abominable girl in triumphant possession of the field. If anything, it will surely convince her that she was in the right of it.''

"She will think that no matter what I do," China said with conviction. "I only hope that when she is married to Prentice, she and I may meet as seldom as possible.''

Jack gave an unamused laugh. "I begin to think she deserves that fate. She'll have a lot more to occupy her than vindictiveness toward you once that event takes place. From what I have heard of that young buck since I have been here, Purdham will lead her a merry dance, I'll be bound. I admit I've wondered that Wrexford countenances the match.''

"There is not much he can do to prevent it since Amelia will be of age in two months' time. The best that can be done is to keep her on an allowance until she is five and twenty. But then she inherits the whole of her fortune whomever she has chosen to marry.''

Jack's brows rose. ''And Purdham didn't balk at that? You surprise me. He's a high-flyer, no mistaking. That and his penchant for deep doings won't make much of an allowance.''

''What do you mean, deep doings?''

Jack shrugged. It was not really his affair, and knowing of Amelia's hostility toward China, he was perfectly content to let her lie in the bed she was so willing to make. ''Let's just say that I wouldn't want a sister of mine married to his sort. The only difference, in my opinion, between Purdham and Bovell is one of birth. Purdham is a Captain Sharp with a title to make it palatable. He hasn't even been above setting his own future brother-in-law up for a fleecing.''

China had once again almost forgotten Amery. Her expression sharpened with interest. ''Has he? I know they are friends; they have known one another all their lives. Surely Prentice would have a concern for that, especially as he is to marry Amelia.''

''You'd think so, wouldn't you?'' Jack said with a sardonic smile. ''I have heard it said that Purdham has more than a participant's interest in one or two gaming hells in town, particularly the one that is all the rage just now, Mrs. Willoby's. They say she is his doxy, so it would not be unlikely. Sir Amery has been known to frequent it quite a bit of late.''

''I have been worried about Amery,'' China admitted, not sure just yet how much to confide in her friend. But if Jack knew more about the darker dealings of society than she, he might not only shed some light on what Amery had been up to of late, but even have some inkling of his present whereabouts. The time she had given for Amery to return before she took any action was steadily growing shorter. ''He has been keeping odd hours of late and coming home foxed more often than not. In fact, it is the reason I may have to delay leaving for Nottinghamshire. I want to assure myself before I go that he is not in any sort of trouble. It does not appear that he has been home since Thursday evening, and he is not really of an age yet for that not to occasion concern.''

Jack was looking into the distance beyond her chair and it was clear that he was mulling over something in his mind. ''I'm not certain I should be telling you this,'' he said slowly. ''It isn't the sort of thing one goes about blabbing to the female members of a fellow's family.''

''Oh, for heaven's sake, Jack,'' China said, her concern making her voice brittle. ''You know me better than to suppose that I would turn missish if Amery had gotten himself into something unsavory. I have been imagining all sorts of horrors since I learned this morning that Amery has not been home in two days. I have nearly come to the point of seeking out his friends to find him, even if it means going to Lord Prentice or Mr. Bovell.''

Jack was shocked. ''Good lord, China!'' he ejaculated. ''Don't do that. It would make Rawdon look the perfect cake to have his stepmama hunting him down all over town.''

''Then you had best tell me what you know,'' China recommended tartly. ''I shall come to the truth of it one way or another.''

''Very well,'' he replied with a short sigh. ''You shall probably find him at a tavern called The Longtree in the Haymarket.''

''The Haymarket,'' China repeated, appalled.

Jack nodded. ''It is not as low a place as some in that neighborhood, and there is a set of bloods, of which Purdham is one, that have made it a club of sorts for their less reputable revels. Purdham keeps rooms there to stay when he can't find the road home except flat on his face, and his friends make use of them from time to time for a similar purpose or when they have outrun the bailiff. I have heard that Rawdon has been there quite a bit of late.''

"He can't be perpetually castaway,'' China said alarmed, wondering if, after all, this was Amery's principal difficulty. He never seemed to drink much in polite company, even by the standard of the times; it was only when he was out with friends mostly unknown to her that he returned in an inebriated condition.

"For some it is a means of forgetting, or at least delaying, other unpleasantness,'' Jack suggested.

Her chair could no longer contain her. China got up and stood before Reid. "For God's sake, Jack, stop being coy,'' she said, speaking to him in a tone she had never used to him before. "You are vexing me to death. If you know what unpleasantness it is that is turning my stepson into a sot, tell me at once.''

Jack did not take umbrage at her vehemence. He looked up at her, his expression clear of emotion, and said, "Rawdon has been playing deep and I have heard the ugly rumor that he can't meet his debts of honor.''

China sagged a bit with relief. The possibilities involving unsavory entanglements or worse had genuinely frightened her. "If it is only that . . .''

"Only,'' Jack said with a bark of laughter. "To a gentleman, honor is everything,'' he added with a trace of self-mockery. "What did you imagine I was going to say to you?''

"I—I don't know that I thought of anything in particular,'' she said untruthfully and a bit disconcerted. She saw from the ironic gleam in her friend's eyes that he did not believe her. But he let it pass.

"I think you are upsetting yourself overmuch,'' he said as China sat down again. "It is most likely that in the end Rawdon will screw up his courage and go to Wrexford for whatever blunt he needs. Wrexford will certainly comb his hair for him, but it is unlikely he will refuse to pay. Perhaps it will be unpleasant enough to teach the boy a lesson and cause him to choose his friends more wisely in the future.''

China would have liked to agree with him; it would certainly have been convenient to do so. But she found she could not shake off her responsibilities so readily. She still felt guilty at having failed to take a greater interest in Amery when she began to notice that he was not conforming to what she had thought to be his character, but with Morgan and even Amery himself making light of it, it had been too easy to dismiss it as the behavior of a young man bent on having a few flings in his salad days. ''I must go to this place,'' she said with sudden decision. ''The Longtree, did you say it was called? I could not be easy in my mind until I know that Amery is safe and home again.''

Jack's eyes widened. ''Don't be absurd, China. You can't go to a place like that.''

''But I shall,'' she said, rising again and going to the bell pull. ''Will you come with me, Jack? I admit I do not much like the idea of going there myself.'' She saw from his expression that Jack was on the point of refusing her, thinking, no doubt, that she would yet hesitate to go alone. ''I shall go with or without you,'' she said in a voice that made it clear that she meant what she said. Jack agreed reluctantly, and when the footman arrived in answer to her summons, she ordered her town carriage to be brought around at once.

''Do you know,'' she said when they were alone again, ''I nearly forgot why I asked you to call on me in the first place.''

''I thought to warn me of Bovell's lies and innuendos.''

''Yes. But it was more than that. If it will not inconvenience you too greatly, Jack, will you escort me to Nottinghamshire? I know it sounds silly for one who has traveled over half the continents under the most appalling conditions to be uneasy about journeying alone in country such as England, but I would be much easier if I had a friend I could rely on with me. The English set such great store by propriety that a woman traveling alone—unless she does so with great consequence, which I do not wish to do—is looked upon askance, and I have no idea what manner of reception I shall receive when I reach Myerly. I assume there is some sort of staff there, but they likely know almost nothing about me other than my existence and they might well take me for an imposter and show me the door, if you will not put your foot in it for me.''

Jack smiled at this sally. He wondered just how proper it would be thought for her to travel alone in his company, but if China intended to put herself out of society, he supposed it didn't much matter. England was not Macao, where brigands lurked behind every tree and hillock, but there were dangers, not the least of which were highwaymen or unscrupulous innkeepers who might find a woman of obvious substance traveling alone easy prey. Even the dangers of the road itself were real, and he did not like to think that China might find herself on some lonely road with a broken axle or a missing wheel and no one to offer her protection except disinterested servants. ''If you are as set on going to Nottinghamshire as you are to the Haymarket, I suppose I must, if only to keep you from getting into scrapes.''

China was so delighted that she hugged him and it was at this moment that through the door, which was already opened, stepped Barrett. They did not spring apart like guilty lovers, but the intimacy had doubtless been noted by the butler. His voice when he spoke was the impassive one of the well-trained retainer. ''My lady, Lord Wrexford has called and wishes to speak with you. Since I knew you had already sent for your carriage, I thought you would wish me to inquire if you are receiving.''

China made a small vexed sound. In different circumstances she might have thought Morgan's unexpected visit opportune—it was perhaps more appropriate that he rather than Jack accompany her to the Haymarket—but if he disapproved of her actions, he might find a way of preventing her from carrying them out that Jack could not, and it might also be that Amery, if he were in some sort of trouble, would not wish his cousin to know of it. She did not really wish to speak with him at all, now that she had made her decision to leave for Myerly. She would leave it for Lady Wrexford to impart that news to her son and let him think what he would of it.

"Do you think you might tell Lord Wrexford that I have already left?" she said to her butler. "My business is somewhat urgent and I don't wish to be delayed."

The butler bowed himself out of the room, still retaining his own thoughts. Jack stood next to her near the mantel. "Was that wise? I would have thought you would prefer Wrexford's company to mine, at least on this mission—or do you think he would be stronger than I and not let you go at all?" he added as if he had guessed at her thoughts.

China's smile acknowledged his perceptiveness. "It is not just that. If Amery has not already gone to Morgan for help, he may have his reasons for not wishing to do so. I would rather find him myself first."

Within a few more minutes the town carriage awaited them and they were soon traveling through the streets of London, gradually leaving behind them the relatively clean and well-ordered avenues where the denizens of society dwelled for streets as noisome as any China had observed India, Africa, or China. As the elegant equipage pulled away from Rawdon House, the Earl of Wrexford stepped from behind a dray settled before the house to the left and regarded their retreat musingly.

In a manner of speaking the Longtree Tavern *was* a

step above many of the rather decrepit buildings in its neighborhood, but it was still not a place that China would have stepped foot inside of for any reason less pressing than the one she had now. There was some difficulty at first convincing the landlord to permit them to go up to the rooms regularly let by Lord Prentice Purdham, and he refused flatly to tell them if they were now occupied by Lord Prentice or any of his friends. But finally, by a fine mixture of threat and bribery, Jack convinced the man to turn a blind eye to their ascent. It might not have been as dreadful a place as China had feared, but it was bad enough, and as much as she wished to find Amery, she had a half-hope that he would not be here.

Jack counted the doors as they walked down the long, narrow, ill-lit hall and stopped at one before the last. He knocked loudly and there was no reply. He and China exchanged glances, his plainly asking her if she wished to acknowledge that Amery was not there. China shook her head and Jack knocked again, this time calling Amery's name. There was still no answer and Jack tried the handle of the door without this time questioning China. To the surprise of both of them, it opened at his touch.

The room was so dark that they stood on the threshold a moment allowing their eyes to adjust to the diminished light. It had a stale smell of unwashed bedding and alcohol, and from what China could make out in the dimness, it looked as if it had been ransacked. Jack paused for only a moment and then he crossed the room, nearly falling over some object left lying in the middle of the floor, and went directly to the window, pulling off a blanket that had been tacked on the sill. The room flooded with light, which was as blinding as the darkness had been. But in a few moments, China was able to take stock of her surroundings and she was dismayed. The room was not only messy, but appeared dirty as well. The bedding was in a tumble on the floor, the mattress was stained with what appeared to be red wine, clothes were strewn about, and numerous glasses and plates, many with the remains of long-ago eaten meals, covered what few flat surfaces were to be found. The room appeared to be empty and China scarcely knew whether to be relieved or disappointed.

"It would appear our bird has flown," Jack said philosophically as he returned to China, but something caught his attention over her shoulder and China turned to see what it was.

Amery stood framed in the doorway with a look of surprised chagrin. He was stripped to the waist and he was frozen in the act of drying his arms with a dirty, threadbare towel. "China! What the devil are you doing here?" he said in a voice gratifyingly clear of any signs of present inebriation.

"Come to see what you are doing here," China replied calmly and walked over to him to gently take his hand and draw him into the room. "If you are in some sort of trouble, Amery, I wish you will confide in me."

Amery shot an accusing look at Jack. "You told her where to find me."

"It was no more than a guess," Jack said, unconcerned by the implied censure.

"Don't be upset, Amery," China said. "I wish to help you if you'll let me."

"There is nothing the least the matter," Amery averred, embarrassment making him brusque. "I was a bit up in the world last night and thought it best not to risk falling down in the street or, worse, footpads on the look for easy prey."

"I have learned that you have not been at Mount Street since Thursday," China said quietly, and watched as Amery's still boyish face crumpled so that for a moment she thought he was going to cry.

But he recovered himself and said, "I was gone to a prize fight with some friends near Melton Mowbray.

I told Hopkins, but he must have forgotten to give you the message.''

China regarded him with patent disbelief, and Amery, after an apparent inward struggle, gave up his pretense and sat down on the bed, burying his head in his hands. ''I didn't want you to know about this. I didn't want to face you or Aunt Alyce. I'm done up, China. Properly in the suds.''

''Gaming debts?'' China inquired, and he raised his head to stare in astonishment at her perception.

Amery nodded glumly. ''More than my entire allowance for the next year. I find I cannot be like Prentice and not let such things overset me. I haven't a hope of paying them, and even though I don't think I came by them honestly, it is play or pay and I have no choice unless I want to make matters even worse by calling the bounders out.''

China felt alarmed by both his words and the bitterness with which he had spoken them. She sat beside him, ignoring the disreputable appearance of the mattress. ''What do you mean, Amery? Do you think you have been cheated?''

''I am certain of it,'' he said, a furious light kindling in his eyes.

''Then of course you must not pay,'' China said reasonably. ''It is no disgrace to honor to refuse to pay someone who has deliberately fleeced you.''

''Even if that person is soon going to be your brother-in-law?'' Amery asked mockingly. It was plain that now that he had made his confession, he was not going to observe any niceties of discretion.

China looked over her shoulder at Jack, who had perched against the arm of a chair otherwise laden with various debris. He smiled at her acknowledgment of his perspicacity, and straightened. ''I suppose you became dished at La Willoby's,'' he said matter-of-factly to Amery as he came around the bed to face them. "You know about Purdham's interest there, I take it."

"I do now," Amery said with self-disgust. "As I know that he had need of money to pay debts of his own. Well, he has it now," he added bitterly. "I heard a bit of talk now and then about Prentice and Maeve Willoby, but I thought it was just an *affaire de coeur* not a mating of thieves. He put up the original investment for her to start her bank when he had a run of luck of his own, and they have been lining their pockets by milking their patrons since they set up shop. It is the wine, I think," he said, as if considering this for the first time. "I noticed even at the beginning that whenever I drank when I played there I had the most godawful headache the next morning and couldn't seem to remember much of what had happened the night before other than that I had lost a good deal more consistently than I am used to do."

"Do you think they put something in it to drug you?" said China, shocked at the notion in spite of being willing to believe the worst of Lord Prentice Purdham.

"I don't know," Amery admitted, "but there is something havey-cavey going on, I am certain of it. I heard once or twice that rather nasty comments are being made about the luck of the house, but I just put it down to the chagrin of bad losers. Now I know it is too good to be true."

"Do you really know something," Jack asked seriously, "or is it just assumption?"

Amery shook his head. He got up, went to a low table, and taking a shirt off the top of it, extracted a small pile of paper from amid a jumble of other objects. The papers were tied together loosely by a bit of stout string. He held them in his hand as if offering them for inspection, and China rose and took them from him. "I don't know why I took them from Albermarle Street. I don't fancy myself as a blackmailer, but I was feeling desperate the night before last when I managed to crawl my way out of that veneered bordello, and it seemed at the time that I might find a way to use them to my advantage. I really didn't more than half-guess at the truth until I found them in Maeve's sitting room," he began to recite as China opened first one and then another of the letters and scanned them quickly. "I must have passed out at a fairly early hour. I was drinking fast because I couldn't afford to play any longer and I didn't have anywhere else to go—I've been fearing for days that you or Morgan would question me more closely, China, and learn that I had gotten myself into a stupid mess. I suppose I thought that if they thought me disguised enough to disturb the other players or cast up my accounts on the rug, they'd let me stay there to sleep it off. It had happened before."

He sat down again on the bed. "I don't remember much except rising from the table and then waking up in a bed upstairs. This time I was alone; other times I had a bit of company," he admitted, "though I usually couldn't remember much of that either. I wasn't sick, thank God, and I managed to get myself up and looking a little less disheveled. It was very late, but I could still hear people downstairs. I meant to duck down the service stairs and leave without Maeve or anyone seeing me if I could. I had to go home sometime, at the least to change my clothes. But I heard someone coming up the main stair and I went into the first room I passed with an open door. It was Maeve's sitting room."

"Was that where you found the letters?" Jack queried. He divided his attention from the boy unburdening himself and China's obviously growing distress as she made her way through the missives.

Amery nodded. "I had moved quickly and it unsettled me. For a moment I thought I would be sick if I didn't sit down for a bit. I was afraid it was Maeve coming up, but it wasn't. There was a small lamp burning in the room and she must have intended to return to it soon. It was the first time I'd been in the room and while I waited for my head to stop whirling, I looked about and saw a desk in the far corner of the room. There were a lot of papers about, not scattered but put together in an orderly way, and what looked like account books. I suppose because it was already in the back of my mind that something was afoot, I decided to have a look at them.

"Nothing on the desk meant a thing to me, of course," he said with a thin smile. "But there was a small drawer half open near the top of the desk that looked as if when it were closed it would blend in with the carving, and I got it into my head that it was some kind of secret drawer and I might find something there to interest me. That was what I found," he said with a brief nod toward China, who was now gathering up the letters and tying them up again with the string.

"They are letters from Prentice to that woman," she said to Jack. "Nothing terribly incriminating, but rather mostly instructive and very full of himself and his own cleverness. It makes it clear at the least that he has a financial interest in the hell and a more personal interest in the proprietress. He mentions Amelia several times, not in a very becoming light."

Amery gave a sharp crack of laughter. "That's understatement. Even Amy wouldn't be able to swallow him calling her a dowdy long meg with more fortune than fairness, which he does in one of them."

China rose and put the letters back on the table. "Why didn't you come home when you left Albermarle Street, Amery?"

"I felt like such a fool," he said, staring at the worn carpet. "Not only was I deeply dipped, but I had been such a green 'un that my own so-called friends had been able to lead me down the garden path. At first I thought of going to Wrexford—he wouldn't take the willow to me and he'd cough up the dibs—but I couldn't bear to face him with the truth and I couldn't let him pay his money for me without knowing it.''

"Will you let me pay it?'' China asked him.

He looked so startled that it was clear this had never occurred to him. "No. Of course not! I don't hang on a woman's skirts,'' he said, plainly disgusted at the idea.

"This is hardly that,'' China said with a crisp note in her voice. "I am your stepmother and your guardian as much as Wrexford is. If your sensibilities are too nice to like taking my money, think of it as your father's instead. It is as much for him that I do this as for you.''

Amery was obviously struck by this thought, but still confused. His expressions were mobile and rapidly changing. He wanted to take the easy solution that China offered him, but he had yet to reconcile it with his already injured sense of honor.

"Don't be a nodcock,'' Jack advised him, seeing from the way both turned to look at him that they had all but forgotten his presence. "I learned from my own experience with my family when I fell out of grace several years ago, that I might have saved myself a deal of pain and trouble if I had not been too proud to accept their understanding when it was offered to me from the first.''

The young baronet still seemed uncertain, but the look he turned on China was such a plea to her compassion that she impulsively sat beside him on the bed again and hugged him unrestrainedly. He returned her embrace, shyly at first and then heartily.

China found her eyes misty when she drew away from him. "I am afraid I shall have to disappoint you in one thing, Amery,'' she said. "I am not going to Brighton, after all, but to Nottinghamshire to see my estate. Your Aunt Alyce is coming to luncheon today and then I shall tell her and Annabelle and Amelia of the change in my plans. You are welcome to come with me to Nottinghamshire, of course, if you wish, but I think it would be best if you went to Ferris with the others. You are much closer to Amelia than anyone else, and she may need you.'' It had not been mentioned, but it was tacitly understood that the use he would probably make of the purloined letters would be to open Amelia's eyes to the true nature of her ''beloved.''

''Now you must come home with me,'' China said, rising and holding out her hand to Amery. ''As soon as you have washed and changed, we shall talk and you will tell me what I need to do for you before I go.''

Amery agreed, but begged her to give him a bit of time to make himself more presentable before returning to Mount Street. It was decided that Jack would remain with Amery and see him home and China would take the carriage back to Rawdon House to be there in time to receive Lady Wrexford when she arrived for luncheon. Jack escorted her back to the waiting carriage.

''Do you think everything is all right now?'' China asked him as he handed her into the vehicle.

Jack nodded. ''There is no vice in the boy that I can detect and I think the experience has sobered him, which is all to the good.'' He squeezed her hand in a comforting way. ''You may go to Nottinghamshire with a clear conscience.''

He closed the door and stood watching for several moments as the equipage pulled away. Neither he nor China took any note of the hack carriage on the other side of the narrow street, nor of its driver, who sat on the box nodding as if overcome with boredom or weariness while waiting for his passenger on what was doubtless some disreputable errand, nor of the man who sat in the shadows inside of it, his expression set as if in stone.

21

AMELIA WOULD probably not have come down for luncheon even though her Aunt Alyce was present if China had not sent her a summons that would have required open defiance to refuse. It was so preemptory that even she recognized that China would likely come to her personally and demand her presence if she did not comply, and she wanted no exchanges with her stepmother at all if she could prevent it, even to avoid her company. It was a quiet meal, but not constrained. China, having made her plans and knowing that Amelia would soon be more deserving of her sympathy than her censure, was at peace and not even Amelia's preserved silence had the power to affect her. When they were done eating and settled in the comfortable saloon at the front of the house, she told them of her change in plans.

Lady Wrexford was surprised in one regard, perhaps, but not in others; Annabelle was disappointed that China was going away so soon; and Amelia, as China had come to expect, made no comment at all, not even to disclaim at having to go to Ferris instead of to Brighton where Prentice would be staying with his brother and sister.

When Amery returned they talked as planned, but this was abbreviated by a call from Thea, who sailed into the room quite unannounced and certain of her welcome. Amery plainly had more to say to China beyond telling her of his debts and tried to speak with her again that day, but China, supposing that he wished only to appease his guilty feelings with another out-pouring of gratitude which made her mildly uncom-fortable, put him off, and then went out to her evening engagements without seeing him again. When she came in for the night, there was no light at his door and she did not know if he were out or already abed.

Jack was punctual the next morning, as she knew he would be. Even in a well-sprung carriage with an ex-cellent team, it was at least a two-day journey to Not-tinghamshire and China wished to be on the road for as little time as possible. She arose when her bed-chamber was still swathed in darkness, and the large traveling carriage which Lady Wrexford had lent her for the journey arrived at her door to be loaded with her baggage before most other households on Mount Street were even stirring.

It was an uneventful journey. None of the potential hazards that Jack had iterated occurred, and they made excellent headway, stopping only to change horses and once or twice during the day for a bit of refreshment. It was late in the day and darkness was finally begin-ning to overtake them when their carriage finally pulled into the courtyard of the inn where they had decided to spend the night.

It was coincidentally in Melton Mowbray, where Amery had lied about attending a pugilistic exhibition, and it turned out that just such an event had taken place only that day. The landlord, seeing the crested carriage and recognizing at once the obvious quality of Lady Rawdon and her "brother," apologized pro-fusely as he led them in to the common room for hav-ing no private parlor free to accommodate them immediately. "If it weren't for the fact, my lady," he said sorrowfully, "that one or two of my gentlemen guests had decided to head back to town tonight in-stead of waiting for the morrow, I should not even be able to offer you bedchambers, and that would be a shame indeed.''

He led them to a quiet corner near the hearth, and though a number of heads turned as China, dressed in a royal blue traveling dress and a matching bonnet with a flirtatious feather, passed, she paid no attention to their admiring stares.

"I'll see to it that you are kept undisturbed over here,'' the landlord assured them as he assisted China to her chair, "and it will be nearly as good.''

Frankly, China didn't care whether or not they had a greater privacy. She was weary from the long hours spent in the carriage and extremely hungry after only a light luncheon of lemonade and biscuits, and would have gladly refreshed herself in the tap if it had been the only place available to them.

Their dinner arrived more quickly than they had supposed it would, delivered by the landlady herself, who assured them that their rooms would be ready for them by the time they had finished eating if they wished to retire early. Lucy had gone upstairs at once with China's portmanteau, and China had no doubt that she would find warm water for washing and her own sheets on the bed when she went upstairs for the night. It was a very comforting thought.

During the day-long drive through the English countryside, discomfitting thoughts which had virtually been banished by her activity in preparing for the journey and the settling of Amery's difficulties came back to haunt her. Morgan had not called again to see her before she left, and though this was what she had hoped for, it lowered her spirits quite ridiculously to realize that it might be several months before she saw him again.

It had been one thing to resolve to put him from her mind forever when she had assumed that he had not loved her enough to ask her to be his wife, but now that he had declared himself and she had rejected him, she could not prevent her doubts from surfacing or the little inner ache whenever she realized that it was really finally at an end. The prospect that she had after all made a wretched mistake in refusing Morgan teased at her and made her head ache. But she would not let Jack see her preoccupation, and she behaved as if she were in perfect spirits, with no thought for any of the unhappiness she had left behind her.

Her assumption of serenity, however, was not destined to last. When the waiter had removed the covers and they were awaiting brandy to be brought for Jack and tea for her, the landlord returned to them and informed them that if they wished it they might after all retire to a private parlor. "A gentlemen of your acquaintance appears to have recognized you, my lady," he explained, "and when I told him of the situation, he persuaded his friends to give up their apartment so that you needn't sit in a common room."

China was both pleased and surprised, and perhaps a little dismayed. She had not noticed anyone who was at all familiar to her, but she supposed it was not wonderful that some man of her acquaintance from town would be here for the match. She felt a faint qualm, though, that whoever it was would think it odd for her to be traveling in company with Jack, but it was too late for such concerns. "That was very gracious of him," China said, thanking the landlord for his interest in her welfare. "Did the gentleman give his name?"

"No, my lady, but that is he at the table near the hearth with his back to the fire."

China turned and something inside of her seemed to grow cold when she beheld Dana Bovell, who was staring back at her with a smile playing on his lips which was quite deliberately meant to be offensive. It was plain enough what he was thinking, and his offer very likely was more in the hope of embarrassing her than from any generosity of spirit. She turned back to

Jack and his eyes questioned her. If she wished to refuse the offer of the parlor, he would not have objected. But China weighed the alternative, which was
to remain in the common room with Dana Bovell
watching her and Jack with malicious interest, with
being able to shut herself off from his effrontery by
closing the door of the private parlor. He would likely
infer something nasty from that as well, but since he
was already convinced that she and Jack were lovers,
it hardly mattered.

China rose to follow the landlord, and Jack followed
suit. At the table by the hearth, she paused; she could
not in decency do anything less. "Thank you, Mr.
Bovell. There was no need to inconvenience yourself
or your friends on my behalf, but since you have, I
express myself grateful."

It was a formal speech meant to dampen his pretensions, but the smile he gave her was intimate and in-
sufferably insulting. He raised his glass in
acknowledgment of her thanks. "I know what it is to
wish for privacy when one is surrounded by the uncomfortable stares of strangers," he said.

There was really nothing in his words on the surface
to give offense, but China felt her hackles rise. She
had no doubt that their intent was insolent. "Or even
of acquaintances," she said dulcetly, and turned her
back on him and went into the parlor, feeling no contrition for taking his gift and repaying him with rudeness.

"The devil take Bovell," Jack said when he came
into the room behind her and beheld her stormy countenance. "Of all the inns in England that we might
have put up at, we had to find the one where he was
staying."

China sat down on a chair beside the table. "What
difference does it make," she said, sighing as if releasing her anger physically. Dana Bovell, she had decided, was not worth the effort of being incensed.

"What can he possibly say of me that would be worse than what he has already done? He has painted me as a murderess and a whore, and in this country I am not certain which I should be more greatly condemned for. Please, let us speak of something else."

Jack obliged, and when their brandy and tea arrived, China soon found herself in spirits again. Yet again this proved to be short-lived. There was a knock at the door some half hour later and China, assuming it to be the waiter come to take the tea things away, called for him to enter. Dana Bovell stepped into the room.

"I came to assure myself of your comfort," he said. He spoke in a friendly manner, but China was not deceived by it. He had hope only of further discomfitting her.

"Let us have done with pretense, Mr. Bovell," she said icily. "You came in the hope of finding Jack and me in some compromising situation so that you might have more grist for your mill. I have no doubt you have been regaling your friends this half hour with the whole of my history as you have chosen to perceive it. I don't give a damn for your opinions or your attempts to discredit me. Dragging me into the mud will not make you rise above the gutter; it is a simple fact of breeding."

An angry flush spread over Bovell's cheeks, but he feigned injured astonishment. "My dear Lady Rawdon, exhaustion from long travel must have disordered your wits. Your reading of my character is quite irrational."

Hot fury sprang into China's eyes. Jack placed a restraining hand on her arm, but she shrugged him off and rose. China rarely gave full reign to her temper, but tiredness and days of anxiety and despair had finally taken their toll. "You are not worthy of my steel," she said in a voice barely controlled to remain low-pitched. "If I were a man I would take my whip to you. The only reason you found any acceptance at all in Macao was because Clive had a good heart and took the trouble to see to it that you were received even though he knew that you were nothing more than a common adventurer. And this is how you repay him. You could not bed me, or use my credit to your advantage, so you take revenge in attempting to ruin me. But it is to no purpose. You may say what you will of me, but your quarry has gone to ground, and you may find as well when you return to town that the friends you thought to use against me are worthless tools or on to your game. Your teeth are drawn, Mr. Bovell, and your poison with them."

Jack watched Bovell's expression change as China spoke, and there was something ugly in his eyes that made Jack rise and come to stand beside China. Bovell ignored him, his eyes, blazing an anger to equal China's, were solely on her. He spat out a vile epithet that China, in her rage, did not flinch from, but before Jack could act on her behalf, a voice, gentle in contrast to China's heat, came from the doorway behind Bovell.

"This, I believe, Mr. Bovell," Morgan said with a coolness that was clearly a mask for a stronger emotion, "is a matter for naming one's friends. However, there is the annoying restriction of only being permitted to kill another gentlemen in an affair of honor, and that you plainly are not."

Bovell had whirled about abruptly at the intrusion and was facing Morgan for most of this speech, but at the end of it he was lying on the floor clutching piteously at his stomach, with blood flowing freely from his nose and onto his shirt front.

Neither Jack nor China had noticed that Bovell had left the door ajar and neither could have been more astonished if Morgan had materialized like a spirit at a seance. Jack was not loath to let Morgan take up the task he had intended for himself, and he was quick to assist by nipping behind that combative gentleman and closing the door before any sound of the altercation could reach into the common room.

Morgan had shrugged off his driving coat and stood splay-legged before the prone Bovell. "Get up," he said in a voice so menacing that China shivered. But when Morgan reached down to drag Bovell to his feet only to strike him again with a punishing left, she did nothing to prevent Morgan from hurting him even though he appeared to be too stunned to be capable of defending himself.

Morgan went after the hapless Bovell again, dragging him roughly this time into a chair. "Fight me, damn you," he said in a voice that was almost a hiss. "If I'm going to kill you, I want the satisfaction of its being some challenge to do so."

Bovell made an attempt to rise, one arm swinging out wildly, but his knees played him false and buckled beneath him. He crashed to the floor yet again, and this time he was still. Morgan, breathing heavily, reached down for him, but Jack caught at his left arm, the first already formed for contact with Bovell's face. "Leave him be," he said quietly. "He's not with us anymore."

China, hearing these words, felt a moment of alarm that finally cut through her amazement at Morgan's opportune arrival. She had not the least objection to Morgan's knocking Dana Bovell down or to making his face look as if it had been kicked by a horse, but she did not want him to kill the man. It was not compassion for Bovell, but a fear of the consequences for Morgan. She hurried over to Morgan and Jack. Bovell's face, where it was not bloody, was unnaturally white and he lay so very still that China felt her heart jump into her throat.

She looked up at Jack, her eyes widened by fright. "He's not . . ." She could not quite bring herself to say the word.

"Dead?" Jack said with no such compunction.

"Unfortunately not, but if he does meet an untimely end, I would rather it were not at the hands of anyone I know."

Morgan looked up at Jack as if seeing him for the first time. "How did he come to be here?"

"More to the point," Jack said, speaking China's thought aloud, "how do you come to be here?"

"I followed you," Morgan pronounced as if with great logic, and turned and went to the table, poured himself a generous amount of brandy, and drank the better part of it off in a single swallow. His eyes were still unnaturally bright, but the murderous rage had died from them, and China thought that if he meant to murder her and Jack as well, he would at least not do so at once.

"Then you did so uncommonly slowly," Jack said practically, not at all perturbed by Morgan's violence or any possibility that it might be turned on him.

"You had more than two hours head start on me. When I called a little before eight at Mount Street, Barrett told me where you had gone."

"You called at eight this morning?" China said with surprise.

Morgan smiled for the first time, albeit with considerable dryness. "I had something important to say to you." He did not add that he had slept little the previous night and had risen from his bed at an hour as early as China had left hers.

China felt as if her heart leapt within her but she willed that organ to be still. This was not a moment for foolish hopes when she was not even certain yet what it was she hoped for. But Morgan's attack on Bovell, the fact that he had called on her at so unseemly an hour and on learning that she had left for Nottinghamshire had gone after her almost at once and followed her such a great distance could only lead her to believe that he had not accepted her rejection of him and that he had had no change of mind or heart in the feelings he had professed to her in Green Park.

For the first time she found herself wishing she had not persuaded Jack to accompany her. If he had believed before that she was Jack's mistress, he must be even more convinced of it now. But she felt instantly guilty for her craven thought. Jack was her dear friend, and as she had told Morgan, she would not deny Jack to convince Morgan of her innocence. Morgan must believe in her of his own accord. A vestige of her lagging certainty that she had done the right thing to refuse Morgan's offer of marriage in Green Park returned to her, making her wish now that Morgan had not come after her, whatever his reason.

Jack looked from Morgan to China and decided he was *de trop*. "I think I had better seek the landlord and procure a basin of water and some sticking plaster. Bovell looks rather like he has been one of the pugilists in today's exhibition."

This elicited no response and he left them, quietly closing the door behind him. China felt suddenly shy and she turned from Morgan and walked to the hearth as if a hearty fire burned there, though only ashes lay in the grate on such a warm June day. Morgan followed her as she knew he would.

Without turning, she said, "It must have been something very important indeed that you wished to say to me if you thought it worth your trouble to travel so far to do so."

"I called at Mount Street this morning to cast your lies to me in your face," he said baldly. "This isn't the first time I have followed you, you see. I saw your carriage arrive at the door yesterday only moments after Barrett had informed me that you were already out. I don't know why I waited to see you leave; I certainly had no intention of following you then. But when you came out with Reid, I hailed a passing hack and did so. I saw you go into the tavern and remain there for the better part of three-quarters of an hour. I thought you might have found a less disagreeable trysting place,'' he added in a tone so cutting that China flinched inwardly. ''I was not as certain what I wished to say to you yesterday as I was today,'' he continued, and she heard a self-mocking note in his voice. ''I think I had almost succeeded in convincing myself that I had misjudged you about Reid. Perhaps I only wanted a bit more reassurance to complete the belief. I don't know, but after I saw you and Reid go into that place together, I told myself I was every sort of fool.''

He had come a little closer to her again and China, not wanting his disconcerting nearness, moved away from him again toward the opposite side of the room from where Bovell still lay unconscious. ''So you came to Rawdon House to deliver your final reading of my character,'' she said bitingly, thinking herself as great a fool to have supposed that Morgan still wanted her. ''I think it was unnecessary to carry it to such a length as to follow me here.''

''That isn't why I came here,'' he said, and the angry bitterness had died from his voice. ''Amery was coming down the stairs when I called and he insisted on speaking with me, though I tried to fob him off. He told me what you have done for him.''

China wondered that Amery could have been so anxious for Morgan not to know of his disgrace that he had been willing to face ruin for it, and then, once out of his difficulties without Morgan ever needing to be the wiser, he had volunteered the information after all. ''I know Clive would have wanted me to help his son in any way that I could,'' China said with a coolness that belied the sincere affection out of which she had acted. She began to feel foolish for attempting to avoid him in the small confines of the room, and sat down on a small low-backed wooden bench near the window facing on the courtyard.

Morgan came to stand in front of her. "Is that why you did it?"

China forced herself to smile. "Of course not," she said with false flipness. "Even women of my character have some compassion for a fellow in difficulties."

He sat down beside her. The bench was narrow in width and their bodies could not help but touch. She wished she had chosen some other place to settle.

"It wasn't to thank you or to condemn you that I followed you today, China," he said with a strange intensity. "I know that you went to the tavern on Amery's behalf. I want you to come back to town. You belong there with Annabelle and Amery. And with me."

China wanted to flee him again, but she made herself look at him. "Is this another gracious proposal, my lord?"

"Are you in love with Reid?" he demanded, ignoring her sarcasm.

"No," she answered truthfully.

"Then why have you rejected me and turned to him again? Give him up and marry me. I don't believe you are as indifferent to me as you pretend to be."

China's soft laugh was genuine. "What a puzzle you are, Morgan. You alternately spurn me and pursue me. Is it challenge that makes you so persistent?"

"It is the realization that I could not bear to know you had spent another night with him," Morgan replied, and there was a chilling note in his voice. "Bovell is an easy and convenient target; it is Reid I would like to have laid out upon the floor, but I would not do so for your sake."

"Or for mine either," Jack said, reentering the room bearing a basin of warm water, some clean rags, and the sticking plaster he had gone to fetch. "I had not heretofore supposed you to be a man of violence, Wrexford," he continued as he set the basin down on a small table beside Bovell, "but you seem bent on mayhem tonight."

Morgan stood abruptly. "Reid," he said in a level voice, "we have matters to discuss."

China rose quickly. "Morgan, no, please," she pleaded, feeling she would be unbearably humiliated if Morgan made his ugly suspicions known to Jack.

Morgan looked over his shoulder at her. "Does he mean that much to you after all?"

Before China could reply, their attention was caught by the sounds of Bovell returning to consciousness. He moaned, coughed, retched slightly, and then pulled himself painfully into a completely upright position, focusing his eyes with some difficulty on his attacker. "I shall see you in a court of law for this unprovoked attack, Wrexford," he said thickly, his speech impeded not only by his foggy mental state but by the fact that his lips were swollen to nearly twice their normal size.

"If you ever dare to utter another word of slander against Lady Rawdon," Morgan told him bluntly, "the only thing you shall see is your maker. The next time I shall surely call you out, dishonor or not, and I shall just as surely kill you." There was such certainty in his tone that though Bovell's expression did not change, he seemed to shrink back from this verbal attack and sat heavily in the chair behind him.

"It is not slander to let the truth be known," he said, this time sounding more petulant than righteous. "If you are the man of honor you claim to be, you should not let your duty be swayed by beauty and a false innocence. Clive Rawdon is dead in circumstances of considerable suspicion, with only his wife's and her lover's word for it that he died of natural causes. Or does avoiding scandal mean more to you than justice?"

Jack had ceased his ministrations to Bovell when that man had stood up, and he stood holding a wet,

pink-stained rag in his hand looking down at his ac-
cuser. "Bovell is right. Clive did not die of an infection," he said so quietly that his words barely carried
to Morgan and China at the other side of the room.
"He died of arsenic poisoning."

There was a brief silence in the room, born of shock.
Even Bovell appeared stunned by the admission. Finally China spoke, without fear or distress. "Jack,
you must not."

"Why not?" he said, turning to China, his voice as
calm as hers. "I am not bound by any deathbed promise. The lying has gone on long enough. It is moot in
any case. I have already told Amery the truth about
his father's illness and death."

"I know." It was Morgan who spoke. "Amery told
me this morning. It was another reason I came after
you, to tell you that I knew."

"He was Clive's son, he had a right to know," Jack
averred defiantly, "whatever Clive's eccentric belief in
his own disgrace. It has placed an unconscionable burden of deceit on you, China, and it is time it was at
an end." He turned again to Bovell, who was attending avidly. "It is not your affair, but since you have
made it so, I shall tell you as well. Sir Clive was a
dying man in any case. I am not certain of the nature
of his disease, but it was wasting, and in the last
months before his death he was becoming increasingly
ill, though he could still get about enough to hide the
truth from most. He might have borne the physical
pain stoically, it was self-disgust with what he perceived as his body rotting while he still lived that he
couldn't bear. He confessed to always having had a
dread of sickness. I think it was as much the memories
attached to his first wife's illness that made him flee
from his home after her death as it was his grief at
losing her.

"He took the poison himself which he had procured
on a trip to Canton, not even telling China of his in-

tention.'' Jack smiled wryly. ''He should have asked me for help if he was so bent on his course. I could have told him that arsenic was not the best instrument. Instead of killing him at once and in his sleep, it made him violently ill first, and gave him a shortened version of exactly the sort of lingering, wretched death he most feared. He was fairly lucid at first and after confessing to China what he had done, extracted from her a promise that she would never divulge the truth to anyone, particularly not to his family as he did not want them to know that he had taken the coward's way out of life, before he would permit her to send for me. The truth could not be kept from me, of course, but I, in my turn, promised China not to let Clive know that I was not deceived. My collusion in the lies that followed were for her sake, not his. Poison is a frightening thing. I feared there would be suspicions and that it would be better to list the death as natural. What did it matter after all, once Clive was dead, how he had died?''

He walked over to China and took her hands in his. ''I am sorry, dear, but it is better than deceit and innuendos. A dying man has no right to put the living under such heavy obligation.'' He glanced toward Morgan. ''There is one last matter that needs clearing up. You think that China and I are lovers.'' His smile was bittersweet and infinitely self-mocking. He brought his eyes back to China's and smiled sadly into them. ''I think I wish it were true. A sweeter, more beautiful mistress a man could not ask for. But not all men are affected equally by a woman's beauty. For some it remains ever aesthetic and unapproachable. To my chagrin and that of my family, who must accept that since the death of my brother there is no hope of our line's continuing, I am such a one. Some call it unnatural. For me, it is just a part of myself that I too have had to learn to accept. I love China dearly, but it is as a friend, not as a lover.''

There were unshed tears in China's eyes. "You did not have to do this, Jack," she said, the trace of a tremor in her voice.

"Yes, I did. I won't let your life be ruined for loyalty to me or to Clive." He turned again to look at Morgan. He was more pleased than he thought he would be to see understanding in that man's eyes rather than condemnation. He released China and walked over to Bovell. "We are *de trop,* my friend," he said with a return to his more usual manner. "If you have a bed waiting for you here, it is time you sought it."

He held out his hand for Bovell to rise and saw the other man look at him with a mixture of distaste and speculation. Jack's smile was sardonic. "Don't imagine you can make gain out of this night. I don't give a damn if you put a notice in the *Post*. I have no ambitions for society nor a taste for it."

Bovell ignored the outstretched hand and stood somewhat shakily. "This is not the end of it, Wrexford," he said, but it was so obviously bravado to save what was left of his face that neither Morgan nor China regarded him. Casting Jack a look of blatant disgust, he went out of the room unassisted.

"The wolf has lost his bite, I think," Jack said, pausing at the door as he made to follow Bovell. He grinned. "I hope you mean to invite me to the wedding," he said, and left them.

Morgan and China both stared at the closed door for several moments as if neither could find the words to speak their thoughts. "I have indeed been every sort of fool," Morgan said at last, but more to himself than to China. "I have no right to ask you to forgive me."

"No, you don't," China agreed. She had never in her life felt a more curious mixture of emotions. She felt far more relieved than upset that there were no longer any secrets to keep, though she had tacitly if not actually betrayed Clive's trust. Her pride wanted her to refuse any renewal of Morgan's declarations of

love for her; he must believe her now, but only because Jack had risked himself for her honor. She knew
intuitively that if she did so it would be the last time
he would speak to her so. Morgan Rawdon was not a
man to wear the willow or to make a career out of
unrewarded devotion. Since their familial ties would
mean that they would continue to know each other,
the day would doubtless come when she would have to
bear seeing him give that love she had spurned to another. This was as unbearable a prospect to her as
Morgan had claimed it was to him that she should
continue what he had thought to be her *affaire* with
Jack.

"But I do," he said, taking her hand in his and
bringing her palm to his lips. "I love you, China."
He laughed softly. "To think you once accused me of
neglecting to say those words. I can't adequately apologize to you for a lifetime of cynicism and a career in
which one advances through mistrust, but I can promise you to try to change these failings. Let me spend
the rest of our lives proving to you that I can make
amends for my pigheadedness."

"You don't have to prove anything," China said,
keeping her voice in control with effort. "If I loved
you I would forgive you without promises."

"Do you?" His voice was level, but she saw in his
eyes the intensity with which he waited for his answer.

All at once she felt light of heart. Her pride could
go to the devil. If she were making a mistake, she only
hoped it would be a very long time before she discovered her folly. "I should not," she said, looking down
at his waistcoat, not in shyness or coyness, but to quiz
him.

He put his hand under her chin and forced her face
up to his. "Damn it, China," he said, vexed and
amused at once. "No more games. Do you love me
and will you marry me?"

For reply, China closed the minute distance between

their lips. She kissed him with all the fervent passion of a realization that she had nearly lost the love of her life. She broke away from him and then drew him fiercely against her again. "Yes," she whispered into his ear, "Yes, yes yes."

His laugh was triumphant, and without any protest from China, he bore her from the parlor and up the stairs to her room. They were not observed by the landlord or landlady, who might have objected, and a few of the stragglers still in the common room there was none to know that they had not every right to seek their bed together.

Their lovemaking that night was both more passionate and gentler than it had been before. Then it had owed more to desire, now it was the satisfying consummation of acknowledged love. China lay naked in Morgan's arms, too happy for quick sleep, and knew peace in her heart at last.

22

JACK DID NOT return to London with them in the morning, preferring to go on to his home in Sussex as he had planned to do from Myerly once he had seen China safely settled. They had no sight of Bovell, who either was in his room nursing his wounds or had left before they had come down. Morgan had come without a groom on his mission, so he had no groom to drive his curricle back to town, but he left instructions for its storage until it could be collected. He would not hear of China's enduring so long a journey in an open carriage and he preferred the company of his bride-to-be to a solitary drive. Passed in each other's company, it seemed a much shorter journey than that of the previous day to them both. The weather held good, they were fortunate in their job horses, and it was only a little after nine that night that they arrived at Wrexford House.

Morgan had insisted that they stop there first before taking China to Mount Street for the night in the hope of finding his mother at home so that they might share their news. "She will be pleased, I think," Morgan said. "She sees more than she says and she has once or twice made some comment to me to make me think that we have not been as successful at disguising our feelings for each other from her as we were from each other. Annabelle and Amery will doubtless wish us joy as well."

"But not Amelia," China said, not wishing to shy from that reality.

"Probably not," Morgan agreed. "In fact, for a time her resentment at our happiness may be the greater. I don't think she will be marrying Purdham after all."

"Amery has shown her the letters?"

"Very probably by now. Now that the scales have fallen from his eyes about the false friendship that Purdham offered him, he will take whatever measures he can to keep his sister from throwing herself away on that loose fish. But we can't expect Amelia to thank him for it," he said with a sigh. "In her heart she must know she has been lying to herself about Purdham's character and his claims of devotion to her, but the truth will hurt too much for her to reason clearly that she is better off to know it."

But in spite of the possibility of unpleasantness from Amelia, China felt no trepidation upon entering Wrexford House. They found Annabelle and Lady Wrexford in the latter's sitting room taking tea and doing needlework while they talked. Annabelle exclaimed in happy surprise at their entrance and Lady Wrexford set aside her sewing and rose to greet them before they had come all the way into the room. She kissed her son and China in turn and then, a beaming smile on her face, led them to a sofa near where she and Annabelle sat.

"We were not sure we would find you at home," Morgan said, "but you act as if you were expecting us."

"I was," the dowager said placidly as she poured out tea for China and something stronger for Morgan, which she had ready to hand. "When Amery told me you had gone after China into Nottinghamshire, I knew what the outcome would be."

Morgan laughed. "I am glad you were so certain, Mama, for I was not."

"But China is in love with you," she said as if speaking to a slow child, "and you with her. And you are both very sensible. I knew that whatever your differences were, you would not let them come between you. Shall you be married from Ferris or here in town?"

Morgan looked at China and the smile she gave him confirmed his own thoughts on the matter. "In town. At once. I intend to get a special license tomorrow, if possible."

"Oh, dear, such haste," Alyce Wrexford said, but without reproach. "I know, though, what it is to be in love. Well, you may still go to Ferris for your bride journey, or perhaps you would prefer to go to Myerly after all to be alone."

"We will go to Ferris, I think, if China does not object," Morgan said. "It is certainly big enough to give us our privacy when we wish it while still sharing our happiness with our family."

China agreed, and then answered Annabelle's eager questions about the romance that had been going on under her nose without her guessing at it. It was perhaps a quarter-hour later when Amelia joined them.

China had actually forgotten about her, assuming her to be out as Amery was for the evening. But Amelia was clad in her dressing gown and her face had a slightly puffy appearance, as if she had been crying, though not recently. She entered quietly and sat at the edge of a chair across from Morgan and China, as if proclaiming that she did not intend to stay and join in the happy conversation.

"I heard you arrive and decided to see why China had come back to town. I stood in the hall for several minutes and listened," she admitted without a blush. "I gather you are to be married." This speech was addressed to Morgan—Amelia had not so much as looked at her stepmother since coming into the room.

"Yes. Tomorrow or the next day by special license," Morgan replied evenly.

Amelia took a deep breath and let it out again. "I think you are making a mistake," she said baldly. "But perhaps I am not the best one to advise you on such matters. I am not to be married."

"I am sorry, Amelia," Morgan said sincerely.

"So am I," she said, and it was plain that she was near to crying again. She stood up. She finally acknowledged her stepmother. "I don't like you, China, but I wish you well," she said and got up, walking from the room with a dignified gait that China knew must have cost her dearly in self-control.

"Well, that passed much better than I had hoped for," Lady Wrexford said, speaking their common thought aloud. She put down her needlework again and patted Annabelle's hand. "Come, Puss. It is time we were abed."

Since during the Season Lady Wrexford rarely retired for the night before the small hours of the morning, it was obvious that she wished to give Morgan and China some time alone before he escorted her to Mount Street. She guessed that they might already be lovers, but she knew her son would not commit the impropriety of going to China's house alone with her before the wedding now that not even the young Rawdons were there to give them some degree of countenance.

Annabelle made a moue of disappointment, but she went quietly enough with her aunt. Morgan waited only until he had heard the click of the door latch catching before gathering China into his arms. "I am almost prepared to fear that Amery will make an appearance and object to the match," he said when he had released her a little and was able to speak again.

"Why should you think such a thing?" China said with a surprised laugh. "I would expect him to be as pleased for us as are Annabelle and your mother."

"Because everything today has gone too well," Morgan said darkly. "From the beginning, every time I indulged in happiness at our being together, something has occurred to draw us apart. Experience is the teacher of superstition."

"If we were drawn apart," China said severely, "it was because you had not the broad mind that should have come from broad travel."

"It is doubtless because I came to my share of the Rawdon wanderlust at an advanced age," he said contritely. "Perhaps we should go abroad again to complete my education."

China shook her head. "I have had quite enough of a nomadic existence. I have learned enough for us both and shall endeavor to teach you."

"Then let the lessons commence," Morgan said with a smile that made China's heart melt within her.

As if on cue, the door of the sitting room opened and Amery stepped in.

Morgan had been about to kiss China again, but he looked up at his cousin with wary expectation as if he really wondered if his teasing prediction were about to come true. But a slow smile spread across the young baronet's features. "Good," Amery said, and stepped out of the room again and shut the door.

Morgan and China looked at each other for a moment and then laughed simultaneously. "Good," Morgan echoed, and completed the act at which he had been interrupted.

About the Author

ELIZABETH HEWITT, who comes from Pennsylvania, now lives in New Jersey with her dog, Maxim, named after a famous romantic hero. She enjoys reading history and is a fervent Anglophile. Music is also an important part of her life; she studies voice and all of her novels for Signet's Regency line were written to a background of music from the baroque and classical periods.